Dark Places of the Heart

Christina Stead / Dark Places of the Heart

Holt, Rinehart and Winston
New York   Chicago   San Francisco

Designer: Ernst Reichl
88107-0216
Printed in the United States of America

For my Friends

Anne and Harry Bloom

Dark Places of the Heart

Some Persons

Pop Cotter, Thomas
Ma Cotter, Mary née Pike

Their children:
  Ellen (Nellie), marries George Cook
  Thomas
  Peggy

Simon Pike, brother of Mary,
  Jeanie and Bessie

George Cook
Eliza Cook, his first wife

Mrs. Gwen McMahon, houseworker
Georgiana, her little daughter

Venna, a prostitute in Southwark
  (does not appear)

Robert Peebles, Nellie's editor
  (does not appear)

Bob Bobsey, an old woman

Camilla Yates, a dressmaker

Caroline Wooller, an office worker

Johnny Sterker, a strange woman

Other women

IT WAS a Saturday, a fine March morning. Two women and a man were in the basement front room, Mrs. Nellie Cook, a journalist, Mrs. Camilla Yates, a dressmaker, and Walter, a window cleaner. Mrs. Yates was making a blue dress for Mrs. Cook.

Mrs. Cook said to the window cleaner, "It's fresh today, pet. Did you try on that leather jacket of my brother's? I had a fit of conscience and wrote to him and said, I gave your leather jacket to Walter, do you mind? And he wrote back, You know me better than that."

"I gave it to my brother. He sold it and bought some vegetables. He's rented a truck," said the man, with a questioning glance.

"I'll give you a suit, too, love, though there's moth in it somewhere. Ah, but I ought to make you give me your spattered denims in exchange, for my husband George. It would bring me fine George nearer to humanity. He wore them once, down on the docks; and now, nothing but tailormades. It was he started me on the primrose path, Mrs. Yates, love. I was told the other day I'd lost all me personality since I married George. But marriage is an incurable disease; and it drives out the others."

Mrs. Yates said it was not incurable.

Walter asked if he could pull the curtains apart in an alcove; he did so. A four-year-old girl was sleeping on a cot there. The window showed a brick wall, some bare trees.

Walter did the window quickly, went out to the kitchen and at the foot of the stairs stopped, "I took some hot water, Missus."

"That's all right, pet," said Mrs. Cook.

When he had gone to the attic, Nellie Cook said she wished he would wear a safety belt. It was a big drop. She didn't like to

[9]

talk to him about it for fear of putting the idea of a fall into his mind.

"We're creatures of our figments, love."

He was not a professional window cleaner. He had chest trouble and needed outdoor work. Because he needed the money, he came round too often. He knew he came too often and made a concession. He got a pound each time.

Nellie said, "I'm ashamed to grudge it to the poor fellow. Besides, he admires George; and is always asking him his political opinion. I'm afraid he hasn't the head for it. He'll ask the same question several times and then he'll repeat what George said, word for word. Is that your opinion, Mr. Cook? It's touching. He followed George home from a meeting once—the same as I did meself! And he'll reassure me to this day, 'Don't worry, Missus; I didn't come to do your windows; I just wanted to ask the Mister what he thinks.' And the way he'll listen to him standing and won't sit down; and then quietly go and you can see him mouthing it over to himself on the doorstep—it's pitiful Camilla darling—I may call you Camilla, love?"

The man dodged into the doorway, brought Mrs. Cook her purse from the piano and pocketed his money with thanks and a strange smile. At the door he turned and with yet another manner, mincing like a Chelsea aesthete, he said he'd be round in three weeks.

"And how is the Mister? I miss his talks on politics."

Nellie said heartily, "Do you, pet? Ah, bless you. It does me good to hear it, Walter. The bugger's on the continent yet, Walter, living on the fat of the land, touring the world as a representative of the working class of Great Britain. The call of England Home and Beauty rings feebly in his ear. He'll be back, pet, in a couple of weeks; but I can't tell you when. He wrote he's drunk every day from midday on. That's his world of the future. That's your sex for you, Walter."

The man gravely nodded and this time glided away without a smile. In a moment they heard the front door close.

"I wonder if that's worth five shillings or whatever informers get," said Mrs. Yates, looking down at her pattern and picking up a sleeve.

"He's a pet, poor man," said Nellie.

"He gives me the creeps; he's not natural. I wouldn't let him in," said the dressmaker, good-naturedly. She was a powerful woman, in her early forties, with a straight broad back, a small classic head on a strong neck, low forehead and short nose in line, dark hair and eyes.

Nellie impatiently stumped out her cigarette and reached for another.

"My test of a person is their opinion of George Cook! I stand high there meself. Eh, Walter's no better than the rest. Mrs. McMahon told George that Walter tried to kiss her and wanted to take her to the movies and asked questions about the boss; but what she wouldn't say. Gwen McMahon's a loyal soul. I could do with a cup of tea."

She drummed on the table with her tobacco-stained long fingers.

Mrs. Yates remarked in her pleasant voice, "You see? A dick. That was my first impression. He's all patches, a makeshift. I said, Now what act is that? And trying to get intimate with the maid."

"Ah, no, pet; it's no good, Camilla. No, no, your suspicious mind can't turn me against Walter. We're old friends. And Mrs. McMahon's no maid, pet; she's our friend. She's been with us since before we were married."

Mrs. Yates held out the dress. Mrs. Cook shed the faded overalls she was wearing and stood in her cotton shirt and long fleecy bloomers, holding out her arms. Mrs. Yates stood back and looked at the hang of the dress.

Mrs. Cook said absently, "You're nervous, Camilla. You feel hunted. So you think your husband is divorcing you, eh? You must be the headlong sort; you rush into the baited trap."

"I married for love."

Nellie now undressed again, was smoking furiously, hanging on to the mantelpiece, waving to the child in the bed. She said rapidly, "It's a grand thing, aye, I don't blame you. Will I do then, pet, in that dress? I won't be an eyesore at the airport when I welcome home my hero? I'll go and make a pot of tea and we'll sit down quietly. You've earned your crust. I'm glad to take it easy on my Saturday off. I'm generally on some off-the-record assignment, or visiting a sick friend, or fixing up the income tax or the mortgage, or running messages for me carefree lad.

"Eh, Camilla, there's a rooster in the hencoop! I expect they were glad to get him out of the navy. He laid out a plan of action for the admiral, or they feared he'd commandeer one of the lifeboats and sail for Tahiti. There he is making the French dames step to his tune. Eh, what a man, what a man! And do you think, Camilla, I'll do in that dress? For I want it now to go to see me mother in, to show Bridgehead, me old home town, that I'm respectable. For there's a skeleton in me cupboard. George and I lived together before we were married, pet. A cat and dog life it was; we didn't think we'd be able to stick it out. Eh, what a bloody egotist, love; but what a man! And to meself I said, My lass, you must submit, you must give up the fine free-lance life. And the wonder of wonders happened, Camilla; the perfect marriage, the perfect counterpoint, aye. Well, before that, I had to tell my folks that I was married, for I had my sister down here to visit, and Bob Bobsey, the dear old elf, who's now gallivanting with me boyo, you don't know her, a real pal, who looks as if she was a shriveled soul, but what's inside is as the meat of the walnut. Bob was in Bridgehead and she called upon my family, the Cotters, and she had to answer my mother's thousand questions. What time of day was it? Did it rain or shine? What dress did Nellie wear? For she swore to my mother that she'd been present at the wedding. Bob's a glorious old bohemian, but she's old fashioned and she didn't approve of us living in sin. It would break my heart if a daughter of mine did it, she said to me solemnly, shaking her dear old head, that great old stone face that's like the face of Grandmother Fate—"

"She must look like a gargoyle," said Mrs. Yates laughing.

"Ah, no, pet; that's your acidulous nature. She's my standby in storms; loyal and staunch. And she said to Mother, being up against it, Your daughter wore a nice blue dress. Every time since, when I go up home, Mother harps on it. Why don't you wear the nice blue dress you were married in? Because I'm keeping it in camphor out of sentiment, I said. So take the tacking threads out, darling, or you'll ruin me; and I've bought a cake of camphor to rub over it. My mother was always a foxy little deducing creature; that was her compensation for a life of defeat." Nellie, in her long bloomers and cotton shirt, went out the back to get tea.

There were three rooms on each floor of the little three-story brick house. Down short stairs here on the ground level, was an old-fashioned W.C. with the handle in a wooden seat and a blue flowered bowl. There was no light and no window; so that generally they sat with the door slightly open looking at the grassy back yard. At the side, a long paved kitchen. There were no windows; the door to the yard was usually kept open here, too. The small back yard was enclosed by brick and low stone walls and contained two small trees and a couple of sheds. On the left, dark old terrace houses with long back yards ran at right angles. They were occupied mostly by immigrant workers, Cypriots, Maltese, Greeks, doing sweatshop labor. On the right, along Lamb Street, were big garages, filling the space of houses knocked down by the bombs. The houses in Lamb Street, all low and narrow, like Nellie Cook's, were occupied mostly by machinists and other garment trade workers. Mrs. Yates lived across the street, with her two children, in two rooms over a small grocery shop. She lived separated from her husband. Her lover, a painter, a tall bulky ungainly man, visited her every day, ate there, used her as a model, looked after her children.

Nellie was a strange thing, her shabby black hair gathered into a sprout on the top of her small head, her beak and backbone bent forward, her thin long legs stepping prudently, gingerly, like a marsh bird's, as she came over the hogback ground floor, stairs up, stairs down, to the front room with her tea tray. The tea tray was neatly set, with a tray cloth; and she had cut thin bread and butter.

Camilla sat with her head bowed over her work. The hooded daylight came from the areaway into the middle of the room and shone on the bright wiry hair. Her neck and curved strong shoulders, dull and smooth, bent down in the plain blue cotton blouse, gathered on a cord and rather low. Her long thighs were apart to make a convenient sewing lap. Opposite her sat Ellen Cook, slouching, her elbow on the chair arm, her fingers to the cigarette, her nose and hair sprout in the air, the other hand on her hips. She spread her legs jauntily apart, in their gray knee-length bloomers, wrinkled black stockings. She wore pointed black shoes, the toes turned up, the thin heels turned down with wear. The light fell on the hollows in face, neck, chest and bony arm and darkened the exhausted skin. Her small eyes, dark blue, looking out sharp between half-closed lids, were tired. She sat smoking, drinking tea and nonchalantly ruminating. At length, she mentioned that she had had a budget of mail that morning, something from George. He had been to Geneva, looking for a job in the I.L.O. office, and was back in France. He was not coming home yet but was going on with the dear old elf, Bob Bobsey, to Florence. Bob had the money.

"He promised it to her long ago, and she says this may be the last time. Eh, old age is a high wall you can't climb and she's coming to the foot of it."

To save money George and old Bob had taken one room with two beds in their travels through France. George went to the Gare du Nord to meet old Bob and brought her to the hotel. Everyone in the hotel ran forward to have a look: *Mon Dieu, ces anglais!* George thought it was a great joke. When they went out for breakfast in the morning again everyone ran to look at them. George thought they admired him for being above prejudice.

After a pause Nellie said that she also had a letter from a sweet friend Caroline, she wanted Camilla to meet.

"She's known the tragedy of failure and the dead end on the lonely road."

Not long before, Nellie had been working in the offices of the Roseland Estate Development in Buckinghamshire. Nothing had developed. There they all sat in the naked old villa, with grass growing over the old avenues; but no new house had yet been built.

"It's all bourgeois waste and caprice anyway. Someone taking the ideas of some Frenchman, great blocks of flats with angles and courtyards, a brick prison, it won't suit England; no fire-places, no chimney and everything laid on from a center. Suppose there's a strike! The whole place can be without fire or water or heating; the mothers and children sick and the fathers grousing. All they have to do is sabotage and hundreds of families can't get their tea or wash their faces. I've seen pictures of it in France. It's the home turned upside down. The British, Camilla, will never give up their fireplaces and their cosy little back rooms. You sit in front of the fire and look into it and you begin to relax after the day's work. You throw in your cigarette ends and your rubbish. How will they keep the place clean? You'll have matches and cigarette butts all over the floor, and where will you relax? Ah, Camilla love, there's nothing better than to come home when you can't go on anymore and brew your pot of tea and sit before the blaze and dream. With this Corbusier there'll be no relaxing and no dreaming; only a soul-less measured-off engineer's world with no place for us."

She lit a fresh cigarette. Through it she murmured, "Caroline, aye! There's a beautiful soul, Camilla, who didn't see the wrongs of it. She believes in the world, she wants the world to be beautiful. She's lonely, aye, living there in a wretched room with a wicked old landlady. Ah, the landladies! And what rooms can you get in a one-street country village? So the only reality to Roseland is a broken-down villa with grassy rises and a landlady's damp cell with peeling walls. I've made her see it. You won't help the world, I said, with building stony streets of barracks with stone cells for the soul of man. They're tearing down the tenements, I said, to put the workers into prison; won't it be easy to isolate and machine-gun a workers' prison? There'll be no freedom then; and no desire for it, I said. Just watch your step and watch your neighbor. She's leaving it. She's coming here for a few days. She's not happy. No; there's another cause. A broken marriage with a dull man, a wandering man."

She sighed and continued, "The parents are the innocent cause. She had a hopelessly middle-class country parson background. You don't venture to say the Queen has unsuitable shoes: *But it's the Queen, dear.* And the big thing to look forward to, taking a stall at the fete to raise funds for the church hall. Aye, she tried to escape. But can the bird break the iron bars by fluttering? You are likely to see bloodied and broken wings; and the close tendrils of parental love were in this case iron bars."

Nellie sighed and blew smoke; "The old, old problem, sweetheart. Even here, where the parents are of a fine old type, the father's word obeyed and the Bible called upon to prove and refute and have the last word; and the mother with a life of unquestioning frustration and the daughter a full-blooded woman with the passions sealed in."

"How old is she, the daughter?"

Nellie hesitated; then, "Twenty-eight and she was married; but not a woman, a girl. The husband tried to get her away; but he hadn't the appeal. He took her to America; but they wrote and they begged. Poor things! She felt the guilt. She came back; but then it was, You'll go back in the spring; you'll go and pay him a visit when the American summer is over; and then, Our dear daughter could not bear to leave her parents alone. Ah, poor things!"

Nellie brushed the tears from her eyes. She drank her tea and said dryly, "Caroline's only outlet is what she thinks is writing. She's published a thing or two, little clouded mirrors of life, that no one ever heard of. I've asked. No one ever heard of her. In one she tried to show her husband; it's pitiful. Life—no more like the stormy, hot-blooded, passionate, unruly, unbridled thing it is, Camilla, than a cup of tea is like a river in flood. But she's fine, and it's a damn shame to see her the prisoner of sterility. Aye, she took my advice. She left home and took this room; and the parents too have nothing. I'm sorry for the older generation. Ah, true marriage, pet, when it comes, is perfection. To think they never knew that! So many generations of wasted joyless lives; and only in our own day and here and there, the perfect flower of married happiness, a rare unforgettable thing, the only earthly joy. It's a grand thing, Camilla, perfection in union; to know each other as man and woman in perfection."

She placed her hands on her knees, leaned her topknot forward and looked earnestly at the dressmaker. Camilla gave her an enquiring glance and bent to her sewing.

Nellie, in the same posture, said, "What George and I have is the flower of perfection. Physically, George is a wonderful man. It's joy, it's heaven; there's nothing like it when it's natural and sweet; a blessed union. That's what I have with George, perfection."

The dressmaker made no reply. After a short silence, she said, "Try this on, Nellie; let me see."

She made some marks with a piece of chalk. Nellie took the dress off and sitting down, smoking away, she continued to make comments along the same lines, until Camilla gave her an irritated glance. She then went on to talk about parenthood and its solemn responsibilities. Our parents, she said, were poor, pitiful, frail human creatures.

Here she was interrupted by a bad fit of coughing. She got up and lounged over to the sofa, where she lay prone, her head hanging down, coughing and hawking, gasping and puffing.

She got up, came back to the chair, picking up her cigarette, "It's me bronchitis."

She took a few puffs, inhaling deeply, and continued, like a chant, "They brought us into the world in sorrow and ignorance and haste, young people then, with their lives before them, taking us like packs on their backs, along the pike; and from then on destiny had only one voice, it came out of the crying mouths of little children. Taking a strange dangerous chance with us, fighting against poverty and death with us in their arms. That's the thought, isn't it, pet? It's pitiful. We must take up the burden of repayment. We've not fulfilled their hope, I'm afraid, darling. That's beyond our poor human powers."

Camilla, won by the inner melody of the northern voice and its unexpected cry, its eloquence, considered her. Nellie was looking into the smoke. She had paused and settled herself in a businesslike way. She cocked her head, like a journalist envisaging his paragraph.

She continued, "My brother Tom doesn't think like me. The poor lad's grown heartless, nothing but the flame of the moment, a poor trifler, out of work and living like a tramp. I had a letter from him this morning, Camilla; a sad change. He was my friend. We were together in everything. I led, he followed. I led them all. But he wandered away from me. He left his beliefs in socialism, the light went out of him: a spendthrift, a ne'er-do-well, an unemployable, a mischief-maker; that's what it's come to. The poor lad, Camilla. A tragedy. Stumbling after happiness, which eludes him like a will-o'-the-wisp, getting deeper into the swamp and clutching at a straw. The misery of it breaks my heart. He's in the clutches of a harpy, Camilla, wandering round the country, like two gypsies with no home, desperate that this iron ration of happiness will be taken from him." When she spoke of her brother, she used the home accent. She said puir la'ad.

"What is she like?" enquired Mrs. Yates.

Mrs. Cook rose and stood at the fireplace swinging one leg and shaking ash into the fire.

"No good, I'm afraid. It's the case of the snake and the fascinated rabbit. She's much older than he, though she doesn't look it; the cosmetics and the hairdresser. She'll leave nothing undone to hold him, every excuse to keep him from humanity. Persuades herself of the higher motive. She's woven him into her web. She's taken the poor helpless fly and made him her parcel. She's carrying him away to death and beyond! That's the type, that preys upon men. And he's promised to die with her!"

She leaned her head on her hand on the mantelpiece.

"What!" said the dressmaker.

"Ah, Camilla, the tenacious, bloodsucking, unscrupulous harpy! It's hard to understand; for he's a bitter man, disenchanted. He's not like me, pet, apt to glamorize everyone."

She sighed.

Camilla, sewing, said, "Yes, you must feel it to lose a great friend like that!"

Nellie stared. She turned, put her hand behind the clock and drew out a tan envelope, took out a sheet of engineer's squared paper and held it out to Camilla.

"There! It came this morning from my brother. It'll show

you the hopelessness. Spending the little they've got on every quack remedy, a typical woman's trick. And there's no black or white in her mind, every method is fair. A superstitious roving, looking for the impossible; and costing George and me money. There's a London doctor in it and we footed the bill to the tune of forty pounds. Read it! You'll see him like a fly in the gluepot."

Camilla, after hesitating, took the sheet of squared paper and read,

Nellie:

I am sorry Mother is sick but I cannot leave Marion now. We must try everything. We have hope in a cure we are trying now. I had to bring her away from the nursing home and she depends on me. In two or three months we will know if this salve will work. It is supposed to cure third-degree burns. She is fighting it out. She will take no drugs for she says the doctors will kill her. I don't know how she stands the awful pain. I cannot leave her. If she begins to mend, I will go up to Bridgehead and see Mother.

Affly, Tom.

The dressmaker read this slowly.

Nellie sat with a sparkling angry face and said, "You see? You see the situation? Relentless to the last."

"It's a terrible thing for the poor man. Is he alone with her?"

Nellie put the note away, saying vaguely, "No, pet. I think there's someone else. They've no money for a nurse. It's a case of destitution."

Camilla bent her head over the dress.

Nellie said, "You see what it is? He has no reason for living and he goes off the deep end over a thing like this."

She got up and lounged about the room. She came and stood near Mrs. Yates, looked down at her, said melodiously, "I'm the guilty one. I brought him to London from the home climate and everyone doesn't transplant. I was the pathfinder. I thought I'd go out and find a way for them, my brother and sister. I threw up the college work because they kept grinding our noses

[19]

into the footnotes on Shakespeare. It's the living word that matters in our day. That's the way to disgust you with Shakespeare. And then, pet—there are some things that it is not right, even in Shakespeare, to offer to innocent minds. It's enough to make you think ill of Shakespeare. It did for me. I walked out and got a job. I was getting five pounds a week when most of them had nothing a week; and I was the leader, I was the dashing Jack Malone. So I influenced them too much perhaps. I knew I had something in me. Aye, I was guilty. I walked out of a good job with me poor mother depending on me pay. Me Dad, the old soldier, was wearing out his strength lifting the elbow. He made good money but it went down the gutters of Bridgehead one way and another. Ah, the grand old humbug; he's been the plague of our lives. I never liked it here, pet. They still make me feel like an invader from the north. But I had to come. It was my destiny. There it is, pet, in a nutshell. Now you understand us."

"Is it cancer?" said Camilla.

Nellie turned away for a moment, took a puff, said, "It's cancer, pet. And there they are traipsing around the country after quacks. It's all illusion: there's no reality to it."

"I'm sorry for him."

"Don't be sorry for him. His life is nothing but a dancing in a hall of mirrors."

Camilla looked at her, not understanding.

"And so I must go to see my family now. My brother's let me down."

She went out, came back again and leaned against the doorpost. She had put on a pair of blue overalls to chop some wood in the yard. She smiled at Camilla and an old-fashioned expression came into her face, like the charm of the delicate-faced crop-headed stage stars of the early twentieth century. For the first time she had a lick of beauty. She went and chopped the wood.

Presently, she came back dressed to go out and implored Mrs. Yates, "Don't think badly of me, Camilla, for leaving you alone. The house is yours, chick. Have some lunch. Mrs. McMahon will be along after lunch to clean up a bit. She's an angel and she'll beg you for work to do. She's a real friend, chick, remember. Her life's hard, poor soul. Married to an older man, a good man, but it's not happiness. And this is her home away from home. And yours too, Camilla."

"Well, I'll stay to finish this, and leave it for you. I may go away next week to see my father-in-law; he may do something for the children; I'll leave them with Edmund. They obey him like a father. They don't obey me."

Nellie gave her a sweet, open, doubting look, "Eh, Camilla, you're a damn good woman. I don't know how a man can leave you."

"Well, they say they can't. But he did," Camilla remarked in good humor.

"Were you hard-hearted to him?"

Camilla laughed.

Nellie went away shaking her head, "You're my idea of a beautiful woman! I wish my poor brother had fallen for a woman like you, pet."

Before she left, she came back with a book in her hand. She placed it beside Mrs. Yates.

"I know you've seen the world, Camilla. I'd like your opinion on this woman. Was it injustice? Was she guilty or not? She says they hounded her. We don't know what is a criminal, or how the criminal suffers do we? The law will never tell us who is a criminal. When I see someone branded I hear the hounds baying. I can't shake it from my mind. I'd be grateful for your opinion."

She took a little canvas bag, her shoulder bag and left. When she had gone Mrs. Yates looked at the book. It was the account of a murder trial at the beginning of the century; the trial of a French woman, Madame Steinheil, for poisoning her husband. A French President, Felix Faure, a friend of hers, she said, died of an overdose of aphrodisiac in a brothel. There was also trouble over a diamond necklace she said was given to her by Monsieur Faure. Mrs. Yates glanced through it and put it on the shelf. On the shelf was a book by Frida Strindberg about her life with the dramatist. On the flyleaf was written in Nellie's flowing hand,

I thank God every day for George, for a man of genius who is human and tender and great. What if I had found one like this? Read it again and again and bless the fate that traced my lines. I was spared all suffering. From him only goodness.

When there was trouble in the industrial north, Northumberland, Durham, Nellie's newspaper sent her up there. She was able to get a week there now, some of the Tyne shipyards being struck; and after getting news along the River Tyne, she went home to her people, the Cotters, in Bridgehead. She had a cup of tea at the Bridgehead Station refreshment room and made for the hill leading to Hadrian's Grove, a long suburban road above the river, and lined on each side with small brick houses, all alike, with bow windows, picket fences and roomy attics in the sharp tiled roofs. Whistling, striding, her shoulder bag flapping, she passed the church and came to Number 23. In the front yard was a grass patch, a tree; a few springs of parsley grew by the doorstep. The multiple curtains in the bow window were drawn. She tried her latchkey. The door was bolted; she rang. A dog barked and Nellie called, "Eh, Tom! Where's Peggy?" When the door opened, there was a struggle. Nellie edged in with the door against her, while a furious young sheepdog jumped up and down snapping at her gloves and scarf. He got a glove and tore it quickly. Nellie called soothingly, "Eh, there, Tom man, down man, eh, ye dumb dog, how are ye, Peggy darling? Where's Ma? Stop it, Tom then man, sure he knows his old Nellie! Eh, Peggy darling, call him off, pet!"

Peggy, a short doughy woman with dark eyes and brows in an oval face, and in apron and pink rubber gloves, said she was just doing the silver. "I didn't hurry," she explained, "because I thought it was Pop; and I thought if he can choose his time, I'll take my time."

"Well, sweetheart," said Nellie cheerily, "so old Pop Cotter's going to come home early? It must be the year of the comet. And where's me old sweetheart, where's Mary Cotter, where's me Ma?" She pushed open the door of the front room, where as well as the piano, the expensive leather suite with sofa and smoking chair, the little tables, the sideboard stacked with bric-a-brac and books, there was a double bed in which lay old Mrs. Cotter.

Simon Pike, a little lean man of just on eighty was bowed over the kitchen fire reading the *Daily Mail*. The kitchen was a small narrow room with one window looking on a little tree and asphalt patch under a high wall. Opposite the window was a large fireplace with an old stove and boiler in it. There was a gas stove alongside, cupboards and a dresser in the corners, a kitchen table under the window. The hall door and the back door made a through draft. The brass rails and fender, the stoves, table and sink, and all things but the window were very clean. A ceiling clothes rack had been let down nearer the fire and the damp clothes touched Uncle Simon's head. He sat in a straight hard armchair in which he could not fall asleep and which almost filled the space between the fender, the kitchen table and the sink. When anyone used the sink, he was spattered and said sharply, "Don't splash me!" His chair was placed with its back to the back door which led to the pantry, scullery, vegetable racks and the back yard. When this door was opened the cold wind blew on his back and he muttered, "Shut the door!" Next to his seat were the coal scuttles, a pile of wood which he had split, the firedogs; high on the mantelshelf were bundles of lighters made by him and in the oven a few newspapers to dry. Uncle Simon made, tended, mended and raked out the house fires.

It was about nine thirty at night. Simon heard a sound, got up, a bowed and cramped little man, with his spectacles on, half-opened the hall door and sat down again, looking towards the door. Someone came in by the front door. Simon shrugged slightly. Mr. Thomas Cotter, Senior, hung up his hat and coat on the hall stand and said, "Well, well, well, well, well," in a fine loud baritone. There was no answer. He came down the hall to the kitchen door. "Where's Mrs. Cotter?" said he.

Simon looked him up and down, a long look for Thomas was just on six feet tall, and very broad; and then he said, "She's been in bed all day and she's asleep now or ought to be, if ye didn't wake her." He went back to the *Daily Mail*.

Mr. Cotter, in the door, turned cheerfully to call, "Are you there, Peggy? Where's Peggy?" He turned back, came in saying, "And me, a hungry man." Simon looked at the hall door. Cotter came in, pulling it to, and looked down at the fire. "Good evening," said Mr. Cotter.

"Good evenin'," said Simon; "your dinner's in the oven. It'll be warm."

Cotter said, in a jolly tone, "Must I get it myself with women in the house?"

Simon said, reading his paper, "It's been waitin' for ye."

Mr. Cotter sat down and at this moment the dog Tom came through the hall door and after growling a little at Cotter and a little at Uncle Simon, but only for the form, he looked in his various saucers, drank some water and came to the fire. Cotter said to the dog, "There's a bad dog, there never was a worse dog than that. Like dog, like master. If they'd given you to me, Tom, you'd be a different dog tonight." The kelpie turned round and barked at Mr. Cotter.

Quickly Peggy came in scolding, "What are ye doin' to him, man?"

"Well," said Cotter, "it's the gaffer! I'm hungry, gaffer. She's the gaffer now and we all have to watch our P's and Q's. Where's my dinner, lass? Do you mean to say a man comes in late and nothing waiting for him, eh?"

"You could have come before, we all ate hours ago."

"And a house with women in it and I must serve myself, is that it," said Cotter tenderly, looking round.

"If it's the women's food you're eating as well as your own, I don't see why not," said Peggy, at the same time getting plates out of the oven. "Will you eat here tonight?"

"Thomas Cotter eats in his own dining room," said he graciously; "and I hope you haven't let the fire go out; don't say you haven't laid the cloth for me?"

"Now don't get excited man, I'll lay it," said Peggy, "but you leave the dog alone, Mr. Cotter."

Mr. Cotter said, shaking his head, "It's a bad dog, that dog.

If you'd give him to me, gaffer, I'd make a dog out of him; but that's a bad dog, he's spoiled. Look at him now." He flicked his clean pocket handkerchief at him.

Peggy said, "He's a bad dog because he sees you're bad, that's all, Thomas Cotter; a dog knows a man. Now don't tease him man, or I'll make you regret it to your dying day."

As she entered the hall with things on a tray, there were steps running downstairs and Nellie's lively voice called out, "Is that you, Pop Cotter? How are you, me bold lad?" Half smiling, Peggy went into the unlit dining room where the fire still burned and a snowy starched cloth was laid for the man of the house. Nellie skated down the hall to the kitchen.

Mr. Cotter sat monumentally in his chair and, as his elder daughter entered, calling, "Hello, Pop Cotter!" he said, "Ah, Mrs. Cook, that was a bad thing you did, there was never a blacker day for this house, than the day you brought that dog in the door. You know what I think about that dog? It's a bad dog! But if the gaffer would only give him to me, I'd know how to treat him. He needs training." Meanwhile, he had fished a red handkerchief out of his trousers' pocket. He flicked it at the dog who growled at him, so that Mr. Cotter was able to kick out with his large boot and prod him.

"Couldn't you see Mother, Pop," said Nellie. "She's waiting for ye, pet. You know she doesn't sleep till you come in."

"Yes," said Mr. Cotter, "that's a bad dog and that was a black day, Mrs. Cook, when you brought that dog across the threshold, Nellie. You never did a worse thing."

Nellie laughed loudly to oblige him.

Peggy came back to the kitchen and said to her father, "Now you leave that dog alone, man, and I'll leave you alone." She opened the drawers of the dresser and asked good-humoredly where the silver was. "I had it all out this afternoon; and I suppose Mother took it away."

"Look for it in the grandfather clock, pet," said Nellie, "that's where she had her shoes this afternoon."

"Then that's where it'll not be; it is vexing."

"Do go and see Mother, Father," said Nellie. "She should

have been asleep long ago; but she stayed awake for you, now go on."

Mr. Cotter heaved himself up and went along the hall to the front room where his wife had been sleeping since her fall on the stairs. She now spent her days there, sometimes walking about a little in her nightgown; he slept upstairs still in the fine front bedroom. They could hear him crooning and cajoling, "How are you, Mary, are you better? Are you feeling better now, this evening, Mary my girl? Are you going to sleep? Now that's right then, sleep now, my girl; are you going to sleep now? Now, that's all right, now will you sleep if I tell you, will you promise?"

Peggy had found some knives and forks done up in a parcel in the cleaning drawer, had laid the tray and got the dish from the oven, a full plate of meat. "It's still hot," she said, "that's good; the fuss he makes! He thinks the whole henhouse must wait up for him."

"Now then, pet," said Nellie, "it's his right, he's the head of the family." Uncle Simon laughed at this and read his paper.

Peggy said, "As a father of a family, he's a disgrace. Why should he get it when he's spending it all in the pubs?"

"Hush, pet," said Nellie, "he's the head of the house and you must be grateful because he's always kept a roof over our heads."

Now Mr. Cotter could be heard in the hall, still crooning, "Are you all right for the night, then, Mollie? Are you comfortable, Mollie? That's right then, dear. Sleep now, sweetheart, have a good night now and please me."

Nellie smiled, "Ah, he's a pet."

Peggy said, "If he worried about her, he'd stay at home and entertain her at nights."

"Now then pet, it isn't the custom of the men in this town as you know; you can't blame the puir old lad for doing what the others do."

Peggy hrmphed. "I know he can't do any wrong with you, but he can do wrong with me. He can do wrong with her. And you can all do wrong with me, for I know what's under it all."

Nellie said, "No, you don't, darling. You don't know that."

[26]

"I know," said Peggy, "it's selfishness, it's nothing but self. The dog there has a better heart than you all."

Nellie said, "Now then, pet, now there he goes into the dining room. I'll take it in, pet, and you'll bring the tea."

As soon as Nellie went out with the tray, the dog began to torment Uncle Simon, by barking rowdily and snatching at his hand. Peggy said meaningly to the dog, "Don't do it, man, don't do it, man!"

Simon said sarcastically, "Don't do it, don't do it, do it!"

"If you didn't torment him man, he'd let you alone. He knows what's what."

Simon said, "Knows what's what."

Peggy cried, "Don't mumble there at him, man; it drives him silly. He's not responsible. He knows you mean harm, man! He's a young dog and he's sharp; and he knows what ye mean. Besides, doesn't he know as I know, ye kick him in the darkness of the hall? I'm on to you. Don't play so hypocritical, Uncle Simon, man. I see through you, man. Let's have a bit of peace, for God's sake."

"A bit of peace for God's sake," said Uncle Simon.

Peggy continued, "Now he doesn't mean anything. That's just his fun. He's got to play, man. He's young. He's not old and shriveled up and ready to die like you. Man, remember when you were young." And this she said in a didactic scolding voice.

Old Simon Pike replied, "When A was young, aye! A wudna be here if A was young." He laid down his paper and began to straighten his back. "When A was young A was oop before six in the marnin'. At six in the marnin' and before A set oot for wark. A was at wark at Armstrong's at six. We all were then. It was different then. Ye wudna see a hoose aboot here then, but wan or two. A've seen snaws here for six weeks, but A was oop every marnin' at five and off to me wark before six. A was a canny lad. Ye wudna catch me here if A was young and if your puir mother wasna so sick and Thomas never in the hoose."

Peggy laughed cheerfully at this, "It's yourself you're thinking of, man. Sitting by the fire and reading your paper; it's not a hard life, is it? That's why you're here and getting everything, your fire and your food and all for only your pension. It suits your pocket, too. Don't make a martyr of yourself, man. It doesn't suit you: you're not a martyr, man. You're selfish like them all. All are selfish and you most of all. A man who was always a bachelor, that's a selfish man, isn't it?"

Simon said, "No, it isn't; perhaps A had me reasons."

"Aye, reasons for spending nothing and keeping warm and cosy, and never taking a chance. You'll understand yourself, man." She cackled. "It's funny to see how the man regards himself. As a fine man. And maybe you saved the family, too, with your savings?"

Simon was still straightening himself and now he rose very slowly from his seat where he had been since suppertime. Peggy looked at him and laughed, "Now, there's no need to rise to the occasion, Uncle Simon, man."

Simon said, "A'm no risin' to the occasion. If A cud rise to the occasion, ye wudna see me heels for dust. A'm risin' slowly to straighten me back and get goin' oopstairs if A'm no welcome here."

Peggy crowed, "Look at the man, now. That's a new act, that's a new song and dance. Now, he's a martyr. Take yourself off, you're more bother than you're worth with your bit of money. No one wants you, you'd be better gone to St. Aidan's churchyard, you would, no one wants you and no one needs you. Puir thing, you think so highly of yourself and you're only a man that has no family and that has been a hanger-on all his life."

Simon was now as straight as he could get and looking not at her, but into the distance, out into the hall, but seeing nothing, his voice shaking out loud, he said, "If it hadna been for me, ye'd all have been on the street wance or twice, ye don't know that." He was trembling and he looked for understanding to Nellie, who had just come from the hall to the kitchen. "There wud ha been no food in this hoose, but for me savin's which A gave ye twice." He looked at Nellie.

She said brightly to Peggy, "Now, what is it, pet? Come in, Peggy, darling, and talk to Father. He's askin' for ye. What is it, Uncle Sime, sweetheart? Sure, ye were always good to us, a guid man. We were always glad to have you, sweetheart. What would home have been without Uncle Sime in the attic? You made the fires for us every day of your life, Uncle Sime, didn't ye?"

Peggy had gone out with the teapot, and Nellie began dis-arranging her blouse to wash at the sink. Uncle Simon looked at her and she, with a bold daring grin at him, fully bared her starved breasts, which she held in her hands and she said in dialect, grinning, "A'm goin' to wash." She went to the sink.

Uncle Simon was not straight now. He was bowed and look-ing downwards. When she returned from the sink, Uncle Simon still stood in the middle of the floor by his chair by the fire. She came and stood in front of him, her breasts lying loose, tempting the ragged old man. He lifted his large faded blue eyes to her sternly. She burst out laughing loudly. "Ye mustn't take the puir girl seriously, Uncle Sime, pet." She swaggered back to the sink, "She's not to blame, pet: we are. We're all guilty, you and me too. We're all guilty."

Uncle Simon sat down and bent over the fire. He tried to control the trembling of his body and hands as he put a coal on the fire.

When Mr. Cotter had finished the plate, he said to Nellie, "Is this all you've got in the house? And what about the roast from Sunday? I need a bit of meat. I wasn't brought up on bits and bacon like you."

Peggy said, "Uncle Simon has a right to his little bit of the roast and you've had all the rest. The rest of us, mother and me, don't touch the stuff. It's not good for us. And it's not good for you or your stomach, except that your stomach's ruined by your firewater and it doesn't matter with you."

Cotter said, "You see what I say? You must look after your-self in this house. In this house you must take thought for your-self, for no one else will bother about you." He examined the butter, spread it on some bread, "It's every man for himself—in this house. Now haven't you got an egg for me? Haven't you got some cheese? Where are your pretty manners, gaffer? Aren't you the gaffer?"

"There's an egg for mother and one for me in the morning," said Peggy continuing to knit.

Cotter said angrily, "I came home the night before last and found no meat on my plate."

"Where would I get meat every night for your plate? Don't you eat all the meat off the joint?"

"Yes, you do, Pop Cotter," said Nellie; "you get more than your fair share, pet; you must think of others."

At this attack, Cotter turned to Peggy and said thoughtfully, "You see, gaffer, times aren't what they were and the money isn't coming in as it was. You must cut your cloth, gaffer—you must cut your cloth—"

Peggy cried out, "Cut my cloth! It's like your cheek, Pop Cotter, to talk about cutting my cloth. It's you who's cutting a big swath in the cloth and no cloth for anyone else. It's like your cheek."

"Now, you say it's like my cheek," he returned graciously, "now it isn't like my cheek. You must cut your coat according to your cloth, now that's well known."

Peggy said, "If forty-five shillings comes into this house, you spend fifty in drink."

Cotter went on, philosophically, gently, "You must cut your coat, gaffer. You, you, Mrs. Cook there," he said appealing to Nellie, "my daughter, you, Nellie Cotter, that's known as Cushie Cotter, now. Do you know what happened to me last week? I was down in the—football club—and a young fellow there said to me, Mr. Cotter, there's a C. Cotter writing in the papers, in the labor papers, is that your daughter? She's got an article saying that over in Sunderland there's a family—a couple with eleven children living in one room and when the beds are made for the night there's no room to walk. Now that's a libel on us and it's printed in London. Is that your daughter? No, said I, that's Cassie Cotter, she belongs to those other Cotters who live near Newcastle, she's not a daughter of mine, she's no Durham Cotter, Mr. I don't know your name. There was your article, Mrs. Cook, as large as life for every man to read, with your name in type at the top, C. Cotter. Now you could have used the name Cook; but I'm not against your using the name Cotter, Miss Cotter; it's a matter of principle. Now you listen, Mrs. Cook, you don't understand. When you've had my experience, you'll understand, Mrs. Cook, that that's a very bad thing. You can do as you please, think as you please, think what you like; but keep it dark. That's good sense and good manners, Mrs. Cook; don't wear your heart on your sleeve."

"Ah, Pop Cotter, you're talking rubbish," said Nellie.

He went on in his deliberate, gentle manner, "There you were earning fifteen pounds a week in that housing business, that Roseland Development there, and you had your principles in your pocket with you and no one asked you what you thought. You could write articles on the side; and now, look where you are. You're getting five pounds a week. We could have used the margin here at home, if you could do without— and you've got nothing for it. Don't wear your heart on your sleeve! Now a fellow asks me, Is that the same C. Cotter, my daughter and I say, No, my name's Thomas Cotter and I have no daughter of that sort. What I'm thinking, he doesn't know and doesn't ask. That's a matter of principle only; don't wear your heart on your sleeve."

Nellie said, flicking away her ash, "That's all right, Pop, that's all right."

Cotter went on with the calm power of a tall strong man, "Now I'm not against your having opinions; a man and a woman's got a right to opinions; this is a free country, isn't it?—but it's just humanity not to wear your heart on your sleeve for daws to peck at. They don't care about your principles. You listen to your father, Miss Cotter; he'll give you good advice. What good did it do, your wearing your heart on your sleeve and dropping ten pounds a week? No, said I, I'm Thomas Cotter and every man knows me; but that Cotter's another family over Newcastle way that I happen to have met, I said. But I don't know that C. Cotter."

"All right, Pop Cotter," said Cushie.

Cotter said more directly to her, "I'm not arguing for your turning your coat; I'm arguing for your not wearing your heart on your sleeve. I'm not the man to say a man hasn't a right to his opinions. And so you see, Miss Cotter—you see—the money's not coming in and I don't know if there will be a fresh newlaid egg for your mother's breakfast; for the gaffer there has not learned to cut her cloth. You see what you've done, Mrs. Cook? Now wasn't that a fine thing to happen to me right down in the—"

Nellie said, "The football club; all right, Pop Cotter."

He continued, as if he had not heard her, "This young fellow comes up to me. Are you Thomas Cotter, said he. I am, sir, I said, that's my name—"

"And you said, Don't wear your heart on your sleeve. I'm sick of your blather, Pop Cotter," said Peggy.

"Now, that'll do, pet," said Nellie to her young sister.

Peggy continued cheerfully nagging, "And when you set the police on us to bring us home when we were young here, you didn't like our opinions."

Nellie said, "Hush, sweetheart; we were eating his bread."

Cotter said blandly, "Now what you're referring to, gaffer, is just what I was saying. You wore your heart on your sleeve and that was for daws to peck at, a danger to the community, so a loving father with my experience, I—"

Peggy said, "You set the police on Nellie and young Tom and me: that's the kind of father you were."

Nellie said, "Now, hush, pet, you'll not speak to father that way. He's our father and he kept a roof over our heads, no matter what; and in the blackest days he fed us."

NELLIE HAD brought some money with her to buy a new pair of shoes in a Bridgehead shop that suited her; and when the money started to go for the family needs, she thought she'd get her shoes cobbled at the reliable old family cobbler's; but that money went too; and she returned to London, to her paper, in the same queer broken-soled shoes with the twisted heels.

As soon as she had turned in her material, she took a few drinks and then hurried home. She had written again from Bridgehead to her friend at Roseland Development, Caroline Wooller, to throw up her job, to come and spend a few days with her and look for a room. Caroline could get a room near the Cooks', get a job in housing, if she was still interested in that, and Nellie would guide her.

Nellie said to herself as she went along, "I love that girl; I'm so susceptible, aye. I hand out my heart like a blooming throw-away."

She rushed into her house on Lamb Street, with parcels in her arms, a cigarette in her mouth, cheerily calling out; but it was too early. No one was home from work. There were letters from George: he was traveling south, hoping to get a job in Rome. There was a little scratch from her brother, three lines, which made her angry; and one signed Johnny, and written by a woman she had known long ago up north, a ragged, dirty, big-faced, black-haired woman who hated the world and was determined to live on it for nothing; a bold, harsh, fearless tramp whom Nellie admired. Johnny was on her way south and expected to stop with Nellie when she reached London; but she was vagabonding and might not be in for months. Johnny wrote once every four or five years.

Nellie stretched out on the bed, shook off her shoes and lay smoking. She was flattered that Johnny had not forgotten her. She thought of Johnny and what Johnny had taught her, of a girl who had died for Johnny; and of others, a person called Jago, a man of forty who had taught Nellie what the world was, when Nellie was sixteen; and of an Indian boy in the Jago circle who had died a terrible death; and of things that would never come out now. Yet she suddenly began to tremble. She jumped up, "Ah, no! Ah, no!" She was loyal to comrades in the unnamed rebel battalion she marched in, outcasts, criminals, the misunderstood, women not one of whom could show a clean record; but she wished Johnny were not coming. Johnny did not believe in marriage. Nellie had not seen her since before her marriage to George. George would not tolerate the tramp woman; and what if he found out, suspected something? George was aboveboard, intolerant, and had no use for castaways, for the aimless refractory suffering bohemian. But Johnny's contempt and wrath were sufferings Nellie could not endure, either.

She walked up and down, went downstairs, presently got a bottle from a locked cupboard and began to drink. The cupboard was locked only against herself, because she was short of money at present and liked to have a drink for visitors.

Someone opened the street door. Nellie washed the glass, put away the bottle and called from the kitchen. It was Caroline Wooller. Nellie at once became joyful, told Caroline to go upstairs, she'd be up in a jiffy with tea and sausage rolls, and she lifted a gay tender face to Caroline as she went upstairs.

Caroline was a tall sober-faced woman, with thick loose fair hair, blue eyes and a small mouth.

Nellie came up to the front room in the attic with her tea tray, sat down and told about her family in Bridgehead, putting everything in a dramatic light; and then while Caroline lay back on the bed, seeming very tired, Nellie began smoking furiously in silence. Caroline sighed.

"Well, chick, what happened to you? Were you all right while your Nellie was away?"

Caroline exclaimed, "Nellie, I've got a job! Right away! Joseph—that man—recommended me and I got a job at once with the Rehousing Committee. It happened they needed someone at once."

Nellie was not pleased and said nothing.

A strange thing had happened. Caroline wondered what Nellie would think of it. Her friend Belle Coyne thought it very strange. It happened through Belle Coyne. Belle who was, she said, descended from a bastard son of one of the old English kings, was a girl in the Roseland office who had befriended her after Nellie left. She knew Caroline was looking for a room in London and brought in a newspaper with a remarkable advertisement in the ROOMS TO LET. It said, special low terms and homelike conditions for colonial and dominion girls; and quoted a very low rent.

"Belle came to London with me. I could never have found it without Belle. It was in a street, a broad street with villas running down to the Thames; but I can't tell you where, except that it was near a bridge. It was a big dark red house of brick with four stories and a slate roof and with a lot of ground in front. There was no front door. The entrance was at the side, a flight of steps under a glass canopy. You see, as I had been out to America, Belle thought I could say I was from overseas. I had my tartan silk dress on."

She paused, thinking about the event.

"Aye, pet."

"The woman who opened the door was not what we expected. She was handsome, dark, proud, well dressed—she looked us over and told us to go upstairs, peremptory, like the headmistress of a girls' school. She said she had one room, one for me: and showed us up to the second floor. I was rather pleased that she was a lady. She didn't seem to like Belle. The second floor was nearly all ballroom, with a number of small plain doors opening out of it; another staircase going up."

"Go on, pet."

"The woman showed us into a little room at the side, very plain and small with a skylight, no window. It must have been over the entrance. It was too small. I said it wouldn't do. She said, I might get a bigger room later on; but for the rent it was good. There was no running water. I said, But I will never get my luggage in here. She seemed surprised and said, Have you a lot of luggage? I said, Yes, I brought my whole trousseau back with me from overseas. This is true."

"The woman hesitated, then said she would go downstairs and find what room they had for luggage. While she was away Belle said to me, Why is there no lock? Why is there just a bolt outside the door? I looked and saw that's how it was. When the woman came back, I asked, Why is there a bolt on the outside of the door and no lock inside? The woman was angry. She said it had been a closet and anyway, no one locked the doors there; they were all friends. So we left and said we'd let her know. She was very angry and said I must let her know at once, she had plenty wanting the room. But when we got into the street Belle said it was very funny about the door; and only a cubicle with a skylight. So I have stayed on here, till you got back, Nellie."

"Aye, I'm glad you did, chick," said Nellie dryly.

"What do you think of it?"

Nellie said curtly, "I don't know, pet; it beats me."

After a short pause, she suddenly became very gay, cajoling and sweet. She told Caroline that she needed a friend, not someone like Belle Coyne, who though no doubt kind, would get her into trouble.

"I see, I see very well, you need me."

Nellie said she'd get some drinks, they'd have supper and a nice long talk. But after tea they went out to a local tavern where Nellie was known; and there she was busy exchanging jokes with customers, or arms akimbo, head cocked, watching the men playing darts. The men talked, laughed and glanced sideways at the women. Coming home, Caroline said they were very nice people. She had only been in a public house once or twice in her life.

Nellie was bored, murmured, "Aye, chick; she's a strange old witch, London is. Look at her now, glamorous with a veil of mystery, the long sameness of the streets end in a soft dream. We need the mists here."

Caroline laughed, "Then she would be handsomer in a pea-souper."

"Ah, no, none of your cynicism. Don't tear down my illusions and my loves. I love London because it's all trial and error like my life; terrible mistakes and blind turnings, beautiful prospects and when you look at some stony reality you can glance aside at a beautiful broken dream."

Caroline laughed a little, but said, "You're fey, I suppose, coming from the north?"

"Ah, no, not that. I'm not fey. There's one crowd that despises the fey Scot and that's the plain Scot. And we're only half Scots. I'm a mixture of the soft and the hard, though the soft dominates; and so I lose what I've gained. Aye, that's me."

Caroline said that she felt much better since coming to London. "The dreariness out in Roseland at night! The long country street, a few housefronts, go to the movies, come home early, sit in your bedroom reading a library book by the dim light. Now I know I will be able to write again. I see people. I went to the Rehousing Committee for my interview and sat with the people waiting for homes. Oh, Nellie, what I saw and heard!"

Nellie said good-naturedly, "You're all alike, you amateurs. Everything is grist to your mill. You don't see the warm natural human material. You see a subject."

"Isn't it a subject for you? A news story?"

"That's different. They have great faith in the press; a lever to move things for them."

"But today one of the men said to me, Write about this, what you see, write a book about us. I told him I wanted to. He said good."

Nellie, not heeding, broke into a blackbird whistle, a headless and tailless motif and went striding along. After a while, she slowed down and said protectively, "I understand the urge. But you'll need more experience. That's not enough, the seamy side. You can't butcher them to make a holiday in print. Writing's not just a case of self-expression or conscience clearing. The muckrakers did their work. Now we want something constructive. You see, sweetheart, just to photograph a refuse yard with its rats, that wouldn't help the workers one tiny little bit. It would only be glorifying your own emotions."

"What would you write about, I mean given your experience? Of course, I can never rival your experience."

"No, I've been up to my ears in it all my life. I always knew reality."

"Well, what would you begin with, say?"

"You just write what you see, Caroline sweetheart. Stick to reality; and when you've got the hang of it, you'll be all right. I knew I had something to say when I started out, pet; but when I saw the paper-spoilers, I said, I'll never do that, so perhaps something great is lost; but that's my feeling."

"I have to see it myself, I know."

"Aye, but you don't want to dress it up in romantic illusion or disillusion. You want to give stark staring reality, straight in the face. And no destruction, nothing depressing. The lives of the workers are depressing enough. You want to cover it with a rosy veil, a mystery."

"No destruction. Yes, I said to myself I never heard talk about retreat and failure from Nellie Cook. And I wanted to come and learn from you."

Nellie was charmed, "Did ye, pet? That was wise and good of you, sweetheart. The workers, pet, were walk-ons in all this glorious history. Their play has got to begin."

"That's well put."

Nellie declared with false melancholy, "No, pet, I haven't fulfilled my promise to myself. Let's go in and get a beer at the Queen's Head. Caroline, I'm dry! And I've got to take a pee."

She rapped Caroline on the shoulder, pushed her into the next pub, and ordered for herself, first a sherry, then a whiskey, then a gin.

"You'll be ill."

"No, I'm just beginning to come round. The social quack Robert Peebles, me editor, blue-penciled half me article. What are ye doing, I asked him, tailoring reality closer to your theories? The air here is thick with theories; you want to get out into the fresh air of dockside: it's a long time since you were there. Ah, pet—give me a minute."

For a while Nellie worked on some notes she had to take in in the morning. She then slapped her book together, gave a huge laughing sigh and ordered for herself a whiskey and a gin.

"And now let's have a good talk. Are you hungry? Or can you hold out for a bit so I can get to know you."

Caroline looked round the room, said it was nice and friendly. "My parents would think it sinful to be here. But here they're just nice ordinary people, kind."

Nellie stretched her legs out and said a perfect friendship was a fine thing. Had Caroline ever had a friend?

"I had plenty of friends, at school and in the church, everywhere. Dozens I suppose if you count them all."

Nellie said earnestly that was not what she meant, "You can't have dozens of friends. You can only have one, one true friend. Have you never had a true friend?"

"Oh, yes, when I was about eighteen I had one. We used to take long walks together. We were both interested in serious questions. She was lovely: so true."

"And she was your true friend, pet?"

"We got on because we weren't too close and weren't alike. That's best. Our lives ran parallel and never met: no friction. And she's loyal and so am I."

"Ah, no, your lives didn't run parallel; they met."

"No, my life never met anyone's till I met Barry, my husband. He was more like a best friend. I was very happy. I knew the risk I was taking coming home."

She paused and Nellie waited. Caroline continued, "We live through everything. Sometimes I think life is a strange disease that attacks different people in different ways; and at different ages it attacks you differently."

"Aye, but with a true friend you can fight off that disease; you can hold on to the true solution, the cure."

"What's the cure?" Caroline laughed sadly.

"There are two, sweetheart: love, and death."

"Oh, both those are diseases, too."

"Ah, you're depressed, love. You see, you never understood what friendship is. The friendship at school and at church, that's good; but it's the loaf of bread; it's not the wine."

"My parents loved me. They couldn't understand why I left home. I heard Mother saying one day, with such an undertone of joy, that their dear daughter had never been able to bear leaving her own home, where she was so loved. I had already secretly begun to save up to come away."

Nellie said, smoking and drinking, "Yes, family love is painted as a smooth green shallow valley of comfort and it's full of abysses; you've got to watch your step not to slip in. But pity is the answer, Caroline. We're responsible for them, their failures and pitiful disappointments. They were young things when they had us, ready for life and we were the first burden on their thin young shoulders. I don't understand those who don't feel this terrible tender guilt towards their parents. It's a crushing burden, darling: it is. It breaks many people; but we have known life and love and it was denied to them."

"I am sure my parents love each other. I even wondered how they could see me there without a life of my own."

Nellie said excitedly, "But isn't that the proof? That they never knew the complete perfection and joy which our generation knows ought to be marriage? Of course, chick, it's rare even with us, a rare, rare flower, shy and difficult. Ah, darling, when I think of my poor grandmother, uncomplaining, a splendid human being who showed us the stuff of life, taught us what a woman could be, held our hands spiritually and physically through our hungry thirsty youth! When we wanted knowledge and were looking for it in all directions, cheeping pitifully like young birds, she fed us from the spring of life, she taught us, a noble human soul, enduring, closest to us all, a noble wife and mother—to think she never knew the meaning of sexual pleasure! Such people, generous and fine, miss the grandest thing of all, for they sacrifice out of ignorance of self, out of goodness. Sacrifice must be done, darling! But pain goes with it. Discovery is the keyword: the world is there to be found. Self-denial is not the modern answer. To know all and to understand all, the good and the evil alike, that is the modern answer. And to pity all. We do not know what lies under the actions of the just or the unjust. Not scorn but pity. All suffer, but the criminal suffers more; all his life is suffering. And one must know joy too, otherwise the crown of perfection is missing. I often wonder at my strange fate to be born into the first generation that understood humanity's birthright, the perfect consummation. If a woman has that with a man, darling, then you can't ask more from life."

"But the classics are full of it. I was interested in love always."

Nellie scowled, "I left the university, pet, because of teachers abruptly enlightening the young, ignorant, questioning minds; that is the reason for many distorted lives. A teacher there—what she said combined with what we knew—and the classics! The Rape of Lucrece, and Venus and Adonis—it was a crime—the corruption of youth."

Caroline looked at her thoughtfully, did not know what to say. Nellie went on in a sweet thin craven tone, asking if Caroline thought they could be friends.

"You're missing something if you haven't a friend."

"But we are friends, aren't we? I know it's early."

"It's early for an ordinary companionship, aye; but where there's a genuine basis, it ought to begin at once. It only needs the act of willing and knowing. Would you say we couldn't be friends now?"

Caroline looked at her, still puzzled.

Nellie went on in a dreamy coaxing tone, "It's no good playing the ascetic, no; the thick armor of self-sufficiency which you have, pet, covers a wound, a scar is there. Self-knowledge must be struggled for. Confess what you know, confess what you don't know. You need a friend for that, to tell your inmost secrets to."

"I'll tell you the truth," said Caroline and paused.

"Ah, now, that's better: let's be frank."

"I've written to Barry, but had no reply. He never caused me any pain. I feel quite sensible now. It was harmony with him, as you say. If he is free, I would go there now."

She looked at Nellie as if she had told her whole story.

Nellie said, "Then there's no hope for us as friends?"

"Why not?"

Caroline looked at her eccentric face and topknot and the glasses standing before her sympathetically. She added, with warmth, "You know, I think it is you who don't know about friendship. For a woman the best friend is a man. There's no deeper feeling."

Nellie cried in a rage, "That's a damn hypocritical superior attitude. I won't take it from you or anyone else. So women are second-class citizens. Like families in slums who need housing. Subjects for pity!"

Caroline sat up in angry astonishment.

Nellie cried, "So that's it. Women are inferior, incapable of friendship. Of all the goddamn backward bourgeois attitudes. A woman's not the equal of a man. I resent it. You can't put that over on me. So we're second-class citizens to you."

Caroline said indignantly, "Well, if it seems that way to you."

"You see what a bourgeois you are? The superiority feeling in everything! You're incapable of a decent human relation with another woman."

Caroline did not reply.

Nellie began to lament, "You see how contorted your attitudes are? You're formed by the middle-class marriage hunt; man first, last and always. Aren't you ashamed, a little ashamed? Ashamed to put your sisters on such a level?"

"I can't see what you mean. If Barry answers, he will be all to me."

"That's a terrible confession."

Caroline said, "A confession?"

"A confession; a terrible confession."

"Of what?"

"Of weakness, inferiority, of needing the superior conquering sex."

Caroline began to laugh weakly, "You make everything so unusual. I want to get married again; that's all. I'm glad to have some women friends."

She felt she had hurt Nellie and added, "We were brought up so differently."

"Yes, we were. I was not brought up with pretty pictures painted on me eyelids."

"If you're my friend, shouldn't you try to understand me?"

Nellie said bitterly, "I understand you very well. You're

[42]

smugly satisfied to be enclosed in the shell and never get out. You don't want experience. You don't want discovery. Experience is a difficult woman to woo: you must leave your mother and your father and your milksop ideas of romance. No good will ever come of your writing unless you open your eyes. You'll get no respect from me. You must rely not on yourself but on others; on me. I can show you the way; and if I don't, if you alienate me, your last chance has gone. You'll be the blind led by the blind. You'll be writing the mutterings and screams in a nightmare, no reality. There are enough paper spoilers. I could show you the way. There is a way. With just a little, you could be close to the warm skin of humanity. But you can't take it. Your soul and heart are second rate. You're weak. You want to follow the way of the mothers, the grandmothers, the pathetic imprisoned Eves."

Nellie ordered another drink and they sat in silence till she had finished it, tossing it in with curt desperate gestures. Then Caroline said, "Shouldn't we go? Didn't you say you had to go and see someone tonight?"

"Yes, I have to go and see someone you'd never go and see. It's an unfortunate woman, miserable and despised. She lives in a prostitute's hotel in a bad street in Southwark on the marshy side. And I don't blame you. I don't know any bourgeois woman who'd go and see her. And yet she is my friend and no man ever was her friend. To be her friend I did what you would never do. I told her I was a streetwalker, too. I told her I had a different district. She thinks I walk the streets round here!"

She ended in a tone of bitter heart-rending misery.

"Let's go then," said Caroline Wooller, getting up.

"I must go home first; I must take her some eggs and a jacket."

They headed home. When they were some way along the street, Caroline noticed that Nellie was crying. When they reached the door, Caroline offered Nellie the house key, thinking that she had offended her too deeply; but Nellie begged suddenly, in her pretty quick tones,

"You'll stay tonight? Let me make it up with you, Caroline. Did I offend you? Did I go too deep? I'm a bloody fool, darling,

I'm so sincere. I cut across nerves. Will you forgive me, pet, and give me another chance?"

"I'm so unused to talk, you see; I'm afraid I'm ridiculously touchy. You're right, that it's not human."

"Eh, darling, you're all right; you're a fine woman. You remind me of my grandmother, the woman I honor most. Let's have a cup of tea and a bite. I've got to unpack me legs and get going, but I must eat something. The poor woman won't have anything. She's waiting on me."

While they were eating Nellie said vaguely, over her cup and cigarette,

"Yes, my grandmother, as I was saying, Caroline, was my guiding star. I resolved that that great life should not sink unrecorded into the dust of millions. That's my high resolve: to make a beautiful drama of it. It's me great play. She will not have lived in vain."

Caroline asked about the plot; but Nellie did not tell.

"There are things, pet, which cannot be reduced to words, though that spites our poor scribbler's vanity."

Someone came into the house; and Nellie explained that it was Eliza Cook, George Cook's sister. She had a back room on the second floor. She was working now as a door-to-door salesman and had many friends who kept her out.

"You'll get to know her, Caroline. Stay here. I need you both. I made up me mind to get drunk after facing that chamber of horrors at Bridgehead and if there wasn't a homing letter from my George. Wait up for me, darling. I'll bring a bottle and we'll drink it together. We'll steep our tribulations in gin in the good old way; and then we'll look at them fresh. There's nothing better. It keeps you from a world of black. And what faces me in Southwark, Caroline, is pure tragedy. She doesn't see why she should live. She has stuck her knife into the carcass of men's truth; and what's in it, is unspeakable. Only the brave can face it. Ah, I couldn't tell you yet: you haven't faced life yet. . . . Aye, and from tragedy I took the train down here."

"I'm sorry about your mother."

"Ah, she's aged before her time, poor pet, the doctor said. It's my father that's worn her out with his women, his pubs and his debts. They should never have married; that's the root of it all. And the way she clings to him, it's pathetic. It is that. I saw a sad ruin. And she's alone there, I feel so guilty with only my poor sister there; and me brother as good as a deaf-mute to it all."

"And how is your sister now; Peggy—is it?"

"Aye, sweetheart, it's Peggy. I don't know, I don't know. Not much better, I'm afraid. That's the terror and it haunts me. I feel so guilty towards the poor pitiful creature. Ah, the poor thing. The frail white camellia. It's a house of storm. I have bloody dreams; and I wake up in terror, all in a sweat, every night in a sweat, dreaming she's over the edge. The beautiful thing that she was, an early bloom, pure white, and now like a flower crushed by a rough hand, only a dark shred where there was a miracle."

"Isn't she likely to marry? She's young yet, isn't she?"

"I'm afraid not, sweet; no, darling; that's not likely now. She's not interested in those things now. You see, it was a bloody rotten, hanging fire affair with a bloody teaser of a man that did it; eight or nine years he had her hanging on and her mind bent. Ah, poor pet. No, no that's impossible now."

"But there's your father. Isn't he at home?"

"Ah, he's at home in a sense: that's his address. He never had any heart. He's out to his football club—wine, women and song it is. He betrayed her with women the first week they were married and she, poor pet, never knew; at least not then. Perhaps later, and it twisted her. It made her the ever-ailing, complaining headachy, artful little thing she is, calling us the guilty ones when we were little: for she worshiped him and never would admit the guilt in the house was his."

Nellie broke into her piercing sweet whistle and lit a cigarette. This started a strangling cough, which shook her thin body in spasms. She took no notice, meditating all the time through the smoke and coughing. She sighed, "Ah, yes, it's a bloody tragedy, you're right. The frustrated lives."

"You're afraid she won't live long."

"It isn't that that worries me, Caroline. It's the bloody harpy he'll drag into the house the next week. I'd like to take ye with me, show you a bit of England with the lid off, no Roseland, the furnace beneath the green moor that'll blow up into a blistering volcano one of these days. Aye, it's a bit different from your green and pleasant fields. But it's a very normal tragedy."

After a while she laughed; "But I didn't tell you about Uncle Sime."

"Ah, he lives there too, then?"

"Certainly he does. He always lived there. We daren't speak to him remember. He'll never answer us, pet. The kitchen's his sitting room. He sleeps up in the attic with the bats, always did. He doesn't get up till eleven."

She began to speak faster, in deeper dialect; "He goes and sits in the kitchen, speaking to no one. He's queer in the head and a penny spared, puir lad, a confirmed bachelor, one of life's beached wrecks, aye. Eh, he'll never forgive ye if ye turn the gas up on the stove; that's his field of action. He's a reactionary, puir pet, he never knew any better. You'd never get on with the ould lad: the best thing is never to take notice. I'm afraid the picture's depressing. It's a house of terror and storm."

"Poor old man; I like odd people. They go their own way."

"No one could like Sime: no one ever did. But then he never had a woman, darling. It's a bloody awful shame in a man's life: it makes him an old maid. He belongs to the generations that had no happiness. Eh, a poor elf."

After a moment, she said, "I'd like to show you Bridgehead, but if you said to me, Remember Bridgehead, I'd say, not the Cotters and their woes, but some blue, red and white advert over the rivers or a dockers' pub down between the quayside railway tracks with some sandy youngster laughing at ye, like me own brother. He was a canny lad—but they twisted him, the bloody women!"

She wiped her eyes, "It's not the High Bridge, nor the coaly Tyne. I'd say, D'ye see that place with the bloody fake Corinthian pillars? That's the Atheneum Club! Old Pop Cotter was peeing against that wall one night when the cops got him. They took him to the lockup. What a man! You can't do this to

[46]

Thomas Cotter! They must have done it for a bloody lark. And he ran amok in the station and gave one of them a broken jaw and one a black eye; and he was in all night. It's like the kids sing, What's his name? Tom Cotter! What's he got? Whooping cough. And what else? And a black eye. And what else? And he got run over. They took him to the hospital and put in stitches and sent him home without his britches. He'll tell that story over and over and say; And they did that to Thomas Cotter. For he knows every cop from South Shields to Peterlee, that's his proud boast; and he can stop his car and say, How are you? What's the time? And the cop'll say, I'm fine, it's twenty to twelve, Mr. Cotter. That's his achievement. Eh, but he's a darling! Fuddled every night, the ould humbug, and me mother polishing the hearth and the woodwork and the brasses; and him without eyes but for the brasses in the pub. Eh-eh-eh! What a lad, what a lad! A fine-looking lad, the Tommy Atkins of me heart. And a big handsome dandy he was, until he ran into the back of a tram and lost the argument; and the drink's done for the rest."

She finished her tea; "So will ye stay a bit, then, Caroline; and give the house a soul?"

"Why not? I'm lucky. It's a new life here."

"Ah, bless you, pet; that's sweet."

Nellie, going out, paused at the door and looked at her, her deep-carved half-moon face pale against the door frame; "Then you like me, pet?"

"Why, Nellie, you're pure English, old English. Why, if they elected the Queen and she wasn't born to it, they'd elect you."

"Sweetheart, you're an angel born."

She went out, with a deep smile.

Nellie returned when the night was not old, with a bottle under her arm and came chirping up the stairs to her friend's attic room, where Caroline was in bed.

"What were you doing, pet, whiling away the time?"

"You're not late after all."

"Ah, no. My friend had to go to work."

[47]

"She works?"

"It's work. Tramping her feet to the bone, doing what none of you would do; taking chances with the vultures."

Caroline looked at her with compassion.

Nellie said, "Come on down to me boudoir; we'll have a drink and a chat and get to know each other; and no misunderstandings this time."

The Cooks occupied on the floor below, a front room and a bedroom. As Caroline entered the front room, she noticed a large painting of a short-haired grinning boy in blue overalls coursing on a bicycle. It was a talentless painting, but spirited; and she exclaimed, "Who's the handsome boy?"

Nellie turned quickly, paused; and with a brilliant smile, "That's me, love."

"Who did it?"

"A friend, my friend Vi. I'd like you to meet her. She's the daughter of me old friend, Ma Pelley. A genius, born into a family of three dull boys. She's married, but there's no hope there, Anthony, a man with a rattletrap tongue and no stuffing. Eh, what a struggle! When I was there last, Ma Pelley and I sat in the kitchen and opened our gin and dropped our tears in it. The house, love, is like a battlefield fought over by vegetables and rags, all torn, muddy, dead and rotten. Vi's no idea of housekeeping, her poor Ma had to go to work to keep them and the poor waif cannot cope. The place is coming down round their ears; but there's no help for it. He hasn't the interest and she hasn't the strength. Eh, the poor man can't help it: no steady job and a psychological down-and-outer, a frail waif. Ye can't blame them."

Nellie opened her bottle and poured out the drinks.

"My friend Vi took me to Spain to write me play; but I couldn't, for the misery of the people; and she came back for him and married him. Eh, eh! And now children and the life of struggle."

"What does he do?"

"Who, love?"

"The down-and-outer, the man."

"I don't know, love. What he can. He's a mechanic by trade,

[48]

I think; an honest sort, a guid man, but no ambition. Poor waif! Aye, Anthony Butters."

"Anthony Butters! Not the one who was in the papers this week? He's fighting for leadership of one of the big unions. They say if he gets in it will be the ruin of England."

"Ah, I don't know, pet. It might be. I don't know. But he hasn't the go. The wasted lives."

Nellie handed Caroline a glass of gin mixed with lime juice, "I take mine plain. You drink that and I'll go and get off me outdoor things. Thank goodness this is my late week. I can stay up and talk out me troubles."

Before going out she gave Caroline the brief letter from her brother Tom; "Read that and you'll understand partly what I mean. He's coming to London. And not alone; but with that bloody leech that's taken every penny and now is coming for some of ours."

She brushed her eyes and began to curse heartily; curse her brother for his treachery and weakness; the woman, for her treachery and vampirism. In the beginning, her brother Tom brought the woman to see her; he liked to have her approval; "And when I heard it was an older woman, that was taking an interest in the poor lad, I was grateful to her and found out where they were staying and sent her a spray of orchids and she came here, the bloody damn traitor wearing them on her shoulder, and full of charm. Aye, she's got charm and spends money on dress; young for her age and knowing all the tricks. She came in here, the—" and Nellie cursed her. Nellie had been charmed and kissed her and begged her to be friends and she had promised; but she meant not a word of it. She had come only to pull the wool over Nellie's eyes, the better to trap the poor baited fish. She had stayed there three days and Nellie had felt sure of her; she had begun to love her; and then, she, Marion, the woman, had gone away with Tom and never come again.

"I resented it bitterly. It was as if she came to spy me out and try me weight and then when she had me weighed up, she knew how to plan her campaign."

"Is she pretty?"

"Pretty enough; big dark eyes and a taking way."

"He didn't marry her?"

"She's married. She's got two of them," said Nellie dryly.

She went into the bedroom, and was away a few minutes. Caroline sat with her back to the door, taking in the room, a low broad room with two windows on the low-built street, the flat night-lighted sky over the flat roofs like an old engraving. The room had bookcases, a record player, a piano and lamps, a daybed; the walls were covered with dark red paper. A large vase, dark blue with a white flower design, was on a stand in the corner. She got up to look at the books and took out one after the other eagerly; all fascinating titles, new to her; *Merrie England, The Ragged Trousered Philanthropists, Priests and People in Ireland, Fields, Factories and Workshops;* one after the other. She picked out one and stood with it.

Nellie returned, poured out more drink and said, "Sit down, pet. What have you got there?"

"There are so many books here I never heard of. I can learn something here if you'll lend them to me."

She came over with a little book in her hand and sat down. She glanced at Nellie and looked away. Nellie, with a lively, hard smile, was sitting opposite, knees wide apart, her eyes fixed on her guest. She was wearing a blue shirt, as in the picture, and a pair of riding breeches, horribly bloodstained. Her hair was tied up with a colored handkerchief, her feet were in Spanish rope slippers, and, leaning on one elbow, she held a cigarette in the air. She leaned forward and told Caroline that what she had with George was a wonderful thing, a rare rare thing, the perfect union; and that if you hadn't known that, you hadn't known what life meant. She shook her cock's crest knowingly, her face darted forward with delight; "Ah, Caroline, if you only knew what a man George is, a real man, he's made for ecstasy. If a woman has a man like that, she can't forget it."

She paused, waiting for an answer. Caroline replied nothing; but got up and went to the bookcase and began looking through one book after another; and then said, she was taking one to bed, *The State and Revolution*, because she had often heard about it; "I always wanted to understand that."

Nellie had launched out on a description of some friends of George's, a writer and an artist living together, two women.

"Me bold hero is a great one for the dames; they're at his feet and no wonder; but what he has is the rare gift."

It turned out that these two women had had a general servant and this servant was Mrs. McMahon; "George saw she admired him and just like you, pet, she wanted to learn something, better her condition. So she came here for one day a week; and presently she gave them up and came to us. That was ten years ago and there she is yet, the good old faithful, the true, loyal working-class woman, better than ye read about, for she's a beautiful loving soul, patient and uncomplaining. Ah, but she thinks the world of George and he is very patient explaining things to her; and what a womanly care, love, for his bits of copper and pewter and china. Such simple devotion. Aye, I'd be jealous if I didn't know the woman's pure loyal heart. But the idea of wickedness never came to her."

Caroline said, "If you're so fond of her, why should she think of wickedness? Among ordinary people there isn't any wickedness, is there? I've never seen any."

Nellie was silent for some time. She suddenly said, in a rough tone, "You see slums full of rats and you don't believe in evil? That's weak, isn't it? There's your rose-painted specs again. You see? How you're tainted to the bone with the fairy-tale pink? It's weak, it's selfish, it's wrong."

"Yes, it is weak; it is wrong."

"Aye, but you won't set it right by signing papers in the Rehousing Committee; or reading *The State and Revolution*, as if it were a goodnight story. The truth is not in books; the truth is in humanity. You're sticking your eyes in a bookcase, you need eyes like a crab on stalks and you'll see nothing but the bottom of the sea. I'm disgusted with you!"

Caroline turned round in frightened anger. But Nellie had not moved; she said, in a melancholy voice; "And the truth's right beside you!"

"What truth?"

"Sit down, love; and I'll explain to you."

Caroline came and sat at a distance from the strange woman. Nellie smoked and said rapidly, "My life's been one of cycles. I look back on it and I try to divide up the tracts of time I've crossed. There was the era in Bridgehead, the era of wandering round the country taking one job and another; then the London era; and now, if me bold lad's going abroad, I'm going too; that will be the fourth. I often think I'll write about it. My mother came to London on her brief honeymoon and now time has come full circle, I'm in London myself. I was probably conceived here in the brief sad two nights of her first and only trip from the grime of her native city. Ah, the poor pallid waif. Taken from the convent at eleven and sent to work in the houses of relatives; and then to the aunt who kept a boarding-house and that's where she met the big gallant Tommy Atkins and that was when for her the meteor fell from the sky. Me uncle Geoffrey went to the Continent to work on overcoats when he was a young man and that's where George is now. Our life is a mysterious thing, Caroline; there are cycles and moments. There are fatal hours. If a man's destined to it, he dies young. It's a fact, pet; one can't shut one's eyes. You may talk about forgetting and losing yourself in a lot of cock-and-bull stories like an infant, for what is revolution to you but a pretty pink teacup in a sitting room, something to toy with? Your life is moving in cycles now to a certain end and you can't escape it; though you run howling and bawling through the universe that's closing in on you. No, it's a fateful thing you went to Roseland; it's a fateful thing you met me; it's fate you lost so many. For haven't you, pet? Haven't your friends dropped off from you; like him too, like Barry. It's your fate; and they're weak creatures; they feel your fate. They feel the death in you. Don't give up, Caroline. Know it; face it. It's been well said, if you don't confess, you must commit suicide and suicide itself is a confession; and not to commit suicide is a terrible confession. But you haven't the strength to confess, have you?"

"Confess what?" said Caroline wearily.

"No, you haven't the courage to deal with your own life. I have no faith in you. That's why I wanted to talk to you. To make you face the stark staring realities. You're wandering. You haven't the strength of soul I thought I found in you. I'm comparing you now with my Southwark friend; what a woman, what a soul! She knows the black. She'd walk boldly right into it."

She brushed her eyes and blew her nose.

"You couldn't. I see. The path's narrow and dark, you've lost your footing, the swamp mud would fill your nose and ears and eyes—"

Caroline was staring at her. She said, "Why?"

"Because you're turning down the hand that's offered to you. No good will come to you. Don't you want, Caroline, to go deep down into yourself and find out what is there? Is this surface thing you? Find out. Then you will understand; then the way will be clear. Come, let us introspect."

But Caroline refused. It was very late. She was exhausted and she found it hard to understand Nellie's words.

"Well, all right, Caroline: you need sleep. We'll talk it through tomorrow."

She rose with a gallant bright smile and kissed Caroline on the cheek, saying, "Bless you, darling."

Mr. COTTER had not been feeling very well, as he told it in his Sunday and Monday, his Tuesday and Wednesday pubs, his Thursday, Friday and Saturday pubs; in the Atheneum and football Clubs; to his clients and colleagues in the insurance business; to the Mother Superior, and to Mrs. Riggs, a divorced woman who had been acting strangely since her divorce; and to all the policemen after whose health he enquired and who kindly enquired after his own. It was no surprise therefore when Mr. Thomas Cotter went into hospital and it was in the local newspapers as an item of interest; Thomas Cotter, who as a young professional footballer had played for Wales.

Mr. Cotter had an anesthetic and went under the knife; and when he came out of it he was worse than before. "They kept me in the hospital," the big man said genially, between spasms of agony, "for they had to empty the liquor out of my veins and put blood in before they would operate. They tested me: they found I was ninety proof"; and when his visitors twitched and paled to see him lying down there in such terrible pain, he said in his large way, "It's not the worst; the very worst is Tuesday, when they'll be talking about me at the *Cross Keys,* if I'm not there, as if I were a dead man. It's Tuesday and where is Thomas Cotter? I don't like to think of it." His next operation was to be in a few days. The first had been a success; "If that's what you call a success," he said, jumping at a stab of pain; "I was all right, I was just a little down, till they started on me and found out all my secrets! And now they can't stop; they've got to go on and on." But on Wednesday, he couldn't help feeling depressed that he was absent from the Princess, his Wednesday pub. What would they be saying, that Thomas Cotter was a goner? On Thursday, the night before his operation, with his stitches and his pain, he got out of bed at eight o'clock at night, put on a hospital dressing gown and telling a taxi driver he knew, whom he found outside the hospital gates, that he was discharged, he got him to unload him at the Ravenscourt, his Thursday pub. There he had a fine time, half doubled with pain, but of interest to all, before the taxi driver, struck with doubt, and the tavernkeeper, struck with compunction, insisted upon getting him back to hospital; for now, for the lark and for the pain, Mr. Thomas Cotter freely admitted that he had climbed the wall, fooled the sentry, escaped from jail. He got back somehow and pretended that he had only been a bit of time in the men's room; and the next day, he died under the anesthetic, so that he would have felt himself quite justified in going out for his last drink, if he could have known.

There never was the funeral of a private person in Bridgehead or surrounding districts, like that of Thomas Cotter. All his friends were there. There were those from the assurance company, colleagues and clients, a group from two of his pubs, the Tuesday and Saturday, and a big wreath from his fellow drinkers of the Thursday for whom he had given his life; and it was thought very small of the lessee of one of the others that he had sent nothing when asked, with the excuse that he did not believe in mourning. He was obliged later to place a wreath in beadwork on the grave itself. The cricket, bowling and football clubs were represented; the policemen, and the Atheneum Club had delegates. It was a fine day: and the firemen sent a band; and the dogs and all the little boys ran along with some long-legged skinny little girls, merry and mean, whose skins and lungs would never quite lose their present coating of Bridgehead gray. That evening, the sports edition squeezed their figures and forecasts to get in some fine glowing remarks about the man who had played for Wales, his subsequent soldierly career, his fine family; and they passed over the misfortune of Cushie's wearing her heart on her sleeve. The sun set on a glorious murky reddish day, with the dark gray river, reflecting in sulky oils its fires and greening. Mr. Cotter was quite right in his life. He lived respected and died as a great man; and for the next week or two, even the next few months, Nellie Cook and Thomas Cotter, Junior, were able to get little concessions from the landlord for the two women left in the house, Mrs. Mary Cotter and Peggy. The assurance company, the football club and the police thought about getting up a subscription. Nellie and Tom gave their mother and sister all they had in the bank and then they had to go back to work.

With old Mrs. Cotter after the funeral, time had been, time was and time might be again, but it was all one time: she knew no difference between the living and the dead. Sometimes she did not recognize the living and sometimes the dead fled from her. She recovered her strength, they moved her upstairs, but to the back bedroom which had been Peggy's; and now Peggy slept with her to attend to her in the night. The fine front bedroom with the oak wardrobe and the air still faintly scented with Thomas Cotter's lotions, pomades and soaps, was empty. There was a lock and they kept it locked; but she found the key; or else her brother Simon gave it to her when she asked for it. The lock soon got broken with the way she treated it, rattling and pecking at it with the key; and then Simon would take the lock off, lay all the parts out in order on the kitchen table and put it together, clean and strong. Mrs. Cotter always had to look in to see if the room was in order and to see who was there. Her husband Thomas Cotter was often away now. Sometimes he was away to London or over the Border on a trip; or to Teesside, sometimes to Wales to see his brothers in business there. Often he was up there too, but asleep; and he was tired, with his traveling; she didn't want to disturb him. The room had to be orderly though; for he was fastidious, even vain, always titivating, as she said with a slight laugh, "a man proud of his looks and with a right to be." Sometimes when she found him out several times running, it occurred to her that something was wrong; and she would climb the stairs to the attic to see if her sister Lily or her own mother was still lying there as they had done for years. When she found no one there, she would hasten down to the kitchen, laugh and say to Simon, "Yes, now I have got it right, Lily is dead and Tom is out on business; what was I thinking of?"

Simon was anxious, for she spent a good deal of time on the

stairs where she had had her fall; and he encouraged her to do her polishing, which she did when she was too tired for climbing. She would be down on her knees polishing the fenders and the grate, rubbing a duster on polished wood and on mantelpiece, scolding Peggy for tarnished silver or a spotted tablecloth; and if she could not find a bit of chamois leather, she would wrap silver up in paper.

"You mustn't let the house go to wrack and ruin just because I'm not watching," she scolded Peggy. She worried about the disorder which she imagined was somewhere, things left on plates; and if she found food on plates, she'd throw it into the fire, for to throw scraps on the fire is a local housekeeping custom. There were days when anyone who wanted to have his dinner would be obliged to walk around with his plate in his hand. Only one thing was not in danger, the pot of tea, sacred in the house; but she would even throw the dog's food in the fire. Perhaps there was, as Peggy said, spite in it; for lately she had turned against the dog, and yet kept calling him Timmie, the name of a long-dead spaniel she had liked. She hoped to show Peggy by example, that it was wrong to call a dog Tom, after a man. On the more fretful days, her sisters would come and argue or console; but everyone was uneasy and ran around like pets in a cage. She would sit stubbornly in front of her own plate, fall into a dream, wake up; and when no one was looking, she would throw it all into the fire, scrape the plate, run to the sink and set the clean plate, fork and knife in their places. Sometimes she got the idea that they had done with this house and were going "to the other house." They had been in this one for forty years and once Thomas Cotter had spoken of moving higher up, near the Moor, where the air was good.

Then the restlessness of everyone upset her. They kept coming in their numbers, knowing what the food situation was; and then kept out of sight, feeling themselves unwanted; they went up the stairs, kept close in the attic, made no sound. She did not want them to feel unwanted and felt she had to offer them something. It was hard for them to come and stay up there overnight, or for a few days and be out of work, or sick;

and not be offered a bit of food. At least, she could offer them tea and biscuits or cake. But there weren't always such things, unless it was the weekend and the order was in; or Nellie and young Tom had sent the money. Uncle Simon had his pension; but she had never applied for hers, for she would have been obliged to tell her true age, which she had concealed at her marriage; and what would Thomas Cotter think, coming home and finding that he had a wife older than himself? Nellie spent freely and was always broke by the middle of the week, but she brought or sent plenty of things at the weekends. Nellie was here today and gone tomorrow; and then young Tom was never at home. The young people of today were very restless, she told Simon; they didn't know whether they were coming or going.

In the afternoon, there was Nellie in the house again, stamping and blowing. Mrs. Cotter had often said to her that men didn't like that behavior in a woman; and a big, scrawny, screechy fowl she was, thought her mother, chuckling to herself at her own funny ideas; a queer bird, more like a rooster or a turkey than a girl, traipsing about, tearing up and down the street running, hallooing beside processions, walking in processions, shouting, yodelling and yelling, climbing fences and telling lies and teaching the others to lie; though Mrs. Cotter always wormed it out of them and of Nellie too, with her nose in the air and her rowdy-dowdy ways. "To think that Thomas Cotter could have a daughter like that," her father said one day; and he stretched her out on the dining-room table and looked her over from head to foot. "Let me look at you," he said. "Anyone would say a flatfish at the end of a fishing rod; but you've got the Cotter nose!"

Mrs. Cotter laughed to herself when she saw Nellie go past the fence, just like he said. She was sitting in the bow window of the front room, waiting for her husband. He was coming home at very irregular hours, she knew, because he had been ill; and probably for the moment, he just took the air a bit and went to the football club, and the pub of course; and then he would come home to see how she was getting on. He had been very attentive to her since her accident, which showed how good he was at heart.

"Are ye there, Mary, pet?" cried Nellie, in the front door and Mary Cotter sat there smiling; she could hear the father in the daughter's voice. Nellie in her bit of velvet toque, on her ear, her topknot, her earrings, her cigarette, her high spot of rouge, her long legs like a stork, stood grinning at the door. "Are you coming, pet? Your tea's waiting for you," said her daughter.

She got up smiling, looking her daughter up and down. "Isn't your hem down, Nellie? You'd better put a stitch in it." "Aye, I will, Ma, don't fret about it," said Nellie in the tone which meant it could be hanging down next week still. Mrs. Cotter could see her rampaging around there till she was forty or fifty with her ways, not settled down. "Now come along, that's the style," said Nellie, "that's the style, pet. What were you doing, watching the world go by, Mary?"

They went into the back room and there, to her surprise, were her sisters, Bessie and Jeanie, who had come in without saying a good day to her and now were installed at the tea table as if at home. But she was very cordial as usual, since she was in her own home. She looked curiously at the furniture which had changed its place—or else—no, no, there she was losing her memory she knew and she was now—probably gone visiting with them; that was it. She remembered that she had been sitting in her own window, someone had come for her and then she had come out—forgotten something and—now of course, there was Nellie with her hat on. They were visiting. She herself had left her hat and coat in the hall. Here she was in her house-dress! She sat down in painful embarrassment and tried not to look at her dress. How absent-minded she was getting that she actually had come to visit her sister in her house-dress. They would never forget it; it would be a family joke for years. She sat there, vexed.

"Sit there, that's the style, chick, that's the girl, that's the way," cried Nellie. "Now then, that's it, eh, she's fine, you'll be dancing a jig yet, Mary, pet."

"Aye, she's doin' all right," said Bessie.

[60]

"What are ye worried about, Mary?" asked Jeanie; "I can see she's worried about something."

"Now eat your egg, Mary pet, and we'll all sit and watch ye," said Nellie.

"But you can't spare an egg, you need your own," said Mrs. Cotter to her sister Bessie. "Aye I can spare you your own egg," said Bessie, laughing.

Nellie said, "You've got to get strong pet, go on now, that's the style! What, Peggy? Where's the butter, darling? Have you got some bread cut out there, pet? It's all right. Don't bother then, I'll get it myself. You were afraid of Uncle Simon's sermons, is that it, pet?"

Peggy said dryly, "The tea's made; there's bread cut from lunch, the butter's in the kitchen."

"Aye, is it pet? I'll get it then. But you should have put it on the table: we've guests to tea. Have your egg, then Mary, me sweetheart, and we'll go and get the butter and cut some bread with instructions on the use of the bread-saw from Uncle Simon." And Nellie went to the kitchen.

Peggy said, "The cloth's on, the tea's made and you're strong enough to pour out your own teas, I suppose."

"Now, lass," said Aunt Jeanie, "there's no need to take offense. I'll do it if you don't feel like it."

"You invite yourselves to tea every other day now," said Peggy; "and I'm sick and tired of waiting upon ye. Ye aren't visitors, you're in and out of the house as much as we are. We pay the rent and you come and make merry."

"Aye, the girl's all right," said Mrs. Duncan, a neighbor who had dropped in with some cakes; "it's all right, Peggy, it's no great matter; don't fuss, we'll manage. I should have brought some tea, I had it: aye, the girl's all right."

"I think that's very rude, Peggy," said Aunt Bessie, a round little woman, getting red and bouncing up, "when I've come all the way from Sunderland. I didn't come for you but for Mary and you ought to be ashamed, putting people out of the house."

"It's nothing to me whether you're in or out of the house

making a nuisance of yourselves," said Peggy gaily, picking up her knitting; "it's nothing but tea, tea, tea all day long. I'm fed up with tea."

Nellie returning, caught this and she soothed her, "Aye, but we've got to have it, pet, we've got to get things done."

Mrs. Cotter laughed suddenly and said, "Done to a T."

Nellie laughed. "That's it, pet, that's the spirit, now you don't call that eating, do you? Come eat it up. Why I thought when I came back, there'd not be a speck of egg left. Now, eat it up while I go and get the butter, while me back's turned. Eat your egg, Mary."

The old woman said deliberately, "I do-ant want no more egg."

The dog, lying across the doormat began to bark, leaping up and down. "Let him out," cried Peggy to her aunt, "let him out, man, can't you move? Are you paralyzed already with the paralysis of the Pikes? I see," she continued; "I see, man, pet, what it is: it's only Uncle Sime teasing you. Open the door, Simon Pike, man, you fool. Nellie! Uncle Sime's standing behind the door teasing the animal. I know his ways."

Uncle Simon and Nellie together opened the door and Nellie said, "Come in, Uncle Sime, pet, are you taking your tea with us, then, Sime?" Uncle Simon was unkempt and disordered. His coat, waistcoat and shirt hung open, showing his thin hairy pigeon-breast. He had a week's growth of beard. He was haggard, his eyes dirty and red. He said, "A got me tay in the kitchen, thank ye kindly. A'm bringin' youse the butter."

Peggy said, "You needn't bother, if that's it. We've got legs to walk. Don't come nosing in, man, where you're not wanted."

Nellie said, "That's kind of you, Uncle Sime. Sit down with us a minute, sweetheart; there's a pet."

"A'll not, thank ye," said the uncle.

His sister Mary laughed and in a cooing voice enquired, "Who wud he sit by? There's no room to sit by himself. It's a long time since Simon took a bath and he lets you know it."

Peggy said, "Though he spends an hour and a half or two hours in the bathroom every day, worse than Mrs. Riggs in

Race Week, going up to see who's strolling on Newcastle Town Moor and to catch a man in front of the Eastern Harem sideshow."

"That's enough, Peggy: you don't know what you're talking about," said Nellie.

Simon said, "A've got no one to get meself oop for; A'm not a young gel and it an't worth the trouble for you here."

Peggy said, "And if ye got up at a reasonable hour, but he's there in his bed to all hours."

Simon said, in a broken tone, "And who sets the fire for ye? Who gets the tay for ye in the marnin'? Isn't it me, takin' ye a tray oop in the marnin' for ye both, when ye're in bed? It's for you, Mary, A do it: for she won't get oop." He turned to his other sisters, "She lets her poor old mother lie there withoot a cup o tay."

"And why should I get up?" said Peggy. "Isn't it allowed to sleep in this house? And what should I get up for? Two old invalids, that's a pleasure for a young woman? Do you think I want to look at your face, Uncle Sime? Go away with ye, man. There isn't and never was anyone wanted to look at ye, man, let alone a woman; and even the very dogs bark at ye. No wonder, Tom, poor man, barks at ye. He hates ye: he can't stand the sight of ye."

Mrs. Duncan said good-humoredly, "Well, there's a good girl, Peggy; now don't get yourself excited. Never mind your uncle, Peggy."

Mary, who had been sitting for some time with a dim smile, spoke up, "And what wud ye be doing in your bed, Simon, so late and so early?" She laughed quietly.

Simon said firmly, "Do ye know what A do every night, Mary?" Mary laughed at this. Peggy listened hungrily.

Aunt Jeanie said to Mrs. Duncan, "You know us well, and you'll gather, too, what it is, why he can't get up. He's been at it for years, eh, he's a character, he is, he's a funny fellow: there's a man for ye. No wonder he likes his bed"; and all the women broke into accustomed laughter, while the angry, half-naked old man looked at them without flinching.

[63]

"Every night before A get to me bed, Mary," he said, "A go down on me knees and A pray to God for ye, Mary. A pray for me poor old sister and pray he'll take care of ye and not let ye suffer; that's what A do."

"Pray for me," Mary cackled, "it's a fine prayer, that."

Peggy said, "I can't stand his nonsense."

Mary enquired, "Why wud you pray for me?"

Simon said, "A pray for ye to get rid of your fancies, and that you'll be right in your mind again, Mary, and have a quiet end: and that's the words A put in me prayer. And A'll stay here till that day to see ye're all right and then A'll go meself. A often wish," he said bitterly, looking at his sisters, "when A get up in the marnin' with me coughin' that it was me last day. A can hardly crawl up and down the stairs and sometimes A'm seized with a fit in the middle of the stairs—oh, A'm afraid of breakin' me neck. And she wishes it too," he said, looking at Peggy, "she's only waitin to be shet of us both, for that girl is not a normal girl, she's a mad girl: or she wouldn't stand that daft dog."

Jeanie cried, "Simon, Simon, none of that language here."

Peggy stood up and shrieked, "I'll not let him say that of me and no one has the right to say that of a dog that he's daft. That is a wicked word: you're a criminal, Uncle Sime, and it's daft and mad you are to say that word: no decent man that hadn't a heart full of blood would say that word. I'll not hear it, I'll not hear it—"

Aunt Bessie said, "There, there, now, girl, sit down, Peggy—"

Nellie said, "He didn't mean it, pet, ye know that not one of us would use such a word."

Mary scolded, "Shame on ye, Simon, don't dare say a word like that here to the poor girl. Hush! Shame! That's no word to say to a young girl. Peggy, come here to your mother."

"Well, well," said Simon, "A take it back. Ah, stop it, damn the dog—"

Peggy had begun to sit down but shrieked again, "Leave him alone; he's more sense than you. He knows what he's barking at: he knows what's in your mind, he has more sense than any

[64]

of you and let him do what he wants, he knows what he wants, he knows what you all are!" They hushed her, much concerned, while she screamed, "Get out, get out, get out."

"A'm gannin'," said Uncle Simon.

Mary said brightly, "I'm gannin' too. Let's go now, Peggy. Where's me hat? Where's me hat, where's me jacket?" She got up and looked over the sideboard where Bessie had put her hat: she tried to make her sisters move on their chairs. "Where's me things?"

"Now what do you want your hat for Mary?" said Bessie.

Cushie said, "Eat your egg, sweetheart. Go out, Uncle Sime. You've upset us all. You don't mean it, Sime, but we're not often honored by your presence, you see."

"A'm goin' then," said Simon; "Peg'd be better, A'm tellin' ye, if she wasn't so coddled, if she was made to behave. She was better when she was goin' out every day. She's a smart enough girl."

"And where would I get a job having to stay at home looking after two old dying people who should be dead long ago? A young woman shut up with two corpses that are on their feet and won't lie down still?"

The aunts protested under their breaths at this; and meanwhile Mary was getting more and more anxious and now she held out her hand to her sister Jeanie saying, "It was very nice, thank you, but it's getting late and I must go home now. My husband'll be home soon, it's getting on to his time and I've got nothing ready and he's always such a hungry man." She gave her sister a tea-party smile, "Where's me supper, he says, I can't eat you! Where's me meat? You're nothing but skin and bone, not a mouthful in you, you won't do!" She tittered. "I ought to know where I left them," she said fussily; "where did I put them, Nellie? I can't remember"—a society smile—"My memory's so bad now, I'm getting old: old age is creeping over me." She laughed self-consciously and whispered, "Where are me things, Nellie? Let's get them and run out." She took a parcel off the sideboard.

[65]

Her sister Bessie laughed, "Where would you be going with that, Mary?"

"I'm taking me things and I'm going home."

"Aye, ye'll be goin' home," said Simon, watching her.

Cushie said, "Now, Mary, pet, this is your home and you're not going home anywhere else."

Mary whispered to her nodding, "Show me me things, Nellie and I'll slip away. Did I leave them in the hall?"

"Never mind your things," said Bessie laughing, "come and finish your tea, Mary. Eh, she's a scream!"

"It's so late. I've been here so long. I can't remember when I came," she simpered at the women. "I'm afraid he'll get home first and find no supper. What's that?"

"It's nothing, pet, it's the wind," said Cushie.

"Who's there?" said Mary, much struck, looking towards the hall.

"It's nothing, Mother: come and sit down and finish your tea. My head's bursting with all this clatter. I never saw such people for making a noise about nothing," said Peggy. "Sit down, Mother, for the love of Mike: it's enough to drive a body from home."

Mary heard nothing of this: she was still listening and she said, "Did you hear, Nellie? It's his step!"

"There, sit down there, Ma, and never mind what you hear."

Her mother began nervously tying a string round the little parcel, "I've got to go, I've got to go, Nellie. Don't stop me. I must go. Suppose he comes home and I'm not there? It's never happened. I never stayed out late. He knows that about me. He'll begin to think something's happened. He'll worry."

Simon was upset, "He's not worryin' about ye now, Mollie!"

"But he will! There always was a woman in the house when he got home."

Cushie sighed, "Aye, that's the truth; too many women waiting for to serve him. You wore yourself out for him, Mary. You're right at home now, Mother and it's here you must wait for him." The mother, half-convinced and puzzled, sat down and looked round at all the faces. Simon went out to the kitchen and a few minutes later Mary came out into the hall where she began arguing with her two daughters. She ran down the hall, laughing foolishly, and said to her brother, "Let me past you, Simon, I'm going the back way. They won't let me out. It's a queer house I'm in. He's home now, it's dark. I must see him."

Simon said, aye, he was home now but she wouldn't be seeing him yet a while.

"I'm goin' to him," said the widow.

"You're not goin' and ye'll never find him. It's dark and dreary, it's blowin' up cold. How would ye find your way to him by yourself in this night?"

"Surely I know me way home after living in one house for forty years and more since my wedding day: I never was away from it except to go round the corner to visit Lily, in all my life. I'm the old-fashioned woman." She laughed at herself, "If you won't let me go, I'll go and get Lily to take me with her. I know the way that far, surely."

"Aye," said Simon, "but ye don't know the way to St. Aidan's churchyard which is where she is tonight, and he too: and they're not expectin' ye or wishin' for ye to join them. Leave them in peace, woman, and go and finish your tay like anyone else."

Mary burst into healthy laughter. "St. Aidan's churchyard? You're daft, man. What are they doing in St. Aidan's? Are they courting in the churchyard?" She turned round hurriedly and said, "Where's my parcel? I can't stand talking daft here. I'm going round to see Willie. He'll understand me. You were always silly, I could never talk to you, Simon."

"He's not there and he hasn't been there for a long time."

"Don't be daft, man: I've no patience with you, saying such a daft thing," she cried out angrily.

Peggy came along the passage with her dog and said, "Lift up your foot, mother, man, lift up your foot, like I tell ye." Her mother, in surprise, lifted her foot, "Don't ye see, man," said Peggy, "that you're wearing one brown and one black shoe?" She quickly slipped off one of her mother's shoes and

[67]

said, "Here, Tom man, go play!" tossing the shoe to the dog. The wild dog seized the shoe, dashed off down the passage and up the stairs where he stood panting, while Peggy called, "Don't be daft, ye daft dog, drop that shoe, man!"

"Eh, you're a wicked girl to tease your poor old mother," said Uncle Simon.

"Eh, mother, look, the dog's got your shoe," said Peggy; "mother, man, ye can't go visiting now, can ye? Now be yourself, woman, and get your tea."

"Tea! I'm sick of tea, nothing but tea, it's a load on me stomach and it gives me a headache, I can't sleep," said the old woman, dreadfully confused and worn. She let Peggy take her arm, but suddenly stopped and dragged her arm away. "No, no, he's waiting for me. He's sitting there by the fire waiting for his dinner."

"He's lyin' down," said Simon, "in the cold, in the ground, woman, and ye must recognize it in the end: and ye do recognize it and know it and ye know you're never leavin' your good home in the night to go on a fool's errand."

"That's a crazy thing," said Mary bluffly, "ye must be a crazed man: his wits are going: he's old."

"Aye, it's me wits," said Simon.

Mary said, horrified, "He's saying wicked things: get going, old wicked man."

"A'm gannin' oopstairs," said Simon. He turned his bent old bony back and stood looking at the dog racing in the hall. Mary suddenly laughed youthfully and raising her arm into the air, she brought it down as if with a knife, to her brother's back.

Peggy said, "Quit your tomfooling, Mother man, and sit down, for Pete's sake. And sit down, Uncle Sime, and don't mix in things that aren't your business. Always meddling. You get nowhere with that."

They went out and the old man turned back to his cold cup of tea which he drank before the fire. It was not fresh, but had been poured off cold soaked leaves from the morning. He looked beaten; and when Jeanie came down to say goodbye he said with tears in his eyes, "Ye see what happens? You're always in the wrong. Ye can never get anythin' but blame."

"Eh, Simon, cheer up, you mustn't pity yourself," said Jeanie cheerfully. She was a short solid dark woman, bluff and busy. "The poor girl's not responsible; she thinks it's for the best."

"Aye, for the best," said he. "Goodnight then: watch the step when ye go oot."

I T WAS October, getting cold and Marion had set out with-out her furs. They did not find the healer at Norwich; he had gone to Glasgow. They turned south to go home to the orchard farm where Marion Ilger lived. But now she wanted to go to London, to Nellie's house.

"I want to ask her about my play; and you could see some agents."

"But you haven't written the play, Marion."

"But Nellie knows how. She has her great play. She can tell me."

Tom laughed, "Nellie hasn't written a line."

"Are you very tired, Tom?"

"I often wonder if I'm in a bad dream. I don't recognize a place I've passed a couple of hundred times in my life. But if you want to, we'll go there."

In the next town he sent a telegram. At the next fork he took the London road. The lights flashed up and down showing the house fronts and hedges that he had seen so many times coming from the factories and airfields to her, so that he knew each one to come; and laughing would say, "And now—" The lights had already gone out. People went to bed at nine or nightfall anywhere outside London or were in at the television. Some sat on the doorsteps till the light faded; and then to bed.

When they reached the Islington street she could not get out; so he carried her up to the back room on the second floor, at-tended to her terrible wound and went down to get her some-thing to eat. He fed her and sat by her bed till she fell asleep with her opiates. She took them now. Then he went down to the kitchen. He was there crouched between the stove and the kitchen table, poring over a newspaper in the bad light, when the key turned in the front door. He didn't stir, indifferent to the family, indifferent to everything, but to Marion upstairs in the dark.

It was Eliza Cook, a short rosy woman, about fifty. She had been a factory worker, then had a clerical job but needed the fresh air for her lungs and now worked as a door-to-door salesman. She beamed when she saw Tom.

"I thought you were disgusted with all of us. Why, Nellie said that London was plague and poison to you now."

He told her the story; they had been a long way looking for the healer.

She sat down comfortably and began to eat a piece of ham. She said, "Nelllie has a great idea. She gets a big piece of bacon and boils it; so we have all the ham we want. I do love ham. We never did get it at home. I'm a great eater of ham. I'd give up all the fowls and steaks in the world for it now. It's a craze that's on me; I'm getting fat." She said *hahm* and *faht*.

Tom told her he'd like to keep Marion there till he found out about the snake venom. He had a pamphlet showing sad-faced sufferers who had been cured. She told him she was glad to be out of the office job where she got no air, light or peace with the telephones ringing. The tramping tired her and she hated arguing the poor people into buying; and she worked after hours, arguing against the atomic bomb; and upstairs, downstairs, ringing bells, working for the Labour Party. She was hot-tempered. Very often at night, she'd lie awake in a sweat, at what men and women had said to her. "I don't mind the words, Tom, I mind them being so foolish. For fear of the landlord, they think it's bad manners to talk about the bomb; and when I say your children will be destroyed, burnt up, they shut the door in my face, because I must be a bad woman. But I give it back to them; I show them up to themselves. I've argued a few into their senses. But it's very wearing. What is wrong with the Londoners? They have more percentage of sun than we do up north, don't they? But no fight with it."

"And ours? They're good at straight talking like the Scots; but what do they do, Eliza? The men do the pools and the women gossip. We're just one nation."

Eliza had been using the room Marion now occupied; she said she would move her things in a jiffy.

"The poor thing. I think you're grand, Tom. I told Nellie she was acting like a jealous sister."

"What did Nellie say?"

"She got into a flap."

"She thinks she does it all for someone's good. I can always stop her by letting her know I'm angry. She's afraid of losing me," said Tom.

Eliza said, "You're a good man. It's rare to find such good men as George and you; though George is a tough nut to crack and I often want to crack him over the nut. That's why we got divorced."

"Who got divorced?"

"George and me."

Tom kept his bright burning face turned to her and began to smile.

Eliza said, "Oh, aye, you'd left home and were out of touch. It is for Nellie's sake I say I'm his sister. She said the people up at home, your people, never would understand her having a second-hand man. No one knows very much. I wasn't writing to my family. George wasn't speaking to his. But I can tell you because I like you and you won't let on."

"And you don't mind living here with them?"

Eliza said comfortably, "Well, Tom, I am going to get out. But Nellie wanted it, she wanted me here. She thought it would keep him home; if there are more hens in the barnyard, he'll stay at home. And Nellie is a love, a dear. She is such a bright, go-ahead, loving soul, she wouldn't think of wrong. She thinks it's a consolation for me to be here too. She didn't want me to feel out in the cold because I'm divorced. That woman is a lovely soul, Tom. But, the fact is—"

She went on to tell Tom about her new man, a grocer's assistant.

"He's not much of a catch. He's going bald and has had a few women, not divorced, living apart, he's got bad feet too, used to be a postman; and younger than me. But I can't stand out against him. I've got to get a room. And I make George angry. We always did fight. I don't know what's struck me, Tom. Is it me age, do you think? I feel the same. He's forty you see, a bit over."

She flushed. They talked on. Tom thought he had better telephone a nursing home in the morning.

"How much would it cost, Eliza? I'd sell my car, for one thing. I've got some books I can sell, a couple of good trunks I picked up at an airfield, a wristwatch. I don't need anything."

"Isn't there anyone to help? What is she—a widow?"

Sulkily, Tom said she had a husband. "But he could only sell the orchard and then she'd have no home. And I want to do it myself. She's mine. She made them let me bring her. She can make them do anything."

"Them? Who's that?"

"Her husband, Ilger and her brother, a big sulky man who's there, Patrick Hall. He used to be an airman too; but we never got on. I don't like him."

"But wouldn't you take money from them?"

"Yes, I'd take money from anywhere. But they haven't got it. It's in the house and orchard. And they're hers. She bought them. She taught her husband—Connie, the man there—to run it; she taught Patrick accountancy—she made him learn accountancy. She can make them do anything. It's her personality and her charm."

"And what about you, Tom?"

"She wanted me there and I went. It was love."

"Aye, I know."

When he went up to bed, Marion was awake trying not to call him. He brought in some bedclothes, made up his bed on the floor. He was too tired to sleep; but dozed and several times during the night she called him.

She said, "I had a terrible dream; but I heard your voice all around me as if I were in the sky and you were all around."

Another time, she said, "Talk to me."

"What shall I say?"

"Tell me some of your horrifying experiences."

He hesitated for a moment, not sure what she meant; and rather annoyed, when he realized what she meant. But he said;

"In the war I had a friend named Cotter. We met in the train and were surprised we had the same name; and we became friends. He was going to my previous airfield. He had finished the service for which he had signed, that is, two thousand flying hours and he was grounded. He said he would never fly again. Plenty of them are like that. You couldn't get me up in the air again.

"They were giving him a celebration that night; and in the afternoon, as it happened, a crew of fourteen lost one of their men through sickness. It's the rule with crews not to take on someone else but to give up the flight and disband for the time being. However, this time a few of them knew Cotter and came to him: Come on, Cotter, this is your last flight, you can fill in for us this time. Others did not want to go along with him on his last flight. But it was an important flight and had to be done; so he agreed. It was an airfield up north, near the sea, on a coast like the Cromer coast, I was thinking of it today when we were there. It had flat grass sloping straight into the sea and was dangerous, especially with mist and low ceiling. However, they had had no accidents while I was on the airfield, though I heard they had two afterwards. This was one. Cotter was coming back ready to land, with the wheels out to land, and he flew into the ocean a few yards from the shore and drowned everyone, including himself.

"I don't suppose you're sleeping much there on the floor," said Marion.

"Oh, some of the best sleeps I ever had were on the floor. When I was grounded they had me in one of the test-beds for a while and several times I lay down on the planks and slept for hours, a good sleep; no one could have done it but people used to the engines roaring. There were propellers driving the air through sometimes at a hundred miles an hour; when you walk, you lean on the wind. I had one laborer who gave a lot of trouble," he said, laughing, and he started to think about it and laugh.

"How?"

"He was always missing. He would go away and never turn up till I sent all over the place; and then he'd come back with some excuse, he'd been to the factory or to get some cotton waste and I never could find out where he got to."

All through he gave his little laughs, reminiscent and teasing: "There were doors about thirty feet high to those houses; and we opened them according to the velocity wanted. They were always part way up; and we shifted them up and down. Well, one day I found out by accident, that he climbed right up to the ledge from which the blind rolled, and slept there. I don't know how he got there, unless he climbed up the blind; I don't know how he slept there. I suppose he shifted his back. One day I ran the blind down fast and I heard a shout. He was a tough fellow, really tough. When he came out of the army he was out of a job and the labor exchange sent him to wheel out an old lady who was paralyzed. Imagine the sort of job—a big husky coot like that! So he wheeled her out somewhere near Norwich or somewhere—I was thinking of it today when we passed that church and I laughed! He got so fed up and repressed, that one day he lifted the old lady out of her chair, hung her up on the church railings and raped her."

Marion laughed.

He ended; "Imagine that, he hung her up like a bundle of skirts and she couldn't do anything. Of course, the next day, he left. He didn't wait to see if she left him her house and garden. And the funny thing is he never heard anything about it. She never told the police, nor the sexton, nor anyone."

"More."

"He used to tell me stories by the hour. They all happened to him. It was interesting at work. He said he didn't mind the trenches; he used to tell stories by the hour; and he got through the five years without a scratch. We used to forget the work. One day he got me into serious trouble. It was that story about the church railings he was telling me. The engines were revved up and they got too hot."

"Any more?"

Someone opened the front door. "Holy Mackerel, what time is it? Is that Nellie?" He whispered, "Let's lie still; or she'll brew a pot and keep me talking all night." They fell asleep.

Marion awoke in the morning to see the light falling on his wasted rough face. His personality was asleep and he looked like hundreds of poor fellows trudging to work through the dirty air, along the dirty pavements. His hair hung about like straw. She pondered; how could she have fallen so much in love with such a thin, sad manikin? Then she put her hand over her eyes and began to cry for him. He awoke soon after and lay for a while looking like a weak little bundle of bones and wind-dried skin; then a smile flowed into his face and with it, the flesh, the energy, the youth.

He presently went down to make breakfast. It was a fine day and he thought he could start off at once to visit the healers and quacks. Time was short. They were willing to try anything.

Eliza would be home at lunchtime. Eliza said, "Nellie was so pleased you were here. She had to go out early. She'll be back. Could you wait for her, Tom? She said she had a bad night, had a row with the editor, he threw out her stuff, it was a bloody shame; she told him all theory and no practice made Jack a dull boy." Eliza burst out laughing.

Then, "Poor woman. It is a bloody shame. She got a good story and no place to put it. She waited at the office till nearly one in the morning. She said, She must see your poor girl, and she must hang herself round your neck just for once, before you go north."

"I'm not going north."

"She said you were going to see your mother. She said she knew you couldn't stay away."

He looked stern. "What about Marion?"

Eliza paused. "I said that. And then she said Marion had a home, a husband—and they have money. She never told it before."

She looked at him earnestly.

"Marion is my wife; she comes first."

The doorbell rang. Eliza went. There was a flurry and they heard Nellie's strained yearning voice, "Left me key, love. Is young Cotter here?"

She rushed down the hall, tumbled down the steps to the

kitchen and cried out at the door, "Hello darling!" There was already a rich false sound, while she flew to him, folding him in her arms and saying;

"Ah, how are ye, pet? I thought you were going to give me the slip!" He disengaged himself with a smile, noticed her triumphant expression. He looked away. At the door, with Eliza standing behind her and frowning, was a short, dark, fleshy woman with a spotted black veil. It was Estelle, his former wife. He said dryly;

"Hello, Estelle."

"I brought her, chick; she wanted to see you."

Nellie smiled and breezed about, fixing chairs and looking for cups. She said to Eliza, "Bless ye, darling. I'm dying for a cup of tea. Now, chicks, let's punish the teapot before we start chatting. I set out this morning with only one cup."

She set Estelle in her chair and eyed Tom. Estelle still wore the veil. Tom turned on his heel.

"Where are you going, chick?"

"I'm late already. I'm sorry I waited," said Tom.

She hurried after him, cajoling. In the front hall he turned, said sternly, "Did you know that Marion is here?"

"Marion? No, pet. Is she here pet? Why didn't you let me know you were coming so soon, chick? I wouldn't have gone away last night. It's a great honor, chick."

He looked at her and something flashed across his face, "I saw my telegram on the mantelpiece. You knew."

She could not help the clever grin. Her big mouth twitched, "Now, pet, don't get me wrong. I was over at Flo's and Estelle was staying there with her. Poor pet, she's in terrible trouble, the poor darling and she begged me to bring her over."

"You begged her to come over," he said calmly.

"Ah, she got cold feet, pet, and said she couldn't face you; but it's best to get it over. I know you've got plenty of troubles, Tom; and it's no question whether they're of your own chosing; but you mustn't be concentrated on self. She's in very great trouble and she claims you're the cause of it all; so you must do your duty, lad. It's a tragedy, Tom; and we've got to help."

"I've got to take Marion to the doctor. It's like Bridgehead;

like the old aunts sitting in the back room. What have ye been cookin' up?" he said, dropping into the home accent.

"Now, pet, you've got to face the facts of life. You can't live in your dream world. There's a human tragedy here and we've got to help her face it. Poor Estelle is very ill; it can't wait."

"Send me the doctor's bill," he said, climbing the stairs.

"Ah, no, pet. you can't get out of it that way. You've got to face the music. You're in it too. It's no laughing matter; it's for life and death. It means isolation, loneliness. It means you cannot touch man or woman: and you're both in it."

"In what?"

She poked her face forward with the bold queasy excited air of the scandalmonger. "She's been afraid of men and never went near them, Tom Cotter; and there are things that take a long time to come out. It's a terrible skin disease; and it's that, Tom Cotter. It's what men give to women."

He said in a high voice, "Is that it? If you've been stewing over it all night, you should have thought up more than that. It's not worthy of you."

"Aye, but it's the truth; and you've got to face it. The poor pet wears the veil outdoors and in. It's the shame and the fear."

"Oh, bunk."

"Ah, but the face, the face!"

"She's neurotic."

"Ah, ah, no, no."

He continued upstairs,

"I hope you girls have a good time. Maybe I'll have the DT's, too, when I come back."

She said hurriedly, looking up at him, "Tom, you had something years ago, when your feet were so bad; and now you never show your feet because it's bad there."

He stopped and looked down, "Does Estelle believe that? Who's been talking it into her? You know nothing about medicine."

"Aye, but it's true, lad."

"Look at my hands, look at my face."

She began to gabble, turning her face away from her brother, who seemed radiant and handsome to her, bending her head and unable to account for the despair rushing up through her. "At any rate, at any rate, Tom, she's got something very bad. She says it's from that time with you and I'm not earning enough money now for the clothes on me back. You've got to help her. She can't go out any more; she sits at home veiled. She went into the street, she was looking into a shop window. A man tried to peer under her veil. She felt such a deadly shame, she ran home. She says it's from you. You destroyed her."

"I don't know what's behind this; but I'm getting out of here. I'm going to take Marion home. It's safer."

Nellie straightened up.

"Ah, no. You have no right to touch Marion. Telephone whoever is with her. Let them come for her. You must never touch her again. Who knows where it came from? Perhaps from you? You don't know what her sickness is, running to the quacks. How do you know what it is?" She peered fiercely up at him, her face sharp and pale.

He went up and into Marion's room. Nellie stood for a moment ruminating and then ran upstairs after him, ran into the room, crying out, "How are ye, Marion sweetheart? Why did you stay away so long? I'm sorry to hear you're not well. You don't want to go away and leave us, pet? The house is yours, pet. This is your home. Eh, Marion, you don't look well. We must look after ye. Stay awhile and let us see you and Tom. You'll be better off here than roaming the roads, won't ye, pet?"

Marion welcomed her gladly. She said they had so much to talk about. She was feeling a bit better, and if they had the room, she'd like to stay a while and get her advice. She had a good plot for a play.

Nellie said feelingly, "Aye. It's damn good of ye, pet, if you'd let him go up to see Mother. It may be the last time, Marion: she's very weak and low. She's worn her life away for us all. I don't understand George and Tom who think we shouldn't feel guilty and responsible towards our parents who kept a roof over our heads and fed us, chick, when we were little."

"What else are they there for?" said Tom.

"No, chick, I don't understand ye. But Marion understands

[80]

me, don't ye, sweetheart? And I'm damned glad you've got a good girl, there, Tom. Ye always were a waif and a stray; he's always been in the sideshow of life, Marion; aye, it's damned good of you to take an interest in me brother. So you trust me, Marion, pet? You'll stay here with me while me brother goes up to pay his respects?"

Marion said she'd be glad to. There were so many questions she wanted to ask Nellie. Nellie was delighted to hear this.

"Then it's all right, Tom. Bless you, darling. And Tom, I want ye to take something to Peggy, the poor chick, running the whole house on her own, as if she wasn't a sick girl. Come out a minute, Tom; I want to speak to ye. We don't want to disturb Marion."

Marion was curious, "Oh, you're not disturbing me."

"No, no, it's better, pet: just domestic matters."

Tom followed her out.

"Now, Tom, me puir lad, you get off as quick as you can and Lize and I will look after Marion. Estelle comes first. Now, Tom, you pack off, get off to Bridgehead; but you get away from Marion. Give me her address and I'll telegraph her folks. I'm ashamed of you."

Tom said, "Estelle would never have fallen for a thing like that when she was with me."

"You're very cocksure. Didn't ye have a friend in the war had that?"

"You think you catch it like measles? You don't know a thing about it. So that's it? You told Estelle that story. You know what I say, Nellie. If one of my bad stories gets out, I know it comes from you. I know you've betrayed me again."

She looked both ways, wanting to deny it. "When did I ever give you away, Tom? I'm your best friend. You always trusted me. You told me what you could tell no one else."

He said, laughing, "And you always betrayed me. But I can't help trusting you again. It's my weakness for you."

"I never betrayed ye, pet."

He said kindly, "It's your mania for confessions. Whenever I see them asking how it is that people confess in political trials, I laugh and think: Whoever caught Nellie, she'd confess.

[81]

She'd confess so much they'd have to stuff their ears, stop the case, shut up shop, they'd hear such a damnable Arabian Nights, they'd go out of—they'd go out and get drunk."

She said angrily, "Now don't go twisting my words, Tom: making me out a fascist and a secret agent. Now you're not going to worm your way out of this. You've caused enough misery with your mischief-making. If you don't go off at once as is your duty, I'll tell Marion everything."

"If you cause Marion any pain at all, I give you my word you'll never see me again. A lifetime of affection and trust will go. I mean it."

"Ah, I'm not like that pet, causing pain."

He said, "I'm going then, but with a heavy heart; and with looking back at you. If you betray me, you'll never see me again. Now keep away from Marion. Lize is going to look after her. I'll just spend one night there and I'll be back tomorrow."

Nellie beamed;

"Ah, dear Lize. Ah, she's a darling; that woman is an angel. Now get going, Tom. I'll bring me parcels down to the car. I want you to say a few words to Estelle, pet. It's her right. When you get a divorce, you don't shed all human feeling. She thinks it's from you and even if it isn't, think of her solitude and misery; she fears all men, pet."

Estelle sat in a corner of the front room between the couch and a tall bookcase built into the wall. Tom sat in the middle of the room facing the fireplace in which a small fire burned; and Nellie, gay and eager, sat smoking on the other side of the fireplace. She looked benevolently from one to the other.

At last, in a low agreeable voice, with a melancholy drawl, an Irish note, Estelle said, "Tom, you know I'm very ill, I have an incurable disease I caught from you."

Like a lesson, thought Tom, who sat attentive, leaning forward a little to look at the red rash up her cheeks and along the jawbones. It was unsightly.

"I can't believe it is what you say, or what Nellie says. I wouldn't believe it without three opinions and a specialist. What you've got is some skin trouble; that's very common with nervous women. The men in camp had plenty of nervous skin diseases. As for me, to satisfy you, I'll send you a medical report as soon as I get back."

Estelle said bitterly, "You run it off like a record. You sound as if you explained it a lot of times." She said to Nellie, "I see you prepared him. You'd do anything for Tom. You'd betray anyone."

Nellie continued to deny everything and pretended to cheer them up.

Estelle said to Nellie, in her slow heart-rending voice, "You never gave us a chance. You always sat in on our marriage, pouncing on every mistake and talking it over with all your friends. You were jealous when I married Tom and you weren't satisfied till he left me."

Nellie was very much surprised by this attack; and countered it with a great number of warm exclamations, assurances, denials, chicks, pets and sweethearts; to which the two concerned listened as if they were using up unwanted tickets at a play. Nellie kept glancing eagerly and anxiously from one to the other, to get the affair going again; but Estelle was resigned, Tom determined; and they spoke to each other on the plane of marriage, so that Nellie did not seize quite what was going on between them. Tom said, "It's like old times. It's like Westbourne Grove. Estelle and I in trouble and Nellie post-morteming for all she's worth, wringing the juice out of the corpse. Now I must get off. I'll pay all the medical bills, though it's a hunk of non-sense. I pay you alimony. I can't do more."

"Aye, but money isn't a compensation," said Nellie.

Tom said, "It's enough for me. My life before me is a series of weekly payments till I'm an old man. That counts for me."

"Ah, don't talk that way, Tom. That's not the humane plane, chick. Don't put human life and love in terms of pounds, shillings and pence. She's got an incurable sickness. You've taken her out of the labor market. She's afraid of men because of you. Have pity on the woman. She needs you."

Tom said, "Pounds, shillings and pence are an incurable sickness."

The wife said, "I think you owe it to me to look after me. I'm terribly alone and what difference does it make to you?

[83]

You told me you didn't care for love; sex was overrated. You said you never wanted to hear the word love again. You told Nellie you wanted to look after the sick, that you didn't know any other way to fight the troubles of our epoch; that you'd never fight again, you wouldn't inflict any more pain. You said you'd be a stretcherbearer, an orderly, a male nurse. You said you'd go off to a sanitarium or a leper colony."

Nellie said, "Yes, you said that, chick, and I thought it grand of you."

Tom said, "Very well; find out what's wrong with you before we set off for any colonies. Now I must go. It'll take me I don't know how long at this hour to get to the North Road and I won't get into Bridgehead till late."

Nellie ran after him, "And where were you all last night, pet? Where did you sleep?"

"On the floor, by Marion. I've done that for a whole year, slept near her to hear when she calls."

Nellie was embarrassed. "I'll get ye the parcels, Tom; and be easy in your mind. You can rely on your old Nellie."

"I know that," he said, laughing.

He shut the door, fixed his pockets, lighted a cigarette and started the car. He had maneuvered Nellie into an uneasy state of mind; but as soon as she contemplated her two invalids and George's acquiescent Eliza, she would feel strong again; new combinations would occur to her. He laughed.

Tom moved out of Lamb Street, started up towards the main road, backed into one of the crossroads, came round the Square and in a few minutes was blowing his horn outside the house. The door was standing open and he could look straight through into the backyard. Eliza was standing at the top of the back steps singing, *Canny at night, bonny at morn*. Estelle and Nellie were on the stairs going up to the attic, to Marion of course.

Nellie ran down and out, "Did you forget something, pet?"

"Yes, Marion. I'm taking her with me."

"Are you playing games, you fool?"

"Yes, playing games."

Estelle came downstairs and slipped into the front room. She had not seen Marion. Eliza came upstairs with him to help him.

She said, "You did the right thing, love. What does she want with us? She wants you. Though I never saw a friendlier woman. You can't take her far, Tom; not to Glasgow. She's not got far to go."

"I'm taking her home."

"Aye, good."

They helped her downstairs. Nellie came running after them with presents for Marion. She begged; "And where are you going now, pet? Where will you be?"

"I'll drop you a line, Nellie. Or to Eliza."

"But where, but where?"

"We're going to Glasgow to find the healer."

Marion said, turning her wasted energetic face, with a smile to Nellie, "I'll send you the play and you'll type it out and send it round won't you?"

"Aye, pet, I certainly will. Yes, love."

"It's a good idea. I know it will go," said Marion.

"You send it along, pet."

Tom started the car. They were nearly home before Marion realized they were not going to Glasgow. She became upset; but Tom promised to leave at once for Glasgow himself to see the faith-healer.

Eliza and Nellie were having tea. Eliza said, "What will he do when she dies? He's spent years living only for Marion. He told me all about it. I don't cry for myself, I don't cry for others; but tears came into my eyes."

Nellie was putting up her hair into a thin sprout on top of her head.

"It isn't that that worries me: it's the harpy who'll get him after she's gone."

She stuck a comb into the back hair and pinched up her small bright eyes this way and that, to see the effect.

"If I don't do my hair better, so George says, he'll up and leave me, the blighter! What gets into the men? They study the soap adverts; and every decent woman has to look like a bloody painted post."

The women laughed. Eliza said; "Where's the harm? I ought to look after meself a bit better. Look at me waist."

"Aye, darling, but it's harm; I've changed for the worse, since I fell in with your George. I'm not a free woman. Soaping and mending and painting and powdering and putting jeweled combs in me hair—is that a decent woman? Is me bodice clean, are me drawers clean, are me stockings wrinkled, are me heels over, is me skirt buttoned? I never was a fidget before. I've got no character left."

Eliza teased, "I saw you on Fleet Street with a pair of gloves the other day."

"Vi says I've gone back on my past; she has no respect for me anymore. But I don't know what to do, now George has got to running around Europe with the bourgeois dames that go to congresses. The buggers should never be allowed into politics, running after the men, the blinking bastards."

Nellie lamented, "I had a letter from me gay cavalier. Do you know a bourgeois dame lent George money this last trip and expected him to take her to lunch, in return? And I've got no respect for your George, Eliza. He was grateful for it. I'll leave you, I wrote to him this morning, if I catch ye drooling after the bloody bourgeois dames, buying men with purses fat with their husband's money. He got into a taxi and halfway along the street he sees the bourgeois dame. She can speak the lingo; he can't. George is too wedded to the doric. So he hails her and she gets in and she wants to go to lunch at a real workers' restaurant, patronizing the workers, the blinking bourgeois bleeder and the damned innocent has no more sense than to take her along. They rode all round Florence and the taxi driver took them to a workers' restaurant and said, It's all right, no charge, comrade; and the bloody dame insulted him by paying him; and afterwards she found the food wasn't good enough. What does me loyal husband say? He's learning something, he's learning to appreciate good food; she was right; the food was not good enough. I told him, Don't come home telling me about good food. In Bridgehead we didn't know what good food was. We had better things to think about. And now he tells me we must start to collect cookery books. That's no library for a trades union man to have."

Estelle now came down to them and said she was leaving. She was going back to Crewe, "You got me here Nellie, but when I saw Tom today I had a feeling of dread. He goes about weaving women into his life and then something dreadful happens to them."

Nellie said in a strained voice, "What do ye mean? What's wrong?"

"I expect he's right: it's a skin disease. But I never want to see him again. He'll kill me. I'd never go away with him. He draws life out of you. There's nothing there and he feeds and feeds on you. I'm terrified of him."

"I don't understand you," said Nellie.

Eliza said, "Neither do I. Tom's a dear. I love the lad. There was only one man born into the world with the heart of Tom."

Estelle said bitterly, "If you really love him, I'm sorry for you. You'll have weeks and months of tension and bedlam; and he'll feel nothing of it, but sit there with a pleasant face like a rose. When you're suffering he'll go and look at himself in the mirror and wonder what is wrong with his face that he can't get round you immediately. I used to conspire with Nellie to get him to come and see me—"

"You didn't conspire, pet: it was your right."

"He came. He sat there looking at me, pink, fresh, untouched by life. He did nothing. He was kind. He went away; and I was sick and horrified, full of nausea. He had only to sit and look at me. And I felt doubt, sorrow, sickness, hopeless love, emptiness and blackness; such a gulf! Yet when he's there, you're happy. He begins to smile and glide and haunt with his voice; and tell you his tales. Before you know it, he's walking by the mirror and looking in to smile and coming back to you like a man out of the mirror and he eats your heart away. Other men seem rough and loutish. You could never love another man as you love Tom. Unless he is just such another man. And he brings you old age, sickness, despair, I don't know what. The worst is that he lets you know what's wrong with him and begs your forgiveness that your love is an incurable disease."

"Ah," said Nellie.

"Love for him is hopeless love," said Estelle despondently.

Nellie was again embarrassed and covered this with chat, "The boy's all right, the boy's all right, he's no ghoul. It's just that he's got in with this ghoul, this damn silly little vampire. We must reclaim him."

"I won't. I've had enough," said Estelle.

"Why, think of the good times we all had together in the old days, you and Tom and me and Vi—"

Estelle said, "They were terrible days."

"Why, love, we used to sit there laughing and chewing the rag till morning."

"You sat in our bedroom all night to separate us; and early in the morning he had to go to work."

"But, pet, we had all to live together! You didn't want a petty bourgeois marriage, with all our lovely friendship splintering apart!"

"I never had a husband. You made him yours early and I didn't know enough. I was right out of the convent."

With a delighted expression, Nellie got up and said, if Estelle was going, she'd go along, too; she had to be at her newspaper office at eleven. She'd be home late and she'd bring a bottle of gin.

She said once more, "I'm a bloody fool, Eliza, to care about my George, but love's an incurable disease. I made up my mind that if I didn't have a letter from the sod this morning, I'd get roaring drunk. So get in the beer and lemonade for your shandy, Lize and I'll drink my gin. I ought to dump George overboard, but I'm too fond of the two of you. Ah, Lize, I don't know where you get your sweet ways from. Well, I'm gannin'."

She went.

THE AFTERNOON of the funeral, Constantine Ilger, Marion's husband, took Tom to the local station in the farm car. At the station, Constantine helped Tom with his luggage, asked him if he had the right change, said goodbye very kindly.

When Tom had his ticket, Constantine said, "Give me your name and address, if you like and I'll write to you one of these days."

Tom wrote and handed him a little card.

"Thomas A. Cotter?"

"Yes."

"Well, of course I knew your name wasn't Tom Green."

"I knew you knew."

"It was for her and I didn't mind. You were very good to her."

Tom said, "I wanted to be."

"You were better than Patrick. He went off and he knew she was dying."

"Yes, I thought a brother would not leave a sister. Even a half-brother."

Ilger said, "You did not know he was not her half-brother?"

"I was never sure. Her mother remarried twice."

"She was engaged to Patrick, when he went to the war. She met me and she liked me. We got married; but she never told Patrick. She kept on writing to him. She said, it wasn't fair to hurt him. When he came back, he found us married. He was quite broken up. She said we had to look after him and so we took him here to live with us. That's how it was."

"She could have told me. I would have understood."

"Marion always thought it was better not to go into things."

"Yes, I know."

"Well, goodbye and good luck, Tom."

"Thanks for the fowl."

"It was fresh killed this morning. I did that before the funeral."

"Thanks."

There was a train leaving King's Cross near midnight. He sat in a café till it was time, and had an interesting conversation with a man counting pennies in heaps, perhaps a newsboy. He was able to stretch out in the second-class carriage. Now that he was on his way, the last terrible days at the farm became real to him; and yet seemed weeks away. He was very tired. There were moments when he felt he had been happy there. "But the man's a fool who expects happiness or the happiness to last; I'm grateful for what I had."

One of his first thoughts was that he must look for another woman at once, who would take him and hold him, so that he could turn his back on the past eight years and begin again. But where should he look?

The train rattled along in the night and he thought for a while of the dark trains he had traveled in during the war and after he got the car, the dark roads, a hooded glimmer all that was allowed; but he had never driven into the ditch. How one's senses developed! And then it was to Marion he had traveled, by train and by car.

He slept as well as he could, waking not long before Bridgehead. "Back to Bridgehead gray," the color of his youth. It was a dark morning, the docks, bridges, ships were lighted. Different shifts were going to work and coming away; and he passed a stand where he got a cup of sour gray tea, "stewed water." He got to his old home before seven. The boy hadn't been around; the empty milk bottles were still standing there. Uncle Simon was some time answering the door; and when Tom heard the old voice, "What d'ye want?" he smiled.

"It's Tom."

Uncle Simon let him in, coughing. "Ye can get in now without that dog tearing the seat off your pants."

"Back home!" smiled Tom. He pushed his grip into the front room and took his parcels to the kitchen. His uncle was too polite to notice them at first, though he cast a few glances under his spectacles.

The fire was not going too well. A newspaper was fastened across the front of the stove and grate. The house was cold but it was warm enough there. The sky was black with smoke fog which had not come down. "If we had a decent government, it would do something about this weather," said Uncle Simon. He was heating his old tea from the night before on the stove and was about to pour some for Tom when he said hospitably, "A'll make ye a fresh pot. Did ye come in your car or off the train?"

"I'm off the train; I sold my car."

"Aye." The old man put one of his three kettles on the gas stove and turned the jet very low under it. The kettle had been sold to Simon as a gas-saver. "It'll be ready by the time the milk gets here." He then got out the bread and his own bit of butter which he set before Tom. "Would ye like some bacon? A haven't touched me bit. Put your washin' on the dresser, ye'll get it spotted."

"That's not washing, that's a chicken I brought for you, Uncle Sime, for Peggy to cook," said Tom.

Uncle Simon said nothing. "It's for you and mother, Uncle, you know Peggy wouldn't touch it."

Uncle Simon looked at the kettle, turned the gas up a little and fussed at the stove. "Thank ye, thank ye." His hands trembled. "A had a bad night: A coughed a lot, A thought A'd die. A ran out of me syrups of quills and me drops." The black coaly sky frowned at him.

Tom said, "How's mother?"

"She's sleepin' too much, not eatin' enough, wanderin' about on the stairs and she sees the dead. Your sister stays in bed till eleven most days; but A wake them with a cup of fresh tea and some bread and butter. Mary needs it. A'll light the back-room fire for ye if ye like."

"I'll sit with you, Uncle Sime. I'll go and see Mother when she wakes."

"She's probably awake now and starvin', but that gel never gets oop for her mother."

When the milk came he prepared the tea, while explaining to Tom about the bread-saw, "They don't know how to coot it: ye

[91]

move the knife backwards and forwards withoot pressure, it does the cootin; ye can get any thickness ye like." The kettle boiled after a long while and Tom took the tray upstairs.

The dog lying inside the door made a fuss. Peggy said, "It's that silly old man scratching on the door to tease him; all right, Uncle Sime man, wait a bit, can't ye?" and she opened the door. "Oh, lord lovaduck, it's Tom."

"Is it Tom?" said the mother quickly.

"It's Tom: Tom's here. When did you get in?"

He came in, without smiling. "Hello, Peggy, hello, Mother."

The old woman had started to get up and was trying to arrange her little white plaits. She had the brush and comb in her hands and she turned to Tom with a lively amused expression.

Peggy was excited, "Well, the lad's dropped in from the sky."

The old woman observed the young fellow calmly, put back the brush and comb and slid back into bed, "Well, put it there," she said patting the bedside table, "I'm not so hungry."

Tom did as he was told, "How are you feeling this morning, Mother?"

She made a trifling little scoffing smile, "The doctor told me to stay in bed in the mornings, but for all the good it's doing me, I'd rather be up," she said crossly, "up at me work. I don't know what I'm lying here for. Get up, Peggy: aren't you ashamed, in bed, with people here?"

Tom said he'd pour out for her. He sat down on the bedside, but she seemed uneasy and said, "Take a chair, there's a chair there"; and when he held the cup for her, she said, "It's very kind of you."

Tom sighed and looked dispiritedly around, at the plain walls with the children's photographs, the nice dressing table of which his mother was proud, the sickly little tree outside the window, now bare between brick walls. It was still quite dark. "Don't get up yet, Mother," he said, "it's a bitter raw morning, real Bridgehead."

Peggy wanted to know if he was on holiday.

"I'll be here a few days, I came to see how Mother was."

"What struck ye, man?" enquired Peggy sarcastically, "something must have bit ye, ye thought of coming to see your sick mother."

"I expected that kind of welcome."

"What kind of welcome would you be expecting? The flags put out and the fatted calf? After not coming near us at Christmas; it was a black dreary house for me in the festive season. We all stayed in bed all Christmas Day and no one near us. I suppose you had a gay time at Christmas."

"Yes, I had a very gay time."

"Well, it certainly is an unexpected pleasure in a black February day to have a distinguished visitor from London," said Peggy who had got back into bed and was finishing her breakfast. She wanted to know if he had a holiday from work.

"No," he said wearily, "I'm out of a job just now."

"You've not lost that job too?" she cried. "Eh, man, you're hopeless! Well, there's no unemployment round here yet, you'd best try to get a job here and live here. At least we're all paying the same rent and you can help with the house a bit: I'm sick of it. It's not fair a young woman like me never getting out or getting a chance to see anyone."

"I'll think it over," he said; "I don't see why I shouldn't. What else have I got to do?"

"Eh, you're hopeless, just hopeless," cried Peggy.

"Yes, I am," he answered.

"What sort of a future have ye, man?" she enquired anxiously, "if you're such a trifler and so restless at your age?"

"That's a good question."

"Ah, be serious, Tom, I'm worried about ye, man."

"Thanks for that," said he seriously, "that's kind of you: you don't know how kind that is."

"Eh, Tom, I'm not trying to harass you, I'm worried about ye, I don't doubt you have your troubles."

"I'll never forget those words, Peggy," he said getting up to hide the tears in his eyes. "I've had an awful time: it was horrible."

"Well, take it easy, man, don't go imagining tragedies. Pluck up courage, man, try to be like I am. Look at what I have to face every day in this house with no one to stand by me! You had bet-

[93]

ter make up your mind to stay here and the troubles you think you've had will be nothing to the troubles you're going to have with these two crazy old people at ye day and night and not one word of sense from one year's end to the other."

"You're a great consoler," said her brother, going to the door, and smiling faintly, "I had quite an experience once: a friend of mine took me to an undertakers' annual banquet. I'm glad I was there now: I can see there's humor in everything."

"Ye sound like Uncle Sime, now watch out, man, you're getting on in years, thirty-three is not twenty." Tom burst out laughing. The dog rushed out the door and escaped downstairs where he began a savage barking.

When Tom got down there, Uncle Simon was standing in the kitchen near his chair, with bowed legs, looking desperate, while the black dog leaped at him. "He's gettin' warse and warse," said he. "He won't let me move. A'd better go to bed. A go back to bed as soon as there's someone aboot, for he doesn't come into me room. A've made up the fire, Tom, and A'd better get to me bed, that's where they want to see me. They don't want me to get up again."

"All right, Uncle Sime," said Tom, "you go up and rest a bit and I'll be muttering to myself down here."

"Don't let the fire go too low and see your Mother doesn't put it out with flingin' food into it." He offered Tom the *Daily Mail*, and though Tom refused it, he left it on the table for him, "It's a good paper, there are some good items in it today. There's another air accident. You mark my words, Tom, they'll give it up, this flyin'. A man is not a bord. Ye've seen it yourself: there's something loose, they haven't time to attend to it, and it goes to pieces in mid-air."

"Yes," said Tom, "all right, and I'll see they cook the chicken for us for lunch or dinner." Uncle Simon slowly made his way through the hall, muttering his thoughts to himself and very slowly got upstairs, being held up halfway by a bad fit of coughing.

Peggy and her mother came downstairs about half past eleven when the house was warm. The street lights were still on; and everyone was coughing. Tom sat in Uncle Simon's chair by the fire, looked at the *Daily Mail* and thought how tired, betrayed and unhappy he was. Marion, after all her loving and his loyalty, had used him, and perhaps despised him. And then she had always thought she was clever, cleverer than the men she brought round her. She lied to them all; that was her idea of running things efficiently. Efficient she was, even at the end, in her misery. At the very end she had given the three men—her husband, Connie, her half-brother Patrick and himself—each a beautiful engraved champagne glass. They stood round her with the glasses in their hands. "Drink to me!" He, too, passed as a half-brother. Connie had the orchard and farm, Patrick had gone away a few months before; he, the so-called half-brother, had looked after her to the end. He didn't mind that: he was glad of it. When she died, he broke his glass on the stone floor of the kitchen.

Tom heard them all coughing. He said aloud, "Marion, Marion, why did you do that? You could have told me. I would have forgiven you." He thought, "I am going to fall immediately for another woman. I hope not some woman out there in the murk of Bridgehead." More likely someone in the sprawling smoking garbage-tip London is in winter. "She'll be the wrong woman and I'll run to her blindly, just to forget myself."

When Peggy came in, ready to fight if he would not stay in Bridgehead and look after the house and work for them, he shouted that he was not going to spend his life in the back kitchen of a sooty back-to-back, though she wanted to leg-rope him there, "like the rest of the Bridgehead women." Peggy said she had never seen such a thing in her life, a man of his age hanging about a kitchen fire, expecting his tea to be poured for him: she wasn't going to wait on him.

"If you're out of work, you'd better get on relief."

"I've never been on relief yet: not even on the dole in the bad days. I always found something. I did anything; I never got there."

"Don't brag, man, ye'll get there," she said.

He was glad to shout his lungs free and run out into the passage, like a boy again. Uncle Simon hid from the fight. The mother came downstairs with her gentle superior smirk. "Dogs

[95]

delight to bark and bite," she said in her aged voice, getting distant now as it drew off to another part of the universe: and she looked about for her duster.

"Tom's out of work and he's come home to live off us," said Peggy when he was at the front door. Tom came back and laid on the table all the loose change in his pockets, about twenty-seven and six. He kept only some notes and fifteen pennies for telephones: then he took back some change for cigarettes. The two women quickly and delightedly picked up the money and before he got to the door again, he saw them with joyful secrecy putting the money away in an old sewing box which fitted into the back of the linen drawer. There they kept the money paid by the insurance company and the weekly allowances made to them by Nellie and himself. Uncle Simon's pension covered the rent. He strolled out into the filthy air, full of coughing black smudges which had been born to be men and women; but it choked him after the fresh fields and hills round Market Orange where he had been living with Marion and Connie. He suddenly wondered if his mother had thrown the chicken into the fire. This made him hurry back.

Peggy was sitting by the back room fire knitting, looking very pleased with herself and whistling. "What mischief has she been up to?" thought Tom. His mother and uncle were in the kitchen. Uncle Simon had his felt slippers on the bright fender and was making weak tea. The old woman in a clean apron sat by a clean empty cup.

"Have some tea," said the old man, "I've got some milk of me own, lad, if you're hungry."

Tom said he had eaten a "businessman's lunch," consisting of sausage and French fries.

"A sausage is very tasty sometimes," said Uncle Simon.

Tom found a cup and saucer and poured some tea, using Uncle Simon's milk that afternoon.

"I know ye need the money, lad: ye can share with me," said the uncle.

"Bread's enough for me, I can live on bread," said Tom, "I don't want to get fat; I've been idling for three months now."

"What've ye been living on, relief?" said the mother.

"It's demoralizin' to take the dole, lad, if ye can get work," said Uncle Simon. "Ye can stay here, if ye like and get a good job here. There are plenty of places, and ye're the right age, just the right age; a man of thirty-three is what they want. Ye could get in at Armstrong's. It's not a question of how fast ye are, but how good ye are."

Tom sat down and drank his tea. Three pale, long, blue-eyed Pike faces looked towards the dirty window and the black air. There was a sickly holly bush in the bit of ground round the tree and some bones and crusts at which birds were pecking. "The mice come out and eat Sime's bones," teased Mrs. Cotter.

"There's mony a dead bord in this black fog," said Uncle Simon, "and mony a dead old man and woman, too. It's carryin' them off."

"Did you hear from Nellie, Mother?"

The old woman looked in front of her, "Nellie never coom, Tom never coom: I've got funny children. I washed and scrubbed and cooked and yet they are not grateful: they don't understand. Their wings get stronger, they fly off."

The back-yard bell rang and Uncle Simon got up. "It's Charlie," said the old woman smiling. "He comes for the messages, his mother's very sick and he helps her: he's such a good boy," she told Tom politely.

Uncle Simon returned with a well-grown smiling boy about ten, with shining black eyes and hair.

"Hello, Charlie," said Mrs. Cotter. "You know, Mr.—" she turned to her son, "I'm sorry, I didn't catch your name?"

"Don't be silly, woman, it's your own son, it's Tom."

"Don't you be silly, it's Charlie," she said rocking with laughter. "You'll be the death of me, Simon, you'll be forgetting your own name. He's no son of mine; it's Charlie Rockett, isn't it, hinny?"

"Aye," said the boy smiling.

The old woman went to a drawer and looked eagerly into it. "Who's been turning this drawer upside down?" she asked merrily.

"It's yourself, Mary, and no man else; what are you looking for?"

"For the chocolate for Charlie."

She found the chocolate presently and gave two pieces to the boy, to whom Uncle Simon had now given the grocery list. He impressed upon Charlie the name of his drops, not to forget them and to get them at Burns's, the corner papershop, not at the chemist's; and he carefully counted out the money.

"Eh, give him the money, Simon, don't be an old miser," said Mrs. Cotter, rollicking: "he won't cheat you." She said to her son, "He's a real good boy to his mother; I give him the change for his mother. Now keep a bit of chocolate for your mother, hinny."

She said to Tom, "My own boy Tom used to bring me chocolate when he came home from singing in the choir at Saint Aidan's. He had such a good voice, a real talent; and they always gave him a piece of chocolate and he came running home to his mother; and he used to bury his head in my lap. He was always a mother's boy."

"Don't you know me, Mother?" said Tom. "It wasn't chocolate, Mother. The way it was, was this. We had to be on time and if we came late, we got bad marks, a mark a minute; and if the choirmaster came late, we got pennies, a penny a boy. With my pennies I bought you chitterlings of which you were very fond; that is what I brought you."

She looked at him and laughed, "Chitterlings! They're very good. I like dumplings, too. Mother used to make very good dumplings."

"Aye, she made them in broth and she made them in boiling water: Mother was a very good cook," said Simon.

"I wish she was cooking for us now, I do," said Mrs. Cotter: "I'm hungry, I get really hungry these days, it's the weather coming on to spring."

"It's a fine spring day in Bridgehead, Mother," said Tom laughing; "it is raining black diamonds. I was out; but came back fast."

"Eh," said Mrs. Cotter looking at him, "well, I'm sorry you must go so soon. And look at us sitting in the kitchen!"

"Now gather your wits together, Mary," said Simon indignantly, "ye complain he doesn't come and when he comes ye take him for the grocer's boy. It's ridiculous, that's what it is, A'm ashamed of ye. Ye always were a great one for play-actin' and now it's got the better of ye. Ye want to tell the plain truth all your life, woman, and speak straight and see straight; otherwise ye get to seein' double. Put on your glasses, Mary, don't be ashamed and look in front of you and stop wanderin' among shadows."

"Oh, leave her alone," said Tom, revolted. "What does it matter? I came, didn't I? It doesn't matter if she doesn't know it."

"No, I don't know it," said the old woman to Tom. "There are a lot of things going on in this house I don't know. They're here and they don't come downstairs. I don't know why. It's as if we were strangers. They don't tell me anything; always going and coming. They've got wild since they grew up and Nellie has got them into bad ways. I'm all alone in the house and I don't know what's going on. I don't ask, I don't interfere, but it makes me look funny. I say funny things when people call. People are very kind, very sociable, always visiting; but I'm worried that I'm going to make a fool of myself, put my foot in it. Then they laugh. You see, Mr.—excuse me, my head is so bad now, Mr.—?"

"Cotter," said Tom.

"Mr. Cotter," she said surprised, looking at him; "are you one of the family? You do look like the family."

"Mother," said Tom.

"Don't bother her now," said Uncle Simon; "it's surprisin' how fresh and clear she is often in the marnin' or late at night; but ye mustn't bother her. Peggy's been a very bad lass today and it's got her worried. She can't stand the shoutin' and the cruelty. She was always a timid woman; it's been too much trouble for her."

Tom brought out the chicken and said they ought to have it for supper. The old people were delighted and excited; but Uncle Simon said he'd never cooked a chicken; though he once knew a French woman who cooked a wonderful chicken and he could still remember it. "Though it was thirty-five years ago," said Tom laughing.

"It was thirty-eight," said Uncle Simon, with dignity. "Her

husband was a German, a strange sort of man. He went away as a German soldier and he came back after the war. A never did trust him."

"With a chicken cook like that, I'm not surprised he came back," said Tom.

"Now, Simon," said Mary, rocking with laughter; "you're surely not going to try and tell us at this late date that you had a sweetheart who cooked you a chicken dinner?"

"A had a friend who was a good cook," said Simon, straightening himself and looking at his sister. She kept on laughing and gently pinching the plump white flesh of the fowl.

"How do you cook a chicken, Mother? Do you boil it or roast it? Which is better?"

The old woman laughed till she cried; but in the end she said, "I can't remember: it's so long since I cooked one."

"Probably forty odd years," said Tom; "I don't remember ever getting one at home."

"A roast with vegetables is best for the weekend," said Uncle Simon, who did the weekend cooking; "one good healthy man can eat a whole chicken at a meal and crack the bones too. A had a friend who did that, cleaned up like a dog, cracked everythin' with his teeth."

Tom called upon Peggy, who at first screeched at the idea of cooking flesh, but eventually was persuaded, because it was good for her mother.

"I'm hungry, too," said Tom.

Grudgingly she hunted for a cookery book which had belonged to Aunt Lily who had died in their attic five years before and who had lain there for four years before that. Fortunately, the chicken had been cleaned by Connie and the giblets were inside it; but no one knew what to do with them; so Tom asked if he could give the chicken heart to the dog. "Chicken heart? What is that?" asked Peggy dubiously.

"Chicken heart? Heart of a chicken."

"Heart of a chicken? I never heard of that." She was very puzzled. She turned it over, with her rubber gloves on; and at length said that if it was cooked he could have it, she thought.

"What would go with a roast fowl or boiled fowl?" Tom asked. Peggy said it would be better to have whatever was in the larder. They got out two halves of cabbage which Peggy had cut into for raw vegetable salads, and some potatoes. The mother declared a hankering for dumplings; they would boil the fowl and put the dumplings in the water. "And the cabbage?" They could do that in a separate pot, but they were not sure how. Peggy had given up cooking vegetables long ago, having read that cooking took the good out of them. They came to an agreement presently. Tom would try his hand at dumplings out of the cookery book; Uncle Simon would boil the fowl and cabbage; and they were forced to accept his view that all these things would do best on a very low gas; "then you won't lose the goodness." Gradually, the watchers departed, leaving the old man in charge. They could not go to the nearest aunt and ask advice, out of pride and because there would not be enough to invite her. Peggy foresaw that they would give a bone to the dog and kill him. Tom thought they might have potatoes too.

Tom went out to get a beer when the beer shop reopened at six, found dinner was not ready, said he'd take a stroll. When he returned at seven thirty, Mrs. Cotter said she was hungry and they decided to dish up. The water, on Uncle Simon's low gas, had never come to the boil. Assuming command, Tom sent Peggy to lay the table, brought his mother to the kitchen to superintend the dishing up, agreed to divide the fowl himself. Simon said that he would eat by his own fire in the kitchen and remarked that it made a lot of dishes. The old mother wrapped all the necessary forks, knives and spoons in a brown paper parcel and put them with Aunt Lily's book in the sideboard in the front room, just after the potatoes were drained. During the hunt that followed she very slyly, with a pale little smirk, tipped the potatoes into Simon's fire, washed and polished the vegetable dish and put it back in its place. They were recalled to the kitchen by the smell. Tom had to finish the table while Peggy, scolding, stood guard and Simon tried to right his fire. The fine young hen which had been put on in cold water, with no salt, for Peggy thought it bad for the blood, was heavy, leathery; it did not seem cooked. The cabbage when dished up was hard, almost crisp. "You should have turned the gas up a bit, Uncle Sime," said Tom pleasantly.

"And lose all the good juices? A don't hold with the modern way of doin' everythin' fast and tasteless."

"It's better for your stomach if the cabbage is raw," said Peggy.

Mother said it smelled very good, it made her mouth water.

"The dumplin's are very good," said Uncle Simon taking a bit of one. Some had fallen to the bottom, others had spread about in the water. "The taste is very good, ye are quite a hand," said Simon.

"You must be very hungry, Uncle," said Tom, smiling sadly. He carried in the hen to divide up and after ten minutes called to the women to bring in the vegetables. "Surely we can do a simple thing like that without your powers of direction," shouted Peggy.

"Very well," said Tom and sat down to wait.

Half an hour later they were all eating what they could, while the dog constantly had to be threatened with the leash; and when the chicken was carried out, Peggy had to stay in the kitchen to see no one gave him a bone. Meantime, she lectured them on the evils of flesh-eating; but she had eaten a lot of cabbage, onion, cheese and was in a good mood. "You'll not want anything to eat for a couple of days," she said; "such guzzling and gobbling, you'd think it was Christmas." She cleaned up efficiently as usual, with the gloves to keep her hands white; and then sat contentedly by the back-room fire to knit. She let them hush the dog, without bursting into fury.

The two men who looked so alike sat in the kitchen, while Simon Pike told Tom about trips he had made to Durham to install an iron fire-escape and to Consett to put in some boilers; and Tom described to his uncle new alloys he had been dealing with. When Tom, later on, took his bag out of the front room and went upstairs, to go to his father's room which he was to occupy, he was startled to see a woman's figure quite still on the dark mid-landing. It was all dark above; below, only the pale light from the street lamp beyond. He stopped. "Who is it?" he said as quietly as he could. No answer. His heart began an irregular beat. "Who is that?"

His mother said in a very low voice, "It is his image standing there."

He did not understand at first, he laughed low, "Yes, yes, it is."

"He just stands there, it's so strange," she said almost in a whisper. Tom went on past her, up the stairs and said casually, "And who is it, Mother?"

"It's Tom. He won't come in because he's waiting for the dog to go. He never could bear that dog. That's a bad dog, he said."

"Yes."

"He couldn't bear anyone to have his name. My son was called Tom and he made us call him Jack. Jack we always called him." She looked up rather brightly and said jokingly, "Hurraw, Jack!" Tom put on the bedroom light and then the stair light.

"You oughtn't to be going upstairs in the dark, Mother."

She looked at him quietly and said, "Jack, couldn't we sell him? We don't want him."

"Who would buy him?"

"Timmie was a good dog," she said; "but this is a bad dog; there never was a worse dog."

When he came down, he sat in the back room with his cigarette and tried to talk to Peggy who had put on superior airs for some reason. Presently two of the aunts came round. Everyone began to talk of the dinners they had had; and Tom, lively, mentioned that Uncle Simon's sauce had been a combination of Friday's roast, juice from the boiling, touched up with a little bottled sauce and they never did get to the salad; perhaps it was for tomorrow. He burst out laughing hysterically.

Peggy flew into a rage, supposing he was laughing at her. He said he was laughing because he was a hollow man. "Is it to be fed ye came home?" He'd sold his car, she cried out and had eaten it, when it would have been useful for taking them out of the house; and just when she expected a bit of a rest, they were going to have two Uncle Simons.

The aunts took this seriously and spoke to him. When he eventually withdrew to the kitchen to make them all some tea, and to see why Tom the dog was making such a noise, Peggy came rushing out to say that they were two worthless lazy men taking out their sour crabbed natures on a young animal.

The next day things were much worse. Tom came downstairs at one moment in time to see Uncle Simon shrink back and Peggy strike him on the temple with a greasy saucepan which she had put in the oven the day before "to keep it from the mice." Uncle Simon had reproached her for not washing it.

"Ah, Peggy, how can you hit the poor old man," he shouted, running in.

"I'd gladly strike him dead and never would be remorseful," said Peggy. "It would rid the earth of a great nuisance. What use is he? Are you such a weak thing, you're afraid to see someone hit? I often hit him. It's good for him. You'd better learn the facts of life. Life is not soft and easy, man. You don't suppose I can stay here with these daft old fools and keep my temper like a sister of charity? I suppose it would be better if I let him drive me back to the Home."

It was a terrible scene and Tom, with a heart fallen as low as it could be, thought there was no help for it, he must get a job in Bridgehead and stay here to protect them. He had no doubt at all that Peggy would get rid of them in her own way if it suited her. But what was the use of increasing the misery by his own? There must be some way of organizing the home so that the old people would be taken care of and Peggy got out of it? He went for his evening walk and walked a long time, with his back bent, his hands clasped behind him, his nose down, with long strides, as was his habit in his lonely ambles. He looked bland, leather-skinned, old, glancing neither left nor right, along the streets he knew from childhood, stopping, walking on automatically with thoughtless precision, just as he drove, noticing old landmarks without comment. After some time, because of his meditations about the past, present and future, he reached a two-story building in an enclosure, with an isolation hospital and locked gates, some trees, a secret place he knew well, the Home where Peggy had been nursed from her twenty-second to her thirtieth year.

Thomas Cotter Senior had never gone in those gates. "It is not my daughter Margaret Cotter that is in the Home, but a girl belonging to the other Cotters across the river" and so for eight years. The nurses had liked her. She was a good-looking, softly charming, and foolishly excited girl, rather clever at that time, going with them everywhere. Then she had lost hold of things, like her old mother now. Bridgehead is a gray town: the women are sensible and salty. Peggy's early blossoming was an event: the men all looked at her and she threw herself to them. They both stood out like scarlet patches on the gray tatters of those years; Nellie too, with her gawky Bohemian toughness, putting out cock's feathers of charm on demand: "Chief Chickenhawk," he had called her to her delight.

He had had ambitions too, running on the muddy winter fields against the sooty sky, with the team in blue and yellow against some team in gold and black or scarlet and sky: notice-able, with his red cheeks and glittering fair hair. He had hopes that though he was a little man and a Pike, he'd play national football because he was tough and relentless: he never gave up. Women had begun to have the strangest effect on him, not as with other boys as far as he could see. Women began to love him. It was a surprise and a release from the back-kitchen world and the aunts. They never thought well of men in the Pike fam-ily; and men, in Bridgehead, were just regarded as work horses. He did not know, in his heart, quite why it was that women's eyes followed him. "I do nothing," he said to himself; "and I give them very little." He often wondered about it with a faint sinking of the heart. Suppose this mysterious charm were to desert him? Of course, it would some day and probably very soon. He must get himself fixed with a woman he could live with for the rest of his life. It had startled him to hear that Uncle Simon had once had a French friend. On the empty day which would bring him nearer to Uncle Simon, make him like him, he was afraid he would not be able to see his way any more.

They had had too many privations as children and adoles-cents. He was skinny, feebler than he showed now; and he had never done anything he had meant to do. For one thing, as a boy, he had admired Carlyle, they all had; and he had thought of writing something in that vein. But now at night, when he came from the works, he could often hardly keep his head up. And the food the landladies provided for the men! He laughed at the idea his sisters had of him. They were Bridgehead women in that. Nellie imagining him always in the lap of some woman; a roué, a cheat. What else would a man do? Not think and meditate of course! He chuckled out loud. And Peggy seeing him as a sort of unemployable. At his last job he had had three hundred men under him. He gave it up to nurse Marion, to be with her every minute of the last days of her life. How could he explain that to the women at home? Besides, they didn't care. Their only idea was to see his pay envelope on Friday.

Well, poor Peggy. She had gone earnestly with them to the miners' cottages when they were young, to learn socialism there from one or two; she had stood in the freezing cold and sold newspapers with them. And when she grew a bit, she had laughed with men and fallen in love with a man who couldn't or wouldn't divorce his wife; and she had lost touch through sorrow and they had shut her up. She thought she was imprisoned for something she had done. At one time, she fancied it was a political crime and the police had got her. Pop Cotter had really sent one of his pals in the police to bring them home. At another time, it was a contagious disease she had she thought —that came from talk among the aunts of the consequences of Pop Cotter's endless gallantries. And then, that when she opened her mouth filthy creatures dropped out of it; and that was Nellie, the way she made us confess, even things we hadn't done at all, but that sounded good and rich to her. "Confession, pets, is good for the soul: it purges; introspection is what distinguishes us from the animals." Sometimes Peggy thought she had threatened someone's life. Perhaps she had. "Poor Peggy! But I have to have all my humanity back of me to make me say it."

And he thought of Nellie, guilty, guilty as she said; and really guilty towards Peggy and himself as he knew her to be, seducing children to love; out of her great vanity wanting to be the only one to show them love; so that no one again could take them from her; but not calling it perversion, calling it knowledge, the true way. "I can lead, I know," she said. He knew she meant no real harm. She did not understand; and his love forgave her:

[106]

"the softest tough girlie I ever met," as he said to her; and a most unscrupulous woman, as Pop Cotter was a most unscrupulous man; anything to be the center of everything and hog the limelight. Nellie, though, being a woman, and being so loving, was forgivable.

On his way home, he thought of Uncle Simon and bought some light ale at a beer shop. He preferred the dark himself and got one of those too, though he knew he would hear the uncle's lecture about caramelized beer. "A warked in a brewery when A was a lad and A had me fill of it. A lot of the men lost their jobs through drunkenness and so A took me lesson." But Simon would take a glass for his cough and he might even give Peggy a glass: she loved it and it was forbidden to her.

Tom did not pick out his gate at first, because at the gate there was a bareheaded woman of the dumpy pale Bridgehead type, black hair pulled back and strong eyebrows, talking to a workman about fifty, with cap and jacket on, no overcoat, leaning on the gate. But he saw it was Peggy. She said hurriedly, "It's the painter; I thought we'd have the kitchen painted cream, it's that grimy. He could start while you're here. Uncle Sime won't let him in."

"And get me to pay for it," thought Tom immediately, nodding curtly to the painter, a thin somewhat bent, cheeky looking man. He said, "You'll get cold, Peggy," and went in. Tom the dog was inside the door and began to bark and leap at Tom when he went in. "Shut up, you dope," he shouted angrily so that Peggy turned round and quieted him. He thought, "They all think I'm another Uncle Sime: well, I'm not." Peggy was embarrassed. Why? Was she offering the man too much, so that he'd come soon to the house and chat with her? He turned and called, "Peggy!"

"All right, all right, for God's sake," but she came in, glad to be vexed. He smiled and offered her a glass of beer, at which she became gay, "Eh, it's a gala day: you'd think it was Race Week."

Simon looked up with his spectacles on his nose. "Mind the linoleum! I'll fix it right away. The dog was tearin' at it. There's another terrible air accident here. Flying's against nature: man is not a bord. Bords know how. Ye'll see, they'll give it oop. Will ye have some tea?" Tom offered his beer, but the old man said, "Thank ye, no, no, better not: I used to like it though."

The dog ran into the kitchen and harassed Simon and presently the mother came in, peering and said, "Oh, I thought Mother was here: I'm always doing that."

"No wonder you can't see, Mother, in the fog and filthy air."

"A large proportion of the soot is the result of incomplete combustion due to inefficient stoking," said Uncle Simon.

"And antiquated methods," said Tom.

"What are they using this opencast for," said Uncle Simon referring to the articles featuring local opencast mining. "It's for the papers. There's no use in it. They send it down south where people don't know and find they've got a bit of earth coated with a bit of coal dust when they bargained for coal. Ye couldn't sell that in Bridgehead."

"We just pipe it out of the air," said Tom. Uncle Simon began to cough such a wrenching cough that he had to get up and stand bowed over the sink.

"It's killin' me," he said to Tom between gasps; "it's the raw climate."

"The window's very dirty, Simon," said the old woman; "you old miser, why don't you let the window cleaner in?"

"Because your daughter has no sense," gasped the old man; "the silly girl was makin' a date with the windowman, that's all. A can tell ye now because ye'll forget it. A can't tell it to the silly women, or they'll fly screechin' down me neck. Peggy can do no wrong because the poor lass was unfortunate. But that's no way to treat her. It would send a steady man out of his wits to be treated like a pet dog. It's treated like a grown woman she should be and told of her responsibilities." He came back and began to toast some bread for his sister. "She hasn't eaten anythin' today. A found out she threw her chicken in the fire when me back was turned. It's no good wastin' your money on them." The dog flew at him and he waved the toasting fork feebly.

The mother said, "I can't make out where they are: it's not like them to go out without their tea and without saying goodbye."

"Sit down, Mother," said Tom, closing the door to the hall.

"But we mustn't close them out, the way they have got, they'll feel they're not welcome."

"It's those that died in the attic, Lily and Mother," said Uncle Simon.

They had not sat there long before she got up and began to search in the drawers. She found paper and string and going to the silver drawer, took things out and wrapped them. Simon told her to quit wrapping things. "You're not goin' anywhere; and if ye were, ye couldn't take the whole house with ye in little parcels."

"Don't be meddling where you're not wanted," she said brightly; and winked at Tom. "He never was—" she tapped her forehead: "No one at home: house to let, apply within, no one went out and no one went in." She laughed greatly at this witticism. The dog felt the discouragement of Simon and began barking at him.

Mary Cotter sat down and said it was a black day for that house the day Nellie brought that dog home. Simon told the story of Nellie's finding him running barking about the railway station. She took him to the police station, put in adverts; interviewed people. "The farther they went, the warse it got and George Cook lost all patience; he is not a patient man."

"No," said Tom.

"And the end of it was, no one would have the dog; they had to keep him."

"That's not the way Nellie tells it," said Tom laughing: "according to her, it was a frail little starved waif and a puir stray. Probably the cruel mother of some probable waif, some puir lad of ten, had refused to pay the dog license; and she brought it home thinking that the puir lad of ten was crying his eyes out because of his hard-hearted mother and soft-hearted dog. On the other hand, probably it was because it was year's end and not money enough in the house, perhaps a drinking father or a strike or an industrial accident, or a widow altogether, so that with licenses at hand, they had both, with sighs and tears, to loose him on the street."

"Aye," said Simon, offended, "she may say it one way and A say it the way it happened. Perhaps she doesn't remember with trailing that dog from South Shields to Chester-le-Street to find its owner. Its owner was an invalid who didn't want it and said Nellie could have it. It began by being very spoiled."

Mrs. Cotter said it was not that dog. They argued the point for a while, when she remembered suddenly, and pointing to the dog, said to her brother, "Take him to the door and lose him, no matter what she says. You can't suffer any more than you do now."

"A'm not so sure of that," said the old man. "A don't know where the end of me sufferin's will be. Ye spoil that girl, Mary; ye're her mother but ye give in to her too much. You must know how to handle weak heads."

"Don't you say that word in this house, Simon."

"Aye, aye, A mustn't say a true word in this house: the house wud fall down. But ye can see me beaten and starved, woman, and A'm here for ye alone. Where's your feelin' of flesh and blood?"

"Now it's coming out of the old man," she said pertly, "the vanity and the arrogance. It's funny to see a little man like that so cocky."

"What's the matter with a little man if he's strong?" said Simon. "If A'm not a royal, A've got the right to live, if A'm a good worker, or was—or was."

"I gave up reading the comic papers, when I saw half the jokes were about little men," said Tom. "You can tell a Bridge-head man anywhere in England, he's so wasted and small; he may be strong but he's pitifully wasted and undersize. Now in England the classes are divided by inches. When they're laughing at us little men, they're laughing at the starveling. The seamy side of wit is cruelty."

"Ah, well, A wudna complain if A was somewhere else," said Uncle Simon tranquilly, "we all get on when the gel's not here. We get along champion."

"Would you chase my own daughter out of the house?" said Mrs. Cotter. "Shame on you, Simon."

"Shame on me, shame on me, I hear no other thanks for all A've done. It's funny, that's what it is, it's funny."

Tom said he was going to get cigarettes and took a walk. As

soon as he left the house, the strong sea air, though heavy with smoke, cleared his brain. He forgot them and began to bowl along as before. "I like to breathe, I like bread, I can get along anywhere," he said to himself, "I just like to live. I'm easy living."

When he came back, the aunts were there and began to badger him about getting a job. As he could not explain to them that he had given up a good job to nurse Marion, he began gradually to forget why he had not a job and discussed jobs with them. "I'll get a job any day I like. I can pick and choose. War or peace, I've got work. I tried already. But I'm not staying in Bridgehead. I'll get to another town; and no more country. I'd end up chewing a grass stalk with one foot behind the other."

"Aye, but your duty is here, lad."

He saw one of the aunts home and when he came in, Peggy was worrying about Uncle Simon's cough keeping them awake and giving him a sleeping pill. Tom hung about the house and while he was getting something out of his overcoat on the hall stand, he thought he saw a head dodge around the stairhead, but took no notice. He felt a real insomnia on him and went into the front room to see if there was one of Aunt Lily's old books he had not read and he started glancing through *Old Mortality*. The others were going to bed, soft footfalls up and down, doors opening and shutting. When he opened the door of the front room and came out, he saw the house dark, except in the kitchen, where Uncle Simon was fidgeting, looking over his shoulders and going through a bunch of keys on a large keyring. Again he thought he saw a head dodge round the post at the landing; but he hadn't slept well for a long time: he wouldn't swear to anything.

He said he'd make some tea, get a sandwich and he'd sit up all night.

"Will ye sit up all night?" asked Simon earnestly, in a low tone.

"I might."

"Then ye can watch the gel. She's put paraffin in the backroom fire, so that it will burn for hours. A looked through the keyhole. There's a terrible white flame in the grate and the

[111]

chimney'll be on fire, if we can't get in. See there!" The sooty
brick wall of the next house was rosy at the top where flame from
the chimney lit it. "She's taken the door key and hidden it somewhere." They went out into the freezing back yard to look, but
Peggy had first closed the back-room curtains. Out of the chimney into the thick air came fire and sparks, the shadows of the
chimneypot hopped on the shed roof. They tried the window
but it had been fastened. "I'll get it from her," said Tom. But
as he went upstairs, he heard the key turned: she had locked
herself, her mother and the dog into the bedroom, which was
directly over the back room. There she could hear the fire roaring in the chimney and chuckle at her naughtiness. "You'd better come up too," said Tom to Simon, at the bottom of the
stairs. "If we make a fuss, then she'll feel she's had her fun and
she'll give up the key."

They went upstairs, knocked, begged and shouted, but only
got a few sprightly or angry responses. "It's Uncle Sime's fault,"
she shouted laughing. "He will rake the fire out front and fill
the room with smoke, so I've made a good bright flame backwards."

"Listen," said Tom, "if you set the place on fire in mischief,
Peggy, you won't get insurance."

"They have to pay you," said Peggy.

"No, they don't. Do you think they won't find out about the
paraffin. You won't get a shilling. That's what the spotters are
for. You'll lose everything, your money in your moneybox, your
insurance and everything."

"We've got our moneybox with us," said Peggy laughing; "eh,
don't rack your brains, man."

"Come out ye little fool," shouted Uncle Simon, "your money
will burn up with ye."

"I'll come out in time, don't worry about me, go to bed and
have pleasant dreams," she began to singsong.

"What aboot ye puir old mother, ye daft thing, no one's worried about your skin, you're safe enough."

Peggy shouted at being called a daft thing.

"How much paraffin did she put on?" asked Tom.

"She emptied out her mother's night light."

"I put some on out of the can too," said Peggy listening to them behind the door.

The dog barked behind the door. "The bright intelligent young woman has got her dog in there and he'll be burned up hair and hide, and good riddance," shouted Uncle Simon, hovering about, jingling the keys and trembling.

"Eh, I'm sick of ye all. I wouldn't count the cost of a cup of paraffin to burn ye all up, you're shriveled up like dried-out Christmas trees, ye old rubbish," called Peggy. "I should worry. It's not me, but yourself you're worried about: and your savings."

"Listen, lass," said Uncle Simon firmly, "now listen to what A'm tellin' ye. Oopstairs in the back attic is me toolbox; in me toolbox is me savin's." Peggy was listening. "A never kept them in the bank like A said: they're oop there. This family owes me three hundred pounds from when you were kiddies, but A'm not countin' that. But A've still got a bit there and it's in notes: and it's more than two hundred pounds. If ye don't come out this instant and give us the key, A'll take that money and give it to Tom and that'll be the end of it. Ye'll never get a smell of it. A'm sick and tired of dancin' the dance of death round ye. A mean that."

"I'll come out," said Peggy at once, "if ye'll take me right up and show me the money, so I'll find out if ye're a liar ye old rascal, I'm on to ye."

"Come out and come quick."

She unbolted then unlocked the door immediately. She was fully dressed as if to go out and looked as usual, rather sharper and more blooming than usual, perhaps. They argued about whether she should be shown the money first or should give up the key first, and they were obliged to give in. They went upstairs, Uncle Simon slowly, to the freezing attic, where in the corner lay a toolbox that looked like an infant's coffin, with a catch and a lock. Uncle Simon unlocked it with a key taken from his chest-warmer and going carefully through the bedded tools of wheelwright, ironworker and general handyman, he got out a large envelope addressed to Tom and an old wallet with an elastic round it. "That's the wallet ye made for me

[113]

when ye were learnin' leatherwork as a lad, Tom," he said nodding. "A appreciated it. A never got a gift in all me years in this house but that." Tom stood by, holding the bunch of keys and Peggy looked down into the box with a glittering look. She bent down and picked up a large screw-wrench, "What's that for?"

"Put it down," said Tom. She put it back again with a sly smile at Tom and looked greedily at the other things there.

Uncle Simon stood up slowly and angrily facing the girl, with trembling hands he undid the wallet and showed the money. "There ye are, gel, it's all there. Now give oop the key."

"I'll give it up, Uncle Sime; now don't put on the tragedy act."

Uncle Simon bent down and put the money back, fixed the tools. Peggy stood there with an awful smile. "That's a canny thing," she said, "that screw-wrench. Now what would it be for?" Uncle Simon locked the box. Looking very old, he stood and faced Tom.

"But there won't be much for ye, Tom, for the money there is for the unforeseen for Mary and meself: the funerals are paid for. A don't want a young feller to be stuck with the expenses of puttin' away two old bodies. It's not fair to burden the young with the old; and there's too much of it." He took the key off the greasy cord hanging in his chest-warmer, and handed it to Tom.

"I suppose you think I'll be coming into your room late at night, Uncle Sime, the only woman was ever in your room, eh? and take it off your neck and kill you for your bit of money?" Peggy said. "Well, don't worry, man, I wouldn't go into your room, no one could, it's a hole an animal would be afraid to crawl into."

"Give me the key, Peggy," said Tom. The three of them went slowly down the stairs and when they reached the landing, the old woman was there with a shawl round her shoulders, looking wonderingly at the stairs filled with people coming down from the attic. She went back into her room without a word.

When the fire was out and the house fixed for the night, they all went to bed and Tom rapidly imagined scenes in which he rescued his mother, Peggy, Uncle Simon, the dog, the moneybox, the toolbox, the insurance policies. He felt the toolbox key in his pocket by the bed, got up and locked the door. Uncle Simon had left his door open, as always; but the pill had put him to sleep: he snored.

"Well," said Tom to himself, "I always expected to see this house in Hadrian's Grove in the *News of the World* and it's surprisingly long coming to it." He lay in bed and thought about Market Orange, the town where he had lived so long with Marion and Constantine. He became too tired for that but remained awake. He could not read, could not move, lay there in an empty delirium. About half past two, he was sure he was awake when he heard a door open and someone go downstairs. He waited awhile, no one returned. Shortly after, a car stopped outside the house, he thought; or was it next door? The people next door were gay; night owls. A car door slammed. Then it seemed to him their own front door opened and shut. At this, he struggled out of bed and went to the window. A woman was getting into the car; it did not drive off; it remained there. Tom waited and waited, freezing and tottering with insomnia. He unlocked his door and listened: everyone was asleep. When he looked over the banisters, he saw new firelight shining faintly through the back-room doorway. He went down to the back room and sat there in the chair waiting for Peggy to return. There he suddenly fell asleep. He awoke after an interval, with someone on the stairs. He got up quickly and seemed to see a head over the banisters at the top which quickly withdrew. He raked out the fire and went up: the car was gone. In the morning he asked himself several times if he had dreamed it. He did not wait for them to rise, but went out and got a chimney-sweep and a new electric fire for his mother's bedroom. Peggy was very excited. Uncle Simon had committed an indiscretion by informing her that Tom was not penniless, but was living off his car. Peggy told him they needed a new vacuum cleaner and a hot-water boiler in the kitchen sink.

There was great talk of selfishness and in the end Tom agreed to take Peggy and her mother out for a ride to Aunt Bessie in Wallsend in a rented car. "Though I don't know what you expect to see in joyless Newcastle!" He drove them around for several hours, as far as Two-Ball Lonnen which Peggy had not seen for seventeen years, since they used to go out over the towns and the moors in bike parties; he drove around Tyneside and as far as Whitley Bay, Cullercoats and Tynemouth.

Peggy was touchingly joyful, proud. He took them to a tea-shop where they had a large tea and Peggy bought two post-cards: the two women kept giggling and exchanging jokes and allusions. But he was sorry for them and when he set them down at the gate, he invited his sister to the cinema for the day after. To his surprise, she hesitated and said she'd let him know. The next day, she made an excuse for staying at home: she could not leave her mother in the evening. He desisted and went back to his aimless wandering. He had his "businessmen's lunch," sat on the moor and came home, coming past the cinema to see the program. On the other side of the road, he noticed a pale mid-dle-aged woman with spectacles, a strained face, a kerchief on her head, hurrying forward with a shopping basket. "What a typical Bridgehead woman she is," he thought, his heart drawn to her by her look of indoor privations, all of which he under-stood. Then he saw that again it was his sister Peggy. He was go-ing to shout, when he saw her turn very sharp and go down a long residential road away from their shopping district. She had come out without the dog, although she was always afraid to leave it at home, saying that her mother or Uncle Simon would thrust it out of doors and lose it. He followed her. At the end of the long road, she turned into another busy thoroughfare where she went into a shop.

Idling along, thinking he would get some cigarettes and thinking, too, that Uncle Simon's two hundred pounds would just about cover his cigarettes for one year, if he didn't give the amount to Peggy, he came near the shop and saw that it was the painter's. He thought he'd just go in and find out what the man was going to charge; for though Peggy was good at calculation, far-sighted, cunning, even miserly, he didn't know how far she'd go for a man's company. He dawdled at the door observing things and people, in his way, and turned towards the shop. It was an old-fashioned little place running back a long way with old flooring, counters on each side, a large skylight at the back, where there were stands of linoleum and wallpapers. The man he had seen at the gate was standing close to Peggy, who was talking eagerly into his face. He was dark, pale-skinned, listening with a slight satisfied smile, but uneasy. He put his hand on her upper arm: she kept talking to him, more softly.

Tom went back home and after a while insisted on taking the dog out with him. "It's getting dark and I'm going to get Peggy: where is she?"

"She's gone for some bread."

"And A think maybe she's gone to see that painter again: she's not used to the excitement, Tom," said Uncle Simon reproachfully: "we lead a quiet life here and it keeps her steady." Tom took the dog and met her halfway along the street.

"Where were ye taking him, man?"

"He's just leading me to you."

"Well, give him up, man: he's not easy with anyone but me."

When they got home Uncle Simon started to nag about the painter and the cost; there was a scene. Tom took another walk. He went down to the river, stood by it a long while, crossed it, went to a pub down by the waterside, walked to Bridgehead Station and wondered what he should do. It was getting bitter cold: the air was jags of ice. Bridgehead! Here the rose in his heart had folded its leaves. All the pleasant things in the old days had folded themselves up. He had been married here, secretly, for Pop Cotter would have none of it. He spent his first married night with his young wife in a hayrick in midsummer; and then he went back to his engineering course. He was working his way through. He had no money for a wife. There were two people in their thirties who had been good to him; the wife had liked him and then that rose had withered too. He must get away. It was wicked to leave the old people, but he was leaving them. Coming back, he looked at the drawn curtains through the cracks at the people inside, no longer with yearning, wanting to talk to them. He shuddered and thought, "What wretches! What real wretches!"

He opened the house door. His mother was sitting on the bottom stairs, laughing to herself. "He's getting more than he bargained for, Jack," she said to the newcomer.

"Will ye learn, man?" shouted Peggy in the kitchen above the dog's barking: "will ye learn to be decent with women about?"

Uncle Simon was making short coughing and hiccoughing sounds and saying, "Ye'll be punished in the end, hi-hi-hi, ye wicked woman. Mary!"

"What's going on, Mother?"

The old woman laughed to herself. Tom roared like an elephant. Peggy turned with the loop end of the leash in her hand. "I'm teaching the man good manners," she said firmly: "he'll not expose himself before women any more or I'll go straight to the police."

Tom took the leather from her and pushed her across the room.

"I've had enough of you," she said. She insulted him; but she had had enough of it. "Don't touch me, Tom Cotter; I've had enough of ye all for a lifetime. I do wish I was somewhere else and didn't know any of ye. Stop laughing like an idiot, Mother man, it's more than a soul can bear." She rushed into the back room.

Uncle Simon was standing by the sink where Tom had seen him first, bending over and holding his loins in both hands. "She hit me on the belly," he said to Tom: "she knows what she's doin'. It made me trouble come back. Help me to the chair. A can't walk by meself." Tom picked him up in his arms and carried him upstairs, Uncle Simon saying, "Be careful of yourself or ye'll get me trouble."

"I'm strong," said Tom.

"Aye, A was strong too, a ball of muscle, once; but A'm eighty now and no one seems to remember it." Tom put him on his bed with his knees bent and asked if he would get the doctor. "No, thank ye, A know how to doctor meself." It was a bitter cold evening and somehow he did not feel like going out to the yard to the closet. Supposing them safe and sound in the back room by the fire, he had shut the door and relieved himself in the waste bucket under the sink; and Peggy, always spying to find some fault, so he said, had found him out, crept back like the sly woman she was, for the dog's leash, rushed in on him while he "was still a naked man" and suddenly beaten him back into the corner by the sink, beat him in the face and nose and all over him, "from me knees to me forehead, A was savagely beaten all over, she has a strength in her revenge and malice: she's broken me belly and poor Mary sittin' there laughin' and bobbin' at the end of the hall: A'm afraid her wits are far away takin' a journey."

"The house can't go on like this," said Tom.

"Do ye hear her?" enquired Uncle Simon. The house was filled with Peggy's sweet piercing whistle.

"I'd better come and look after you all," said Tom, in the bitterest tone.

"The house can't go on this way," said Simon.

"Has she been better since I was here?" asked Tom.

"Naw, naw, she's been warse, far warse," Uncle Simon declared. "A'm the head of the family, she knaws, with her tricks, and if A roar at her A can get her to stop; but now ye're here, she doesn't respect me at all. She's got too wild this week runnin' in and oot and thinkin' the warld of herself and drinkin' beer which is forbidden to her: she's uncontrollable. And now she knaws where the money is, and A've given it to ye, Tom, it's done. A'm finished. Sometimes we used to get along champion, but then came your father's passin' and your mother not knawin' the day of the week and she got wilder. And you and Nellie came here, Tom," he said reproachfully, "and ye fixed everythin' up between ye, to give it all to her and never asked me me advice, though A'm the head of the family; and A sat there in the kitchen, thinkin' ye were comin' to ask me me advice, but ye never even thought of it. And A thought, There ought to be some return, A was waitin' for it all these years, and never expectin' any return; but I said to meself, there ought to be some return now. But ye fixed it all up to give it to her; and then she began to think of herself as a monied woman and fixed for life. But still she thought there was me money comin'. And now she knows A'm cleaned oot."

Tom heard a sound and turned to see Peggy standing in the door with a smile.

"Go away, Peggy," he said meaningly. She kept on smiling, and turned away. "Peggy," said Tom, "I'm not taking Uncle

Sime's money. I wouldn't take it. He'll keep it and he'll leave it as he wants later on." She flashed a sarcastic smile at him and went into the bedroom. "I'd better take you with me," said Tom, to the old man. "Peggy is always good to Mother and she can look after her. We'll fix up about the house later. I've got to go to London and try to get a job there. We'll go to a boarding house. There's a pretty good one not far from Nellie's where her postman lives."

"Naw, naw, what wud A do that for?" said Simon. "A wudna go anywhere till Mary goes, she needs me; and then me time's oop. Help me to get oop, Tom."

"No, I'll do anything you want."

"Aye, but tomorrow A must get oop to go for me pension."

"Why don't you let Peggy get it when she takes a walk?"

"Don't be crazy, lad," he said testily; "A've enough of bein' called a pauper; she'd pocket it and say A'd never paid. She'll end oop a miser that gel."

Peggy, in the bedroom, burst out laughing.

B UT TOM COULD NOT leave for a while. He and Peggy received pathetic and cajoling letters from Nellie in London. She could not send any money, she was afraid she was losing her job, she had unforeseen expenses, she wasn't able to get her shoes repaired, she had lost two of her lodgers, Eliza Cook, George's sister, and Caroline Wooller, a poor ill-qualified waif, a middle-class unfortunate, who had wandered away. George did not seem able to send money. She knew Tom would have pity on the poor frail ones in Bridgehead and stand by; and she suggested that old Mrs. Cotter should apply for her old age pension; and Peggy for her "sickness pension." Mr. Cotter Senior had always refused to let Peggy get her disability pension, unable to admit that she had been ill; and Nellie was the same. Tom was worried; Nellie must be in a very bad way to write like this. He decided to go to London within a few days. In the meantime, his mother agreed to draw her pension; and suddenly found she was very glad of it. Peggy and she were very gay the first morning she had to sign the receipt for Peggy to carry to the post office. Tom left them in a good mood.

George had written from Rome to say that he was getting a job in the I.L.O. office in Rome, would not be home for some time and could not send money yet, since he had some debts to repay. Nellie now found a room for Caroline Wooller in a small slum house nearby, owned by a Mrs. Hatchard: and the woman called Johnny Sterker was in the house, living upstairs in one of the Cooks' rooms. She was a heavy woman, with dark hair and a strangely pale face. Eliza had gone to stay with Irish friends who had a basement flat in a neighboring street and who always had a spare bed and a couple of shake-downs for those who came by. Irish girls coming to London came to them, found a job and a room and moved on.

Downstairs, in the basement, Camilla did her sewing. Nellie was hangdog, swaggering, dirty and hungry. She was spending her money on Johnny. She talked in a loud voice in other rooms to Johnny who treated her with a high hand; but she never quarreled with Johnny. Nellie went in to her work, was out till all hours; and now had to go to a hospital in south London to see Venna, her Southwark friend, who was ill. Nellie came home late, wept and cursed, hung about in hallways, would bang the front door: two minutes later her nosy profile might be seen looking into some room.

Sometimes Camilla stayed overnight at the house of an obese rich customer in the West End for whom she was making an outfit. The woman was ashamed to be seen out; and usually wore dressing gowns and gave parties to literary London in her bedroom. The Lamb Street house when silent was astir. There might be a slight wind; a bit of plaster fell upstairs; the staircase creaked. Camilla had a nervous attack so that she could neither think or sleep. She needed the sewing room, the house was nearly empty and yet she felt in the way. Once when she went upstairs to reach the kitchen, she found Nellie roaming about naked, except for the bandanna tied round her "bunch of scallions."

"I was just going to take a tub, pet."

There was no bath in the house. Bathers stood in the kitchen and threw water over themselves from the sink.

"You could have a bath put in; there's room between the kitchen and the W.C."

"There's a swamp underneath there; the house would fall in."

"I ought to pay you something for the room, Nellie. I use it every day."

"I don't come from your class, pet; I don't live off sweating walls and sweating blood."

"If I ever lived in a house again, Nellie, I'd run it as you run this place; I'd see that it was open to everyone who needed a bed or a meal. But then I shall have to marry another sort of man, shan't I?"

Nellie understood this as a disparagement of her house and as a hint that her men, Tom and George, were too poor for Camilla. Her pride suffered that they were regarded as slum people by Camilla. She went away to her friends and put it as best she could: Camilla could never get over her girlhood training, the head-hunting middle-class vanity.

Camilla went to visit Caroline in her new quarters at Mrs. Hatchard's, and coming back said that it was a very nice room, good proportions; but then she said, "It's infamously dirty."

This, too, offended Nellie. Millions in London lived worse and during whole lifetimes; but called it home, led good home lives and called it England; and England it was. Ah, the pitiless Philistine, the bourgeois dame! When she wrote her miseries to George in Rome, she mentioned this too: "this dame you say looks like a memsahib!"

Thinking over these insults and rebuffs, sometimes cursing and sometimes with tears in her eyes, she tramped about. She ate as little as would keep her on her feet. Those feet limped and her knees shook. But she could not stay at home. She had to keep up the walking, the knocking on doors, the miserable complaints. Her nights were all fever and bad dreams about all the people she knew. She dreamed that Peggy was ill; that George was far away, she was penniless and could never reach him. She dreamed that she was back in Bridgehead, taking endless journeys by bus and train south to get a job and get away. On the way she talked to strange people; but when she got to her destination, she was back in Hadrian's Grove.

Tom had come down, saying he would get a job at once and send money to Bridgehead and help her out. He answered advertisements, in London first, and waited for the letters in reply, sitting about the house, filling the empty rooms. But he soon saw that he was not wanted and began his roving, though Nellie warned him, "Keep away from the woman in Richmond; there's danger there for you. Don't go down to the family in Wargrave, pet, you mustn't make mischief."

But he did as he pleased and she hardly noticed what he did. He called on Eliza and on Caroline whom Nellie was not seeing now; he went over to Camilla's to eat. Camilla was doing her sewing at home.

Once when he dropped in at Nellie's, Mrs. McMahon was

there. She was a little thinner, but when she saw him she glowed. Nellie was out; no one was in.

Tom said, "It's nice to have the whole house to myself. Of course, there's you, Mrs. McMahon. That makes it like home."

She had never cared for Tom, whom she compared unfavorably with his brother-in-law; but she sometimes asked him things about George.

"There are letters from Mr. Cook. For Mrs. Cook and one for me. He was mentioning something about the Cold War. What is the Cold War?"

"It's a bad feeling against Russia."

"Oh! I asked my husband and he said the papers were always talking about it but he never knew what it meant."

Then out of her handbag she got George's letter and showed it to him; as if she had to, in her pleasure. It began "Dear Mrs. McMahon," spoke of her last and his last and continued,

I wish you were here to look after me. I have someone to fix things for me but no one like you. My dream would be to bring you over here. I never was so well cared for as when you were in the house: then it looked like a man's home. No such luck here; though otherwise the people are all very friendly. I have a boy to run messages for me and someone to teach me Italian. I am not very fast at it: my Bridgehead burr gets in the way. You Welsh ought to pick it up quickly. The principal thing is to open your mouth and say your vowels pure: now, you are good at that. . . . Perhaps I'll be seeing you soon. I hope Nellie will let you know when I get in; keep in touch with her.

Respectfully, George Cook

"Have you been there, sir?"

"Yes," said Tom.

"Do you think I could pick it up?"

"Yes, I am sure you could."

"Do you think I could get something to do there?"

"With the English or Americans perhaps—you would work like here: or better, if you could do office work."

"That's what Mr. Cook said. But I need a machine to practice."

"My sister has one. She'd lend it to you."

Tom went up to the Cooks' sitting room to look for an interesting book. He found one that appealed to him, *The Hampdenshire Wonder*, by J.D. Beresford, and settled down to it. The front door opened and shut, people went in and out. Suddenly, there was a great noise about a blinking blighter, a blasted blooming bugger, a bleeding bourgeois bitch, who turned out to be (for Nellie was talking to someone) a woman interested in trades unionism and women's causes who had gone abroad to a congress meeting and met George in Rome. George had written to Nellie that they had eaten together in a place called Il Notaio. Why were blistering blasted bourgeois buggers admitted to such congresses at all, either by card or press permit or gate-crashing, when their only object was to manhunt? Why were the beggarly blistered bourgeois bitches ever allowed near the labor movement when no one was safe from them, not even the worker born?

Tom kept out of the way. It turned out that Nellie was exclaiming to Johnny Sterker. Tom disliked her. This went on for a long time. Tom put the book in his pocket and quietly left the house. When he returned there were still noises in the kitchen; it was Eliza who was there now, with Camilla. So it went on. Raving and weeping, trembling, mad with smoke, hunger and sleeplessness, and Johnny's strange tyranny, Nellie stumped here and there and when she could not cry any more to the cruel walls at home, she went elsewhere to rave.

Tom's trunk and his folding cot which Connie Ilger had sent to King's Cross for him, were set up in the middle room in the attic. The front room there was for passing visitors; in the back was a little room and there a bed with a honeycomb quilt, a chest of dawers, a little madonna and some holy pictures on the wall, there Eliza's sick mother had made a long stay. In each of the few rooms were traces of past guests, a pair of cufflinks in a china ashtray from Gloucester, a frayed tie, a pair of wrinkled workshoes.

"I don't know why he sent them. I don't know what I want

them for. I don't want anything. I don't want to live," said Tom, when he set up his cot. He opened the wardrobe trunk and let it stand there. He found Nellie looking at the knitted woolen socks and a cardigan.

"Connie knitted those."

"Connie?"

"The husband. He knits beautifully. He knitted Patrick a polo sweater," he said in a hard voice.

Nellie, looking at the cardigan, dark blue, found a small photograph in the pocket—a laughing woman with black eyes looking through bright tangled hair and it was like the sun shining on blackberries in a blackberry bush. Tom let her look.

"She took a good photograph; any snap was good," said Tom. "It's a scheming face. There's no frankness there; only tactics."

Tom turned away, "I don't want to talk about it. I wish I weren't here. I wish I were with her."

Johnny Sterker, on her wanderings again, presently left; and Tom and Nellie had much time together. Nellie could not help thinking of that trunk always standing open in the attic room. Instead of going to bars or to cronies, Nellie rushed home each day, to keep her brother from suicide, as she told everyone. Tom, though he kept saying he had no future, had gone to several interviews in London and had written off for two other jobs, both in the country.

"I don't know why I wrote, Nellie. It's automatic. I write if I see something to suit me."

"I should think you've had enough of the country. You could go to Bridgehead. There may be a job going, an unskilled job you could get."

"An unskilled job! You don't think I'd take an unskilled job?"

"What else could you get?"

He could not help laughing, "Nellie, you don't think much of me."

"Well, Tom, you've been foot-loose long enough. But stay here awhile, you need me. And I want you to talk it out, get rid of it. If you don't, there'll be another harpy. Introspect, lad, make me understand. If I can see your problem, I can help you.

[126]

You've been under a spell. You've been in fairyland. I've got to ungum your eyes. And what legacy did she leave you, the bad fairy that she was to you? The wish for death?"

"It's too fresh yet, Nellie."

"Ah, you poor bemused victim. What was it? A sort of mesmerism? You, a clear-eyed man, always acidulous and on your guard? I can't swallow it, lad. It's too much for me. It sticks in me craw to think she could have made such a booby out of you. Living there with two others, calling you her half-brother; and the other a half-brother, too; and the husband taking it all. What sort of men were you all?"

"We were all men who loved her."

She plagued him, hungry for relief: she questioned him, day and night, probing into his secret life, suffering as she faced the intolerable truth, that Tom had loved the woman. She made him go over it again and again, repeating detail after detail; but she could not come to understand why he had loved Marion; nor why he had stayed there at the orchard with her husband Constantine Ilger; why he had called himself Green, not Cotter, Tom Green and got his letters, Tom Cotter, at a post office in a village fifty miles away.

"She had relatives called Green."

Why had he hidden himself from Nellie, his family and his friends?

"It is true. I dropped every friend."

"It was your shame, your acknowledgment to yourself that it was a shameful, unnatural love. You wanted no one to know, not even me! You had a reason. What was it? I can't bear it!"

She would jump up, stalk about, smoking, raging.

He remained sedate and sometimes sweet, "But why do you care, Nellie? I don't care. I'm anonymous. I may as well be called Green as Cotter."

"You'll pardon me! Your name's Cotter and you stick to your name, not an alias, unless you're doing something you're ashamed of."

"You've changed your name to Cook," he said, grinning.

"Don't try to wriggle out of it! You know all she wanted was to see how deep in the mud she could get you. You stay there with two men in the house and you're called her half-brother, though you know you're no brother and there's another half-brother and you never guessed! I can't take it, her calling you brother. Ah, ah, no, no. I used to be proud of you. I thought you had the grit to face your fate. I pity you."

A hundred points of the mystery she struggled to clear up, by cross-questioning, by stabbing at inconsistencies, by petulance, argument, by sweetness, by speaking her abhorrence of lies and by weak and piteous ways so that the tears came into his eyes. She begged him to "introspect," to look into himself and remark on the weakness and cowardice that had made him for eight years live with a scheming woman, who had nothing for him and for whom he had nothing.

"But we had something, not nothing. I can't explain it, but it was there. It was not nothing."

She thought his tears were tears of regret, remorse; but they came because Marion would smile tenderly when he said "naw-thing" in his Northumbrian; "A am naw-thing."

Nellie repeated, "It was all illusion, bitter cruel illusion and you fell for it, the sweet candy covering the rotten apple."

It ached in her brain, it kept her awake all night. She wanted Tom for comfort with George away; but Tom sitting there quiet and pensive, in his long mild silences, was spending the time with Marion probably. How could he, so acid, so keen, so slow to make friends (she said), so touchy about his honor, a clean man, so wise about women, have even liked, much less sacrificed himself for this faithless woman, who never loved him, but just wanted to count in another victim? But no matter how she put it to him, no matter how far she analyzed it and exhibited it, the miserable conspiracy, the way he had been tricked, not loved, she could get no more out of him, than, "I know, but it didn't matter."

"And you make so much fuss about people lying and cheating!"

"That's the way of it, Nellie."

"But when you talked things over, introspected, didn't you notice things that didn't fit? Didn't you point them out?"

"No."

"Well, what did you talk about all the time?"

"About ourselves. How I had to live for her. How I wanted to live for her and she for me."

"I can't understand it. It doesn't seem like you."

Every day she asked about it, in her free hours; and it was for that she hurried home, to torture herself over her tea, her cigarettes; crying between her two men, tormented by George's tenacious egotism, and by the intangible in Tom's story. As soon as she came home, she went to find him and made him a pot of tea.

Then, "You've changed so much, you're unrecognizable, putting up with a thing like that."

"I've always been the same, Nellie."

"No, pet, I've thought and thought. I've tormented myself to make you see. For you, of all men to be involved with a harpy. Was it glamour? But she wasn't glamorous: it was all make-up and dress."

"I can't explain it to you, Nellie."

He told her all she asked, because with her he could talk about all of it and in the end, weep. They wept together. He told her that he was himself weak and wicked because he had promised to die with Marion and he ought to do it. He had sent off for two jobs just as if nothing had happened.

"It's just as if she meant nothing."

"She did mean nothing; and that's why you can do it. That's it, the simple raw truth. You think something tragic happened. Nothing happened. And now you want to make it a reality, your poor illusion of life. Aye, it's a conjurer's trick, done with mirrors. Because she wasn't there, not the woman you dreamed of; and you weren't there; and the love, the passion you talk of— you make me so angry, lad, though I pity you, talking at random, using big words that have no meaning for you, to try to get in with me, to equal me, to make me think bigger of you."

He was not offended. He roused himself to say, "Nellie, you're a fine woman, you're honest; but there are some things you don't understand. You want everything black and white; there are grays—and red and greens. If everything were black and white, I should have kept my promise to Marion."

She cried out, "But Tom chick, it was nothing. It wasn't a

great love. It was a shadow, thinner than the films. That wasn't love, Tom! It couldn't have been. That comes once in a lifetime or many lifetimes; it couldn't have been that."

"I agree that it may have been something else."

"Ah, you admit it! You've only got to see it plainly and you'll see there never was anything there at all. No great love, no tragedy, just a weak self-interest that it is an insult to call with the name of love."

Tom said, "I don't know. I see everything your way and yet it was real. It was the only thing that ever happened to me."

"Ah, no, pet, not the only thing; you can't go back on the rest of your life and on me like that."

"I don't know what my life was for, Nellie."

"That's the state she got you into, helplessly dependent. I can't forgive her for that."

"I don't expect you to forgive her, and I have no need to."

"Now, that's where you abdicate all your common sense and I can't sympathize with you, Tom Cotter. This mourning is ridiculous; it's a posture."

"All right, Nellie."

"Tom, it's getting me down. I can't sleep at night. It's the enigma. I worry about you. You've become twisted. I could always depend on you for the sensible flat view. It's the thing that's happened to your personality that worries me."

"Don't worry about me."

"But Tom, I do. I can never forgive Marion for using you, just to let the other men see she had someone else in her power, the weakest of all. What else was it, what but that?" She said this in a yearning, mournful voice.

"I don't know what it was myself, Nellie. If I could only ask her just that one question, she'd tell me. She always told me the truth. I told her the truth. There was a bond. It was no use lying, because we always knew."

"The truth!"

"Can't you be satisfied to leave it like that? An enigma."

"That's the proof isn't it that she didn't love you? She fooled and tricked you. Why, Patrick knew all along that you were no half-brother. And Connie knew it. They must have been laughing at you."

"No one laughed. Patrick hated me."

"Would you sacrifice someone you loved?" said Nellie.

"No, I wouldn't."

"So, you admit you were just a trophy for her. There was no love."

"It may be so."

"And yet you stand up for her, Tom, a man like you. Now, why don't you say straight out, say it to me, confess it, that you condemn her. You know in your heart of hearts she used you and gave you nothing."

"Ah, but she did give me something."

"What! How can you say that? What? Say what?"

"She loved me."

"And so you would die for her? Ah, lad, that's bitter! That's the bitterest word you ever said to me. And you wouldn't die for me, would you? I'm only Nellie, the old sister, the one you left behind in your grand life of adventure and passion. Love! Love! And you use that word for her."

Nellie never could have enough of it, arguing, pleading. She would burst into tears and so would Tom. When she left him she went to talk to others; what was the explanation? She wept.

In the back kitchens and back bars, from north London to south, "He mightn't be there when I get home. To think he's there now listening to a dead voice."

She would do her work and go home and begin again, "If I asked you to die for me, would you do it?"

"Perhaps, Nellie, I don't know. Would you—wouldn't you? I don't know. If it would do you some good, perhaps."

"Ah, Tom, I get it. If love has by-passed you and you've given up your party, life may not be worth living. You don't want to keep trudging through the desert of life without a drop of water. I get it, lad. Ah, Tom, the curtain came down for you before the play began. Dedicated to frustration. And this woman seeing what it was, took advantage of the pitiful situation. Aye, it's a shocking thing. Who wouldn't see the pitiful tragedy? The defeated longing, the love-hungry man, running and crying to an older woman for an iron ration of happiness. It gets me down, Tom. I feel too much for you."

"But Nellie, it wasn't an iron ration; it was real."

"Aye, pet, it seemed real. It's strange, Tom, that the last ten years were the years you and I came to the crock of gold; but mine was real gold and yours was fairy gold. There's a parallel in everything we do, but mine is reality and yours is the shadow. Ours is a strange fate. Ah, Tom, if you only knew the happiness, the joy I met with George, the fruition. And that's why, Tom, I don't want you to take the Dead Sea fruit for the golden apple."

She smoked and waggled her legs and said to Tom, "Well, chick, do you feel better now? Introspection, confession is the thing. Now there are some friends of mine would do you some good. Solid real people. You'd forget the ghosts and embers."

"Now, Nellie, leave me alone. No friends can make any difference. I couldn't go out and start talking about the Labour Party and the housing crisis and Khrushchev's policy."

And she went out again to drum up friends for him, telling them all the sadness, the lonely deceived man, the great illusion, "the black widow spider." Sometimes, they came to the house and saw a sedate, quiet man smoking away; sometimes he went out with them to a pub and talked cheerfully about anything; a countryman he seemed, with his thick boots and tan face.

When the next weekend she had to go to Henley, to Bob Bobsey's, where a great skylarking was looked forward to, celebrating Bob's return, she implored Eliza Cook and Camilla Yates to look after her brother. Go she must: the lazy tyke George had left there an Italian sweater he wanted and Bob had letters; but she would not be able to enjoy the few days off she so badly needed, with the thought of her brother alone and "living the past with the dead." Eliza and Camilla promised.

Camilla had been a little surprised to see in Tom a lean-faced, brown-skinned man of mature age, in good dark blue clothing, careful of his appearance, with clean shapely hands and nails. He had red lips, blue eyes, bright hair. He was polite, affable but restrained: they said good day. She heard him with his sister talking interminably morning and evening. She respected their privacy. The first day that Nellie was in the country, she went into the kitchen to eat and Tom came in. He slid into a seat beneath the long rickety table as if it had been allotted to him by her and gave her a quaint smile, bright, catlike.

Camilla gave him some breakfast without chatting, not to intrude on his despair. When she sat down, she said, "I know that you have just lost your wife and I am very sorry."

"Yes. I lost my wife."

"I admire what you did. It was a beautiful thing to do. You are a brave man."

"I couldn't help myself. I was in it."

After a pause, she remarked; "Your sister says you know England well."

"Yes, I know it. I could show you places people don't know."

"I once saw the mountains near the Cheviot and those dangerous moors; what lovely colors!"

"I know them well."

"Do you know the Border, Allen Dale, Allen Head, the Cumberland side?"

He smiled a little, "All. Cheviot, Roseberry Topping, Ovington Edge and Ockfield Fell and all in the north, on the moors, through the gaps, against the wind, and with the sea-fret hanging, the sinking east coast and the brecklands; even Crewe and London, black Manchester—I could show you places. I went to some of the places because I heard about them in rhymes and songs, like Cwm Elan; and I was curious. I lived in some of those places. When I go first to a town I get to know all the cafés, all the teashops and the alleys where there are little shops; and the old town; and I get to know the people who wait and walk about, like messengers, paperboys, gatekeepers, sextons, policemen—I get to know all the people of that sort. I could show you hundreds of places. I could take you to a lot of people."

She was astonished. "From your sister's description of you, they could have put a hundred men in a line-up and I should never have picked you."

A pause. Then he said, "You are surprised people torment

you. You know them for years and they always torment you. It's the fox under your jacket."

"Ah!"

"If you talk to strangers in a town you learn all kinds of things and they're kind to you. I was invited to Buckingham Palace by a stranger I met in the train."

He gave a curious broken laugh, like a sob. She said nothing.

He continued, "And a horrifying thing happened to me on that occasion. I went to see him. He was some kind of under-butler. I walked in past the sentries and the policemen and the guards and had to begin in the kitchens. I probably began with a potboy. I was passed on to the maids and a housekeeper, I imagine, and then met my friend, who said he would send me up to see the table laid for a state banquet that night, with the gold plate. He took me to a footman and I was passed on and on and we reached a man standing at the foot of some stairs and on and on; and the head butler was very pleasant about it. He wasn't supposed to, but he did. They took me to a door and opened it and there I saw a long table already set with all the crystal, the china and plate on it. The plate was all gold, wonderful to think about, but somehow dead, when there was so much of it. I stood there and then said goodbye to my friend and came out the way I came in. I saw a few of them looking at my lapel but it didn't occur to me to think why. So I came out of the place and into the park and under the trees a Mayflower fell onto me and I looked at it. Then I noticed I was wearing my red star with the hammer and sickle I got in Russia. I suppose they thought it was some sort of order in a civilian department."

She burst into a ringing laugh.

He continued oak-faced, speaking quietly in a low baritone, with his northern burr and inner song, slightly bowed, with his hands clasped on his knees.

"I remember those stairs. I don't like walking downhill; my feet go before me. They slip. I can't get shoes to fit."

"You ought to have them made to order."

"I saw some in a paper yesterday for three pounds. I sent off for them."

"That's not enough to pay."

[134]

"I'm not obliged to take them."

"Are you tired? Do you want to be alone?"

He looked at her anxiously, passed his hand down his cheek, "I put up my cotbed and I'm used to it, but it isn't comfortable. There are no sheets. My head falls over the top of it. When I'm worried I sometimes do the contrary, I get farther and farther down under the blankets and I wake up almost suffocated. So my sleep is broken."

He got up and went to the mirror hanging on the wall near the door, opposite the sink.

He came back and explained earnestly, "I'm small and bony, but I'm very fit. I've always been nothing but skin and bone. My father didn't like me because of that. I told him Caesar and Napoleon were little men; but he wanted me to play football. We weren't fed as children. They didn't know enough. I think I should have died once of inanition but for a movie called *Bill Barter's Adventures*. I had a horrifying experience when I was about fourteen. I was riding on the moor on my bike with another boy when I fell off and broke my arm. I didn't go to the emergency ward till next morning; no one seemed to think to tell me. When I got there, I had to wait and there was a man before me, groaning and bowing up and down with pain. My sister Nellie, and my other sister went away for a holiday and I thought they were punishing me, leaving me at home. I had to stay with an aunt who could not look after me, because of her new baby. One day I walked to our house which was shut up, just to look at it and I walked back to my aunt's. It was a long walk and when I got opposite the big general hospital I sat down on a stone wall and felt so feeble and weak that I thought I would die. I thought, I will die right now; why go any farther? A man in the porter's lodge was watching me for quite a time. Then he called out to me. I was afraid but I got up and went over and he held out his hand to me. He had two eggs in it. Take these, he said; go home and cook them and eat them. So I did that and ate them. My aunt came in and said, What is the matter? I said, I feel so weak, I think I am going to die. She said, Here's sixpence, go to the pictures; there's a boy's picture on. I still felt weak and tired, but I went; and somehow the movie turned the tide for me. It was about a boy's adventures. I don't remember it now; but I never wanted to die again."

When Camilla went to the front basement room to do her sewing, he went with her and he sat there, interested in her work, talking, telling her endless tales, "horrifying things," and she listened, smiled. It was easier to work with him there. He asked her nothing about herself or her children. When she went up for lunch, he went too. He went out for a walk but was back for tea and brought something for dinner. Then he took her out for drinks in a pub and when they came back he went over to her rooms with her, smiled at the children but without making up to them; and she sat, smiling, musing, surprised, while he went on with his reminiscences. When her lover Edmund came, Tom went. Her lover was very busy with an exhibition of pictures, his own and others', and even slept on the other side of town at present.

They spent two days in this way. Tom, who had now bought a cheap, second-hand car, was to go to East Anglia the following week to a factory, where he hoped to get the position of works manager.

"Do you think you'll get it? Have you experience?"

"Yes. I had three hundred men under me in the last job and in the job before that about fifty. I gave up one to come and be near Marion; and then I gave up the last one to nurse her."

"I know nothing about England. Here I sit all day, all the year, making clothes and curtains and chair covers."

"You have West End customers."

"Yes. They're nearly all West End. The workers round here all work for West End tailors and dressmakers. Round the corner in Johnson Street are sweatshops for the multiple stores; it's a different trade."

"You work hard, Camilla. Could you take a day off to go with me when I go, and see the country?"

"I could arrange it."

He thought for a while, looking at the tablecloth as if considering a map.

Then he said, "Well, there is Grimes's Graves, in southwest Norfolk. They are flint mines; and about four thousand years

[136]

old or more. There are about three hundred fifty of them and some of them are lost. I know a flint-knapper there and he prepares the flints just as they were prepared four thousand years ago. It's not a lost art. He introduced me to the caretaker. He showed me how they used to hang axeheads on trees till the handle grew into the axehead. It's a quiet grassy heathland in the middle of a lot of low forest. It's bleak and desolate in winter, but it's lovely in summer. I was just walking there once and I flushed about fifty pheasants. They were sitting there in the grass enjoying themselves. They whirred all round my head."

He laughed. "You ride along. You must keep blowing your horn. The road is thick with grasshoppers. Wild birds and rabbits just sit there, and pheasants stalk across the road in front of you or sit calmly on the fence looking at you. Grimes means something like Peter Grimes perhaps; he's a sprite. And they aren't graves. They did a big trade in flints four thousand years ago and there's a sort of flint track all the way to the river where they shipped to the sea. They dug with antlers and antlers are still there in the mine galleries. Would you like to see that? I don't like to drive alone. I'm not used to it."

She was excited. All her poverty and imprisonment by work was perhaps her own doing. She had never tried to get out of it. So she thought for a moment, studying the quiet man, now fresher looking, younger.

When Nellie returned on Sunday evening Camilla left them together, but in a different mood, as if she had part of him, too. He gave himself so freely.

Later, Nellie, inquisitive, came over to see her.

"I heard you were so good as to talk a little to the poor lad. It's good of you, pet. And where's Edmund?"

"Your brother doesn't seem very sad."

"Ah, pet, he keeps it up before people; but it's an act. It's what the Chinese call face. He's proud. But with me he's different. Now I have to face the night, Camilla, and I don't know if he'll see the morning. There's the awful prospect. But don't think badly of me for saddling you with my family troubles. Where's Edmund?"

[137]

"He's away for about a week. He has this exhibition to arrange."

She said excitedly, innocently, "Ah, that's lovely, pet and you'll be going to have a look."

When she recrossed the street, Tom was on the stairs, saying he was going for a ride.

"Where are you going, pet?" said his sister anxiously.

"Just for a ride."

"Let me come with you. We'll have a chat."

He said in the crooning they both used, "No, Nellie, you stay here. I'll be back later."

She asked and asked anxiously, in her thin wailing voice and added, "I'm afraid Marion will be riding with you."

"Perhaps I won't even think. I'll just ride."

She stood at the door, watching him to the corner.

She went in. She told Eliza, who was staying overnight, "He's gone. I don't know if I'll ever see him again. He's gone to talk to the dead."

"Give him time. I think he's quite sane for a recent widower."

"Eh, Eliza, sweetheart, don't say that word: that's a misnomer. No Eliza, he's no widower. He was not married in any sense, legally, physically, mentally, morally. We must deny he had anything; for he had nothing. Fantasies can grow and eat up the brain. He's out there now, speaking to her now, thinking of what they said to each other and begging her to explain. I made him confess everything. The man's a hollow man, he's not a real man, remember that, Eliza; and let us do what we can to save the poor lamenting thing."

Eliza gazed at her uneasily. She was puzzled, but moved by Nellie's upset. They went to the kitchen for the usual pot of tea. Nellie was restless, kept going to the door and eventually went out. She was headed for a pub up the hill.

Tom soon returned. He said smiling, "I just wanted to breathe."

"You're a funny coot," said Eliza.

She began telling him things he did not know about the early Bridgehead years; and he her.

He said, "When I was ten we had a little fox terrier called

[138]

Doggo. They never would believe me that he was vicious. As soon as we got outside the gate he chased me till I got up on a pile of leaves or dirt and he ran round barking. As soon as he got inside the gate he wagged his tail and turned sweet and peaceful. They thought I made it up."

She told him that Nellie and George had clubbed together to buy her an oak chest because she'd been pleasant about the divorce.

"I didn't like it, that they did it when I agreed. It cost me nothing, not a minute's thought. The chest cost them eight pounds and they couldn't afford it, setting up house. They called me here and presented it to me and told me to stay here, too. It was after the war and I was living in the attic of a house that had been badly bombed. I didn't like living in the house with them. But Nellie insisted."

Tom presently went to bed.

Nellie came restlessly prowling in, "Where's the boy? Where's young Cotter?"

She leaned against the door, looking Eliza over, smoking; and said in a moment, in rather a bullying tone, that she had learned that Camilla was going with Tom to East Anglia for a ride.

"It's good of you, Eliza, pet; aye, it's good of you girls to mother the poor waif. He needs it."

But she was very uneasy, lounged about the house, went to bed and got up.

In the morning, as soon as Camilla came over to her work-room, Nellie went in to see her and asked what day they were going to East Anglia, for the ride. It was to be two days after that, a Wednesday; and Edmund was coming to look after the children. Nellie communed with her cigarette for a while and said, "Talk to him, then, Camilla. You've got the day before you. Bring him to his senses. You're a mother. You've no time for his silly nonsense. I want you to make him see what he's been through and let him see what death is; not a subject for play-acting. It's the end, total extinction, the big question mark. Act the sister to him. But sweetheart, you must understand what he is. He was at a feast of illusion and himself was a ghost eating with a ghoul. You've faced total failure, Camilla: your man left

[139]

you, you had nowhere to turn and but for your children, you'd have been willing to die, because of the misery, the unsuitableness of life as you see it. You're brave, pet. I admire it. And he's not. He's a child playing with a sunbird, in an empty moldy room. Show him. Let him shiver and shudder before it. I'm bloody tired of his weeping and wailing about a worthless dame who deceived me, tried her smile on me to get him away. I sent her a corsage when I heard she was coming and she had the blasted cheek to come here wearing it and smiling at me and calling me her sister. As if I would have a sister like that!

"Then she went off with him, hid him from me. There he was, eight bloody years, without a thought of me or the poor things at Bridgehead, playing like a child with a doll and, now, I have to hear this trifling trash about his broken heart. He has no heart. He's without a heart. Some vulture took it out of him long ago, a woman of thirty when he was seventeen. And long before that we had faced the facts and I made him see he had no one but me, only me for his life long; and he had admitted it. Then he married one of my best friends; and after that, when that failed, nothing but whims and sensual amusement. Ah, Camilla, the suffering of a sincere and loving heart—that's mine; and the shame to see him what he is."

Nellie had been leaning against the doorpost and knew that Eliza was behind her. She did not mind; it had brought on a deeper melancholy.

But Eliza turned red and hit her on the shoulder, "I'm not going to listen to such lies, Nellie. You don't know what you're saying. Why do you run him down? He's loyal to you. I never met a more loyal soul. He has a true heart. Can't you see you're just a jealous sister? You can't bear him to ever have had anyone but you! That's mean. It's so mean, I canna bear it."

Nellie, smoking, turned round, leaned against the door and said, "Ah, bless you, darling, for your good heart. You pity the poor waif; and I'm grateful. But don't be taken in with his rainbow stories. The women are. He's a great hand with the women, telling his heartbreaking tales."

She spread her arms, took in both women, said, fierce and strong, "Ask him if he has a heart! See what he will say! Ask him what and who he cares for? See what he will say! You don't know yet what a burden I've had all these years, Eliza. I've been the leader and guide of the family and he's been nothing to anyone, not honored a single promise or debt, felt no guilt, no heartbeat. You must forgive me if my bitterness suddenly rises to the surface, Eliza; but I'm tried of the silly flimflam and the shallow corruption of the whole thing."

"I think he's a good decent man and I'll hear nothing against him," said Eliza; and she went off to work, saying abrupt goodbyes. She was quite upset.

Nellie said, "Ah, Camilla, Eliza's a good true soul; there's a heart without corruption. Bless her. She'll always be true working class, not like her big bluffing brother George. What a pity, Camilla, that she never married, didn't become a mother. She's had men, aye; but pitiful little travesties of love they were. There isn't a man good enough for her; and the men don't see pure pearls."

Camilla looked at her, hesitated, and then said, "Don't you remember you told me that Eliza is George's first wife. I do think she's a wonderful woman. Not many would do what she does."

This unbalanced Nellie for a moment. She waved her head, her long earrings, her cigarette, her elbows, her legs, expostulated, exclaimed and in a very sweet voice, kept praising Eliza over and over. Switching dizzily, she told Camilla about the poor pitiful creatures in Bridgehead, with their wasted lives, the frustrated mother and betrayed sister; and in the end Camilla understood that she was excusing herself for Eliza Cook. She forgave her. Nellie with her bright eye cocked, knew when she was forgiven; and at once changed her tone, pleading as if for a very great favor, "He'll have a good long talk with you, with your beautiful common sense and he'll stop talking to her ghost; for her ghost is still here, tearing him away from me. She's upstairs there at night with him. She comes out of that trunk. That's the tragedy of it, that he still takes it for real. And she laughing at him still, a ghostly laugh. I hear it, I hear it."

And Nellie turned to her and laughed a horrible laugh. She startled herself. She paused to light another cigarette, choking, blowing a cloud to hide her face; and when she could, continued in a gentle voice:

"You will do me this favor? Save me from disillusionment. Let the man coming back with you on Wednesday be a sensible man, who admits it all, defeat and hopelessness and the bitterness; but sanity."

"But I don't know why I should," said Camilla, seriously.

"Won't you do what I ask, love? I know him, poor lad. I know what's best. I don't want him roaming the countryside, footloose and aimless and perhaps in some pub, on some roadside pick up some other harpy, instead of swallowing the bitter pill and facing the lonely road."

"I don't understand why his fate should be loneliness. He likes people."

Camilla was stroking in some fine pleats round the neck of a blouse, and she bent over her work, stroking slowly, delicately.

"He's born to it, sweetheart, aye, it's a sad fate. No wonder he's depressed and acidulous. He has missed the best thing in life, the glory of perfect love. Aye, I understand. But—I can't bear, I won't endure the women who ride him wild, dangling in front of his nose the carrot he can never have."

"Why can't he have it?" asked Camilla, more and more puzzled.

Nellie bent over and wagged her head, "Ah, no, it's a tragedy. The man without a shadow. Aye, my eyes fill with tears. It's not for him, love, wife and child. It's hard to bear. Fate is a wrinkled beldame, a cruel stepmother."

As Camilla had not got her bearings and Nellie sank into reflection, no more was said for a while; when Nellie suddenly got up from the doorstep and said in a businesslike tone, "That's right, then, chick. I leave it to you. You're a sweet waif, bless you."

She gestured elegantly with her cigarette. She went out to the kitchen to wash in the sink and to get a bite before work.

At night on Tuesday, Eliza and Nellie sat in the kitchen and waited; but Tom was home very late.

He slipped in, sat down smiling meekly and apologized to Nellie, "I'm sorry I am late. I was thirsty and went down a street I know near Piccadilly Circus. I saw a sort of café near Wardour Street which I knew in the war, but the door was closed. I rapped and was let in and had something; I don't know whether it was coffee or tea. There was a man there, a pimp and three girls outside on parade. The man studied me and came up and I thought, he thinks I'm a prospect for a girl; but no. He said, Are you superstitious? I don't know what I said. The man said, Because a man dropped dead in that chair, this night last week, that chair you're sitting in. He came in late like you and rapped at the door and he looked like you. I thought perhaps the man was warning me off; but he was dead serious. He pulled out a newspaper nearly a week old and showed me an account of it. We got to talking about superstitions and he said he was superstitious. I told him one time I motored up north, I stopped late at night at a hotel in Doncaster and the woman said to me, You were here last week. I said, No I haven't been this way for months. She said, Well, there's your name in the book and the police were here asking for you. And she showed me, Tom Cotter."

"What did you make of it?" said Eliza.

"I didn't know. I knew a Tom Cotter in the war, but he died. When I came out of this café, I saw a bike trying to take a piece out of a horse and I got to talking to the driver and he told me of a good fried fish shop round there. When I was in the ammonia works, there was a jealous horse, one of a team of two which brought round soft drinks for the canteen. This gelding would edge the mare up onto the pavement and try to take bites out of all the cyclists along the road. I suppose that was a bike that remembered. I used to see this jealous gelding working after hours. I had some sugar for him; but I was careful. He had a laugh in his eye."

Nellie sulked. She thought he was teasing her. She humped over her tea and smoked, looking down into her lap and pretending to think about something. Tom said he was coming along a street in Belsize Park when he passed a well-lighted house he knew was a gambling place.

"I was attracted. I used to gamble a lot."

Eliza smiled, "How much did you gamble?"

"A lot," he said evasively.

"How much?"

He said uneasily, "About six pounds at a time. I spent my money in all sorts of ways. Not on clothes. I should have bought a caravan instead. I could have taken it to some river bank in good game country and gone in for living on fish and game."

He said with a gentle smile, "Only I don't care much for catching and killing things. I'd rather have bread and tea. I used to like blue cheese but I got sick of it."

"What about winter, the floods and the ice?"

"Yes. I could move to higher ground. But it isn't practical. I think the best thing for me is to go in for nursing."

Eliza said, "Oh, no! I did it once. It was awful. You get involved with the patient and it's a nightmare. You'd have to join an association of male nurses, get a certificate. And supposing you had a big patient, a man, with delirium say. He might kill you."

He said huffily, "I'm stronger than I look. I'm very strong."

"Don't do it. If you're alone with someone, it goes wrong. It brings out queer things in people. You never know what will rise from the depths. There was that girl Nellie knew. She roomed with a friend. The mother went to bed and pretended to be ill, so that no one could leave the house. What was your friend's name, Nellie?" said Eliza.

"I don't know, pet," said Nellie.

"You told me about this girl, who had all the bad luck. She roomed with one after the other and each got her claws into her, you said. You remember the letter you read me from her?"

Nellie said, "No, pet, you've got me wrong. I don't know."

Eliza said, "You came over to see me, over in Hampstead. We were sitting on the hill and you told me about this girl you were worried about. She had such bad luck. You said there were a lot of you worried about her. You thought some gray fate was waiting for her."

Nellie said nothing.

[144]

"I asked you if she was a lesbian. Or they were."

Nellie muttered, "No, no, pet, no, no."

"I know who it is," said Tom.

Nellie went into a flurry, "Ah, yes, a tragedy there, I'm afraid. No, pet, I don't know about the others, but she wasn't one, she didn't know the word. No, darling."

"Where is she—Lucine?" asked Tom.

"She died."

Tom was upset, "When?"

"I don't know, Tom. Last year. She was living with someone and she got fed up with it all."

"Who was she living with?" asked Tom.

"I don't know, love, don't know at all," muttered Nellie.

Tom leaned back in his chair eyeing her deliberately and shaking the ashes from his cigarette. She seemed to feel it.

She exclaimed, "There was a bloody man in it. She found out he was married and just leading her on; and she couldn't take it."

Tom was upset.

"Why didn't you tell me? I could have stopped it. She used to talk to me."

Nellie turned to him in a fury, "What could you have done with your little smirks and fairy tales? She asked the great question; she got the great rejoinder and she accepted it—something you could never do. She was a woman and she accepted fate. She didn't try to run away from it with a hundred ducks and dives, running in and out—but it's a labyrinth, you can't escape. You'll end in a blind corner whether you like it or not. I won't stand it, Tom Cotter. I'll pay you out for poking fun at what is nearest to me heart."

She got up, lounged out of the room and presently they heard a bottle being uncorked and the liquid running.

Eliza exclaimed, "Nellie's a thrilling woman! She can make you see things her way, though you know it wasn't so. I used to think there was a lot of gimcrack and phony in her make-up, too much of the old man. She's always imitating him and he was a grand phony. But you cannot blame the old Kipling soldier for the character they put on him. And now he's gone, strike me pink, if she isn't more like him than before. Here I am sitting and tearing people to pieces like a Bridgehead back-kitchen wife. Aye, but he wasn't fair to you, Tom, the old soldier."

"He wasn't fair to her either. She suffered because he told her she was a scarecrow. She never got over her love for him till she met—till George."

But the next morning when Camilla and Tom started out, Nellie was in excellent humor. George was coming home at the end of the week to stay for a few weeks.

It was a fresh morning. They started off at seven-thirty to get to Norwich near which town Tom was to be interviewed by the managers of a plastics firm. Camilla sat still with the fresh-faced young man beside her telling her his anecdotes; she was glad to be away. Marion's death was mentioned several times but in an unexpected way.

"My girl had great courage. She didn't want to lose me and we made an unfair agreement."

"Do you think it was unfair?"

"Because she had to and I hadn't. And when it was over, I felt the passion of a boy. I felt quite new as if I had never tasted life at all; it was all to come. I still feel it. It was her death that waked me up to real passion. I burned for it. I'm living for it now."

He slowly raised the lids over his large eyes and stared unblinking in his unnatural way at her. He bent his mouth in a red bow and smiled, "Of course, I had three months' holiday from work and in the country, well fed, in an orchard, you see."

"You must find a friend," said Camilla, about to laugh.

Tom said placidly, "I have friends. I went out with one on Saturday. She does not get much out of life. They're poor and I took her out with her little boy, but the serpent raised its head and I thought she was too young and would suffer. Young women get caught and suffer. I am sure I will find a woman. I am like an adolescent—I can only think about the woman I am going to love and I'm excited about her, wondering."

She was silent, smiling.

"That young woman was awkward and cold and I became cold. I felt nothing for her, so I took her home and I came home."

"I don't like to think of poor Nellie waiting for us until midnight tonight. She is so pale. She is so worried about you."

He smiled ironically, "She is afraid I might make a run for paradise with a woman. Nellie would not like me to get from under her paws so fast. She wants to lick up every last drop. I don't take her seriously."

"Don't you think England is spectral? I am from a warmer place. The light is more golden and red."

"Yes, you can be sitting at tea, with the fire blazing away and the curtains drawn and no matter where you are, it comes over you: your hair begins to bristle."

"You're not a Christian people at all. Like the Italians, you're a very old people. *Christ stopped at Eboli.* Christ didn't come here at all."

Tom said, "I went to Stonehenge. I was there at sunset and it was just like the pictures. I was disappointed. The only interesting thing was a circle of trees on the hill, growing in the form of Stonehenge and I've seen that before too. I don't know what it means. I just sat down in the middle of the stones in the circle and was looking down the hill at the camp not far away. You could see the soldiers. The sun went down and suddenly I felt something awful. I felt some horror was coming in. I took to my heels. If you sit in a grassy hollow and can't see a house, you begin to think of the people who were there thousands of years ago; and you feel them there. You can't stand it."

He continued with a faint sound, like a distant sound of laughing coming over a hill in puffs, "I had a horrifying experience. I was in Scotland. Gone on a trip to Carlyle's country. Go up to the moors, he said. It was a spring day, the sun shining and no wind. I was walking across country taking care because of marshy spots and I was heading for a little town on the map. I came into a little valley, a depression, without anything in it, a few grasses and stones and mostly moss and I could see nothing but the light blue sky. It was springy turf and easy going but I began to feel scared. With each step I took I knew there was

[147]

something wrong. I looked round everywhere but saw nothing. I was glad to get out of it. In the town they told me that valley is full of asps; it is the only one anywhere around with asps. On the same trip I was crossing some fields with stone fences. There was a bush on the other side of a low stone fence and I was attracted by it. I went that way. I was just putting my leg over when I saw four or five stoats standing on the other side of the bush, as if they were talking something over. I knew they were dangerous, and attack people in lonely places. They saw me and they all turned towards me. I turned and ran for my life and when I looked back the stoats were all coming over the fence; one was over. I ran for my life. I am a good runner. I was a good footballer."

He talked on and on about his wonderful adventures. Her thoughts began to play softly among these adventures as if playing in these upland breezes he was piping in.

She smiled when he stopped, "Go on with your horrifying experiences."

"What do you mean?"

"You say that."

"Someone—said that to me a little while ago."

She knew who. They remained silent. After a few minutes it occurred to him that she was trying to make him forget his sorrow.

He began to talk again, "I was out taking a walk one day, the sky very clear and light, the sun broadshed, the birds were flying about and I was thinking of nothing. I was just wandering aimlessly. Clouds of ideas pass over you and leave you; and I was quite dizzy. It was spring. I was thinking I would like to be a hermit. I would like to live in the woods and be a voice to people, tell them things I know. I would talk to the animals and whistle. I can't sing because they made me sing alto too long. People would say, There's a man in the woods who can tell you things that will make it easier for you. If I did that, I could become a healer perhaps. I would have to develop it."

"That is why your voice is like that, floating," she mused. After a while, she said, "Isn't that a pretty hotel!"

It was an old long white building with a few well-placed windows.

"Would you like to stay there?" he asked.

"Oh, yes."

"We could stay there tonight. Let's go in now and have lunch."

She was amused, "How could we stay? They expect us home."

"Oh, we'll send telegrams. I've done it before. Marion and I did it."

They both began to laugh. They had lunch at the hotel. He went upstairs and when he came down said he had been to look at the rooms. They could have a room.

"Goodness, you would get into trouble with Nellie."

"I don't care what trouble they make. I'd do anything for you."

She went out and got into the car. He followed her in his manner, bright and composed.

After they had been driving a few minutes, and were out of the little country town, he said, "I know plenty of hotels along the road. I stopped at a few of them with Marion."

"And yesterday Nellie told me not to mention Marion; but to talk to you about death!" She laughed.

He said roughly, "She needn't worry. I'm glad I knew death in that way."

He became silent.

"How can you say that?"

He remained silent.

"It must have been misery."

"I don't think about it. I'm free. As soon as the earth covered her, I felt alive, really alive, streaming with life, like a young hill covered with grass in the spring rains. The cemetery is on a hill and it overlooks nurseries and planted hills. There was no feeling of death at all. And do you know the only thing that worried me?"

"No," she said timidly.

"What I would do for a woman. She had been ill a very long time."

Camilla looked round at him and then at the long grassy hill they were passing and she smiled, thought of a joke and burst out laughing. He laughed too.

"Why does Nellie talk about death so much?"

"She knows nothing about it. It's just good copy. I saw hundreds of dead men. I used to be the first to go into burnt-out planes: things like that. I could get in through small twisted apertures. I decided never to fight, only to help, to heal, or carry stretchers."

"I'm glad to talk to you. I was lonely. I didn't know it."

He said nothing about Edmund or the children. He went on talking, his voice carrying through the noises of the road, the engine, all through the day.

"She was very ambitious: she would have written a play if she'd lived. Even when she was in pain, she would talk about her ideas.

"A strange thing happened the morning she died. I was just sitting there, knowing I had to pack and get out. The housekeeper came to me and said, Mr. Green, here's the mallet you asked for. I said, Take it away, I don't want it. I didn't remember asking for a mallet. She said, You said, Find it, give it to me and I'll hide it. I don't know what it means.

"It was cold and damp in the church and in the churchyard. I forgot my coat, but I didn't mind. I wanted to feel bad; but I didn't. The clergyman was in a hurry to get inside. We filed past him; I didn't even look at him. I was thinking, It will soon be spring."

They got back to London late at night. He took a wrong turning, got into a maze of one-way streets and it was some time before they got to the newspaper office where Nellie was waiting. She introduced them both warmly and sweetly to her colleagues. She was worn out. She had had another struggle getting her article in, a whole day's work boiled down to a few lines in the midnight edition: and it would come out altogether by morning. But it seemed to her that her story was the most important of all, the real truth about humanity. She exclaimed, waved her cigarette, danced a lanky step or two, hovered in patch and color, like a harlequin among the desks and girls in plain blouses and men in shirt-sleeves. At last, regretfully, she left the office. It was nearly one in the morning. They drove home, Nellie still talking about her wrangles in the office and the pity of it that a real labor paper, the only real one, had no money, while giant presses labored night and day turning out tripe. George had arrived home suddenly, but she couldn't get off.

When she got them home, sitting with her in the kitchen over a late light meal, she suddenly noticed them, it seemed.

"Forgive me, chicks. Did you have a little chat? There's a little brandy in the cupboard. Eliza's sleeping with your children tonight, Camilla, as arranged. We'll have some coffee. Are you unhappy, Tom? Are you feeling all right, pet? What did you talk about, chicks? Ah, I'm glad of it, though; introspection is the wine of the soul: it divides us from the animals. If you don't introspect, the soul sleeps."

Noticing Camilla's quiet and Tom's enigmatic air, she said sharply, "What is it, chicks? You didn't quarrel, did you? You've both had very tough experiences and I suppose your nerves were on edge. I shouldn't have let you go off together. I suppose you worried the sore tooth."

"Where's George?" said Tom rudely.

"Upstairs asleep. I have me orders not to wake him. He says he doesn't want to hear me post-mortems. He telephoned me, though, bless his heart. At the office, twice. Bless the lad. And you go, too, Tom lad. You look all in."

Tom took his dismissal.

"We had a lovely day. It's so long since I had a day off," said Camilla.

He smiled, and went without a word.

Nellie looked quickly at them both and when Tom had gone, began in an undertone, anxious, "Are you sure? Ah, I'm afraid I was wrong leaving you to turn over the blotted pages of life together."

"Oh, it was glorious, Nellie."

"You must excuse the poor lad, he's not himself. He's been twisted. The thoughts of the past are aching in his mind. It's moral neuralgia. I hope he didn't tread on your feelings, Camilla. He can be cruel and hurtful. You're such a sensitive plant."

This was so unlike anything she had heard in her life before, for she was a stalwart woman, that Camilla smiled.

Nellie took in the smile and hurried on, "No woman can mean anything to him, poor lad. It's the empty corridor of time he faces; and only the footsteps of ghosts in it."

She sighed, "Love is an empty shell to him. You pick up a shell on the beach and listen to its singing. But the shell is dead. To have nothing, Camilla! A life spent in sighing and longing. And what I taught him, to look inwards, the healthy introspection, the facing facts, she took away from him. She made him a buffoon dancing in a hall of mirrors. She tried to cut him off from reality to make him her lapdog. I can't take it!"

She jumped up, twisting in her misery. She controlled herself and sat down, saying earnestly, "No wonder the thought of death attracts him. It's a comfort when life has betrayed you. There's an end to the shame and flapdoodle! But he's light-minded. He can't hold to a single truth. That's why I'm glad he has you. You're solid. You've put that foolishness of sex behind you. You're not interested in hoaxing romance. Aye, you're good for him, salutary, a good cold bath for a neurotic fool. But can ye understand it, Camilla, love, now you've seen the boy? He was a truthful, simple-hearted boy, so fair-minded, guileless. When I had him. Oh, he was mine, Camilla; his sister's. Ah, it's the bloody dames, Camilla, taking the meek, poor-spirited boys and using them. Aye, but why do I talk to you about it? You know. Aye, you know. He's been talking to you about it, has he?"

"No."

"No? No, it's a sealed-up life. No, it's rare for him to make friends. No, it isn't that that worries me. It's the harpy that'll be after him next. The lad's weak, he's a nonresister. It's almost a principle with him. Life happens to me, he says. But what did you talk about then, Camilla?"

Camilla became animated; a delightful smile appeared as she told Nellie about the stoats and asps. She became self-forgetful. Nellie listened frowning and her glossy feathers lay down flat and dull. A deep silence settled in her; she became motionless. Camilla began to laugh in her deep southern voice, her splendid statuesque body became that of a living woman, a woman of maternal and sexual passions, the deep-throated woman who could, who would love insensately, "What strange things happen to him! He has only to look out of the window. He's a poet, a singer. I listened to him all day. I can still hear his voice, a thin penetrating voice you can't forget. I felt so much happier. I think it's this voice. I can hear it now. I can see why women fall in love with him: he's delightful. I love him myself. I see why you love him. I don't love him like you, Nellie. It is just a feeling, a simple sort of pleasure. Were you there when the two hundred starving people went down to the Soviet ship in the Tyne for a meal and they all thought themselves invited by Tom, because he knew the engineer and the engineer told him to come for a meal and bring a friend?"

She laughed aloud, seeing the amazing incident again, as Tom had told it. Nellie muttered.

Camilla continued, "But Nellie, he is not empty at all. He is strange, not like other men. He makes you feel like a child at a picnic."

Nellie sat in perfect silence.

"You have shaped him, Nellie; and what he is to you, he is, in shape, to other women. He made me happy. That is his charm. Marion wasn't a spider. She wanted the happiness he can give."

After a while, Nellie roused herself to say quietly, "I have never heard these stories. I am surprised."

"Doesn't he tell you?"

"No, you see, we talk about intellectual things."

"The feeling Tom gives a woman is altogether unselfish. I can't get over the impression—this story of his tenderness, compassion, sacrifice and his love for Marion. This is a beautiful thing."

Nellie sat still.

"I understand your love for him. You love him, don't you?" said Camilla with a note of surprise.

"Naturally, we were close. I didn't think about loving him. It was something deeper, a communion; that comes only once in a life, if it comes at all. He could never have with anyone else what he had with me. We don't have to talk or tell anecdotes. We have a perfect understanding."

Tom now reappeared in a blue paisley-figured dressing gown, blue leather slippers and a scarf. He had settled his hair, shaved; his face was a smooth rose and white; his eyes were wide open, as those of a child. He sat down at one side of the fire smiling at them, sitting bolt upright and appearing to await some comment upon his looks. But Nellie did not notice them. She smoked, flicked ashes and drank tea. Tom's changed appearance, his childish complexion checked Camilla; she did not understand it. Nellie noticed her feelings and her clever mouth twisted into a smirk. She softened and began to unwind the speech she had got ready for them.

In a murmurous voice, she began, "It's so cosy and warm, why, it's lovely having you together. I'm glad you had a good talk. The world's shut its curtains against you. You drop into the wayside inn and there for a moment you have a few words with a fellow traveler. It's all there is, but it's warming. And then the lonely road. But it's the heart-cheering moment. It's wonderful that you two could have an hour together by a stranger's fire. You've watched the lonely black sky together, and felt adrift. And you know that destiny is individual. Destiny is loneliness. It's mysterious and no one can share it. No one can shed his blood for you, no one can die for you, no one can live for you. It's the final truth. It's single blessedness to the end. There's no marriage in death; it's a stark commentary on our sham passions. They're sideshows on the lonely road. Eh, it's wonderful for me, chicks, it makes me humble, to meet two clear-eyed people like you, who do not believe there are any bargains in Vanity Fair. The lonely road, leading right through Vanity Fair. That's a freezing thought! What beautiful souls you are, like saints, like hermits! Eh, I'd like to have your courage. I'd get myself a canvas house, like the watchman on the roadworks, my brazier, my tent, my bunk, my black tea, sitting up all night, musing and thinking; that's my ideal existence. Nothing but the wind blowing, the blackness—that's the reality. You've got such a terrible thing hanging over you both—I thought it would be a good thing for you to talk it out. Aye, I was glad I arranged the trip. I thought you'd help each other.

[154]

You didn't mind me bringing you together, then? Did you have a little talk, then Tom?"

"We talked quite a bit," said Tom.

"Did you, pet?"

She sat leaning forward, elbow on sharp knee, smoking and musing, quite serious now. The others, like lovers between whom something has been decided, sat still, just glanced at each other.

She remarked at length, "Aye, mankind isn't consistent. It's fine people like you and Tom who are consistent. That's how we live; we're inconsistent. But you fine, sensitive, unselfish souls that have left your great passion behind you are better than the rest of us. You're superior. We've got nothing to teach you. You belong to another race. You've gone away beyond us. You can never come back. Your voices will speak to us from another place."

She sighed, "It's lovely, but you've been through fire and flood and life has nothing more to teach you. None of us would have the courage voluntarily to join you. Living is our weakness. It's a wonderful rare loneliness, the thing they've left you. Ah, poor pets! My heart's breaking for you. It's a terrible inheritance, the inheritance of life. Then you know that death is the friend."

Camilla looked at Tom and saw his eyes were wet. Nellie observed this, smoking away, sighing and tossing her cigarette butt into the grate and starting to smoke again.

She said to Camilla who was not wet-eyed, "Don't cry, pet. I feel for you, Camilla. I know what it is. Life for you is a kind of life in death. You work, pet: you're brave. You accept a simulacrum of human warmth, but the real day is over. You would like to sublimate your emotions and work for society. I understand you. Your father was a brave man. He went to jail. He suffered for society. Society rejected him. It did not accept his offerings. The martyr, the agitator is offering society what it does not want. I imagine the suffering of the rejected votary. Ah, society is a cruel god. It can only reject. But you must be true to yourself, Camilla. Every situation has its temptations, they say; and I wouldn't want to see you salve your aching heart with delusions. You're a socialist, Camilla, you're a true heart. You have been about the world and seen injustice and the horror of poor pitiful bereaved homes. But must you think of setting vengeance in action? That's what political action is. You want to change the laws, you say, not upset society. Aye, but isn't any man-made law an iron hand reaching out to squeeze us poor creatures into faceless mud? Isn't any political action the same as fascism, the same as repression? You must repress someone to get your way. Isn't it a paradox, pet? Don't let your regret for human sufferings turn you into a Philistine; you'd lose my respect. For your intelligence and sensitivity; for the unusual individual I thought you."

"My father died in jail but I'm not worthy of him. I am no agitator," said Camilla.

"Yes, you know in your own family that law is tyranny and vengeance and the iron heel. You can't meet tyranny with tyranny, oppression with vengeance. What is revolt? It's tearing open the body of society to satisfy private feelings. It's bestial. You take a bad man and make him worse. He won't say, I was wrong: he'll say, They were out to get me and they got me: the vultures got me. Society is a vulture to the lonely soul."

They were disturbed to see that she had begun to cry.

She wiped her eyes but went on in a mournful and menacing, an excited way, "You don't understand. You're good people. I often tremble when I see the law pursuing someone and I read the list of his crimes and he gets a heavy sentence. He'll come out, not reformed, but worse. He'll say, I was going my way, the way society showed me, and they fell on me. They have armies and police Philistines, the stiff-necked bloody-minded Philistine, the blood-red bystander, the mock civic, and I have nothing, nothing but my own soul. They took me and forced me and branded me. And they've created an outlaw, a man who hates life. Instead of trying to understand her, they've ruined her to satisfy their vengeance; but first they've used her. And their guilt. They're all guilty. She's innocent; or she was till that day. She did no more than earn a crust in their way. You can't be a success in the bourgeois world unless you've committed incessant crimes starting as a child. And what you see around you, Camilla love, convinces you that there is no compassion, no fairness, it's all private self-indulgence, back-yard calumny, public vengeance and the death of the poor creature."

Tom, smoking calmly, said, "That's silly non-sense. That's the kind of stuff we used to talk when we were half grown and you're just coughing it up again now. You don't believe a word of it, Nell."

"Yes, I do, Tom. Political action is wrong. A political man is no good man. You should see Robert Peebles and you'd know. He's a man with a machete clearing a path for himself through a jungle of other egotisms and cutting down the innocent wild creatures in his path, the creatures who know life. It's vindictive and selfish and cruel to pretend to work for the world when you're only satisfying yourself. Ah, man is only a small whirling atom in a universe which itself will perish, and here we all are fighting and struggling and satisfying our petty passions or mangling our sacred true perceptions to suit a Juggernaut and calling it the higher life, the higher perception. It's an ugly picture, Tom. Isn't it all hopeless?"

"You're very tired, Nellie. It's nearly three. Let us go to bed."

With a wild cry, she said, "Ah, Tom, Peebles won't let me be. He's trying to change me and make me give a daub where I see nature. He'll ruin me: I won't be myself. I won't see things in my way. I told him, If you're going to correct anything I write from the armchair point of view, if I'm to become an armchair socialist, dreaming it up in an office and sitting in a classroom at night, I'm quitting. It's not for me. I'm leaving and leave you to go whirling along in your Laputa till you reach empty space. But I'm getting off and staying here with reality and the real people. Your socialism is vanity and conceit."

"You resigned, Nellie?" said Tom with anxiety.

"Aye," she said somberly.

"I must work tomorrow, I'll go upstairs," said Camilla.

When she had gone they faced each other. Tom made another pot of tea and with a contented face, he sat down next to her.

"You looked peaked, Nell."

"Ah, pet, it's all fight, no truce. But I won't give up my principles."

They sat for awhile, resting, in silence.

[157]

Then Tom said, "So you threw it in, Nell."

"Ah, no. They're kind to the ignorant northern sod. They'll give me another chance. It's damnable. I'm tired of the fight. I'll go with George."

But she said it in a reckless bitter tone; and she continued, "I see his point. This is my country and they don't want my opinions."

Tom said nothing.

She continued, "Well, I admit I was upset. Not by him. My friend in Southwark—I had a message and I went to see her; she was home again and all right, but her neighbor on the landing told me they'd put her in the van and taken her away. She's in jail. For what? Because she's a victim of society. Ah, Tom, the poor frail waif, like my own sister to me, almost. And I know why. I know why. I'll never forgive it. I'll never forgive society. Nor anyone that arrogates pride and position to himself, all those that chain up the others."

"You mean the prostitute?"

"Don't you dare, Tom Cotter, put that hard name on her. You, one of the worst of men, going back on me and cheating all the women."

"Well, thanks for the kind words. I'll go to bed. And you go, too."

"If it wasn't for my friend Caroline I wouldn't know where to turn. You're all black hearts but hers," she said bitterly.

When he had left, she put both elbows on the table, squeezed her face between her hands and stared ahead. She brushed her fingers over both eyes, got up, emptied the teapot and went up to bed. Through the night those waking heard her coughing and sighing.

Camilla, sleeping in Eliza's bed, slept well; but she was awakened by strange sounds and could not understand their source. They came from the rug beside her. Nellie was there wrapped in an old eiderdown, bent half over two pillows, her shoulder blades showing through the washed-out pajama coat. She was in one of her paroxysms.

When it was over, she said weakly, "I didn't mean to wake

you, Camilla. I come here when I cough too much, and sleep beside Eliza. When George is here he tells me to get out, or he'll get out. He has to have his sleep straight through or he's wretched all day. And it's me cigarettes. He has a nicotine reaction, dizziness and nausea, poor sod. And it's me talk. So he says. Go to sleep, Camilla. I am sorry, love."

The smoke rose through the air from the floor and began to get sharp in Camilla's nostrils.

She coughed. "You're awake, are you?"

"Yes."

"I've been thinking of you all night," said Nellie.

Camilla smiled to herself.

"But you want to sleep, Camilla?"

"I must work all day tomorrow; and get up early to relieve Eliza of the children."

"Yes, pet. Well, I won't trouble you. You must sleep and work."

She began to get up, pulling her bed things off the floor. With them in her arms, she stood and looked down at her guest, "Do you love him, Camilla?"

"Edmund? I think so. He makes it home."

"But you're not decided?"

"I can't break with my father-in-law. He will help with the children. He likes me. He wants to give me a home. I went to look at a flat in the West End the other day that he picked out for us. There was a room for him too, to visit us. He has the money. But I would be tied up, bound to him."

"So it's not a great love, with you and Edmund?"

"There are so many kinds of love. One for each man."

"I see, pet. Well, I'll leave you to your sleep. Sweet dreams."

Nellie went upstairs. Tom awoke, looked up and smiled.

He yawned, "I was having a lovely dream. I dream a lot: it interests me. How did you girls get on? Did you swap all the dirt?"

She flicked a sharp glance at him, "It's no laughing matter, Tom. I'm afraid the poor woman's a castaway, driftwood, Tom. Driftwood can sink. Give it a push with your heel. Will that be **work** to be proud of, lad?"

He lay flat, his glance shining out of the skylight, her words to him like other bright living things in the air.

He heard her say, "Whom the gods love die."

"The gods sure get around." He laughed lightly.

"Ah, pet, 'tis the final taunt."

"Who's taunting?"

She said solemnly, "Death is, I mean. But what other remedy is there to despair, endless despair? Venna sees things as they are."

"Venna?"

"My friend in Southwark. Or Camilla. Or poor Caroline. All despoiled women: castaways."

Tom said, "You have to keep thinking to yourself that there are people for whom everything is finished. You have to force yourself to realize it. It changes the look of the grass, even the grass. But the grass grows up. You see how green it is. It's the advance banners of new life."

"There's one thing I don't understand," said Nellie, promptly, shaking out her cigarette and getting another.

"Give me one, Nell."

They began smoking in harmony; their long strong fingers played at the cigarettes. Their attitudes and faces were in harmony by starlight, too; neither showed any emotion.

"I don't understand how you could be friendly with a person so long and be deceived. It's beyond me, Tom."

He didn't mind her attentions. He took them as a compliment. "I didn't ask any questions."

"But when you were introspecting, didn't she ever make a slip about Patrick?"

"We didn't do any introspection. She was always making plans."

"But you must have talked."

"We talked all the time—about her projects and affairs. She was a woman like that. We talked about the orchard. Connie—Ilger—was very much interested in Michurin and what Huxley was saying. We talked about books that came out—how we were wasting the resources of our planet. I said I worked in Newtonian factories in an Einsteinian universe. They were interested in that."

"You're evading the issue. You're not frank with me. Confess, lad, tell the truth. You're hiding something. You're ashamed of something."

"I'm not. I told them what happened at work. They liked to know. They were the only people I had to talk to. At work I couldn't tell anyone about the Ilgers. You didn't want to hear. I couldn't mention it at Bridgehead. I had them."

"That showed shame, lad. That's where the rotten patch is."

"She had plans and ideas. She made those two men. Ilger knew nothing; he was like a ward of his mother's, an old bachelor. She took him, taught him farming and orchard work, learned it herself first; she made Patrick learn accounting. I had engineering. She thought we could run an efficient farm that way."

A look of irritation passed over her face. "Come, Tom, when people are sitting alone with each other, you know they talk about fundamentals, serious subjects: they confess."

"She never did. She said it was a great mistake to talk about fundamentals."

"There you are! She couldn't bear the truth."

"It was her life, Nellie. I wanted her to do what she wanted."

"But she was a bad woman, Tom; and you're a good man. Now she's gone—what's left? She took away your name, took you from your family, got into your soul tooth and nail; and for this vampire you left me and told me nothing. If you'd come to me and explained, I could have cleared it up for you. You need not have wasted those years. You wouldn't have this corruption to look back to. Yes, cover your eyes. How could you be fond of such a woman? It's killing me."

"It was just an attraction at first; and it was fading as such things fade, when I found out how ill she was; and we had to begin to try every cure; from plants and snake venom to mesmerism. I took a great interest in it. I learned a lot. I was glad to help and gradually it grew into a great passion."

He shut his eyes, "There never was any question after that of leaving her, or asking questions or of selfish ignoble motives. What is my name anyway, if I don't have someone to love? Do you know, Nell, when I was a boy at school I wanted to change my name; and often afterwards, I thought, I'd like to change my name, be no one, begin again. I did it. I was for her only. She needed me and it was a great joy and relief. It was hard at times; but I made up my mind that that was what I ought to do; and I would do it again and with the same joy, the same passion."

Nellie said impatiently, "Aye, that's very well. I honor you for your good feelings, lad; but what sticks in my throat is they knew the truth and no one there took you into their confidence, when they all knew."

"I see it all as you do; but I don't care."

She continued to reason and upbraid. He was thinking of his past and did not hear her at first. She persisted, trying to get some words from him that would ease her torment for the night; and they spent a long time yet, this night, smoking together and going over things.

She kept saying, "You see, Tom, you couldn't die for a woman like that, just a rag and a bone and a hank of hair."

"It's strange how things can be dead, a thing like hair. She is dead; and I don't grasp it."

"She's got you where she wants you. I'm sick of it, lad."

"Why are you jealous of her, now she's dead?" said Tom looking into her strange face, snowy with fatigue and spite, the rapacious beak, the winking eyebrows, the wrinkled forehead which he admired and loved.

"She isn't dead; it's the vampire mind of her still alive, still at you. She'll kill you yet."

"I wouldn't care if she did. I hope she does."

"Perhaps it would be better than lying about dreaming, living a tatter existence, a nobody's man. I've no patience with you, you're no brother of mine. You're a silly coot running after women's skirts with your tongue hanging out: my patience is gone. And talking a lot of tripe to Camilla when her heart's breaking."

He looked at her with surprised interest, "What tripe?"

"Adventures and sex and such flimflam. I'm ashamed of you.

Teasing a poor woman who doesn't want to hear your trifling trash."

"What tripe about sex?" enquired Tom.

Nellie was embarrassed, "You talked about sex to her."

"I did not."

"I want you to leave her alone. She's a friend of mine. I don't want her confused and troubled by your confessions and nonsense. She's in trouble now, between two or three men, each one wanting his own profit. There's only one thing for her, to leave the men alone. I wanted you to discuss suicide and death with her, because she's on that lonely road herself and I'll think the less of you if you've hurt her seriousness."

Tom smiled, "She was glad of a day out, like any other woman in the house."

"And I've got another bone to pick with you."

He laughed.

"You went over to see Caroline."

"I'm glad I did. I said I'd look for another room for her. That's an evil-smelling slum you found for her."

"But it's near here and she can come here for advice and for a little sincere talk," said Nellie.

"Who is that old stone woman? She said she was from Cornwall. I think she's the last sister of the Cornish giants. I'm going to have a look round tomorrow."

"That's Ma Hatchard. Did ye have trouble with her, pet?"

"No, she fell for me. She's twice my size. She told me her second husband died by falling downstairs. I looked up and I could just see her at the top tossing him down with one hand, a thin fistful of skin and bone—like me."

He laughed his childish laugh, "Oh, I'm *persona grata* there. But I'll snatch Caroline from the fee-fi-fo-fum. I'll have a look tomorrow."

Nellie sighed, "A change of room won't help, Tom. The girl's a born victim. And she worries and gnaws and tears at herself with introspection; she can't face the truth."

Tom said, Well, he'd go and look; and he was taking the girl out in the evening.

No, said Nellie, she thought Tom ought to get out of town,

go to Bob Bobsey's, anywhere. There were too many temptations here.

"No, Nellie, I'm all right here for the while. I'm going out tomorrow and I'll buy a bottle of wine for Caroline and we'll sample it and have a talk at Ma Hatchard's and then see how it works out."

"That's childish."

"What we all need is a good bottle of wine and a good steak, that's all. She's hungry. Camilla's hungry. There are a lot of half-fed people about; that accounts for their troubles. They think it's misery, despair; it's not enough food and fun."

"That's crass materialism."

"That wine's due for slaughter tomorrow night. I'm just going to find out how merry we can be, three candidates for the Exit, according to you. I know a hard-boiled egg can cure the everlasting cold, a bottle of wine the miseries. You're right. We have something to say to each other. Life! Let it come!"

"Caroline doesn't want any artificial moods. She's getting used with me to facing life without cosmetics. I've just had a fight getting her to see the truth of a miserable flirtation that's breaking her down. I can't understand it. Any shameful hope with a man! But I've got her to admit it has no future; and I won't see an honest girl spoiled. I won't have you either with your artificial tricks tampering with my work."

"What work is that?"

She was bitterly silent.

He laughed.

"Poor old Nell! Go and harrow someone else's feelings. Go and have a good time. I'd like to sleep. I drove three hundred miles today."

She turned back and sprang up, "I know your game. I know what you're up to. I despise you, Tom Cotter."

He was suddenly dashed, "Do you despise me? No, don't do that, Nellie."

"Leave the girl alone, Tom. She's innocent. She's been tampered with by this office flirt who's got the women after him. He plays with her and throws her a sop and then turns her off; and then takes her on again and she can't understand the cruelty.

[164]

He can't mean it, she says: he's so good. You're not to play around with her. I'm trying to protect her from the hopeless bitterness; the dead sea fruit he's got for her. The wickedness, the falseness, lies and scoundrelism! Why? Why do they do it? Oh, the poor women."

He glanced at her wild worn face, "All right, Nellie!"

He heard for a while the rush of words and then he slept. She had gone when he opened his eyes. He turned so that he could look at the sky through the open skylight. He looked at the stars as they wheeled and like a child, he smiled at them. He felt blissful.

She was lying on the bottom steps of the top flight, exhausted with her struggle; and trying to collect her ideas for the struggles that awaited her, she had fallen asleep. George, Caroline, the woman in Southwark, Johnny, Camilla and many others, too, that no one here knew about, all going wrong; and Tom too, the gliding, smiling man. She went to bed at last, after roaming the house silently, the smell of her cigarette going into every room, so that wakers knew she was there. She could not sleep. In the morning's mail had been a letter from Bob. Bob wanted George to stay at the cottage because he had promised to paint it for her, dig a garden, make slip; and there was great talk about a chicken run. They had got permission. Bob thought she might sell eggs. She ought to try here first, before they emigrated. At last, Nellie threw herself as she was on the divan in the front room and between smoking and coughing, slept a bit.

NELLIE GOT up early, washed hastily at the kitchen sink, and went striding over to Ma Hatchard's two streets away. She and the landlady had hated each other at sight. Mrs. Hatchard was in her fifties, like a tree trunk lightning struck, gray, powerful, thick, with a creased face, thin white hair, wearing a very long gray or blue dress with a narrow belt and a small white collar. Her eyes were sea blue. She behaved mannishly, in her strength; except when, vivacious with some tidbit of scandal, she put on a new little flowered hat and high heels and hurried off to neighbors she had known in the bombing, neighbors who for the most part lived in temporary dwellings on a bombed-out site. Hovering in the background of her dark street-level rooms was a good-looking but pale and tired young woman, who appeared to sleep in Mrs. Hatchard's quarters. Ma Hatchard herself slept in a remarkable four-poster bed with canopy and room looked like a stage. Ma Hatchard was fond of cats. She had curtains, which reared itself against the back wall, so that the saved cats from hunger and death during the war and subsequent national starvation; her house, unwashed, unpainted with broken leaking walls and crumbling stairs covered with coconut matting smelled of human and cat urine. But though there were no fastenings on windows or doors and the bedclothes were patched and gray with bad washing, she had fixed her lodgers' rooms up completely, with each a little oven and stove, and good lights, each item on a separate meter. The meters ate up the pennies, sixpences and shillings. There was a regular rake-off for the landlady on each meter.

It was in the best room, the large front room on the first floor upstairs, that Caroline lived; a shabby and dirty room, but cheaper than most to be found and "clean"; that is, free of insect pests. Caroline was deeply ashamed of living in such dirt.

She invited no friend there but Nellie. She was afraid of Mrs. Hatchard.

Ma Hatchard let Nellie in without a word. Nellie flung past and ran up the stairs three at a time, with a gay halloo.

"Are you there, love?"

She flung herself down on the armchair with her leg over it and began raging about her brother. How could Tom still go round making experiments with human beings? There was a stormy, seeking time in Bridgehead many years before when they were roaming looking for the road out. "Some people called it Bohemia." That was all right for young people. It was all despair, stupidity and selfishness if they looked homewards. So they looked outwards and saw depression, the dole, the fourth winter of unemployment, many homes broken up, children wandering for work all over England. They had found the answer, she and Tom; but it had formed them differently.

"I struggled out of it; but he never did. He's remained an adolescent and he's killed souls with his purposeful evasiveness. He's dangerous. I'm warning you. You want to be very sure of yourself to cope with him. It was a bad time, a time of many solutions. There was corruption. Tom and I were in all that corruption together. He's no good."

"But Tom is so gentle and good and so gay," said the young woman.

Nellie said bitterly, "Aye, he's an angel—a gilded angel with rotting wings." She flung herself down and hid her face on the chairback, "I've come for ye. He'll pull the wool over your eyes; he's the spirit of mischief. He'll take you away from me."

"Oh, how can you say that? I know what you've done for me. You've befriended me; and I was so lonely."

"There's no standing water with friendship; it's turn your back on me or come forward and be my real friend. There's no other way. It's me or him. Life or death. He's coming here! I know his tricks. He'll catch a poor bloody innocent like you. And why haven't you trusted me? It should be all right between us, I shouldn't have to worry, after all I've done for you. But you shilly-shally. You married a weak man and you hadn't the backbone to stand by your mistake. You got led astray like a Woolworth miss in Roseland. You fell for that bugger in the office. I know you. I have no faith in you. You have no character. You won't look into yourself and see what you are. You won't confess to what's wrong."

"I know Alan has been strange. I don't understand all he does. I have been very unhappy, very. He was so good to me. I went over everything a hundred times. Why should he be unkind to me? I loved him; he asked me and I told him. I do love him. I always will. Would it be love if I became angry with him the first time he hurt me?"

"I pity you. I pity you from the bottom of my heart. I pity you living in fairy stories like a child. If you even think you love him, I pity you. And you'll be easy game for a prinking thing, a smirking toy like Tom. He'll sing you a song and tell you a tale and you'll go straight to the mountebank and forget everything I've told you and been to you."

"I don't understand you. Why are you so upset?"

Caroline was uneasy at Nellie's pain. Couldn't they all be friends? Nellie loved Tom, Caroline liked them both. No, no, said Nellie; she had to choose. The ways lay at right angles. Caroline was puzzled and very uneasy at the misery and passion she saw in Nellie.

Nellie was downright, "He has no need of you. He can do nothing for you and I can do everything. He can't offer you friendship, love or any such thing. He's coming over to play cat's cradle with your feelings. If you knew my wild loneliness, Caroline, you'd come to your senses."

"But I thought you had so many friends."

Nellie muttered, "Not one that understands me. In you I thought I had found the perfect understanding. Oh, Caroline, for someone to talk to, to talk into the heart and leave it there and feel peace."

Nellie talked in this distracted way for some time, when they both had to go to work. Nellie went along with Caroline to the station, begging her to be true to her, not to be taken in by the "pink and white illusionist."

"I'm warning you. It will end badly. He can only harm women."

[169]

Nellie bought the morning papers, sat on a bench till it was time for the pubs to open and presently went downtown to work.

Caroline came out of the housing office at six o'clock and walked along briskly, thinking about catching her bus, though her head was spinning. She wondered if she would have the courage to go into a pub and have a drink, wishing she were home now, at Ma Hatchard's, so that she could begin the routine of cooking, eating, fixing her clothes. She had thought about Alan so much that she had envisaged even the most unlikely possibilities; even that he would tell her the affair was finished. I couldn't face it, she said to herself; then at once, everything can be faced. And he is too good, too kind and I am no nuisance; and he loves me. She had thought of everything, wondering very much these last few months at his strangeness. I don't know much about men. I have to learn.

This afternoon, after talking to her in a gruff embarrassed way, chopping out his answers and questions, he had mentioned a couple that had been ejected from their one-room home and were now housed in different temporary shelters, wives and husbands separately. The wife was having a love affair with the man's closest friend. The husband couldn't grasp it and was disturbed. "He cries without stopping; he cried for three days."

"Oh, poor man. It's overwork."

"Yes, he was doing two jobs to try to get a home. I told him it will be all right. Temporary affairs have no meaning and don't last."

When he said it, she knew at once what he was getting at. They talked for a while in this way and everything had two meanings. He walked to the door with her and she kissed him as she had been doing, though she noticed he drew back. A car honked at her and there was Tom waiting to take her home. She got in and sat down, quite easeful. He noticed her looks and asked if she were ill.

"I may be, but I'm happy and free."

"Who is happy and free?"

They laughed.

[170]

"Would you like a drive in the country?"

No, she had promised Nellie to go straight home.

"Nellie will get along all right."

"No: I promised."

He began to drive. She didn't know where they went; but she realized presently that Tom was talking, talking, the light voice mixing with the street sounds, birds. It stopped when the traffic stopped. He was recounting all kinds of things.

"I'm a lonely walker. I was just thinking about something that happened last time I was in Bridgehead. There was a boy at a corner in the main road. He was in painter's overalls, new, just an apprentice, with a bucket and brush, laughing at the antics of four older painters two houses away, one on the ladder going up, splashing stuff at the others. The boy stood with things in his hand and a rag; his hair blowing like a storm of cornflakes and the rag blowing. Just then a hat came round the corner. It made three hops and it was so funny we all started to laugh; and it hopped into the boy's bucket. A man came round the corner to get his hat which was in green paint. We fished it out and we started to talk. He said, Do you know anything that is going on? He was a local Reuter's correspondent and he said he had no luck. Just the night before, there was a fire in his lodgings, which spread to a few other houses, when he was in the movies. He saw it flashed on the screen. I promised to let him know if anything happened and he gave me his address. The apprentice began to tell him things that had happened in that street. He couldn't stop talking and he kept walking away with the man. I saw them in the distance about half a mile away. I was laughing and turning away when the door of a house opened just across the road and someone began to throw things in the roadway, a vase, then some silver, a picture; so I went the other way. One of the painters said, That is a man who cannot get away from his mother. She never let the husband out of the house; and when he died, she kept the son there. Then the painters asked me where the apprentice was. I said he was about a mile away with the Reuter's correspondent. They began to tell me things and I could hardly get home . . ."

At first there were tears in her eyes: then she fell asleep. He did not wake her up, but she woke when they stopped in front of a Hampstead pub. It was a pretty place, a terrace with benches and bushes.

He laughed, "You say you like me to talk; and you fall asleep."

"I thought I was in trouble; then you were talking and I saw people are living everywhere, and I was glad and I fell asleep."

He looked at her gaily and got her drinks, chatting with everyone.

When they got outside, he said, "To Ma Hatchard's?"

The old woman stood in the door of her den. Tom smiled at her, a light passed over her face, she stood away without a word and let them go up.

"You are not well, you're ill," said Tom.

"I should be ashamed to be ill because of a love affair. I've had plenty of experience."

Tom ran out and up several streets looking for things to eat. He bought food at last in a pub. He came back. He moved about like a cat and seemed beside himself with joy at being able to look after her.

He told her that he thought he could cure people. People believed in him and he wanted to help them. It was a power in him sometimes, not always. Even at moments, he had been able to help Marion.

"Only for a little while."

She asked him what he did.

He got up from his chair, stood near her, leaning slightly forward, spread out his arms a little from his body and began to look straight at her, smiling a deep smile. To her surprise, he seemed to grow upwards and outwards and she felt herself smiling, drawn towards him. His hands and face seemed larger and a feeling of happiness spread through her. He sat down and she began to tremble.

"It is there; but I have to develop it. Marion wanted me to go to India to learn. She said I could be of great use to sick people."

They were sitting quietly by the gas fire, not saying much, a little bored and laughing a little about raffling off the furniture in the dingy room, when there was a discussion downstairs and they heard Nellie's voice. She ran upstairs and burst open the door, looking at them both with a terrible accusing face.

"I knew you were here, Tom. I saw the car downstairs."

"Well, I am here. You were right."

"You must take us all home. I have a room for Caroline. She can't stay here with that harpy. I've explained it to Mrs. Hatchard and I've paid her. Get your things together, Caroline, and come home and I'll look after you."

"Caroline is too tired."

"Caroline promised me to come. She wants to come with me."

"Very well," said Tom.

When he got them home, with the bags, he said he would take Eliza Cook out for a drink. Nellie had not spoken a word to him during the drive and did not speak now.

Tom said, "I'll be back in the early hours of the morning. Don't wait up for me or wonder where I am."

Nellie was pale with rage, speechless; but when Tom clapped the front door to, she flung herself into Caroline's arms and burst into a raucous sobbing.

"It's too much for me, Caroline."

Presently she said that her life was like struggling over a stony hill, stubbing her feet, where the stones were people: that was the Philistine world. Robert Peebles had rejected her article outright. She needed Caroline above all. She kept Caroline up very late talking. George had told her he could not sleep in the house; not only was it that she didn't seem able to sleep at night, but roamed about in the dark hours; it was also her coughing and smoking.

"And that's love for you, Caroline. What the men mean by love is routine and comfort."

Caroline slept at last, in the back room. Tom came home later still and slept late.

When Nellie got home, on her late night a few days later, Tom was waiting up for her. He had received a firm answer from the plastics factory at Blackstone in Norfolk and was to go up there the following week.

"So I won't be a burden to you any longer than next week.

Isn't it time, Nellie, you wrote to George and told him he must come home, or you get a week off and go down to Bob's. You look bad, Nellie."

She looked ragged and devitalized; she was dirty and uncombed.

"I don't know. Things are too hard for me, Tom. The damn worthless bugger ought to be home but I don't know what will bring him. I want to disgrace myself and cry all day long."

Tom said he'd take her to Bob's farm the next day, which was Saturday. They could pick up some drinks and food somewhere. But she refused to go there. She wanted to ride into the country and he said he would take her.

"I've got to be here, see someone who's on the danger list. The consolation is George's with Bob, the dear old elf," said Nellie.

Tom said nothing.

She continued nervously, "I want to talk to you about Bridgehead. The poor helpless pets are there depending on us. I can't send much now. Couldn't you get a job and stay at home, Tom? It would keep you out of temptation."

"I couldn't Nellie."

"I'd feel easier, pet."

"No, Nellie."

"Where did you spend the morning, Tom?"

"With Camilla, the Italian goddess."

"Did you see Caroline? Was she home?"

"I don't know. I didn't see her," he said sharply.

"Be careful of her, Tom. She's such a sensitive, naïve, sweet girl. She couldn't take any more of that. She's off men. She needs a rest cure. Don't flirt with her. She's honest. She's too serious. She can be hurt."

"You take a dim view of me, Nellie."

"Eh, pet, I don't blame you with the seasoned women; but you don't know what you're doing, playing with the sensitive plants."

"Thanks."

"Eh, Tom; we don't always calculate the costs."

"No."

"And Camilla, too, Tom. She's had a terrible lesson. She married in haste and now she's feeling her way; always the wrong man. Loneliness is a terrible blindness."

"You think that in her blindness she's feeling for me?" he said with teasing vanity.

He had her beaten. She could never stand a direct hit.

"Where is Caroline now?" Tom pursued.

"She's all right, Tom. She's about the same. The heart's bruised. She's not made for this world, not your world, Tom."

"She has grit. She'll get over it. We're jellies that survive anything. She was happy with me."

Nellie cried out, "What are you monkeying about for, Tom? I know you. You've got nothing to offer but your own selfish pleasure. You like to pry into souls, show them fool's gold, sell them the sideshows, upset my work."

He said seriously, "Nellie, what work is it you think you're doing?"

"Truth not lies. What are you trying to put into my mouth?"

He laughed.

"I like to see you get into a flap. You're so transparent, Nell. You've got just a little twisted spittling spider thread of sympathy and you try to dangle a whole human being on it."

He said this in the croon they used at home.

He continued, "You don't know any more about Camilla or Eliza or Caroline than you know about Tibet, but you'll never admit it. And if you introspected with them for a hundred years you'd never know anything about them. For it's you, Nell. It isn't them. They don't care for death and the lonely road. And neither do you. It's just your spellbinding; but you'll get nowhere with it. And you shouldn't. You don't know—Nell, it's just as if some evil spirit, some demon were speaking out of your mouth. Those aren't your words; and you don't know what work you're at."

She tossed her head-feathers, the strings of hair and turban and the long earrings, the thin scarf, her bony flying arms; she poked her face, the mere rind of a face, here and there.

"It isn't me nor for me, pet. I'm trying to free them from themselves; that's the only freedom. Then their problems will be over. It's you who want them to live in the world of illusion. I want to free them by truth. Death is the end. What is the use of these tawdry loves, as you call them, and such? Aren't they always disappointed? Doesn't that prove that it's shameful degrading nonsense. It's nonsense they sell them so they won't look straight ahead and see where it is all leading."

"That we are all going to die, is news from nowhere. Is that your great truth?"

"My great truth is freedom from illusion, from lies, deceptions, from hypocrisy, from all those shameful loves, the opium of the heart. I want them to come to me and learn, come to me; I can teach them that there is only one way, and they must find it in pain, but I can help."

He crooned, "And so you dabble in their lives as if their lives were puddles, just to cool off your emotions a bit, Nell; and you talk about death and moonshine the way the old man used to talk about poltergeists and bodiless footsteps; just to get an audience. And one of these days you'll bitterly regret it, because I know you. You don't mean an ounce of harm by it; you don't know what you're saying. You're just trying to get a lot of personal influence so that you can see yourself having a big wailing at your funeral and a big piece in the papers." He laughed kindly.

She continued her flurry, snapped, "Eh, sweetheart, I'm afraid time will prove you a false prophet. It's not my funeral but Caroline's I'm worried about. She thinks she can't escape from her loneliness. It's the bloody men, Tom. It was like the morning of the world, she says; I trusted him. He's only a human being like myself; no more trustworthy than myself. So the victim forgives the executioner. And it makes me smile to think that it would mean nothing to him if I died; she says that. Tom, it's unbearable. That's a crazy wicked obsession, I keep telling her, to be thinking of extinction when you haven't first unraveled the secret of life. I talk to her every night—aye, I've been over, when you've been running out after your temptations. We're friends, let's think this thing over, face it, get to know it, find out what it is in yourself that courts misery, makes you fail with humanity, it must be something in you, not in them—"

"Every night? You went over every night to nag her? Where is she now? In the attic? I'm going to her when we get back."

She ignored him: she said savagely, "Men with dead hearts don't want you, I said. Live with the living, live with me. Confide in your friend. She doesn't sleep. You can sleep if you want to, I said. It's a damn insult to me to be howling at night for the love of dead men who've rejected you. That's the way to make a new one in the company of the lost. With me you'll never be lost."

"Do you really think you have the power? It's unlucky to call on powers: they come. That's no philosophy of consolation. Do you remember the Indian boy? In Bridgehead? One of Jago's circle. He was attracted by Jago's scraps of philosophy."

"Yes," she said sulkily, mumbling her cigarette.

"He talked about death all the time and do you remember what happened?"

"No, pet, I don't."

"You do remember, Nell. You had got us separated by then, Estelle and me. I was sleeping in a cot in the same room and Estelle had adopted that fellow, that returned soldier who couldn't get a job, a misfit. He had no room and we had him sleeping on the floor; then he found a place and went. His name was Bob, Robert.

"One night after he'd gone, when I was dead tired, I woke up to hear Estelle dreaming and calling out, 'Bob! Bob!' She had had a nightmare. She saw Bob in flames. 'He's burning!' she said to me. It took me a long time to get her calm. As it happened, that same night someone else, that Indian boy, was burned to death in the house he had just moved into in Bridgehead. You remember, he had money and we all went to his place to eat and drink. He bought records and food just to make friends. But he couldn't make friends, he was too miserable. The evening would start off gay; we'd be there singing and dancing; and it would gradually get quieter and quieter, with him giving us the food and then standing there, quiet and miserable. He spent all his money on us; and he moved to a cheaper place; and in the end he moved to a condemned house they were trying to get the people out of. They let him a top room secretly. The man on the ground floor used to booze. He came in and upset a lamp and the place went up in a few minutes. Right at the end they heard someone screaming. The Indian boy was standing right on the roof calling and shouting and before anyone could do anything, the roof fell in and he fell backwards."

Tom put his hand over his eyes, took them away, looked at her with his large globular china blue eyes, shining and staring, "You used to talk death with him, Nellie; isn't that where you got this black stuff? You should never have brought her here."

"She needs me. I'll cure her. I made her promise to give up that office job. Otherwise, we might see another bout of sheep's-eyes."

Tom was aghast. Throwing up jobs was one of Nellie's own ways of purifying herself.

Nellie answered him, "You judge too fast and you judge by yourself. You wheedle and coax. I don't. I have something to say; it is to make them see the truth as it is. It's given to me to see the truth."

"What is the truth then? I'd like to know myself!"

"Ah, lad, but you won't face it. It's like asking for a foothold in quicksand. Under you it's bottomless, but you keep afloat because you're a feather. You have no real heart; you can't despair."

"Is that all? To despair? You don't despair."

"We're all different. We go by different paths." She seemed serious. He lighted another cigarette, threw himself back and smoked upwards.

"She's too honest, Nell. You oughtn't to play with her."

"It wasn't me," she said in a deep voice.

"Leave her alone. She'll get out of it. We all do."

"She didn't want to get out of it. She wanted to understand. She sent me a cry for help."

He murmured, "Day and night she cried on me, Fair Helen of Kirk-connell Lea."

"I had to go, pet. It was an emotional morass. She was getting confused and taking false steps and ready to sink in. When I got her back here from Roseland, I thought she was safe. That fellow with his phony book on housing."

[178]

"How do you know it was phony?"

She yelped, "Can you help the workingman living in the slums with a book? It's the landlords! They're glad to see your books and your commissions. Nothing will be done if there are enough books. It's the penpushers justifying themselves with a bit of type; me name's there as a champion of the down-and-outers. So I explained it to her: it's no good. What you're doing is useless. It's hopeless. It's getting nowhere. And that fellow tearing her the other way. And she took that and took his bloody flirtation and thought, I'm guilty, I'm not good enough for a man who writes a book. I can't bear it: ah, the poor waif. I got her out of that mess and at once here some humbugging man starts in again and she can't understand it. She asks me advice. You can't take it again, pet, I said. You'll never take it again. So on my advice she promised to quit the job."

"You're succeeding better than I thought," said Tom.

"What do you mean by that?" asked Nellie sharply.

He began in their horrible croon, "However fast she makes connections with real things, and real people, you cut them away one by one, and soon the whole spider web will be adrift."

"I don't know what you're talking about."

"I'm talking about the soul you're saving. Where did you get the idea that you could save souls?"

Nellie mumbled quickly, "It's no such thing. I need someone of me own, Tom. Where is George and where is Bob? They're saving their own souls and you too, Tom. Ye all have no hearts. It makes me sick and shudder, to see the selfish striving. It's so patent. I have a friend I've been with tonight. There I found understanding; but she's cured of the world, the cruel mean hearts, the bloodsuckers and flesh-eaters. You'll never know what she knows and I see it through her eyes, through love—a friend's love. Her heart is one wound and the world's bleeding to death through her: that's how she feels. And Tom, I must have someone; I can't face it. And she clings to me, Caroline. She believes in me and I'm the only one. I can save her from what no other sees. She's such a credulous loving child. Say the word love to her and she loves. Ah, chick, death's the end of that road, through the fens and the brambles. It's a lonely road, sweetheart; with stumbling footsteps; and if there's despair and disbelief in you, you'll stray off sooner or later into the—"

"Stop it!" shouted Tom.

She hid an ungleeful smile. Her face was very pale, strained. Her small eyes moved about under the narrow lids as if searching for something.

She said amiably, though, "What's the matter, pet. Can't you take it? No, I can't get through to you now. But I make her take it, face it. Aye, she's braver than you are. Women are. And she'll be able to face it when she sees where she is, the fen mists all around and the bog of death—"

She paused, no longer interested, and lighted another cigarette.

Tom said, "Do you remember, Cush, when you got Estelle and me apart, you left us?"

"You're talking rubbish, Tom."

"You went to that hotel in Wales. You got a job there for you and one for Peggy. You made her come out of Bridgehead."

"Aye. She was desperately seeking a way out."

"She was going to dances like other girls. She had boys."

"Never, never! She never cared for those things. It was another sort of hunger. And I brought her out to see the world a bit, to understand. Perhaps I made a mistake. Some are too fragile."

"You got her into a hotel among the men, the travelers, the waiters, and she got into trouble. You meant well; and it always ends in misery. Whenever you dabble in soul-saving, you get someone into trouble. I know why, Nellie. You have a loving heart. It isn't enough."

The next afternoon, a Saturday, he took Nellie for a drive. They had taken a long rising road and were high above the Vale of Aylesbury, which, under a faint vapor, rolled away right and left before them. The road was on a rampart of earth and above it rose an almost naked mound.

Nellie said, "Let's stop here. Let's go up there and get the real fresh wind."

A fair cool breeze was blowing and hissing in the grass tufts.

"It'll be bad for you, Nellie. You shouldn't overexert yourself."

"I'll be fine, chick. Just help me up. Let's sit on top of the world, like we used to on the moors. You always said, I can breathe now. I like to be with you, darling. There's no one like you. You're restful. You help me to believe in things. Ah, darling, it's hard at times. The road is rough."

He held on to her, pulled her upwards.

"Take it easy, Nell."

She had to stop several times; her breath came rasping. She coughed and held her chest while she laughed and protested, "I'll be all right, pet; I'll make it."

He said they never should have come up. They sat down.

She gasped and hawked and said, "Those chimneys spoil the view: see the smoke going into the fresh air!"

"No chimneys and I'd have no work," said Tom.

"Come on, tell me the gossip, Tom."

"What gossip? Nothing ever happens to me."

She said laughing, blowing her cigarette smoke away, "Ah, ye devil! Come chick, let's have your news, don't tease! Tell it in your own deprecating style, at the rate of one hint a half-hour, to be tiresome. Come, what did you do last night, chick?"

"I saw Eliza. We all went to the pub."

"They are a damn dreary lot." She looked restlessly here and there.

"Well, here you are Nellie, on top of the world."

Said she, musing, "I've come a long way. My life's been an unusual story. In a sense it is clear-cut. The five ages, aye. My childhood up to fourteen when I was a sad serious child, very conscious of my shortcomings and the feeling of guilt. That's salutary. Then fifteen when I realized the world and myself in it. Then my work in London and the provinces when I brought you all down, out of it, to get into reality; and perhaps I'm guilty. And then George."

"That's four. And then?"

"Then life without George."

He waited.

[181]

She wiped a tear off her cheek, "He's leaving me in the lurch, the bastard. He telephoned me this morning. He can't fix it for me for a while. He had a letter from Geneva. He's going to Geneva as soon as he gets his papers ready. They don't want me yet. They want him to settle first. It's the end."

She turned round, clasped his neck, sobbing.

"Chick, I can't be brave."

Tom put his arms round her, and kissed her, "You'll have to stick to me, Nell."

"Ah, bless you, Tom, you're a saint. Would you go up to Bridgehead, lad; and I'll try and get a job there and we'll be back in the old home?"

"Not on your life. Why you wouldn't stick it three days, Nell." He chuckled.

She pleaded in a strained yearning voice, "It would do the poor souls' hearts good; and she'd be saner, Tom. You'd take the burden off the poor girl. It's not fair, Tom."

Tom said drily, "I do what I can."

"Tom, I don't understand you. Our parents are only struggling human beings. They brought us into the world. They're not guilty. We're guilty. Ah, Tom, I feel guilty, guilty. When I stop on the doorstep with the frail bits of parsley by it and see the clean window curtains and put me key in the door, you don't know the awful guilt I feel."

"I don't feel guilty, Nell."

"You're hard, harder than I am, Tom. How can you speak so of that innocent flower destroyed in savagery, in thoughtless egotism and that now has nothing to fulfill itself but in stifled bitterness? What is she, Peggy, the poor darling, but a white flower in a black cloth? What is Bridgehead but the black cloth? She's being slowly suffocated, put away, turned brown and wrinkled in a back drawer. Tom—she's my greatest deepest regret. I feel a horrible guilt. I led the way. I meant to show her life. She was such a rosy white child with that soulless merry laugh. Tom, oh my lad, I remember her as she was, not as the poor Bridgehead lass living a defeated life in a back kitchen as she seems now to you. Men cannot see women. They see them with a purpose, an aim, not with pitiful love and an everlasting

[182]

tender heart. I see her sitting there in the dark room knitting; to me she's just a white bird with a trailing wing, a bit between spirit and flower."

"You'd say that about a coal barge in the Scotswood muck if it suited you, Nell," he said laughing.

"Ah, Tom, the poor wee lost spirit; why can't I make you see? Will ye go, lad? I'll give up my job and we'll work together for the home."

"I will not."

"They look to us like hungry birds, now that Pop Cotter, bless his heart, has gone. They don't understand it when the money doesn't come in."

"No, they're not getting me back into that trap. I'm no Uncle Simon."

She cried, in a thin failing voice, "But why not? What have you got in your life, pet? I'd understand it if you had a home; but you're just a wanderer. Look at George. Wandering, thinking of his own pleasure, thinking of some new love! What's in the men? You're degenerate—thinking of it and nothing else! No mercy, no pity. I'm disgusted with you all. The first woman that comes along to look at you open-mouthed and everything else vanishes like burnt paper."

"It's a good life," he said, smiling.

"I know you, Tom. You'll begin to spend your money foolishly and it'll end up in some new Marion craze. It's just monkey tricks and mumming with you from end to end."

"I like it."

"And it'll be some harpy again getting the money, when they need it."

"They get more than their share in Bridgehead. Don't nag me."

"Ah, you're bitter, Tom. I'm thinking of what they never had. Have they had the lovely dreams we've had, seen the sights, known the world? Their poor old bodies sitting their lives out in a smoky chimney corner! It's pitiful, it makes me weep. Here we sit on top of a hill in beautiful southern England and we are free to do what we like. They're chained to Bridgehead."

"And they've turned into chuckle-headed gossips and domestic cutpurses and I don't intend to exchange my experience for theirs."

For a while they sat side by side, smoking and looking at the view. A man was in a glider, rising on geysers of wind through clefts, reaching an invisible billow and wallowing over it. And others; some of them going far up and away, banking and coming back in circles, using the air as birds do, soundless and easy, though not free. The sun was going down over the Vale of Aylesbury and shone sometimes on the faces, or even on a wrist watch of the gliders. It was such a strange sight, like a vision of the future, or of Mars by an old time engraver.

At last Nellie said gently, "Tom darling, you see, pet, if you were to go up there, I could perhaps go with George, if he wants me. I could follow him. Wives are wanted. It's the rule in official jobs. They can't deny his wife."

"Ah, is that it? Why couldn't you come out with it, Nell?"

She said eagerly, "Ah, then you'll do it, chick? Ah, chick, you're a blessed saint."

"I will not, Nell."

"But why not? Tom, your life's empty. And I couldn't send the money myself. George is so hard. He wants me to put them in homes. And he won't send money willingly."

His face was placid, mild.

And now Nellie wanted to get back to London. She had become very agitated. Her friend in Southwark was in hospital again, and very low. Perhaps she was sinking. "I heard her voice just then, Tom; she said, Oh, Nellie, Nellie! Why is she calling me? I must go."

As they turned towards London, Tom began to smile to himself. He had his own reasons for wanting to get to London.

"If I can go, Tom, what am I to do with the house in Lamb Street? How will I keep up the payments? It's ruin I face. I must have me home."

"It's a poser."

"And my poor sweet girl up in Bridgehead struggling along on breadline money. And I'm responsible."

"I'm damned if I know what to do."

"Tom, I must go to him."

[184]

"Yes, I know."

She said in a soft wailing voice, "It's a bloody bugger; pet. He's my weakness. You know I never was like that. Tom; he's ruthless. He overrides me every time. Bob's encouraged him. He's a stalwart, she says. And I think so too; I agree with her. He's a big man. He's got to develop."

Tom said, "I get it. You needn't go on."

"What do you mean?"

After a silence, she said, "You're angry, aren't you?"

"No, I'm not."

She suddenly flew into a temper, "You'd desert your family and anyone, to stay in London and flirt."

He didn't answer.

She said fiercely, "You're both traitors to me. You'd both desert me for the first harpy that comes your way."

"I wouldn't, Nell," he said calmly.

"You don't sympathize with me: you don't care if he leaves me: it's the League of Men."

"No, it isn't."

"You sit there looking so smooth and fair," she complained, "you know I forgive you everything."

"No, you don't."

"I would even love anyone you asked me to."

"No, you wouldn't."

"You don't think I'd do anything to hurt you, Tom."

"Yes."

"But we're two against the world, Tom: there's only you and me."

"No, there's not, Nell."

"Ah, damn and blast you, Tom Cotter," she said flying into a wild roistering banter, "you've got me by the nose sitting there with your meek smirk and saying, No, I don't, and Yes, you do."

"No, I haven't."

"What do you mean by telling all the women your sorrowing tales and talking about sex and mayflower and saying you feel like the son of Venus's son: and that in the country your feet don't seem to touch the ground and such sonnets?"

"Those are not my words," said Tom.

[185]

"Real beams came from Venus all this month: you said that to Caroline this morning: she admired it."

"Those were my words."

"What are you going round telling all the women your poetry for?"

"Because I feel it," said Tom.

Nellie was silent. After a while, she said, "But what's the sense to it, Tom?"

He was looking straight in front, smiling at the red evening.

"What pleasure do you get out of it?"

"No pleasure!"

"Then why do you do it?"

He was silent.

"At your age, Tom, with your experience, you ought to give up this wild dancing in a hall of mirrors."

"This wild dancing in a hall of mirrors."

"And it's an illusion!"

"And it's no illusion," said Tom.

"But you haven't known happiness as I have, Tom: you must grant that. You haven't known the great reality, the one great true experience, the tree of life."

"No, I haven't known it as you have," he said humbly.

"And you never can, it's a one in a million chance."

"No, I shall make another mistake," said Tom.

"Then why try, when you know it's foredoomed?"

No answer.

"Is it right to trouble the lives of these women and go round making mischief?"

He looked slyly at her, a troubling sideways glance.

"If you were honest, you'd tell them to get the hell out of your life and leave you alone."

He looked sideways at her, and she began to tremble with urgency, "Now, Tom, I want you to promise me you won't go and do any more mischief-making."

He looked ahead at the road.

"Eh, Tom?"

"I don't make mischief; I do nothing. I just sit there."

"I don't ask you to restrict your life."

"I don't bother about what you ask."

"What?" she said, astonished.

"Life doesn't restrict itself. It comes and finds you."

"Then you won't make any promise?"

"No."

"I'm ashamed of you."

"To change the subject. My room where I had my last job, Nell, was a miserable bedroom with a light you couldn't read by. The wind howled and blew in the street. The landlord came in and out of the dining room like a dark-colored spook and used to whip the plates at you from behind his trousers like a conjurer. He wore a felt hat and bicycle clips, and his wife used to go to the pub after dinner. I don't blame her. She felt that if they could get away to London they could better themselves. He was interested because the atom bomb didn't injure canned beer. There was a laboratory chemist there who had lost his job and worried because he was getting farther and farther behind. If you're three or four years behind, you're lost, out of it. I used to wake up at night trembling, my heart was jumping about. I knew there was nothing there, but I couldn't help it, I'd lie there without daring to move. It was the loneliness."

"You were born to loneliness, lad."

"And so I think, Nell, I must look around and find a wife."

She said angrily, "You know you're not for women! You can't give. You're a bachelor born. You're cold, stone cold. You're trying to get warm, like poor old Simon at the kitchen fire; but no woman can warm the likes of you; and you can give her nothing," and she said it deep in dialect, "naw-thin."

She continued, "You were born, you will live and die, a lonely man. Ah, isn't it better to accept it, swallow the pill and be yourself, lad? You're out of character, cooing to the women. Be what you were, as a lad. I was proud of ye then. And now I'm ashamed of ye."

"But I think I'll get married. I have my eye on someone."

She sulked. Tom, soon lost in his thoughts, smiled to himself. Nellie, at first absorbed, noticed his expression. She put her thin wrist on his and said sweetly, "You're not going to go where temptation lies, are ye, love?"

[187]

"I'm in a mood to be tempted, Nellie."

She reflected.

Along the London road, passing through a large town, there was a wide green, well kept with trees behind and bushes round a convenience in front.

"I feel like a pee, Tom. Let's get out and stretch our legs."

He waited for her and then strolled across the green, half of which was occupied by circus tents.

"Ah, Tom, I love the sideshows, let's walk on sawdust for ten minutes."

It reminded her of Race Week on the Town Moor, when, poor children, bedraggled but whistling and shouting, they had gone up there with a few pence in their pockets.

"Peggy loved it so much, the darling. And now we can't let her go near: it's bad for her. Ah, the bygone days!"

She said as if inspired, "Do you remember, Tom, the day we all went to Whitley Bay and went in the ghost train? Peggy wanted so much to go on the ghost train and we were afraid, for she was always so excitable; and we went in and what was it but a track running in all the curves over bare earth and you could see it too? Poor Peggy! But I was glad. No spiderwebs, no shrieking spooks. The poor devils, aye, they were packing up, no business; but they took our sixpences!" She laughed, "And do ye remember that day, the prawns we ate at Cullercoats! And the bus conductor who fell off the bus and tore me good jacket; and looked at me so angry! He thought I was going to bawl him out and I said, Go on, love, better me jacket than yours; and he still went on up the stairs, looking back so furious."

She went into shrill sisterly laughter, "I was taken for a bloody bourgeois suing dame that day! It was a nice jacket, all new, made to order, me first and in a good cloth. Do ye ever think of those days, Tom?"

"I never had a happy day there but on the football field. I stand now and watch them in Regent's Park, the lads making a thousand goals an hour, but it doesn't get me any more. And like me, the daft lads think they'll reach the big money that way."

[188]

"Ah, Tom!" she wheedled. "Eh, look there, Tom! Isn't that a grand one. Let's go in."

They had come along the tents and were now at a large loosely boarded place named Palace of Mirrors.

"I've got such a craving on me for those things, Tom. Let's go in."

"Well, you know what it is: it's distorting mirrors."

"Ah, come, love, let's go in. Let's have a bit of fun, just brother and sister, like the old days. It gives me the thrill of Race Week when I was small. We used to beg petty cash for it."

"Aye and once I stole from Mother's purse. You remember? And you gave me a curtain lecture."

There was no one at the booth: it was between afternoon and evening sessions. They rapped and looked, till they found a man in shirt-sleeves who let them in. The entrance door was a mirror, in which they saw themselves, the short yellow-haired man and the tall wedge-faced woman; they looked earnestly and went in. There was a short corridor with different sorts of mirrors, then a rotunda, it seemed. One mirror showed Tom cut off at the waist and very fat; "A playing-card king, just what Patrick said," said Tom disgustedly. "Patrick? Who's that?" he laughed. "And look at me, the spindling hatchet witch," she said, poking out her tongue at herself in the neighboring glass in which her long thin arms, legs and face were fancifully drawn out. Tom looked where it made him a dwarf with a huge head. Depressed, he leaned against the wall and watched Nellie who was looking at herself in every mirror in turn, laughing, posturing, exclaiming, "Eh, Tom, love, I'm a beauty. Tom, look at this black raven! Why, thank god, Tom, it is not the Hall of Truth."

He said nothing. She began to gesture, posture and then dance a strange dance, her own, with knees bent and wobbling, arms akimbo, tufted head going up and down and sideways, like "a crawing creature" she said. Aside and forward she went in the figures of her dance, smiling to herself, beckoning to herself, putting her arms on her breast and with a strut turning the circle. She saw Tom there, stretched out her long thin arms and he came forward in his heavy shoes, took both hands; and they danced a few steps, though he was no dancer, at arms' length, a country dance. Her face bright as metal, triumphant, gleamed and cut into him; very bright, her small eyes peered into his large bursting ones. Then she flung one of his hands aside and began to draw him after her. She stopped a moment, eying a mirror which showed them side by side, shredded, a bundle of dark reeds and a wisp of hay, both with long beaked faces, split like seaweed, on her head a long sprout, on his the dry grass ground birds hide in.

She was displeased, "Not much, is it? They're distortions of human beings! Why do we like it, Tom?"

After eying it for a bit, she screwed up her face, leaned forward and dragged him behind her. "Let's dance!"

So there was a string of them in the dusty narrow corridor, a ballroom of the strangest people, but always the same two. And suddenly, she stopped, dropped to the floor, and leaning on a bent knee and one arm, began to cough. She leaned over, her head to the floor, whooped, almost strangled. Tom stood there waiting. Presently, she climbed up over herself. He helped her up.

She leaned on his shoulder for a breather, "Eh, it's the dust. The floor's thick with the dust of feet," she said.

"Come on, Nell. We'll go home and you lie down."

"It's a drink I need, sweetheart: they must be open now. Take me to the nearest. They're all friends."

"Ye-es, Nell."

"It does me good to have a drink and to stretch me legs in a strange pub. I feel so cosy and so free. Me troubles are outside."

They sat some two hours in the nearest pub, Nellie tossing down one drink after the other, in her own cycle, sherry, whiskey, gin: and Tom taking one glass of wine which made him go red.

Said Nellie, "Must be snobs round here, if they serve you glasses of wine. You'd never get anything as fancy as that in a true workingmen's pub."

After she had drunk two rounds, she leaned her head back on the yellow flyspecked wall, her elbow on the table, her hand turned gracefully outwards, the cigarette smoking into the air;

and she said in her weak tone, "If ye only knew, Tom, how it sticks in me gullet. He's dead and he thought that of me at the last, that I was letting the family down. I'll never swallow that black spoonful. I sup with guilt."

"What is it, Nell?"

"Aye, ye weren't there. Pop Cotter in his big bland way, lambasting me, Tom, because I'd dropped ten pounds a week and there wasn't enough food in the house, nor meat for his plate. I'll have it always with me, Tom. If only you had been able to get a job there, darlin'. I know it's work you want, not a name, I wouldn't have this shadow on me shoulders. It's with me in my dreams, it haunts me in the day, that the money isn't coming in and they look to us like pitiful hungry birds."

He did not answer, looking rosily around, noticing everything.

She did not insist then, but grasped his hand, kissed his cheek and said, "Eh, but that was grand, Tom, just when I needed it. You and me together. That's the way we meant it to be; but it can't be. You can't argue with the world. I need the world, Tom and that's why it all went wrong. Let's go; I must get back. Will ye drive me to the hospital?"

"I'm not sure it's good for you."

"I am the only one she can talk her heart out to. The rest she calls vultures."

When they sat in the car, driving, looking ahead, she said, "I feel on top of the world, now, because you're the one I've given me real heart to, Tom. Don't let me down ever; or I'll think very little of you."

"You know, Cushie, that you've always got me."

"Bless you, pet."

GEORGE, WHILE waiting for a Geneva transfer, had gone back to the Rome office. One day she got a telegram from George, saying that she was to leave for Rome as soon as she could arrange; he believed they had a job for her in his office. This was on a Thursday. The newspaper told Nellie to go at once. Not only had the doctor been in the office and given her warning, but anyone could see that she could not last much longer in this way.

Two days later she was to leave by train. She sent Tom to Bridgehead to say goodbye for her and give presents and make promises. If Tom caught the early train down in the afternoon, he would just be able to say a few words to her before she went. He was to go straight from his train to a delicatessen near Victoria and wait outside. She would go there to buy a few sandwiches; then they could have the parting cup of tea. He left Bridgehead at the earliest possible moment and after the four-hour trip got to the rendezvous with about half an hour to spare. She could be counted on, though she often rushed in at the last minute. He stood there till there were only a few minutes left before train time, with anxiously beating heart, flushing with worry. At last he rushed across the station, where he found a crowd at the barrier. There were dozens and dozens of people there, kissing, shaking hands, calling out, laughing; every kind of affection and momentary tenderness, a feast of love and emotion. He looked eagerly about, straining, calling, "Nellie, Cushie, Cotter!" He asked the man at the gate if he could get in; but this was not allowed. He stood on tiptoe and poked his face through the railings. Nellie did not come and the train pulled out.

This was unprecedented. They had had their last cup of tea

together in every big terminal in England and in one or two in Scotland.

Tom hurried to the telephone and telephoned the house in Lamb Street. Johnny Sterker answered. She said Nellie had certainly taken the train. Johnny had gone to the station with her. "Nellie thought you wouldn't make it."

Johnny said she was glad he had come back. Nellie had left the house in her charge and that was not her line. She was quitting. If he had a key, she'd leave now. Tom was stabbed. Nellie was so anxious to get off to George, that she had not looked for him at all; she had had time for Johnny, though. His back had ached badly all the way down in the train; but it wasn't that that he counted. Perhaps she would not come back for years! He went to the station bar and had three whiskies. He picked up his bag with a twinge and went to the telephone again. He telephoned Eliza; she was always at home on Friday nights, helping her friends with the wash and the ironing. She had friends in the next street, a family in one room with a small wash basin in a cupboard, but no sink or bath.

"Eliza! I was at the train and she never came! I waited half an hour and she didn't turn up and I went to the barrier, but she didn't come and she was on the train."

"Is it you, Tom?" said Eliza.

He sobbed, "Yes; everyone was there saying goodbye, everyone had someone talking to them. I looked everywhere. I called and I waited and I had no one. No one came to me. She went off without saying goodbye. So," he said petulantly, "I got drunk. I drank three whiskies on an empty stomach."

Eliza said, "Oh, she is probably going to cry all the way to Rome because she missed you." But she did not laugh. "Take it easy, Tom; don't drink any more. Why don't you go home now, Tom, lad?"

"The house is empty! I don't want to go there. Who will I talk to?"

"Now come home now, lad, and I'll talk to you and you can come out with us this evening. There's a big party, they're dancing and afterwards they're going to the pub."

"I don't want to see a lot of people. I don't feel like it. I can't understand all that gaiety. She said to wait at the delicatessen. I waited until the last moment. I bought her sandwiches, ham and chicken, the best, and then I rushed over and she never even bothered to look for me. I waited and waited. I can't understand it."

"Come here, lad, and eat something with us; there are a nice lot of youngsters here and some girls fresh from Ireland: they're lonely."

"No, no; that would make it worse! I'll put up at a hotel. Or I'll come home later."

Eliza said, after a hesitation, "Would you like me to come and meet you there at Victoria station? Can you get home all right?"

"No, no, I'm all right, Eliza. Yes, I'll come home to Lamb Street. Goodbye. I wish I was coming to you with no one else there."

"Take it easy then, Tom!"

"It's all right, I just had to talk to someone, I was there at the barrier and no one came to me."

He had another drink on the way home and had been in the Lamb Street house about ten minutes, when the front door opened and Eliza walked in.

"Eliza!" he shouted with joy. He got up, not noticing the pain, rushed to her, "Eliza! Oh, I am glad you came."

"It was just to find out how you are. I felt guilty with Nellie running off to George. Did you eat something?"

"I was just going to eat the sandwiches I bought. I'm glad to talk to you. It was just being left like that. I didn't know I really wanted you. I didn't feel like seeing anyone tonight and I was just going to sit here and mope. But I feel better," he continued brightening and smiling at her. "Dear Eliza! I'm glad you came. That was just the right thing! Just the right thing!" he said in an astonished tone.

"I'll get you some dinner," said Eliza. "Every homeless person in London has been in and out of here so I grabbed something at the ham-and-beef shop. We all live in common over there, there's always plenty. Here it is just one big tent, people walk in and out. Nellie is a wonderful woman; there is no one like her, Tom."

[195]

Tom was standing close to her.

"You are taller than you look, taller than me, but not as fat," she laughed.

"I am much stronger than you really," he remarked, "but now my back is out of order."

He followed her out to the kitchen and began once more to tell her indignantly about Nellie's betrayal.

"I wouldn't do such a thing to her."

After a while he laughed sadly and asked her to forgive him. He was very much upset because an awful thing had happened that day. A young soldier had fallen onto the line when a train was approaching at a station on the way down. His mate had jumped down to pull him back and both had been killed. Tom had seen what had happened. Then his train had moved on. "I didn't know what to do, I wanted to tell Nellie: she could have said something to me."

He had also been in pain all the week, but, "I don't dare lie down, and I don't want to lie down. If you lie down you don't know when you're going to get up."

He sat now on the edge of the chair by the table, twisted so as to give his back ease.

"So long as I can keep going without pain-killing tablets I'm all right. I don't like to give in, and I can't. I've got to get a better job soon. There's Estelle; and there's Bridgehead."

Then he discussed what he could do, if Nellie stayed abroad. He knew enough high-school French to begin with and wages for experienced men like himself, were high enough in Paris, which was a great engineering city. "And I could suit myself whether I kept paying out all that alimony or not. Maybe I could skip the life sentence. Of course I would soon have some other responsibility," he said demurely, with a red little smile, looking for approval. He had studied trades union conditions and wages already: he had been thinking it over. "I sent away for the papers as soon as I knew Nellie might go."

Then he talked about his lonely rides, the wind, the waste, the trees, the hungry wallowing of the vast open skies and country at him, their great formless bodies snatching at a love-hungry man who must spend his life alone. "The sky leans down to suck me up and the country bends all round me and seems to have hold of my feet: I don't know whether there's an ancient horror in the country, or whether it's only summer blowing in on me in my cell. I like work best, there I have company and plenty of space." In the factory he was thinking of, work was going ahead, they were getting army orders. He didn't like it, but didn't know what to do about it: it would be so in whatever branch of engineering he got into. He had helped in the last war, had to, but he had made up his mind to do nothing connected with killing in the next.

"I'll help the sick and wounded, I'll do any social work, helping evacuees, constructing hutments, arranging for supplies, I'll be a stretcherbearer, but I will never bring death to a human being, not even a bird! There was an analytical chemist in my last boarding house who agreed with me." He began to laugh. "I noticed he seized every opportunity of talking to me, and he was edging round all the time to the subject of war and peace. Presently I saw he was trying to get me to understand that war was a bad thing and ruinous for the country: he wanted me to see that peace was a good thing. So I let him go on converting me. He made progress: I told him I would be a stretcherbearer in the next war."

"I hope your back gets better for the next war," said Eliza.

"I'm very strong," said he, displeased. "I carried Marion up and down stairs often and she looked heavier than me—sometimes, that is," he said hastily. "I could carry you."

She laughed. "Eh, no, lad, not now! Would you like to go to bed now? You're very tired. I'll stay here and tomorrow clean up a bit."

He wanted to stay up. "I'm craving for some good talk. I look in wherever the curtains are not drawn and wish I could go in and talk. I like everybody, why can't I go in? Why aren't I let in?"

He sat in his chair sideways getting drowsy, rosy, beginning to smile as if asleep, a smiling, silly, radiant look.

"There's some wine left in the cupboard on the top shelf," he suddenly argued, "George left it there: I'm going to open some."

"Can you take it, Tom?"

"I'm all right. I can drink like a fish."

"No, you can't."

"I get drunk, but I can drink any amount."

She got it because of his back.

"I had to sit up all that way in the train: and when I got there, what did I find?" he said morosely.

"It's all selfishness in this house," quoted Eliza.

Tom was sulky at being ridiculed. "She let me down!" He grabbed the glass she held out to him and took a swallow. "I like wine! With wine nothing can get you down." He put down the glass. "I always knew those bottles were there! I always made up my mind to take one of them. It was there for months and he never offered to open one for me. I brought lots of wine to this house."

"George is judicious about his presents," said Eliza: "he has a very direct mind."

"I know, I'm obliged to stick around, so he needn't buy me. Any time he wants to desert my sister, I'm obliged to look after everything. I'm beginning to feel better."

Eliza was sitting on the couch under the open window which looked on the street. It was still light, a long green summer evening. The back window which looked into Nellie's sleeping alcove was also open and the tree scents blew in. They could see the darkening shape of the top of a tree in the Square, and brilliant stardust.

"What are you looking at?"

"The sky," said Eliza, "over the back."

"Let me come and see it too."

He brought the little table over, put it in front of them: but he couldn't get a comfortable position; he was in pain.

"Go to bed Tom, rest."

"I don't want to leave you; I won't be alone."

She went and sat on the bed in the alcove, so that he could lie beside her and talk to her; and fixed him up with some pillows.

"I don't know what you've done to yourself," she said anxiously, "you may have hurt yourself."

"Yes, I have, I think."

He leaned against her and said he felt better now. He looked worn and wasted. She gave him some pain-killing tablets which he had brought along, but he said, "Don't leave me, stay with me," and she stayed. "Stay near me. I am so tired of being alone."

Eliza had nursed a good many people and did what she could for Tom, who slept for a long time.

In the morning she came in once or twice but found him asleep. She had slept on the couch near the window and not slept well.

He smiled when he saw her, "I slept like a top." He had groaned and coughed all night; he didn't know it. "I'd like to sleep some more."

She let him sleep and worked about the house.

When Tom was awake again, she took him his breakfast. His clothes, blue and white, small and clean, were neatly folded into two heaps; the contents of his pockets were laid out on the table. He went through his lengthy toilet, coming out in the end looking like a fresh youth.

"I'd sit in the sun all day. I couldn't face a trip anywhere today. But I must make a visit over to Kensington. I must tell a woman to get the hell out of my life. She's young and has a child and she's getting too involved. And I can't go down to Bob's any more for a while. There's a woman there, too, I mustn't see any more. I've helped her. I taught her to understand music. I always try to help."

She sat down with him while he had his tea on the couch by the window. He sat talking about his life, various ideas that crossed his mind. He wished he had time to study: he must marry. He had sent a check for some shoes he had not received. In his old job, a firm had sent him a present which he had sent back. He still regretted having taken that job; he had found out that the man in line for his job was a soak, but a good engineer; he had done what he could for the man. To drink was only a substitute for something that had failed, a proof of frustration: happy people didn't drink. The thing he hated in a manager's position, was that you had to sort out people who came for jobs, turn some away. All the time, he sat shrunk into a little chair, soft and young, his eyes no longer inflamed and starting, but large, quiet, full of light.

Suddenly he got up and coming to kneel beside Eliza, put his arms round her,

"Dear, dear Eliza; you give me peace."

He went back to his chair and prattled on, smiling. He must do this and that. The country walks must be pleasant now. Think that one evening, taking a long walk in a private forest, he had come to the end of the road and struck into the green grassy hillside and come to a mound and there a crowd of pheasants had risen screaming, their wings tearing the air up, the heavy bodies whirring. They were all round his head and he stood still with fright, expecting every gamekeeper within miles to be coming over and possibly taking potshots at him. But nothing happened; the perfect stillness returned. He had been just near the shallow grassy valley of Grimes's Graves by himself. He liked the country there. He liked that old, old England.

"Although now you can hardly cross the fields in some parts; the Americans have taken it up. An Englishman can't cross his own fields."

"Aye, we're quartered upon."

He leaned forward and rose again, stole over to the couch and once more knelt beside her, putting his arms around her. She held him to her until he became restless. The host of suppressed maternal feelings which had come back to her during the night rose, their wings whirred round her and she felt darkness; it became love. She let him go. He left her.

He started his remarks again. He must get a job and a girl in the country; all this would not do. He didn't mind if that was his fate; other people lived through it. What did Eliza think?

"Yes, you must. You can't go through such loneliness; you can't be alone when you're sick."

"Oh, I'm very strong. I'm very young. The Pikes are very young all their lives and live long. Uncle Simon looks sixty sometimes."

Eliza said, "I often wonder if I should go back to Bridgehead;

but I can't get over the fascination of London. It has life. Where can you get a cup of tea after six on Saturday in Bridgehead? In the back kitchen. Not even at the railway station."

"I never look at Bridgehead if I can help it. I just go to Hadrian's Grove and to the station. It reminds me of when we were all up there and how the people used to be. The women were kind to me, when I sold the party paper door to door. They'd listen to me; That's rait, it's true, hinny; or, Tha's rait, la'ad; but they looked as if they could hardly stand up; and it was only to please me very often, because they had lads of their own. They don't all even vote Labour, though it's a Labour stronghold. And when they took over the mines but compensated the noble owners, who had been compensated over and over again long before, the miners ran up a flag at their great victory."

Eliza flushed a roaring red, "Aye, but when I see it, I've got to take them by the necks and make them see it."

"They'll be socialists in the end, but they'll import it: they'll wait to see the rest of the world test it first: they're canny and cool."

"Then we need rabble-rousers, like George used to be," said she hotly.

"I'm not a zealot," said Tom meekly.

After a silence, he got up again and knelt by Eliza, letting her hold him while she liked, like a good son to his mother.

She kissed him and he said, "Eliza, I'll never forget a single minute of last night. I thought I was lying in bed with two pistons that throbbed and I thought, What am I doing in bed with two pistons? It was my thighs. I woke up, it was so unpleasant. I had one bad spot when I thought of you and a whole hour had gone; it was between five and six. You were asleep the whole time. Then I slept sweetly. I'll never forget. I couldn't go away today even if I felt all right. That is, if you want me here."

"Haven't you somewhere to go?"

"Well, if you don't mind, I must go over and have tea with a girl and come straight back. Nell wanted me to go and see Bob but I won't do it; I'll come back to you."

She made him lunch; he got ready to go and standing in the hall with him, she said in a troubled way, "You know, Tom, I've fallen for you! I'm not myself."

"I knew that," said Tom.

He opened his mouth wide and pressed it round hers.

She felt faint, "Eigh!" said Eliza.

He went with a clap of sound, closed the door. Eliza was busy with the house, then went for a walk. I like to breathe, Tom always said, I can live if I breathe. He was a mere boy.

A boy bending over his bike scooted past; his thin back looked like Tom's. Another boy coming down the opposite side of the road, nicely dressed for Sunday, shaved, the hairs down his neck gleaming, a clean collar, must be going to see his girl. There seemed to be streams of children in the streets, of ages from four to eleven, a tide setting towards the future, like a swarm of birds migrating in a wide open broad sky. She had not noticed them for years.

When Tom came back, he was full of beauty. She tried to fix for him a little red and blue waistcoat he wore and which had shrunk.

He took her hands and kissed them; "Dear Eliza! I hurried back."

She could not help smiling at him, to see how much at ease and natural he was in being loved. He understood women because he had been loved so much. She finished the sewing, fastened the wool, and he looked at himself in the glass.

"It's a funny little jerkin," she said.

But he didn't like that; "Marion made it for me. She could do anything. She could make a man's overcoat."

Nellie could not accommodate herself to Rome, though she fancied the Italians, a friendly people, who liked to spend a couple of hours before a half bottle of wine in a café, who would say anything to please, as she did herself, who were demonstrative and dramatic. But Nellie caught a bad cold the first night there and could not shake it off. George wore her out taking her to see the sights over the stony pavements. She had not the least interest in the river, the buildings, the galleries. So she came home to Eliza, Tom and Caroline.

"Eh, pet, London's a Rome, too, since the blitz. I see no difference."

She could only get tea in tea rooms for English tourists, used by a sort she was not used to.

And as for the language, "English is a world-wide language, you'd think they'd speak it. They cheat you, telling you everyone speaks English abroad. I felt like a foreigner. You'd think they would have got away from Latin long ago: it's a dead language. At school they told us that Italian is just a sort of Latin, a Latin that came through the army camps; and so is French. I don't understand why they use dog-Latin."

She could have had a job, but only as a typist in George's office; and she didn't want that grind. There were other things; but she never said them all.

"I didn't think I could stick it and told George I'd go home, if he'd try to get a job at home. He said he would and he saw me off very affectionately."

He had given her the house in her name, though it meant she would be responsible if he did not return; but he wanted her to have a roof over her head. He would try to send her money.

"I always said that where George was, there was me fatherland; but it proved me wrong. Ah, George is very active there; but they won't see his point of view; they're feather-bedded, asleep, smothered in tradition. And would ye know, the lively ones want to get away to South America, or anywhere. They don't like it either."

She had to get a job; she worried about the house. Perhaps Tom could get a London job and live there. They could all look after him. Eliza said she could give up her little room with her Irish friends: they could easily let it to one of the Irish workers who are always coming in.

Nellie was delighted. She said joyfully, "Eh, it will do George good to hear his Eliza is back again. Why shouldn't you find refuge in his house? In our house? It'll be lovely to have the family together again, with you and Tom."

Eliza smiled.

Nellie coaxed. "Would you mind Tom around? He's harmless, the lad."

Eliza said, "Don't call him harmless: that's wrong of you. He's a fine working man; he had three hundred men under him at the last place and here he'll have eighty and a gang of twelve fitters and they're relying on him for everything for two factories. Why do you always paint him as daft?"

Nellie opened her eyes; she said gently, "Well, no, pet; it's just me way of speaking."

"Tom's a fine lad. You're lucky to have so good a brother. I've got to know him while you were away and I see you've just been carrying on the family story. Bridgehead is a queer place. The women sit around backbiting the men and the men take it."

Nellie said, "So the lad's been here?"

She began to make enquiries about him, where and how long and when.

"And I thought him safely tucked away at Bob's for the weekends. Ah," she said philosophically, "Ah, he's cunning; he's been playing on your maternal heartstrings, lass. He's a great lad for the older women. I'm afraid I formed him to obey an older woman and that's what he's looking for, the sister to the brother; and I'm afraid it's not been for his good."

Eliza said firmly, "You're no good, running a man down for your own vanity. I won't listen to it, Nellie; you'd better know right off. I have the greatest respect for the man and I love him, too."

"Well, that's all right, chick, he's a fine fellow, and he's me brother. He's got a great way with him; he's very taking; and there's no real harm in him. Ye've seen life, you have your experience of men and the poor lad will be grateful to you: he's so lonely. He makes contacts with reality, he can't make a go of it. It's a terrible injustice, a punishment for the sins of the fathers: it's not his fault, Eliza, but he has caused suffering and misery. He's ruining homes and mischief-making all around, and it's all a shadow show, pet. Ah, don't speak to me about it: it's a sore spot in me heart. Bless ye, pet, bless you."

She smoked her cigarette hard and smiled at Eliza.

"Will ye come here, then, chick and share George's roof with me? That's good of you, Eliza. The hard time's coming for me, I'm afraid. George made his handsome promises, but I'm not sure it wasn't to speed the parting guest. And he's given me the house, which is good of him, too, but it has a resemblance to a division of the estate. I know it, but I said nothing: for after all, he may lose the job and then he'll have to come back to his home, and so I'm glad to have it. I'm not a fist at business, Lize, but I'm going to make a will and I'm going to leave the house to George and then to you. You're getting on, Lize, you're a hard-worked woman. I've seen you at it ever since we were young people; and what future is there for us when the poor old horse has done his day? Who can live on the old-age pension? You've got nowhere to go; I know ye, you'll not live on others. You're the salt of the earth and I can't help thinking about you, chick: I love you, Eliza! I've got nothing else so I'm leaving it to you, chick. I made up me mind on the train; George first, for it's his, or ours, and then you: there's no one else in the world means a jot to me."

"That's not quite right," Eliza said, "I wouldn't rob anyone, Nellie. Do what's right, but don't forget your own family. The Pikes are a very loyal family."

"My own family!" said Nellie bitterly. "I can't begin to tell you and I won't, but I've been betrayed over and over again only by my own family. They deserve nothing of me. I've killed my-self ever since I was sixteen working for them and they sit up there talking about how ungrateful I am that I'm not going straight there, now that I've lost me husband. There's only Peggy that I give a damn for and she's a lost soul; aye, it must have a dark end. That's all. I need you, chick, and you owe it to me. We'll damn George's eyes together."

She laughed and getting up patted Eliza on her plump back. "Forgive me for a quick temper, chick! I've got the sun in me blood, chick! I never could stand the climate. It's the wrong time to go to Italy and George looks like a boiled lobster half the time, but he insists he likes it and he's got himself up in pleated shirt-fronts and colored ties: he'll be wearing a silk band round his waist next and dancing the tarantella. He's got the sun in his blood and spots before his eyes, the bugger. Eh, but it's a pleasure to see him blooming. A shower bath of Chianti daily, too, me dear: it's worth it I suppose, but I tramped me feet off thirsting for an English cup of tea and I was disappointed, I expected to see the Mediterranean laid out before me. I'm not one for monumental bric-a-brac and I can get an eyeful of blasted masonry here in old London if I want it. My idea is to spend a blissful morning on a café terrace tasting me tea and letting the world go by. Come, I'll take ye abroad in the autumn, to see your wandering George, Eliza, what do you say? I'll spend the last of me savings on it."

She put her arms round Eliza and hugged her, "Bless you, Lize, you're the girl for me! You'll come and keep me company and we'll have high old times."

Eliza questioned whether she wasn't likely to get a job in Geneva if George tried for her: they said it was quite cold there in winter.

"No, no," said Nellie: "it's their world—they made it, I don't feel right living on the crust. It's England for me, England without George hey-ho."

She said George had paid everything for her and bought her a blouse, and she herself had brought a blouse and a necklace for Eliza, knowing she had a weakness for them, "Aye, I've got a fat woman's love for gewgaws," said Eliza. "I like striped clothes that make me look wider and tight shoes and trinkets: I'll be the circus fat lady in a year or two."

Nellie rushed in and got the blouse, which had in fact stripes on it, and a handful of cheap jewelry, like a handful of berries. "Take your pick, take it all, chick, if you want it."

Eliza chose and Nellie insisted upon her putting on the blouse and the jewelry immediately. She helped her, pulled the blouse this way and that; it needed perhaps a stitch in the back where it was cut too large, but the embroidery in front was nice: "It shows me red neck," said Eliza.

"You've got a beautiful firm woman's flesh and that's all," said Nellie. "You're shy, chick: it's a pleasure to see a shy woman."

They had a jolly time and Nellie insisted upon getting some beer and lemonade to make Eliza her favorite drink, "Bridgehead shandy." On top of that they had some cognac which

George had sent home and they took their chairs out into the back yard to doze and chat. They slept together in the big bed downstairs that night, so that they could have a "glorious long chat" and Eliza was persuaded to give notice to the family she was living with, for that day next week, "or sooner, if they have someone; your home's here, Eliza. A sweeter woman ne'er drew breath than George Cook's girl Elizabeth. You've cheered me up so much, Eliza, I never thought I could be happy again. There must be something rare in the Cooks. It must have been you in your George that drew me to him first, for he was a fine martinet when I met him in a class of his. The next time I saw him he was giving someone a black eye in a street struggle. There's little of your sweetness about him, Eliza."

"And I think," said Eliza, "there's something rare in the Cotters: you're both wonderful, you and your brother. I don't wonder you love Tom."

After a meditative pause, Nellie said, "Poor lad, he's like a child playing with things he doesn't understand, releasing terrible forces: like a child that opens a sluice and lets the flood waters pour through. It's imitating me. I've got myself to blame. I meant to ask you before pet, but I felt bashful, but now we're friends and going to be housemates, we'll be real pals and I have confidence in you, I can trust you. Ye've seen a lot of cases of sickness, Lize, would you know a skin condition if you saw it or heard about it? Now I've been worried about the lad, he's got a skin covered with red spots, what do you think it is? Would it be a nervous condition, or would it be in the blood?"

"He's very tired, it's just a heat rash; anxiety," said Eliza.

"Aye, would it be? Did he mention it?"

"Yes, he showed me," said Eliza.

"The lad's born for misfortune, an unlucky star shone on his cradle: he was a canny—" She stopped and double-tracked, "Aye, a man's reasons are his own; he's caused too much tragedy already. I'm glad he's leaving the marriageable women alone and that he's made his confession to a sensible woman whose sorrows are over and done with. Am I boring you, Eliza? Am I treading on delicate ground, chick? I'm a bloody fool if I hurt you. Eh? you're a working-class girl, Lize, not one of these bloody bourgeois; I feel at home with you. We can talk and never get goose-flesh. You're a real friend and you can only have one real friend. I feel it in you. I love you, Eliza pet. That makes it all even, doesn't it? Do you forgive me chick? I didn't tread on your corns?"

"Why?" said Eliza frankly. "Because you said I'm getting on? I am getting on. I'm thirteen years older than you and twenty years older than Tom. I remember it. I let my head and my heart both have a go, that way they're healthy and keep a respect for each other. I fell for Tom, he's a dear lad, he could be my son but I fell for him like a girl and love him, that's the truth. It's my old age, Nellie; I never thought it would happen to me. I thought it was a bourgeois weakness, as you'd say. It's a hopeless love, he can't marry me and I'm not free. I have someone, and if I were free he wouldn't have me, and I couldn't have him. Would I be going out and having people looking at us and then asking us with a lark in their eyes, How is your nephew, or your son? I'd have more self-respect, though perhaps he wouldn't; for my boy Tom is an angel, he has no feelings but kind ones. He'd do anything for a woman: and I'd do anything for him."

"Your boy Tom," said Nellie, thoughtfully, looking at Eliza. "Bless you, darling."

She smoked a bit and remarked, "Aye, he's a fine lad, the poor lad. He should have had better luck. Or maybe he's better as he is. He would have cut a wide swathe; his victims would have stretched from Moscow to Peru. He's walked on hearts to where he'll be now, the wailing spirit of the Brecklands."

"He's just a plain workingman, like many another," said Eliza indignantly. "He's honest and true."

"Not so plain, chick, not so honest." And Nellie continued to smoke; "He's got a lot of his mother in him. She was a wily old spider sitting there in the glimmer of the hearth, a helpless complaining little body and drawing it all out of you, word by word, question by question, getting behind you. She made him what he is, afraid of his own shadow, starting at every word, full of deceit and shamming. Aching for love, for she never had a true love, the poor body: and he learned that of her too. He was always mother's boy. She adored him, Eliza; it was pitiful. She groveled before him, as she did before every man of her own. We're a pathetic breed, believing in the men, groveling before them: it's a pitiful sight. When he came into the house from his playing on the moors, his boyish tricks, she'd be after him. Do you want this, love; can I do this for you, hinny? He couldn't bear the house on Sundays because of the smell of cooking; whatever she thought the men would like, pies, and joint and two veg. as they say; the soup and the gravy, the puddings and the dumplings. It made him sick. Give me bread, I'm a plain man, he said: but she couldn't understand it, the love. The weekend had to be a family feast; it was all she had to look forward to. So you can see how it is that now he says, All I ask is to be let alone, I'm a man who is better alone. Give me bread and tea and a lonely walk and I'm myself again. I'm afraid it's like Uncle Sime he'll end up."

"He says he was starved as a child," said Eliza, "and I know it's true; don't I know Bridgehead?"

"Aye, but did you ever meet a boy who wasn't starved?" said Cushie. "I wasn't starved, for I had more to think about; but Tom was always a vapid thing. The boy will do anything to get immediate satisfaction, and then he forgets it like a young dog. He's good at promising and he knows how to promise more with a look than a word."

"I'm not a mad, old woman," said Eliza, "I know he's looking for a job and a girl and that is right and I'm for it."

Cushie asked her, "You'll forgive me won't you, pet, treading on your feelings. I'm sorry, sweetheart. I don't do it to hurt you. I don't want you to be taken in by an angel-faced lad. He's black, Eliza, as black as me; we were in the tar pits, all that Jago corruption together. We thought it was knowledge, darling! What the bourgeois was afraid to do, we did."

Eliza said, "I didn't hear of this Jago circle till I met you and Tom again in London; and then Tom said nothing: hard liquor and dope, he said, and ignorant adolescents playing at vice. There may have been such goings on among the people I knew but I never heard of it. My sisters and I had to scrub, wash and sweep from children; and when I got political ideas from George, or we both got them together, I don't know which, I electioneered and pamphleteered, and did everything they asked me including washing the floor of the hall and knocking planks together and holding the horse's head while they were waiting for the procession to begin to the Town Moor, because my father was a brewery drayman, and I knew about horses. I went out in the usual Bridgehead weather, and my mother graduated from a shawl to a cheap overcoat and felt she was getting on in life, and that's all I know about it. I never would have credited that there was a lot of youngsters getting boozed up, or smoking doped cigarettes or whatever it was you did. What, in Bridgehead?"

"You're right there. And it was a scarlet on the gray that Jago tried to patch. I'm not blaming him. He was only a Bridgehead man; he probably thought he was bringing a little London to our doorsteps. He was forty, Violet says, and it was a shame. But I say, poor human being, he was fighting a pitiful struggle against frustration and failure. He wanted to be a painter, but whoever was an artist on the Tyne? So his bent and twisted impulses tried to create something in us."

"I have no use for devils," said Eliza.

"You're hard and passionate—you're unforgiving. I can't help but pity. Tom is like you; you are both stern angels. But I can't help putting the rosy veil of pity over their pitiful human weakness. I see their struggles. I forgive them. There's good stuff in everyone. Judge not, for the stern judge is a criminal: he does not take into account the terrible struggles: he is sacrificing to the Baal of his selfish pride."

"We all have struggles. I don't think a criminal struggles more than another."

"Eh, we don't know! And it's the weakness of the criminal that asks for our pity. It's like punishing a blind man for his blindness."

Eliza was quiet for a while.

"Well," enquired Nellie timidly, "do you think there's a chance for us, Eliza? Can we be pals?"

"We are," said Eliza.

"I don't mean that, chick, I mean real friends. Do you trust me?"

"Yes."

"You believe in me, chick? You don't think badly of me?"

"Why, you're wonderful Nellie: I've seen your struggles for years. I've never known a better woman. You've overcome sickness and disappointment and with such courage: you'd be wonderful in a resistance movement, I've been thinking. You're the stuff of a hero."

"Bless you for that, I'll never forget it," said Nellie, getting up and coming over to her. "I have to kiss you for that, let's have a good long hug, darling: eh, what it is to find a true woman."

When she came away she stood against the door looking down at her friend, her tall slender body bent like a seahorse, with the tuft and the nose and with a wild sly bright eye; and she smiled with diffident charm.

"I'm afraid I'm imposing on you, Eliza, you're so good. Perhaps ye don't want to live with me."

"I do, though."

"Ye're not offended chick with my ideas about—about Jago, you know."

"I've always had the thought," said Eliza, "that hunger is a greater passion than love; and I've been surprised not to hear them talk about the distortions produced by hunger, the sublimations and disguised forms of hunger. It's a primitive need, you can live without all but food." She laughed. "So it must take very diverse forms in us, especially in a childhood and youth of semi-starvation. When you see all about you twisted and starved and when they enquire into your bellies and send visitors to look at your kitchens—So Jago played on your hunger and I don't blame you."

"Oh, no, pet," said Nellie flicking her cigarette, "man does not live by bread alone. I'm sorry but I can't agree, Lize. No, he wasn't playing on our hunger. He gave us a big spread. That was one of the attractions. We'd go there for the food when we were just hungry chicks. No, he understood that there were bigger impulses working up in us and great aspirations. It was the intellectual hunger, we all felt. It was a great hunger. We went everywhere looking not for food, but for guidance and for knowledge. You see we couldn't find any of it at home. And Jago understood us: he was the only one that did. We went to the Communists and they said, Study, read the history of socialism, learn how society is composed and work for a future society. But I said to the district organizer, What is the meaning of death and hunger? Have you got some words so that I can explain that to a poor mother? Hunger, desertion and death are too stark for words! Your pals, I'm sorry to say Eliza, did not understand us at all. They treated us a bit like pickpockets. In fact, I think they would have preferred pickpockets. They would have been able to work on them. But they couldn't work on us so easily for we were damned serious. It was spiritual hunger."

"We just had no education," said Eliza, "and it was a vague struggle for education and it was a lively time, those days: but don't argue for them. We just couldn't get along on humblepie and humbug, but that's all we knew."

"I don't agree with you, pet," Nellie closed hastily. "We'll have many a good evening wrangling it out. We'll have a grand time, chick. We won't repine. As long as you can stand me, Lize. As long as I'm not boring you."

The evenings were long and light. One time when Nellie strolled home just before the closing of the pubs, though there was no light in the house, she heard voices and one of the voices sounded like George. She turned her key softly in the door and came in listening.

In the front room George was shouting, "Nothing's going to stop me! I've found out what I wanted. I'm only fifty. I know I can. I know I will. I can pick and choose now: they're begging me to accept. I'm going to Geneva. I'm fixed! What do you think of that, Bob?"

"What about the job here? You had one in view!"

"They'll have to get along without me."

"They'll find it's not the same," said Bob with her sea-gull laugh.

Nellie leaned against the front door, with her eyes closed. She had not been feeling well for a long time; she had not eaten all day.

George roared with laughter, "Come on, now," he commanded, "get me some more of that divine coffee, Bob. You taught me about coffee: I owe a lot to you. I'll never forget. I must have my coffee black. Oh, the wonderful coffee you get in Italy. I'm a European bureaucrat now. Flawless service is what I get."

"Take some brandy instead," said Bob.

Nellie heard the drink being poured and she thought this was what she needed.

She glided to the doorway. "Hello, chicks! I heard you, George. I heard your news chick, because I was at the door, though I could have heard it if I'd still been in the tube. Hello, Bob darling! I'm heartily glad to see you, pet."

She kissed the old woman who was sitting against the wall, smoking and drinking brandy. George had a brandy glass half full and was tossing the liquid round in the glass between his two large rosy hands.

"Give me that," said Nellie, reaching for the glass, but George said, "Get your own, I'm warming this."

Nellie laughed, "I'll drink from the bottle! Don't let me interrupt your tête-à-tête. A nip and then I'll just make meself a cup of tea: and then I'll be in to join in the rejoicings. Hand the bottle there, can't you spare a drink for a pal." She began to rally, the light began to gather in her face. "You're a pal, George! Cognac! Ye lucky bloody sod, George, with fair dames plying you with three-star and your ould wife plying her trade along the pavements and in every dirty damp harbor round Britain. I sound like an ould streetwalker and I couldn't be worse off if I was."

"Cognac and tea don't go," said George: "I've learned my manners. You'll be sick."

"With me, it'll go, sweetheart. Don't worry about me. I can drink ax heads pickled in methyl and take a chaser of the black bilge by Armstrong's, but I still need me tea to make me sleep sweetly. But nothing today will wash the taste out of my neck of your going back. It's bitter; but I didn't expect honey. What'll happen to your old wife, George, now you're fixed? What the hell, I don't care! Aye, I care! It hurts and it aches, but I won't try to stop you. How are ye, Bob pet? How is the pottery? How is the farm, pet? You'll be a saint if you take in a tired old grass widow one of these days for a rest. I'll have to take a weekend off."

Bob was sitting hunched over herself, her blue eyes looking very strange through her thick glasses, her white and black streaked hair pulled tight over her large skull. Her thick, aging skin was smooth and yellow-brown from exposure, and the solid bones stood out, making an impressive mask. She looked straight at anyone when she spoke, with disturbing effect.

"You'll be welcome, Cushie," said she harshly, looking at Nellie.

Nellie laughed and tossed her shoulders. "Ah, bless ye, thank ye," she muttered uneasily and turned to George, "So it's fixed up, you've got a new job? That's a nice thing to hear. It's a bloody runout powder you're taking. You know you could work here at home."

"But at home I'd have you and I'm trying to get rid of you, Cushie." George was in great humor. "You don't get the point; you're the burr in the sheep's back. I could have such a whale of a good time without you."

"George, you oughtn't to say that," protested Bob.

"But I mean it. I've been trying to lose the woman for years and this is my big chance." He leaned back, picked up his glass of brandy and held it up before him tipping it to his face and sucking at it. "More, varlet! At once, melord! Make it snappy! Ding-ding-dong! melord."

"Mr. George Cook, late of the working class," said Nellie. "Aye, he's a typical old socialist, trying to be glorious at the expense of the workers. I despise you, George Cook: the back of me hand to you. Did you struggle your way up from the docks of Tyneside for this pitiful glass of brandy?"

"I did," cried George. "A worker's a figment to you, Nellie; it's a schoolgirl dream. It's a vague, dirty, hungering man, weak and a failure: someone for you to mother and maunder over. You're just a plain Fleet Street sobsister."

"That's a bloody lie, you bastard," cried Nellie, springing up, "I won't sit at the table with you; you're on the way over to the other side."

George bellowed with laughter. "But you sit at table with every ex-I.R.A. sellout, who'll hand you a dishful of workman romance. Ah, the British sods, the murderers of the Irish people: what can ye do? Ye must write tripe to fill your unworthy belly and ye must write the tripe they want, the poor beggarly Sassenachs living on king and country, for they know no better. I'm no traitor, I'm just an Englishman who wants to represent his country abroad. In the old days it was the young lords and the promising young scholars and now it's the worker from Blaydon way."

"Why, Nellie, must we shoot the bolts on our own jail-door? He's right. The rich still go abroad: it's only the poor that stay. It's a class law," said Bob, looking pinpoints at Nellie through her pebbles.

"Ah, don't flatter the sod," cried Nellie: "ye can't give him enough: he'll be hungry for more, whatever ye say. It's a fine figure, the self-elected Atlas holding up England abroad. It's not for the wine then you're going? It's for your principles, ye sod? It's a damn disgrace. Deserting your country for the sake of a meal."

"Why doesn't my country offer me a square meal?" said George angrily. "I'm a big man, I'm not a half-starved sparrow. I've worked all my life: I've fought for my class. It's a rule in demonstrations that after you've got in some good hits, you step aside or get off to some other area, you don't waste yourself: you keep yourself so you're there next time."

"I'd a damned sight rather waste myself than make a show of myself as a runaway." But Nellie couldn't find words bad enough to characterize this excuse.

Bob said it was a time when not only individuals but masses of people were driven from their countries or sought refuge for their own sakes in other countries: there seemed to be no end to it, then.

But Nellie repeated that George was hauling down the flag, betraying his class and turning his back on his life of struggle.

"If all Englishmen had stayed home, true to their dear sod," George said with irony, "I should like to know where the Empire would have come from, that's kept us in sugar and tea? We don't grow it ourselves, that I know of."

"You're avoiding the personal point with your grand comparisons," said Nellie.

"And you're trying to drag everything down to the personal plane like you," shouted George. George was angry. "And you're helping them. You're helping your lords and masters by talking a lot of frill about patriotism. Whose country is it? Whose pound sterling is it? Whose indebtedness is it? Whose empire is it? Whose revenues are they? Am I going to lose my eyes and hair and get to be like your Uncle Sime, old scrap nobody wants, and everyone spits on, to save their England? Or to save Cotters' England?"

"What do you mean by Cotters' England?" she cried out. "What's wrong with my England?"

"The England of the depressed that starved you all to wraiths, gave Eliza TB, sent your sister into the Home, got your old mother into bed with malnutrition, and is trying it on with me, too, getting at my health. I never had an ache or pain in my life: I beat their England. I lived through the unemployment, the starvation, the war, I knocked out a few bloody eyes and I got me fists skinned a few times, that's all I ever got: and now I'm going to live for my country. You stay here and die in it. Don't you want to change it? Or is it only the beer-soaked sawdust of bohemia you love? The dirt and sweat of the tear-stained bachelor's bedroom; Bridgehead in all its glory? You don't know what you're fighting for. To change Cotters' England. Wasn't that what drove you on? Or just ragged rebellion?"

"You're a bloody Cook's Tours, that's all you are," said Nellie; "you've got your spoon into the fleshpots; dear old Bob introduced you to it without knowing what it would do to you, it was the grand maternal impulse in the dear old elf; and now the smell of the ragout is all you can think of."

George was irate and humiliated to be slanged so before another woman. He got up, stretched, turned to Bob smiling, under the light, a magnificently built middle-aged man, tall, broad, brass-faced, brass-haired, very red now; and in the cour-

[216]

teous and even unctuous manner he could assume, he said he must go to call on Mrs. McMahon who had been lovely to him and written such kind letters.

Nellie was leaning against the mantelpiece, her arms akimbo, the glass held on her hip, her hair loosed from its turban and her bony cheeks caved in. She had lost weight again and seemed only snowy skin and long bone. She looked at the grate, threw the end of her cigarette into it, looked up at George, dashed tears from her eyelashes and said, "Me sun has set." She looked at Bob and remarked, "There's only selfishness there, the man's heartless: he's leaving me."

"Well, I'm not leaving you till I can get my plane ticket," said George. "Relax, I'm going out. Sorry Bob, I'll see you soon." He went out, whistling, banged the door.

"You see," said Nellie, "his fine, rough, common sense? The man's hard as steel. Now he's going to torment Gwen McMahon, a poor dame who thinks his love is to her, when it was only to his pots and carpets." She sank into a chair and lighted another cigarette. "Give me a glass of brandy, Bob. Ah, sweetheart, I'm not very brave, I'm afraid. Give me a fortnight and I'll swim to the surface. And I am going to fight for him, though I hate to fight. I'm weak. I don't like to fight with my sweethearts." She burst into tears. "No one is really for me. They all think he is going to leave me. I've always known it myself. And when I stand up to him, it's with terror. I'm afraid of that bald blind look of total Philistine intolerance. He hasn't been making love to you, Bob?" she said in a weak voice.

"No, he's not my sort," croaked Bob.

Nellie hardly listened to the answer. She went on, shaking out her ashes, "I'll not sleep tonight, either way. And for once he must stay up with me. Ah, darling, love's an incurable disease, and I've got a bad case. The bugger's got me beat: but you'll see me fighting a grand retreat. You're staying the night, sweetheart? Ah, do, pet: but you know you're always expected."

When George returned, Nellie said, "You can put on your pajamas, George, but you're not going to get any sleep. You've had enough sleep at your desk in Rome, me fine lad. You're going to have it out with me: I'm going to pull the woman act. You're not deserting me without a whimper, I'm not going to be the heroine. I'm going to fight for you."

George wore a reflective smile. He sat down and said, "Where's Bob?"

"Bob's upstairs: she's going to bed."

"I feel like a cup of tea with Bob," said George, who seemed thoughtful and mild.

"No, pet, I'll make it and we'll drink the pot out."

She brought it in presently and found George halfdressed. She sat down opposite and said sweetly, "George, when I married you, I looked upon you as the glory and success of my life, sweetheart, my laurel wreath." She implored him, "George, are you going off to leave me lonely, a wandering woman of forty, fighting by myself?"

"There's a hole in my right sock again," said George, looking at his foot. "It's the toe I stubbed on the table. The doctor said, That'll never grow straight again: you'll have it for the rest of your life. How did he know that at once?"

"I've darned your others: you've got fresh."

"It stops me from going barefoot or wearing sandals," said George, "women used to admire my feet."

"Admired your feet now," cried Nellie, "you beggarly provocateur!"

"Well, if I'm in for it, I may as well enjoy myself," said George.

"I intend to run you ragged, you bugger," said Nellie.

George walked up and down for a while. She tormented him. The bed invited his glowing body over which the hot dusk and lethargy had already come. Her ability to tease and stir was the hold she had over him. Once, too, he had thought her very beautiful in a unique way, strange, shaking with mysterious bells and corollas like an oriental tree, shivering with sunstreaks, racing with windrips from within. He still saw these almost invisible movements in her. His eyes were closing and her darings and trillings, her ingenuous and disingenuous ways, lovely voice and queer oaths, all the practiced art came to him, blew round him, lulled him and made him laugh: and then she would wake him up with a buffet, with sting and roaring in his eyes and ears. He laughed, shouted, sulked and falsely snored; and he did sleep, too.

"I'll give it to you," she cried. She made pots of tea; the night wore away.

At last he said, "I'm getting out of here. I'm going to sleep upstairs!"

"There's nowhere to sleep—Bob's in one room, Johnny's got another reserved for her and Eliza has hers. Caroline's in the attic. You can't go there."

George went out into the backyard where the cool early morning air woke him. There was an immense beach of sky to the east on which were thousands of little sand-colored clouds and the light blue air was swimming off it: and yet it was only half past three. Bob had said, "You must take care of Nellie, it is your duty: she is going to pieces, her moral and mental health is going." What moral health? George had laughed at this, "Nellie always was a bohemian. She can't be shipwrecked in Bohemia." Bob was herself a bohemian: "What's wrong with Bohemia?"

"I couldn't stand it," George had said; "I hate it."

"It's the way out for many people, it's the way they pick up an education."

"Yes, but Nellie's a prisoner of Bohemia. She won't grow. When I met her she was in it and promised to get out: she never got out."

"Take her with you," said Bob, "and she'll have to get out. Take her away from the weeds growing over the ruins. Even Nellie will have to change."

"If I only thought she could grow—" But George didn't think so. She not only wanted to stay in Cotters' England, or Bohemia as he saw it, but she wanted him to stay there, too. "It's like asking someone to stay in a bad place in fairyland: I'm no fairy." George had thought as he said it and caught Bob's gimlet glance, that Bob looked very like a bad fairy.

Now when he came inside to Nellie, he said, grinning, "The roof looks sunken. Let it fall in and even you will see I can't stay."

[219]

"I'd love it if it were only a heap of bricks and rags," said Nellie. "People lived in such places in the blitz, and lived through it and are Englishmen today."

George laughed. "She's hopeless! By the way, Nell," he said sitting down and taking a pull at the fresh pot of tea, "who's this friend of yours, Caroline? There's an attractive woman."

Nellie was quiet for a while, looking at the tea table and swinging a foot, gentle and earnest looking.

George got up and began sorting books again. "I'll sell the Italian dictionary," he said, "now I won't have to learn that; I wasn't good at it. I had a lovely girl to teach me, too. You should have seen the old wolf in the pension when I brought her in. He told the boys at the table, You should see what the Englishman picked out, *bellissima ragazza!* She was a University graduate, a doctor, and too timid to name a price for her lessons. She said I could name the price at the end of the first series. She lived with her family in the new flat houses that were put up after the war and she was rather ashamed of them, because workmen lived in them too. At first I went to a class and in front of us, all middle-aged people, was one of the most beautiful women in the world, a glorious deep-limbed blonde, her flesh just flowed from her waist to her feet, and her feet only touched the ground gently. Her hair curled and flowed on her shoulders: she had long flowing cheeks and neck. She was writing simple things on the board and I thought she was learning her lesson before the teacher came. Who is the teacher, I asked her. I was in the front row. I am the teacheress, she said. She had no stockings. She came to teach me privately and we had conversations at which I was no good, but I asked her questions. She told me she can't marry because she has no dowry. She is middle class and cannot marry a worker. She didn't seem to think the young men were cads: she didn't want to reform them. I said to her, What a shame! I couldn't tell her she was so beautiful that it seemed to me she'd only have to walk down the street in any capital in the world and have men at her feet: for there she was in Rome where they have a sense of beauty. And I couldn't say the words to her: she was too glorious, not merely beautiful. I looked at her and felt the air rushing down my nose and throat; I couldn't get any words out. I worked very hard for her. I never tried to make her. I never made her a compliment. I couldn't. I felt ashamed for men. You know how the young Italians walk about all the time in Rome, up and down, doing nothing. She told me they are waiting for a dowry. When I had to leave just now, I asked her how much and she timidly named a price for the whole series of lessons which was just enough for one pair of nylon stockings. I gave her twice that; I couldn't give her more. She asked me if I would drop her a postcard. She said she knew I was married; but just to get a postcard sometimes from an acquaintance. She said she was so lonely. She was a teacher. She had to teach Americans and refugees: they made silly talk, rough camp gallantries with her. She would just pass it over."

"She seems to have made a hit," said Nellie dryly, but ruminating.

"You can't believe that a woman can be so beautiful that you are very far from thinking of her for yourself," said George, looking at Nellie loftily.

"Yes, I can see she was," said Nellie, mildly.

"If you fell for a woman like that, you would be under for life; I would be a different man. It would be a way of having a new life and being someone else, of course," said George thoughtfully. "I couldn't love her. She is too good for me: she is better than me."

"I wish I had a record of those words," said Nellie unwinding her legs, smoking and looking at George, "because no one will ever believe you said them. I like you, pet: you're a good man. If travel can do that for George Cook, it can do anything. I wish I knew your—what was her name?"

"*La bellissima ragazza,*" said George, smiling loftily. Nellie flushed. George smiled, "In the pension they wondered how the devil I picked out a girl like that. Just my luck. An accident. I'm lucky with women."

"Are ye, ye devil?" said Nellie, frowning and flushing. "I won't have ye pulling my leg, now stop it." She sprang up. "Now listen to me, George. You're not going to keep playing fast and loose with me. Your Ragazza is lucky she got away, but where you're going you'll soon be playing round with another. I won't have it. You all cause tragedy. All of you. You're a race of satanic inventions set on women. Do you know what is the matter with Caroline? She's sick of heartache, she's sick of loneliness, she's sick of a man, or of men, just as surely as a poor pitiful waif of a street girl."

"He dropped her?" enquired George. "Some men are fools."

"Of course, he was a cruel bloody tease; they all are. I know the trouble and the suffering, but what words can be used to communicate with the soul in agony? She thought she was loved. Love is a word I hate because of the way it's mauled. The man was a coquette, George, and she wasn't. The coquettes are happy people. They can live bluffly in a hard world and they're hard. But she is so soft and gentle as a lamb. Aye, I am tender with her; and so I am with your sweet, sainted Eliza; that woman, George, you don't appreciate her, she's full of hope like the morning star—"

George's face opened with astonishment; then "Haw-haw-haw," he began, "Eliza's maybe like the planet Mars, but the morning star—"

"You don't appreciate her, George, she's a sweet angel, and she is angelically soft to Caroline, we all are, all the women." Her voice dropped. She said sadly, "She can't see who are her friends. She has been twisted. Our voices don't reach her mind. She is unable to love anyone after all but herself and that makes her untrue to mankind: it's a frightful thing," her voice rose now, "to put your faith in a heartless man!"

"Pip!" said George. "I'm going back to bed. If we're going into this!"

"You stay here! You stay here! What have you done to this Italian girl? You don't know. Caroline could not believe at first. Yes, but not to me, she thinks: they don't know. *But wha could think sae o' Tam Glenn?* She wrote poems: who cared about them? She just heard no, no, no, on every side, and at first for years she couldn't believe she was cheated, betrayed, turned down and laughed at by cruel calculating coquettes. For what is all mankind but coquettes when you're looking for simple human affection? Some, when they find out what you want, turn rascal and call in others to see the fun, sticking pins into a human heart; it makes them angry to see someone simply suffering and they try to beat the heart and kill it some way or another."

"Ugh," said George, "I did nothing with the Italian girl. I've told you the truth. I not only respected her, she stopped me. She may have been a simple girl but she looked like a goddess."

"And where is she now? What is she thinking now?"

"How do I know?" roared George.

Nellie sneered, "So Caroline couldn't catch her rascal and her heart's dead in a world of rascals."

"I thought she was a bit—twisted—" said George; "a neurotic."

"She'll be better than all of us. Because she'll see through it. I'll cure her."

"Poppycock! That's slush," said George.

"You won't believe! Believe in suffering, George; believe!" Nellie put up her bony arms and bony wrists and wiped her wet face. She cursed, lit another cigarette and went into an insupportable spasm of coughing. She leaned over the bed, flinging her arms and legs and head about and at length got up gasping.

"Excuse me, pet," said she, as soon as she caught her breath, "I'm sorry, pet, smoke and tea went the wrong way. I feel low myself, George pet. Wherever you go someone wants something from you. The bourgeois and the Philistines trampling on your feelings and labeling you. Life's a hard thing, an abomination. There's no hope in it. It's a great, seamy, crusted face looking up at you from underneath, you can't get away from it because you're treading on it, you need it to live on and you're treading on it, and whenever you look you see the great face with the lips; you hurry away to another spot and you see the great eyes neither animal nor human unwinking and you are afraid just the same to walk everywhere on the face of life. You wonder where there's a place for you on the face that's so watchful and whose thoughts you don't know. You strain to find out one of its thoughts, but it has nothing but an awful thinking about the good and the evil and it judges you. In a way the Philistines are closer to it than me, because they are glad to judge you too, and if they understand you it's with a hard knife to your brain. Ah, George," she said, "you're my judge! It's the things you say to me that count and nothing else. I turn my back on them all. What have I got to hold me here? Supposing I am predestined to commit a crime! You can save me. If you take me with you now, you are judging me, you let me off, you see. We don't know what has us in its hand. They are all rascals here. I haven't a friend. Let me follow you like Ruth. Put up with the ould wife. Perhaps she's your punishment. 'Instead of the cross, the albatross about his neck they hung.' Perhaps you committed a crime once, some poor girl died, you didn't even know it and I was your punishment. Take me with you George! I hate England. Take me away from it. Don't throw my life away. Don't put on the black cap when you look at me. I beg ye pet; can you turn me down?"

She went down on her knees, hobbled the short space across the floor and coming up between his knees, and taking his hands, with her queer ugly, fascinating face twisted into laughs and sobs, she looked up, kissing his hands. "Forgive me, George, I'm a damn histrionic bugger, I'm a bloody groveling fool, can ye leave your poor old wife?"

George bent down and lifted her up. He kissed her with tears in his eyes. "Of all the strange, queer, phoney fakes in the world," he cried, "I've surely got the prize. I'll try and get you a place there, Nellie. What makes you think I wouldn't? I don't know what all that means, your line; but I suppose it means something. Do you know what time it is? Now hustle round and get me some breakfast. You'll have to make your mind up on one thing! You'll have to learn to live without tea, tea, tea!"

"Eh, bless you, my darling," said Nellie; "there's nothing like a man for sanity. You set me straight. I'd go whirling wild without you. No one can hold me. I need you. It's been dreadful George without you, a disease. I've had the married moans but it's cured now. Wait till Eliza comes in. I'll tell her her George is a wonderful man. What a family! I love ye, pet. You'll never get another woman, George, to be such a fool about you."

George stretched himself out on the couch downstairs and began taking off the rest of his clothes. As soon as Nellie went to work he fell asleep, and slept heavily. When he awakened Eliza was there, back from work and George mentioned that

Nellie seemed very anxious to get abroad, he would never have thought it of her. And Eliza too, he found, had changed her opinion, she thought Nellie should join him in Geneva. George scratched his head when by himself. He had looked forward to his freedom but he had been sure that Nellie preferred England. He went on with his final plans and thought to himself that he would wait until he got settled into his job, when he would see things very differently. He would try to send money to Nellie, though that was a thing he hated to do, for he always imagined it as flying up to Bridgehead into Peggy's ever thickening roll.

Within a week he had left for Geneva. Nellie weeping and Eliza cheerful, saw him off at the airport. Eliza went back to her work; Nellie went home.

Camilla was sewing long lined curtains for a West End customer. Nellie sat with her. She had got her job back at the paper, though the office doctor had told her to get outdoor work, if she could. "It's only me bronchitis, doctor," were Nellie's words; "if you can't stand a bit of bronchitis, you can't be British." So she told Camilla now; and continued, "I'm afraid that with my figure I'm like the old advert of the fisherman with the cod on his back; that's me, man and cod together; and the codliver oil they want inside me. But I'm no invalid."

She sighed, jigged her cigarette, took a drink and continued, "My brother warned me that if I don't reform, read the beauty hints, get a perm and follow the fads, George will leave me. Do you see the nail varnish? I put it on for the airport. The first time, Camilla. I'm ashamed of what I'm doing for the man. And George says he's grateful to my brother. That's an example of the male trades-union, for they don't care for each other. No. Different types."

"And Tom's not like you."

Nellie sighed. "Eh, no darling, I'm afraid very different. He's a drifter, a ne'er-do-weel, a bit of a troglodyte, crabbed, sour; not like me. Good nature's my weak spot. Camilla, do you advise me to get a perm? Me hair's so brittle and thin from me bronchitis. But Tom says I must."

"Well, try one, once."

She sighed.

"Eh, I know. George insisted. But I don't get much pleasure out of looking like a fashionplate. In the marrow of me bones, I don't appreciate the compliments. I feel petty-bourgeois. I feel more myself in an old pair of pants a bit stiff with dirt. And it'd do George good to wear the same. Do you know, that when we're in bed in the act of love, I know that George is glad that we're pressing his pants underneath the mattress at the same time. Eh, the man with his political ambitions. Eliza saw me in Fleet Street the other day with a pair of gloves. It's for George, I said. Eh, darling, marriage is an incurable disease. Once you're bitten you carry the marks of it to your grave."

"You're both very sturdy: is it the Scots character in you?" asked Camilla.

"Well, I'm only half Scots. I came down here to conquer the capital and the capital conquered me and George too. And they with their soft still nice ways, make me feel odd man out and I think I cut a dash in Fleet Street; but perhaps they're just tolerating a Johnny Raw."

"I don't believe it. They need red blood."

"Ah, darling, that's kind. What I have done, I have done. I led the men out of Smithfield the day of the strike, me at their head. Come on, boys, I said, make up your minds, I'll take you out. And I did. And I got the men out at Covent Garden, one time I went there to report their discontent. Why do you dither? Make up your minds, I said, behave like your own masters. And they went out. I lost a Fleet Street job over that."

"Most journalists are not so downright."

"What I've got in me is something different."

She put her arms akimbo and began to flutter in her brilliant jaunty way, "And George is of that opinion, too; though I don't deserve it. They had hopes of me in Bridgehead. We'll hear of you, Nellie, said me boy friend and loved one, Solomon—he died and I left the place; I couldn't tolerate it—but down here I was out of me element. In Bridgehead they still ask, What is Nellie Cotter doing? But here they notice nobody. Everyone brings his wares to hawk in the capital. So I was not much more than a poor beachcomber, marooned, when George gallantly rescued me out of the street. Ah-ah, if he ever abandoned me, and I think it, I

[226]

shudder and think it—if he did, I could never forget that, nor have anything for him but love and gratitude. I often feared it. I said to myself, If he leaves me, if this is my brief summer, come the winter, I'll go and find a sandy island, stick me toes in the sand and write me book. It will be about a golden man; for at least there is one. I wish that he were here. I do wish it. I would flatter him to his heart's content. And he would find it but the bare bones of truth. Here he's away. I hinny and honey. When he's here I give him the rounds of the kitchen. The ceiling fell down twice, up there, in the very middle of a row. It's my fault though. He's so easy to arouse and I get a kick out of it. And that's why he left Eliza."

"Do you know what he told me, Nellie? About you."

"Come on, love, tell me. What did he say, the beggar? Come tell me. Ah, don't tease me."

Camilla laughed, "He said he never read poetry as a boy, he thought it eyewash, not for the working class, bourgeois weakness, even the Revolt of Islam, the first and only poem he read."

"Well, Shelley was a millionaire and a gentleman and went to Oxford. It is not for us! The poets are not us, Camilla! They are talking to themselves. No, but what did he say?"

"He said, When I fell for Nellie and it was spring, I saw the trees and the leaves on them for the first time. I said, Is it for me? The trees were just hanging out their little green rags. I saw a young thin tree over the edge of the rock dancing. I thought; I know what love is! I didn't know I didn't know! I couldn't forget it. And I imagined a tall, thin tree with thin branches and this tall, strong man underneath it, looking up into the branches with his sky-blue eyes."

"His sky-blue eyes! Just that."

She got up and kissed Camilla.

"To think he has it in him. And won't tell me."

Eliza was home on Wednesday afternoon for a half-holiday. She was doing Nellie's washing and ironing, Nellie having no time at all for herself. In mid-afternoon she made tea and called Camilla from her workroom to share it. Camilla said that she had not known at first that Eliza was George's first wife.

"There's no point in mentioning it: I'm not his wife now. And I respect Nellie. She's a grand woman."

Eliza said they were all from the same setting, knew each other as children.

"I've known Cooks all my life, his Ma and his brothers and sisters; and they're as they were before, living in Bridgehead back-to-backs and spending the weekends at the races and owing money to the little clothing clubs. But George had it in him. He was a choirboy till thirteen, then he read something and became an atheist. He joined the union, the party, the county library, evening classes, anything that was going, to get some polish; and then he went into the navy not so much for love of the sea as to get some education while getting pay. I know he's a bright man. I don't blame him. Now I'm fair, fat and fifty myself and I worked, but I didn't study and so I didn't get on much. I'm blaming no one but myself. You must study. He needed one like Nellie. She used to spend all her afternoons in the library at one time when she was about sixteen. You've no idea how they've changed from the Bridgehead lad and lass they were. They've changed each other, too. You should have seen her up there when she was fifteen and sixteen. She left school because it wasn't life she said. Some of us like George and me were at our jobs. Tom was still at school. She got big money, it seemed to us then, writing little bits for a paper; it seemed marvelous to us, her interviewing the nobs. She stood everyone drinks, she bought food, handed out cigarettes and beer. She was there spending her money, making a great show which impressed the youngsters; and others, too, were impressed, I can tell you. There was a man Solomon and others, political types, who expected big things of her. We'll hear from Nellie Cotter, they used to say. I wasn't close to the Cotters then; but I'd see her in real silk blouses and flashing a big sapphire ring she used to pawn every Wednesday when the pay was gone. She was rowdy with opinions she got out of books, perhaps; but for us they were her own; and she never agreed, always disagreed; and she put over her opinions with a lot of them, who were impressed. I didn't know. I did my work. She was not my type. But she made a big splash; and the youngsters there were so ignorant; and wanting to get out of it. She got in touch with Jago's circle and took others in. That was a pity. She was different then, bony and ugly and wild as a streetboy, ripping out the dirty oaths, with a great charm coming into the drawn lines of her face. Eigh, but that was away above our heads. It was George brought learning into our home." She laughed, "With tomatoes and salad. He taught us to eat them. It was bacon and egg and dripping and the Sunday roast with us and that was all. And they thought it was unmanly and foreign of George, I can tell you, the salad; and I didna like it myself—but I ate it for love."

Eliza became silent, as she spread thick butter and jam on her toast.

Camilla said, "What was this Jago circle?"

Eliza seemed to regret mentioning it.

She began to excuse it, "It was a hungry time then, all ways. It was from the slum to the factory, get married early and back into the slum with your first baby, the only recreation to wheel the baby on the moor on Sunday; and unemployment in the factories, the docks and the mines."

She made an impatient gesture, "George said he wouldn't be caught there; so he got out and I followed him. I came to London where I was like a wild heathen; I knew nothing. But I knew him and I went round the bookshops asking for him. I was lucky. I found him working, out the back packing books, in the third bookshop in Charing Cross Road, I asked in. He came out in a khaki workcoat, we walked out that evening, I got a job and we got married. Neither of us could take a Bridgehead future."

"What was that Jago circle?" persisted Camilla.

Eliza seemed a little angry or embarrassed, "I heard it from Nellie and it was a shame, a man of forty, taking young people, almost children, to corrupt them and say it was culture. Jago is a big name up there; there are a lot of Jagos, and he had family prestige. He had a big room with pictures and rugs and food and drink and cigarettes; and they used to go so eagerly. For Nellie it was the opening up of the world. They hadn't known which way to turn. First they joined the Fascist Party, though George didn't; only the arty youngsters went fascist, because there was what sounded like democratic talk in it, but they were

Bedlamites to us. Then Jago told them that was wrong. I don't know what he was, a fringe anarchist, an intellectual anarchist —try anything, it's all human. It's only the State that puts an iron collar of morality to make you work, marry young and have children early and never look over the brick wall of the slum back yard. Find out about life yourself, life's all around you, everything is life, everything is reality. He filled them with rubbish. Don't take old saws for axioms; and don't take axioms for axioms. Prove everything yourself. You're different, you have a different truth. Introspect and find out who you are. Judge nothing till you've tried; and don't judge others. Don't mistake timidity for morality. Everything was invented by man. The tyrant invented the state, the priest invented religion. All tables of law are human and invented by frail fallible humans. One man's vice is another man's virtue. Nell's told me all. They were very much excited about it; but most of them settled down. Not Nellie. And he convinced Nellie she had greatness in her, she needed to obey no little rules. Well, the young people all faced a hard future and wanted something better. They were sick of the dull narrow horizons and the meanness of family life, the pools, work talk, gossip and one good time a year, Race Week on New- castle Town Moor with the sideshows the only news of outside life: mermaids, dog-headed boys."

"I'd like to go up there. You don't know England in London," said Camilla.

"Aye, but not Bridgehead. You should see Newcastle. It's worth seeing. You see the iron of its ribs and backbone when you first look. The reefs of little houses, the iron-ribbed river. It's a great place, a big city, the capital of an old kingdom. They stand against the Scots, they stand against the southerners and the midlanders: they don't even like their neighbors, the Yorkshire- men; and yet they don't think much of themselves. But Bridge- head or Newcastle, it's the same: they feel nothing great ever came out of there. A canna understand it meself."

Eliza dropped back for a moment into the local talk, as they all dropped back when they began to think deeply of their home place.

"If you can forget for a moment the black coal fog and the

black coaly river, Newcastle, too, has beauty. But it despises culture. They never mention it. It's pure grind-and-drudge working class and a very mean middle class with butlers, a small town sort; you don't get anything from them. If we had famous men, you never hear of them. Why I heard from George, in London, that one of us, Thomas Belt, made a famous voyage in Nicaragua; and that's us, we go everywhere. But as for mentioning it in school, they don't care for it; only the bread and butter. You stand under the High Level Bridge in Newcastle and you think, That's beautiful; with all the trained men, the technicians we have, you ought to get great artists out of Bridgehead, all the engineers and the masters of ships and sailors who've seen the world. But no. So there were only three things: get away to London or get away across the North Sea—because news of big doings at that time came to us across the North Sea and it seemed nothing to go to Russia and see; and there's the Baltic and Hanse ports and boats going across the world; and then the other thing was right on the spot, Jago's circle. I suppose it was like a magic carpet, step off the hard street stones into culture. He knew a bit; all twisted, I'd say, from my earthy point of view. Nellie took Tom and Peggy there, as she took them to hear the miners in the cottages talking socialism. Aye, she was a pioneer; she did all she could and she was only a schoolgirl. Then Nellie fell in love with a boy who died; a Jewish boy who was a socialist and played the violin; and she said lovely things about him. "The Jews can play the violin because it expresses suffering and they suffer." Perhaps it's right. And she fell in love with a lot of other things, some bad; though she thought them all good and she wanted to do good. George and I and a lot of others had no talent that way."

"But now George cares for culture."

Eliza excused him, "Well, you see, what put him off, for he heard of it, was the gossip and scandal about the Jago circle. A boy died, not their fault; a girl died, maybe not their fault either; and to Nellie it was great doings; she was wanting life to be like Dostoyevsky and Gorki; and that made it so. I couldn't keep my eyes open at night to study. When the sun goes down, I'm ready for bed. George sat up studying, though his eyes were closing. I used to give him the rough side of my tongue, there fingering his arty books. He got an office job. I don't like to see a fine man, a good organizer that can get the men behind him, going in for papershifting. The first thing I knew after we were married and he got out of jail after a fight with a fascist, was he had a rubber stamp with his initials G.C.—him, who used to have the men hanging on every word when he stood on a crate down at the docks. I know three men became and remained socialists because of George Cook. A'm ashamed of ye, A canna understand it, I said to him, We had terrible rows. And I wasn't right, I was wrong. He was pushing ahead the best he could. He was getting to be a leader of men, waiting to be selected for Parliament. And I couldn't take what you have to do to be that. One of our worst rows, almost the last, was over a boy that dropped down at a meeting. George was organizer and chairman and speaker and the big man down there: and he was very proud he had an M.P. coming. They had a hall and six boys with big flags, the British flag and the red flag, standing round the platform. They were tall flags with heavy poles; George in the middle on the platform at the little pine table. And just as George starts to speak, the front boy on the right, holding the flag, drops down, faints, straight from work and no dinner I expect, a pale fair tall boy. The other boys, knowing George, stand still, and only one bends his head that way; but a couple of men rush forward, George has to interrupt his opening remarks; and as they drag the boy away and he opens his eyes, George rushes to him and shouts at him his duty to the working class. A cudna get over it. A gave him a taste of me tongue. It still makes me see red."

She laughed good-humoredly.

"I was glad to lose him and him me. He's lucky he got Nellie: and being the man he is now, I'm not sure he deserves her."

"We all deserve one another," said Camilla.

"Ah, well, who knows? I don't believe that, that a man deserves his fate. Otherwise, why would we work and worry to change the world?"

She got up, cleared away and started on the ironing. "Today,

I'm off. Nellie isn't good at ironing and Mrs. McMahon has enough to do."

Later in the afternoon, Nellie came home from a big political meeting at which she had taken notes. She had a rough, shrewd idea of practical politics, an affection for the leaders and speakers who gave her interviews, a contempt for theory. She sat down at once to sketch out her article. She was chalky-cheeked with shadows in the great northern eye sockets, skin drooping round the great northern beak. But she had a cup of tea, invited Camilla, put up her notes, called merrily, "Well, now, what cheer? Is there a letter from me bonnie lad?"

There had been a note for Gwen McMahon. George thanked her for looking after his things and begged her to write. He was lonely.

Nellie sang out through her cigarette, "Ah, bless the lad; he's a good lad. She'd do anything for us, the pet; and she idolizes George. You know my work, Lize, always away at Scarborough and Blackpool and Aldeburgh and Edinburgh and Bognor and wherever they hold their conferences and all the time George sitting at home here an object of public debate—you know, pet, he was victimized and made the headlines—all that time Gwen McMahon treated him like her own child. There's a real working woman for you, Camilla. Her home life is depressing; a good man but dull; an old man, she gets no joy in love—aye, he's steady, he gives her his pay. Now, where's me own letter? No letter for me? McMahon votes liberal, the poor old sod—but George has changed her vote to Labour—"

She got up and looked about for her own letters. She took her jacket, and skirt off, dragged on her overalls, looking for her letter, found it by the clock. She kissed it, tore it open.

She scanned it, flung it down in a fury, picked it up and thrust it at Camilla and Eliza, "Read it, read it, will ye! I'd give a bushel of his endearments for a pinch of consideration. God-damn his corny come hither and his long views."

Picking it up again, she read, "Dear, dearest darling, dearest of darlings! I'm glad I got away! I never thought you'd let me go! I took a week off here just to sleep after the last few nights in Lamb Street with you chewing my ear off about the home of the brave. I'm thinking of you every minute, my dear dearest, asleep or awake; but I'm glad I'm not there when you get this billet-doux to hear your old-fashioned remarks. I'm thinking of you, Nellie, when I ought to be getting down to it. It's for you I take the long view, sweetheart. If it doesn't work out here, you never know, I'm *still* not staying home. I'll find a place somewhere or I'll go to the colonies. I talked it over with Bob. This is an experiment. If this isn't it, Bob will go with us somewhere, Canada or Australia. My God, my God, darling—I've spent fifty years of my life like a toad in the hole, eyes up through the mud. What's that gray foggy swamp up yonder? That's the sky, toad love. Do you know that here the shadows are blue; the people are alive and the sun puts its hand on your bones. Send me a note, darling. I'll cable you. Make arrangements for your family; for you'll hear from me I hope. Wives are wanted; but I must dig in first and it may take months. Don't stay up all night every night chewing the rag; and get rid of that—Johnny. You know I can't stand her. Get some sleep. Don't weep over every cynical tramp. It's my home, too. Your sweetheart ever, George."

Eliza exploded. "By gum! What a trio you'll make emigrating! They'll think they're going to shoot a Victor Hugo film."

Nellie stretched her arms over the table and put her head down. But she was not crying, evidently; her head was sideways and smoke came from it; and presently, words, too.

"Bless old Bob. If I can't bring him back, she will. But I've got to have time to digest me blessings."

"Bob's this old woman," said Camilla.

Eliza said, "Bob's an old woman with thick spectacles, a humpback, she's thick, she limps, she has white hair and black eyes surrounded by circles like coal. He's no fool. She'll leave him her half-acre. It's a damn shame, Nellie." She had flushed and ended up very hotly.

Nellie sat up, "Do you think he'd stay here if he had a half-acre? He might. Perhaps she's canny. Ah, pet, it's not as bad as it looks. They're just pals. Wait till you see Bob, Camilla. She's a pet, just a sweet old waif and no humpback intellectually or

[234]

physically, Lize. She's leading me husband astray from the highest motives. She wants to end her days in the sunshine; and George wants to eat and drink, the bloody gigolo—he's a gigolo now to the powers in Geneva. He could sign himself with truth, Your half-husband George, Remote from the working class."

Eliza burst out laughing, "Eh, Nellie, love—"

"What gets into the men? They lick their lips for the fleshpots. I just had to tick off that damn, pussy-footing, pale pink journalist, Robin Bramble!"

"Eh, Robin Bramble, he's all right; he's a friend of the people—"

"Robin Bramble! Do you know him! He's a first-rate labor journalist," said Camilla.

"He was edging up to me at the meeting making signs and asking me if I was going up north, so he could come along and hide in me skirts; he's afraid of the rabble. And asking me what happened at the housing meeting at Highbury the other day. He had to leave early. What's it to you? I said. Are your silk-stocking parlor pinks behind their Hampstead cottonwool barricades, are they interested in the lives of the humble? Is it a new circulation stunt, using me for a stooge? I know you, mopping and mowing at the left-wingers, afraid the Reds might win before you've got yourself established as the people's champion. Time server, with a foot in as many camps as a bloody centipede. I told him he'd got a lot of closet theory, nicely served up in an ivied quadrangle, when he was young. It's the life the workers lead, not chewed-up paper, not theory, I told him. What's it to them, the history of the British working class, and Jack Cade and the levelers and chartists. Do you think they'd join any of those lots? You've got to go down in the street, I said, and climb the rotting staircase, cluttered with plaster from the ceiling like here, and slipping in the unnameable from the burst waste pipes. Give me a cup of tea, Eliza, pet! That damn dominie Robert Peebles, me editor, says I have to go to classes for three months, to classes on theory! Me! I don't believe in Marxian theory, I said. Can it explain the unknowable? Can it help a working-class mother who has just lost her baby? Can it stop the concentration camps? Can it keep a man in his country? It's too much schooling ye have and too little experience; and that's why I'm the best journalist you've got or can hope to have. I'm from the people."

Camilla said, "Robert Peebles is a first-rate journalist, he's brave and energetic and he isn't fooled by British socialism; he knows his theory through and through. I know him from my father."

Eliza gave Nellie a cup of tea, while assenting to what Camilla said. Nellie took a big gulp and a big puff and said, "All right, loves! I respect you for your principles; but when you're down in the blood and muck, you've got to feel with them that never read a bloody book in their lives and don't know the name of Robert Peebles, nor what I write, to our shame. What is the good of theory? It's not good for you, Lize; you've got the Bridgehead gray in your lungs; you need sun and air and a rest. It's good for George to climb with. Theory is to climb up into the fresh air above the working class. You can be running your extramural forums from now to kingdom come, but it's they who must fight for themselves and you too, without theory. I don't mean you Eliza love, I mean them. It makes me wonder if they're not all playing games, the men. There they sit in their swivel chairs and swop book talk and elbow each other for a seat on the council and only take an interest in an evicted family if they've got a photographer with them. Not one word of their theory can put a roof over that family's heads. There are evicted families living in halfway houses, council barracks, crying for their father, for the other half. Will ye come and say, Here's no father, but here's a good hunk of socialist theory to cheer ye up? This'll put meat in your stone broth. I don't understand you, Eliza, and you a working woman. Wage rises are got with strikes, I said to him. They've got to go out like bloody pirates with a knife between their gap teeth to get anything; and they get it and ye sit there and applaud, the self-satisfied pack of you, leading the working class on your bottoms."

Eliza brought her another cup of tea, laughing, "And what did he say, the poor man?"

"If it's Robert Peebles you mean, he told me I had to show up for the class on theory. A sobsister he called me. Me!"

"And Robin Bramble?"

"Aye, there's the rub. My article was thrown out by Peebles. His is going in on the front page."

Eliza considered, "That's not bad, to get the housing meeting on the front page."

"That's not the way to look at it, pet. It's not a subject for the helping hand brigade. And anyway it's only for the early run. They'll grab it out. And me own boss. The paper's a bloody mess, I told him. With captions and subheads like a damn cough medicine advert. It's degrading the workers. It's a damn wishwashy holier-than-thou Sunday School paper. Where's the meat, where's the drink? If a worker buys your sheet, I said, it's out of pity. He has to spend another fourpence to get a decent sheet with the news he wants. I said, Leave socialist theory on the shelf and take a look in at the men at dinnertime in the yard."

"But Nellie, to organize the trades-union movement, to organize a state, to take over the State, to run a Labour Government, you have to know what you're doing. You've got to have theory," said Camilla.

"When it comes, it comes by itself; the men know what to do. I'd know what to do. And Robin Bramble and Robert Peebles would not know what to do; they'd be off on a trip to the continent, hiding from the rabble and importing a load of foreign theory. You can't teach socialism, Camilla; it comes to you. It comes to one, not to another; it comes by mysterious ways. It is the way; but you can't point it out to another."

Eliza and Camilla burst out laughing.

Nellie said solemnly, "You know if you've got it in you, that's all."

She took a gulp of tea, stuffed her cigarette back into her mouth, began to cough, got up and hung herself over the sofa, head down, as usual, nonchalantly gasping, "Excuse me!"

She seemed to be suffocating. After coughing and choking up the phlegm, as she said, for some minutes, she came back to the table and sat down, saying weakly, "It's me bronchitis! It's the fighting takes it out of you. But I've got to do it. I hate to see them going round with gummed-up eyes. It's me duty."

"Do you always quarrel with your editor?" asked Camilla.

Nellie said mournfully, "It's those on top who don't know. When you sit in the sun, the sun blinds you. People look like blue and white phantoms. You forget."

TOM HAD begun his job in Blackstone when another job came up, better paid. He had started on the first uneasy days in his Blackstone job, was not happy but was feeling his way; and he was by nature a sticker. He went for his interview to St. Faith, a village near Norwich, borrowing a car from the Blackstone company, but though he saw he would be accepted, he could not make up his mind to break. He had found out that he was wanted at Blackstone to replace an elderly engineer who had got into trouble through debt; and he had made up his mind to support that old engineer and keep him on in the factory. At the same time, every day, he saw to it that he was making a stronger impression on the men. He was a good calculator; but he had thought up a trick to help him; he had a slide-rule attached to his sleeve so that he could consult it without anyone observing it. He passed for a mathematical wizard, among the locals; and he had had a bit of luck the first day, fixing a machine; so that already he was looked at, when he passed; and the girls were giggling to get his attention.

Still, he was in need of money. He had to make a decision. He came to London to see it all from a distance and to talk to women. The Saturday evening he came down, he took Eliza to a pub until late; and the next morning he telephoned one of his friends, Frida, to whom he had written. They would go for a drive and he would talk to her about his future. Frida, who worked on the files in a London clinic, and Charles her husband, who did film documentaries, were friends of George. Once they had been very enthusiastic about Nellie too; but he sensed a cooling-off. Nellie explained that they were bourgeois, living partly off unearned income and they cared only for suburban comfort. She had been deceived in them. On the other hand, Frida seemed angry with Nellie.

She had said to him, "I decided never to see her again."

"Surely that shows a weakness in yourself, an unsureness," said Tom.

"No. I have no time for a person who pretends loving friendship and has an ulterior motive. Love between women is unnatural."

Tom said cautiously, "Oh, of course, love between women is unnatural. One hasn't sympathy for unnatural feelings."

The break pleased him, though; he himself never interfered in Nellie's affairs; he respected her passions, her mistakes; it meant more to her than to him.

Frida led a quiet life when Charlie was away, as he was now, doing work on an undersea project in the Mediterranean.

She was a fair woman and this July morning had on a thin green wool suit with white silk blouse and was ready when he got there; and he was there earlier than he said. It was a cloudless, delicately sparkling day. Tom showed her places he had showed Marion, the manor houses, orchards, sunken villages, ruined monasteries, the roadsides where they had stopped, the fertile Lincolnshire lands, the high banks which might overflow.

"I used to get eggs here for Marion—on the way back, I'll show you a famous village—I always carry a pocket full of pennies, so that I can telephone anywhere—here we got off in a field and rested when Marion was ill—do you know the story of the Pedlar?"

He told her the wonderful story of his love and misery; and artlessly, as if with a woman he had known and loved for years, he gave all the details of his life and passion to her, though she was only an acquaintance; everything from his boyhood. They had time: it was a long summer's day.

"The reason Nellie feels this guilt is that Mother tried to make us feel guilty; and blamed Nellie because Nellie led us. I expect she was jealous. When we came home, Mother pried and questioned. She never went out. She got it all out of us. And if we didn't tell enough, she'd send us to bed and say she didn't love us. It hurt us terribly. We'd be there, in different rooms, calling out in childish voices; Mother, don't you love me? And we'd be crying. We believed her. She'd say, No, I don't love you,

I don't trust you. You lie to me. I won't love you till you tell the truth. We'd be begging and calling out, in little voices, like birds, Mother, don't you love me? No, you don't love me. Yes, I do, Mother, yes, I do. And I do, too, Mother. She could keep it up for hours hovering about, not letting us see her. She enjoyed it. She had no other life in that house but what she made herself. And Nellie believes everything. We all cried and felt guilty; but Nellie never grew out of it."

They passed through a village.

He said, "Let's stop here. I'll take that second job, it's near here; and we'll stay here the rest of our lives."

"I'll think about it."

They laughed, an eager, excited, thrilling laugh. He looked round at her with a gay, cunning smile. She looked at him when he was watching the road, surprised. He had a boyish, reddened face.

She said, "Nellie telephoned me last night, very coaxing, and said to remember you were heartbroken. You did tell her after all, that you were seeing me."

He said arrogantly, "Nellie only thinks she knows me."

It was a clear sunset, a large sun, pure gold in a sky clear from horizon to horizon. On the way home he began to talk quickly about all sorts of things that interested her; but when she mentioned places she had seen with Charlie, he frowned. He was suggesting, teasing, pausing, "—she seemed interested, but I didn't care for her, perhaps I made a mistake, but—a Polish girl told me once that she could teach me something, perhaps I should have, but it was at the factory and—there is a Spanish girl down near Bob's—I taught her something about music and—"

He could take one of two jobs, he said; a woman was necessary; the woman might decide the job; but if only one could know beforehand, an impossible thing—how fateful it all was. He went on, all these glittering little tempting figures, the girls and himself, his pointed bright face looking round at her, neatly worked into the illuminated life he was showing her. She kept studying the dry little face, pondering his assurance.

They reached her home and went into a sitting room at the back of the house on the ground floor. French doors looked into a tangled back yard, old vines, old trees. She listened to his prattle, smiling with tenderness; such a very quick, very transparent game; but he was gentle and good. He had taken off his jacket and sat in rolled shirt-sleeves, showing his muscular arms. He moved about a bit and then sat in a chair brought up close to her, looking at her with mock piteous eyes. She thought of her contented married life, this lonely man, the distraught sister, that she did not care about lovers, that he was what Charlie called "a lamplight lover," the visitor and talker and non-doer; but he was a puzzle to her.

"You're not like other women!"

"Why not?"

"Other women ask me what I do."

It turned out he meant about love; he called it passion.

"I don't care, Tom; it's not my affair."

He turned aside restlessly and hurt, "No, it's not your affair."

He began to talk mournfully about the new job. He didn't know. Should he give up the whole idea? What was her advice? He was lost: he'd take any advice.

"I am used to taking advice from a woman. I like to do what they say. They give the best advice. They're unselfish."

They talked about it for a while, but he continued disappointed, gloomy.

He remarked, "But you don't care what I do. It isn't your affair."

She laughed, "Well, tell me, Tom, what you do."

He was pleased and said nothing.

"Well, tell me who are these kind women, landladies, schoolgirls, Kensington afternoon women, artists—"

He listened with a shining face, contemplating all these possibilities. She ended impatiently with grotesque things. He was shocked, "No; nothing like that."

After a while, he said softly and sweetly, that he had looked for love with two or three women the last few days but it had not come off; he felt cold. No one understood him.

She said, "Yes, there is something funny about you. Part is very, very cold, stone cold. I keep feeling the stone cold. That's very unusual in a man. Generally, you can feel heat, like an oven."

She looked to see if she had offended him. No; he was pleased. It was as if he had been waiting for those words.

"Yes, part of me is very, very cold."

He looked brightly at her, a demure look came on his face, "I must be warmed!"

He took her arms, bent his head and hid it in her breasts.

He said, "Yes, that is it."

She was taken by the childlike behavior and reassured him, "I understand. I knew all the time."

He was pleased at that, too. He lifted his head a little to say, "What shall I do then?"

"It's the fault of the women."

He rested his head on her breast again, looking up at her. Then he said, suddenly, "But you don't love me; you're not jealous."

"Yes, I am. I'll poison all those women."

"Would you? Would you really do that for me?"

He was delighted, as if it were all true. He was not quite at ease till he had discussed all sorts of details with her, as if they were lovers.

"In the morning I am full of passion: why is that? I am two men; one doesn't fit the other. Do you want to see me as I am? I don't mind. I'd like that."

There was a long mirror between the two windows. He took off the blue shirt and tie which went with his eyes, he took off everything and with a serious expression, stood in front of the mirror for her to look at him. He was two men, as he said. One was a man all silver in the silvery light, an old man, thin and bony though straight, a wasted hungered man, with the expression of one delivered from hope. The other was a gold man, skin and hair youthful, red lips and a hopeful smile. She stood behind him and they both stood looking thoughtfully into the mirror. But he had meant, a strong man and a frail man; a stone man and a flesh man. "Yes, I see," she said.

He looked at her in the mirror, quite seriously and turned to her,

"Do you like me?"

"Oh, yes. I like you very much. As a kind of love."

Joy filled his face, "I'll do anything for you. So would anyone."

When they went out for a drink, he was manly and free as if they were now united and he was a man. He shouted across the park, with his extraordinary voice, people turned round. "I am going to keep that job at Blackstone. You decided me. I am going to get married."

He smiled at her and looked at her arms and breasts as if he knew his head and arms were still lying there. They sat down on the heath, looking at a distant view; then turned inwards.

He said romantically, "You would have made a good mother."

"I like children."

He understood that for the first time she felt that she was not a woman, she had no children. He was delighted: he was fulfilled. It was as if a child had come to her and said, Why haven't you me? He was the child. He was happy at all that had happened and took her home, kissed her at the door, came back, kissed her again; and made off.

He had a long hasty stride, the stride of a tall man; his long thin muscular body bent forward. At the corner he turned with a smile and waved, crossed the street and at that corner smiled and waved. The smile ran down the folds of his face, spread over it: the smile of a happy confident man.

When he was round the corner he strode fast; but tears came into his eyes as he thought of his loneliness. Frida's husband would be home in a day or two: she had nothing to do but wait for him. She felt nothing real as Tom did; she felt no loneliness, did not know what the thing meant; and women did not; they had only to wait. It was Nellie in her desperation, her gallant attempt to be something she was not, that was closest to him. He passed a mother in the side street, with two children. She was about nineteen, her long fair hair was arranged like a cape, a shortcut Lady Godiva: she had high-heeled white shoes for dancing, banana legs, a short white spongy skirt and a long red-blue silk shirt over it, a dizzying pattern. She looked like the wildest dancehall youngster; but there she was married and complete. I wish I were a woman: life would be easy."

But he was proud of being a man. Perhaps he ought to marry a woman with children, like Camilla. He always said that a man with children, who shammed devotion, was a defeated man; it was no fulfillment for a man.

He would go and see Camilla. The children were away visiting the grandfather. She hoped Edmund would marry her when she was free. The grandfather always seemed to stand in the way. There was even a hint—and he had seen Camilla in very strange moods. "I don't want the grandfather to give us a home; there would be too many strings." Yet she was attracted. I could save her from that, thought Tom. But he wanted a woman of his own; and to tie the woman up, a man had to have her child. Weak women—liking him, but not enough; wanting strings on several men; naturally unstable.

There was one woman he could marry: Caroline, and she was younger than himself. He was near home now and determined to go up and ask her to marry him; clinch the matter before Nellie could put in her oar.

"You are so good, so kind; there's no one like you," Caroline had said.

But he would prove he was a lover, too; a real lover, a man, firm and aggressive. He reached the Cooks' house and went upstairs. At the turn of the staircase he looked across and saw Camilla at her window opposite. He hesitated; then went on.

Caroline, with her loose light brown hair over the pillow, her arms open and her breasts almost uncovered, was lying in bed, looking sick. She didn't know what was the matter. She felt miserable and restless; she had no strength. She couldn't get up to make soup or tea.

"You have a temperature! I'll get the doctor!"

Nellie was over at the hospital: she had received an emergency call: her friend was on the danger list. Her Southwark friend had said Nellie was her married sister. Tom called the doctor, stood about quietly; Caroline went to sleep. Nellie came in, at last, in a very black mood, so he left her to herself. When the doctor came, Tom went out for the medicine; came back, tended

Caroline, and went downstairs for food for her. He brought it back, fed her and gave her the sweet shadowy comforting look he had given other sick ones. He was joyful; and made up his mind to ask her as soon as she was a little better. He would give her a new life. He would have to find a place in Blackstone first. Things could happen; he could decide to come to London. Should he do so? Avoid the dull, ignorant life of the country town, which was proud of its decline? "We've been going downhill in Blackstone since the year one thousand." And all around were the buried roads and ramparts, the abbey walls weathered to bogeys in the wild winds of the piney lands; a miserable place in winter.

The "temptations" of London would not matter if he were married. But the woman? Once a woman married she became unsettled: so there must be a child.

"Well, I can give her a child; I know that."

He sat there, delighted to be united with her in the sickroom silence, and thought now about Nellie. Angry with him for coming downstairs so tardily, after her return, perhaps, she had given him a gruff hello. She had on her blackest face and she was wiping away tears. No doubt, some letter from George. Perhaps she would be pleased that he was taking Caroline away, no longer be open to all those temptations.

"She is right to worry about me."

Caroline could work at first: there would be money for Bridgehead.

Downstairs, there had been a discussion. "When are you going off, Tom? You won't be coming down for the weekends for a while, will you?"

"I'll be coming down, Nell; but I'll bring my own fodder, ducks, geese or pheasants. All I have to do is chalk up on the board, *The engineer wants a brace of pheasants,* or ducks maybe, and they turn up. Where they are got is not for me to ask. Nearly every one of my workers is off the feudal estate."

He laughed.

She said briefly, "We have no one here to cook birds of that sort. Gwen McMahon never saw a bird in her life, but a chicken to take over to the priest."

He volunteered, "I'll cook them. I'll have enough for you and Camilla and Caroline."

She said earnestly, "Now, Tom, I want your solemn promise that when I'm away on this Labour Party conference, you'll keep away from them: you'll do no mischief-making with Caroline and Camilla."

He laughed, "Oh, I can easily do that. I am going to ask Caroline to marry me. I think she'll say yes. I came here for that this afternoon: but she's ill. It won't do now."

She said violently, "You'll do no such thing. Do you want to cut her mind to pieces with such rubbish? She can't understand. This is her weakness. I foresaw some such tripe. I've arranged for her to go away and stay with someone reliable, a friend of mine, while I'm away. Keep away from her. I won't let her backslide now."

"When she's my wife, you won't have to trouble. I'll take care of her health."

She said rudely, "I won't tolerate it. So that's where you were? Talking spoony to her. I'm going straight up there now. Behind my back, under my nose, it's the same story. I'll undo your nonsense at once."

But he said she was asleep, she had influenza, was weak, and to have a future with him would make her happy; if Nellie started her nonsense he'd be very angry.

"What do you mean by my nonsense?" she said indignantly.

"Now I'm taking a walk, Nellie, and I'm coming back to look after her. I won't ask her now; but it's on the record; and I'll ask her next weekend. It's settled. You know when I mean a thing."

Nellie, sitting twisted at the table, smoked and stared at him; "You mean, then, that it's all meant nothing to ye, all I've said? You're going on with your trouble-making? You're not going to do your duty by Bridgehead?"

He stood, looking at her calmly, waiting for her remonstrances. To all she said, he smiled; and repeated he was going out for his walk and would be back.

"And perhaps, in view of what you've said, Nellie, I'll ask her tonight. I'll get it settled. I don't want any of your counter-plots!"

She burst out indignantly: she was honest and fair, the only honest one that she knew in the world. There was another one —she paused; she got up and turning her back went to the fire-place, where she stuck her shoe into the empty grate and looked down.

Then she turned back, lifted her head proudly and said, "She's just died, Venna, me true sister. The world's a black-guard. I see nothing else. The vultures got her. Oh, Tom, if only I could get them. If only—oh, Tom. And ye said counterplot. What counterplot is there to beat them? Go away, go out, I'll stay here till me feelings fly screeching up the chimney and I wish I could fly with them."

"Let me stay with you, Cushie. You won't see me: I'll be in the other room."

She exclaimed passionately, "You! The bloody bystander! Aye, easy for you to drop a bamboozling tear. Where's your heart? Isn't there a torn place in your jacket on the left side? Someone came along and tore it out of you and since then you've been wrenching the hearts of others. You were born without one or it was taken from you as a child."

He said calmly, "Aye! And you were the one who took it, Nell. And that's a thing you can't give back. You took it from me and lived on it, and now you're scurrying around from one body to another, hungry and thirsty and you'll do anything to still the pain."

"It is pain! Struggle and pain—and now I feel what I never felt before: everything is repulsive that isn't struggle and pain; for that's the real world. And I can't submit. Ah, leave me. Take your walk, go to your pub. Leave me. What is here is too real."

He went out. But he was troubled, worked up, sorry and angry though he had kept calm before his sister. He waved to Camilla who was sitting in the window sewing. He wondered why she was not using Nellie's basement room. He thought he would go in and find out. Camilla rose when she saw him, placed a seat at the second-hand wooden canteen table she had bought for her sewing, and began to prepare a rabbit.

[248]

"Do you like rabbit?"

"I did; till in the war we began to get those warren rabbits tasting of dirt."

"What's your favorite dish, Tom?"

"I like herring, plain herring. There's nothing better."

"Yes, but they're bad for children with all those bones."

"As a child, I had strong teeth and I chewed the bones."

She went on working.

He chatted, "Your hair's lovely Camilla, now it's loose I can see how nice it is. But why are your eyebrows a different color?"

"Eyebrows often are. This is my natural color. I'm not dyed."

"Ye-es. I knew that. What wonderful teeth you have, Camilla."

She said laughing, "I see Nellie has been talking me down."

He said nothing. She continued, "Nellie has been roaming the place in a bad temper, so I made myself scarce. She's missing George. I thought she would be over here for me to make it up, but she hasn't been. She doesn't like Edmund."

"Where's Edmund?" he said in a hard tone.

"He's got a mortgage. He's buying a house in Chelsea. He wants me to go there. I can't. The grandfather would never swallow that."

"Did he ask you to marry him?" he said, as before.

"Who?"

"Either!" he said angrily.

"Neither."

She looked at him, smiled, parted his yellow hair and kissed the parting. He said, "I knew that was going to happen."

"You sit waiting."

"I know something is going to happen. I don't know what. I'm waiting for it."

She laughed.

He said nicely, "I'm thinking of getting married. I have someone in mind. What do you recommend? I've been having an affair. It didn't work out. My feelings changed. This is someone who needs me."

She studied his face, "Someone in London?"

"Someone who needs me."

She went out. He heard her chopping something on the chopping board. She came back with stuffing for the rabbit.

"It's all right, Tom. I wasn't serious with you."

He said somberly, "I know: it's not serious with you. You don't care for me."

"You're wrong. I love you—in a way."

He sat by the hearth in a low chair which eased his aching back and mused. He seemed hurt. He got up presently with difficulty, barred the way as she crossed the room, put his arms round her like a child. He said with a sob, "Oh this is so real, so natural." He said, he'd go: he felt upset.

"Do you feel bad?"

"I should like to feel worse."

"Do you think good and bad has anything to do with it?"

"How do you know I'm saying what I mean?" he asked, recovering himself and beginning to smoke.

"It doesn't matter."

He looked at her as she moved about,

"A friend of mine up at Blackstone wouldn't approve of you, Camilla."

"Who is it?" she said proudly.

"A policeman. He has no stripes because he has never sent in a report. He can't shop anyone. They are trying to make up their minds to get rid of him; but he hasn't done anything bad either. He lives in a shack and makes papier-mâché maps of the district. When he was a boy a teacher taught him that and he's been doing it all his life. He joined the cops thinking he'd have a lot of spare time and could get about making maps. He has a savage dog at the front gate to bark when any policeman comes to spy on him. That dog hates policemen. It likes me."

"Why should he disapprove of me? Perhaps he could try to do me in papier-mâché."

Tom laughed, "Yes, it would get him out of the rut. But he's very moral. He's full of moral ideas. He's very rough on women. He thinks a bad woman makes a bad man."

"I'm not going to make you bad," she said.

She moved over suddenly and kissed his head many times, "No one loves you as much as I do."

[250]

He said restlessly, "I don't know. I'm not really passionless. But I can't settle. I'm waiting. I can love. I ought to stay in my swamp in Blackstone. It's cold there all times of the year. It suits me. I'm miserable and don't have hopes."

"Don't do that."

"There's a bird with a most awful cry, a shriek; it must be a bird, on the heath at night. There's a fog there I've never seen before. It rises thick white, straight out of the ground and hangs about shoulder height, so you can just see a head moving towards you."

He put his head against her and said in a tremulous voice, "In the evening, it's a strange sight. They talk of other towns as if they were a hundred miles away and not even in the same century. They say that in Wisbech—"

He laughed lightly.

He went on, "You can hear sounds, things moving round your feet, in the fog. It might be a bush. You might stumble over something, the remains of masonry. You can't see your feet: you feel as if all the parts of your body are going along separately. If you take someone's hand, it's just your hand holding a hand. You lift your hand up over the fog and there are two hands holding together."

"Now, in July?"

"No, but I've seen it," he said flatly. Then he confessed that he had been in a camp near there during the war; "It's a bad climate: half the men had what I have, lumbago and back pains."

He bent his head, kept close to her.

"Tom, I don't know what it is, you give me a feeling that I can't stand. It's in my heart, a cold slipping struggle. You're taking me down with you in your swamp," she said with a slight laugh.

"Oh, I hope not," he said sitting up.

"You're a man could kill a woman. I don't want to marry you. I don't know what it is. You're only playing a game, you're cold and indifferent. You have smiles that no serious man has."

"I couldn't kill a woman, or anyone else."

"You're like a painted Christ in a blue and pink oleo."

"Beware of the man with the painted heart," he said seriously.

She said, "How can you be so cheerful and do what everyone asks, when you're so unhappy and lonely."

"I'm not happy. I never was. I don't ask for anything. But I like to feel all I can: I like to see a fireside sometimes, the air of the moors and heaths, strange people. Any sort of person can be strange."

He lighted a cigarette and began to chat. "You have curious experiences up there. I came down in a train that stopped at every dog-kennel. There were very few people in the train. We passed some lonely looking heaths with dark trees. At one stop a man and woman got into the carriage with a lot of luggage; so I thought they might be going to London. The man sat opposite, the woman sat next to me. They didn't say a word, but each got out a book. The man read very slowly; the woman was a fast reader and got to the end of her book before the man had turned three pages. Then she got down a bag, put away the book and got out another book, which she began on. She read everything, the title page, the foreword, and then started on chapter one. It was a novel I'd never heard of. As we were coming in to the next wayside station I got up and went to the other window and at that moment an express rushed past in the other direction; you could see people in different postures, doing things, scraps of actions and smiles. It was like a play.

He sat with a contented air, looking at her, "When I turned round, they had gone, their luggage was gone; and I hadn't heard anything. They had just traveled one stop."

He laughed outright, "I asked myself if they'd been there. But I wasn't at all sleepy. I looked to see if my chicken and eggs were still there. I take a glass of beer about once a week in Blackstone. I just go into the pub and take one glass and stay a bit. A man said to me the other evening, You're the man who came down from Scotland with a child nine years old, aren't you? I said no. He said to me, I recognize you because I happened to be over in Wisbech and you were there and the child was never heard of again. That's the kind of thing that can happen to you and get you a reputation. They don't know what I am. They think I have a Scots accent. And anyone who comes from ten miles away is a rollingstone. Because I come to London they imagine orgies. If anything horrifying takes place, I'll be the first man questioned. They give me the creeps too. They're off ducal estates, or else they're descended from Lady Hamilton's lackeydom. I hate Lord Nelson. Everyone talks about the national hero. I don't. He ran a navy manned by press-gang crews."

Camilla was at the window: she exclaimed, "I can see Nellie: she's in that top room. Caroline's there, isn't she?"

Tom jumped up and stared across the street. The window was open and Nellie seemed to be forcing Caroline out of it. Tom rushed out of the room, downstairs, into the house without closing the front door; and presently Camilla saw him struggling with Nellie and Caroline at the window. He closed the window. Astonished and frightened, Camilla sat down in Tom's little chair. Who were they and what were they doing? She sat there for a time, grew cold and tugged out of a chest a great black shawl she had once had for the theater. There, like an old Italian woman, she sat till it was time for the roast.

Tom got Caroline back to bed and ordered Nellie out of the room in such a tone, that she went, looking wild, hollow-eyed, insensate. He heard her talking on the stairs.

"To think one quiet girl should cause so much passion," said Tom.

"Yes," said Caroline, sinking into her pillow and drawing a breath.

"Sleep now. I have something to do."

The girl did not answer. He went away, leaving the door ajar. He asked in the kitchen, "And now, Nellie, what in the world were you doing?"

"I was showing her what you were. She wouldn't believe me. I said to her, Is that your wonderful man? Can you see him over there, with his make-believe, with that middle-class wanton, that harpy who's got her clutches into three men already and is now living with a love, keeping a tight hold on a man who wants a divorce and playing for marriage with a rich man, the grandfather. Do you see him? And there she was kissing you, fondling you, the old woman. Caroline said her eyes were heavy, she could not see. I made her see. I opened the window and pushed her over the sill to see you standing there with your harpy."

"Does she think I'm a wonderful man?" he asked.

"Aye, the poor sick brain. I love Tom. I'd die for a man so good. So your little fairy story makes its way. It's their desperation and they call it love to death. I can't understand you."

She went to the stove to put on some hot water to wash, came striding back, flung herself down and went on raging at her brother.

"It isn't you: it was this Alan in the office. It's the desperate seeking. It's not love. She doesn't know what it is. There are those who never know. Then they must learn to face life without it. What is it, this dirty swamp they want to sink in? I'll die for him. Aye, she'll have to. For this Alan picked for himself one of those cream-cake strawberry-filling dames."

"I'd go for that sort myself," said Tom, amiably.

Nellie blackened and told the story of Alan and Caroline again with spicing and stuffing, "I despise and loathe and have complete contempt for the knight-errant and minnesinger who goes around playing with things that are so deep."

"Am I a minnesinger? I like that."

He began a Northumbrian tune in his aeolian voice.

"What's that rubbish?"

"A song about me, the man without a heart," he smiled.

She became very earnest, "Tom, you had a chance, the best chance a man ever had, to be a decent pure man. I was so proud of you. Before you make another mistake, lad and ruin another life, like other men, hurt and harm, won't you take the beautiful chance you were given? You could have been always a brother to women, like you were to me, a beautiful thing: they need it. You need never have harmed any creature. You had a heart and head of gold. I always used to see your gold head all the way down the street and I thought, There's my own lad, a sweet true boy. Why were you tempted when you grew up? You threw away all that sweetness and purity. Let me plead with you now, to keep away from the women for ever, do them no harm. Oh, it would be a lovely thing to see such a man; I grant ye, you don't know all the harm men do; I know now. You mean well, you think. But you can do nothing but harm. Wouldn't you like to live alone, to meditate, to find the way for yourself, the truth? Don't go down the slippery steps again and sink into the mud. I beg ye, Tom. You'll never do any good unless you are a pure man, never touching a woman; and why should you? If only you would reconcile yourself to a beautiful destiny, to the purity of loneliness."

"Like Uncle Simon! No thanks," said Tom.

"I can't tell you what I've been told. I wouldn't spread evil and contaminate," she said bitterly, chewing her cigarette and her lip together. "You ought to do what I ask without questioning. I know. You know I know."

"You've heard a lot of dark stories from a—from an unfortunate friend, and that's all; it doesn't happen to everyone. There are happy lives."

"There are no happy lives. Those that are happy are blind and selfish. They're blind," cried Nellie.

He said he was going out. She told him not to come back before midnight; and then tomorrow morning early to get up to Blackstone; and to stay there. He was not wanted here by anyone, least of all by her.

"I'm staying for two days. I've got to go to the Industries Fair for the firm. What's more, I'm coming down every weekend," said he.

"While I'm away at the conference, too?"

"Every weekend, first train out and last train in."

"Then I must put an end to it."

He took no notice of this threat; but went out to see a friend of his called Monica. He had made up his mind to put an end to that affair, to begin with.

Nellie tried to sit with Caroline the two nights of the weekend, smoking many cigarettes to pass the time; but it was hard for her to sit without talking. She would go downstairs for tea or brandy, cut a wedge of bread, walk about whistling softly and ruminating. At last, she stretched out beside the sick woman and slept restlessly, coughing and uneasy; she had no covering.

When Caroline woke in the early hours, Nellie made her some

tea, cut thin bread and butter and brought them up and put them beside her friend on a chair. She was too heedless to have a sickroom manner; and waited impatiently for Caroline to lie back, which she presently did.

Then Nellie said, sweetly, with a sigh, "I'm glad you're here with me, darling; me poor brother's off gallivanting again. I'm a fool, I must be to trust him. But when he's sweet to me, I trust him again. Aye, we women earn our troubles; and why was it I wonder that Nature gave the men those sweet ways to cheat us to make us the doting weak things we are? Otherwise, we'd see them as they are, no doubt. That must be it. It's the law of survival: aye, it is. For don't we naturally trust each other, more? So there has to be something to lure us; and if the man's your brother, no matter what he is, you can't help the love and pity."

"Yes, I can never forget how nice Tom has been to me, Nellie. You're a beautiful pair; you're a real brother and sister."

"Aye, you feel it, do you, that we're alike, that we have something in common?"

"Yes, goodness and compassion."

Nellie glowed; then lamented, "Yes, I have it, love. But he has not got it, it's a simulacrum: it's the veil of cheating I was talking about. He caught it from me, it's me shadow self, but it isn't him. Any word he says to you is false, for it isn't him and it has no outcome. If he were to say love, it doesn't mean love; things aren't what they seem: things are the contrary: if he were to say marry me, it would be nothing but the joke of a silly, yellow-faced, garlanded clown dancing in a hall of mirrors, but in all these hundred shadows, love, there is not one man. You can't marry him, for there is nothing to marry. If you stood up before the minister or went down to the Town Hall, it's no difference: you'd be the world's most miserable woman. He was married, did ye know that? And the marriage at once fell apart for he cannot play the husband's part; and the poor girl, always a girl, is left to mourn. Did ye not know that? Did he not tell ye? And because the poor simple creature, doomed to loneliness, cannot bear to face the truth, he will play the cat and mouse with all the women. Will ye marry me? Would ye marry me? Could ye marry me? It's a game; and playing the game he knows the women; and there's your lure and dead end of life for you, darling. Don't think of him! Root him out if he's put down root, crush him if he's made a paper flower in your heart, for it's nothing, there's nothing for a woman in him. I can't tell you, love, for it would crush you, the names of the women he has taken in and what has happened to them. Ah, don't let me see you join them. I couldn't bear it with you. I can't bear to think," she said stormily, "that he is doing this to you and to me, when we were so close, close as sisters, we were reaching the perfect understanding, the true love."

Caroline had understood that Tom might propose marriage to her very soon and Nellie's exhortation confirmed it. She became very agitated and said Tom was good and they were fond of each other.

Nellie began to croon, "Marriage is an illusion, it's not the paradise of women as they thought, the poor pitiful mothers and grandmothers. Ah, pet, if ye could have seen me poor mother down on her knees, waxing the lino and polishing the brasses for a man who had eyes only for the harpy's red smile and the fake brilliant in the false gold on her finger, you'd understand me. I see you going wrong. I've seen it before and let it go on, for I'm a great believer in destiny; but I've been punished for it and I'm punished now if ye go wrong. He has no need of you, me weak and wicked brother, Tom. He can do nothing for you and you nothing for him. But I can do everything, I'm the doer and seer. He can't offer you love, not even friendship, he's only playing with your tangled feeling to get relief for a moment, the moment of a cigarette's burning, love, from his own tangled confusion, the contemplation of his wasting and loneliness. I know it's a pitiful thing, I admire you for your kind heart, but it's the kind hearts are taken and consumed."

She leaned forward sharply, bent with her bright fierce little eyes over the sick woman, shaking cigarette ash on the bed, "Heed me, darling. I can see into hearts and I know what is in his and yours. You're not for each other: you're both for the lonely road."

Caroline with a soft and blasted look, lay on her pillow, her large watering eyes fixed on Nellie's, blinking, shutting, opening.

"Nellie, let me rest a bit? I'm so tired and weak feeling, so depleted."

Nellie broke into a humble croon, "It was the memory of me sister, Caroline, forgive me. Can you excuse me, darling? I tried to lead her into life, I wanted her to get the feel of the world, to interest her in social matters; it was wrong. I tried it with you, it was wrong. You see it for yourself or not at all: it is a matter of fate. I tried to lead you to Marxism: it was wrong. You cannot be led. It must come of itself, the vision and the way. I have always been punished for interfering with fate. I've been black and blue, striped with the thongs of fate, it's come back on me. But beware of the false vision. Ye bend over looking into the well of illusion and ye see a face, a dark significant face, but it's your own, it's the reflection of your loneliness, there's no one there, love. Ah, it's a terror, it's the lonely terror. Haven't I told ye about it though, haven't I faced it myself? Aye, I know what it is. But it's my Peggy I'm thinking of. Even now, I wake up in a sweat, every night sweating for her and I think of her destroyed by her trustfulness, her innocent longing for glamour and love, like you, just like you. I am guilty of that, too. I thought all she needed was escape, like you escape from the dear Dead Sea fruit of your parents' love, which turns bitter and poisons a young life. But ah, it broke her; I'm afraid it has broken you. I can never do too much for her, nor too much for you. Every look and word you grant me, darling, is a blessing to me: for it shows me you trust me, you've forgiven me for any accident of mistake.

"You'll forgive me, won't ye, love; for warning you about Tom? Let him go and trust me, you'll find peace when you've had it all out, seen it for what it is, rooted it out, confessed and told me everything and faced the music. You've got a long way though to go to get out of your mess, I'm afraid. You're not ready, not willing."

"Why do you say that?" said the woman, feverishly and vaguely.

"Surely you don't think you've succeeded, Caroline? Or are you giving up the struggle?"

"I think the best way for me is not to think about myself and all this trouble, but to get a job in social work as I had before and work for others. And I know I must watch my feelings. I control them and they betray me on a lower level. I never can keep them in hand."

Nellie beamed wickedly, "Muckraking and exposés and the helping hand of the good women are the delight of the Philistine middle class, it's pleasurable pollution and sedative holiness for Sunday: to see the workers rolling in their wallows and pity them so that you can rough-tongue the char on Mondays with a good conscience. There's a gulf between them and us: you can't bridge it over with paper. Is that what you want to do with your life, already wasted so far? The muckraking and social-worker epoch is ended: you've come too late. You can't put ointment on your sore any more with that. The workers understand you. It's your own fate you have to face, not theirs. They know about theirs and they know about you. It's the courage you lack to face yourself. But I'm going to help you. I'm going to make up for what I did to me sister, in my devotion."

"It's hard for me to understand all this," Caroline said feebly, "because I've never really met evil, or I didn't see it, I didn't think there was hate or jealousy or envy in our world; I never saw it. Recently, with your help, I've begun to see it. I know I must face the reality of the world."

"Aye, it's a hard, malicious, lined old face, the world. It's got no smile for you. It's to others, your sisters, to those who understand and pity ye must turn, not to the world."

"And there are things I don't understand even in you. Now you say you love your brother, Nellie. I know you love your sister and family. But you say your brother is selfish and light and only making a game out of his passionate beautiful love for that dead woman, a trifling and skipping you said, a borrowed air on a tin whistle. I can't see it. It's because of that I believe in him. If I can't think that's true, life wouldn't be worth living; I think he's true. That's what I thought existed in the world; and he has it."

"What he's planted in you I've got to tear out bit by bit. He's not what you think, unfortunately, a lover in a poem. He'd like to know you thought that. He never even tried to get you out of that beautiful cell of dream you live in. He's only blown you up with self-importance and vanity, a lot of silly tripe. This sudden whim shows a great weakness in you, you're ready to cling to anyone who'll feed you the moonshine you want. You're cling-ing to any fairy tale. I'd blush to say such a thing. You have a desire for death and the end; that's noble and true; that's con-nected with the best and deepest in life, that's realization. It takes courage to face what I see is in you. You're trying to run away. You wouldn't have the courage to make a death pact, even as he did. He's a weak, poor creature but had the courage to do that. I admire that. He'll always have my admiration for that. If he did that for a worthless, wicked spider woman, what would the poor lad have done if he'd met the right person. But life is not for him. The booth with the puppets is for him; he's good at voices, aye. Let him go through the world with his songs and games if he doesn't hurt anyone. But he does. He doesn't say, This is my Punch and Judy show: he says, This is real, this is love, this is what you want. So he's the meanest and most danger-ous of mountebanks and charlatans. But when the woman played up to him, Will you die for me? he said yes. And would you die for me, pet? I said, Aye, he said, for you if it would help you. For that's what he is. Sterling in the essence. And you, though, you have not that courage. Would you die for someone who loved you, do this for me because I ask you? Aye, I've heard of such things. I've gone down on me knees in holy humble re-spect, I've hidden me face for the joy and shining in it, before such a thing. And if ye could do such a thing, I'd go down on me knees before you. But would you? Has my love and respect been misplaced?"

"I could," said Caroline, faintly. "I think so. I wouldn't want the world much if someone I loved in it, died. I don't think it's my fault you don't think me brave. There was the war; I lost Barry; I lost my family. I changed towns and jobs. I poked about looking for something; I had a sort of social consciousness in me; it came from the church perhaps. Now I see that's no use, at least coming from me. But I do believe in something, though I don't now what it is. I love someone, though I'm not sure who it is."

"Ah, no, ah, no; you can't have it both ways."

Caroline was puzzled by this and said nothing.

"Am I keeping you up, when you're not well, sweetheart? Are you tired?"

"I'm a little tired, Nellie. It's the flu."

Nellie put out the light. The faint starlight coming in over the low roofs opposite showed the whereabouts of the hair on the pillows, the sheet turned down. Nellie leaned against the bedhead. Opposite, Mrs. Yates was looking after one of her children. Nellie mentioned it, "She's a darling, Camilla Yates, but too effaced. She's a pet but she doesn't like to talk, it's reticence, it's reserve; and she feels she's getting older; her time is over. She's absorbed in the thought. The men don't let her alone, poor waif. Her first husband was once Governor of some province and to him she's a province he's won and won't free. And she, too, got the manner, the great dame manner; she can't sink to the human level. Poor woman! A lost life."

Caroline was beginning to sleep.

Nellie said it was heaven to be talking to someone who understood and who was not afraid of friendship, after Tom's behavior making her so angry, teasing her in her pitiful state, "I'm afraid I blew my top!"

Caroline was grateful for her talking. She was sinking into a sweet exhaustion. Everything was peace now after the strange winds that blew through this house.

"Am I disturbing you, pet?" said Nellie, low.

"No, Nellie."

Nellie was grateful: she sang her praises. There she had been looking for a friend and the gods gave her Caroline.

"But don't you feel the need of a great friendship, the perfection communion, Caroline? Then everything would be clear as morning. You would have joy."

Nellie's voice roved about the room sweetly, almost like a breeze. She had marvelous endurance; she could sit up all night talking. Did she get it from the white nights of the Bridgehead summers? "We used to do this in Bridgehead: it reminds me of fine summers gone." Nellie saw nothing strange in it. It was truth, intellectual aspiration, the right thing to do. Souls who needed to find true love, vision, a way of life, did it.

Caroline woke up, Nellie had become excited. Caroline must give her an answer now, whether she believed in friendship. What other answer was there to the loneliness of the human being? Men offered it and tore it away again; aye, it was cruel. You set out to sea with one sail and the first storm blew it away and you were left to your fate.

Caroline, in confusion, listened and fought to understand. Poor lonely woman, sitting up all night trying to stir passions in sluggish souls, singing for herself, a nightingale, the victim of her song. As soon as she opened her throat the same passion poured; ears opened, but she went on twanging in the dark: it did not seem to matter who heard. These sympathetic thoughts fluttered over Caroline but she was too tired: she didn't care now what they both meant, this pair, the singing brother and the singing sister. She knew George had been there for one night and had now gone off to Bob's farm; and even Nellie had said, Does he think he'll get the farm, the cadging bugger? Everyone thought, it was clear, that George was going to leave Nellie, Nellie thought so; and George didn't care what he did: for himself, and his ideas were trained puppies that ran beside him. Utterly spoiled by women: Caroline had noticed his ways, Bring me this, Caroline; Mrs. McMahon, I want to see your smile; Nellie, my shoes need cleaning. And yet he was a fine man, a great fighter and a great orator, so they said.

And when he and Nellie were together in the rooms downstairs and she could not hear their words, their voices were perfect counterpoint, it didn't matter what was said; you could hear the music; it was the music of the male and female, true, poignant. The music might hold them together; it was the only thing.

Nellie was saying, "I lost George when I gave up my fifteen-pound-a-week job and took one at five. He's more like Pop Cotter than he thinks. He calls me a sentimentalist."

Caroline went to sleep. Nellie called her awake a second time, with her keen lilt, with her northern song: on and on about friendship, wearisome, poor thing, talking senselessly, restlessly, so that she couldn't think about George's doings. If he leaves me, I'll need a friend as never before. I never was happy before. I didn't believe in it. As you have more, there is more pain; perhaps it's better to have nothing like the poor women before me, and so you do your duty."

"Am I bothering you, Caroline? You don't want to hear lucubrations?"

"Yes, yes, I do."

"But you're silent: you're judging me. You're deep in the heart of that beautiful crystal shell where nothing can touch you!"

"No, I'm drowsy."

"It's only as high as the room and as broad as the house, that's your world. Private worlds! If you only could break out and come into ours. Friendship would do that for you. But there you are nursing your soul as if it were a toothache. I had a friend, Caroline, who used to inspect the timbering in the mines. The men elected him and he did it for thirty years; men's lives were dependent on him; He said, I hate to come to the surface, for life seems gaudy and shallow; down there, it's real: men's lives and their families depend on me. He said to me, Cushie, get out and do things and you'll be more of a citizen. Don't stick around the pithead, writing notes about surface life. That's what I did. He'd never be able to talk to you, Caroline. But he'd know by looking at me that I'd followed his advice. Now, my life's been a life of adventure and taking chances."

"I know it has."

"Aye, but knowing isn't enough. The miners would never talk to a woman like you; you don't know the words to appeal to them. I do. He's my friend but he'd be disgusted with you. If the timbers aren't right, the miners die. No matter how many papers you shift and sign, no one dies and no one lives, you least of all. It's Gimcrack Castle, it's smirking into a looking glass in your clean collar and new make-up; it's wage-rape."

Caroline lay there, baffled and gloomy.

Nellie continued, "The life of the office worker living on the back of the true workers is a sapsucking thing. They regard you as a parasite, someone who never works and the hollowness and shallowness reveals itself in your feeling of defeat and failure. You have no life-aim. That's it in a nutshell, why you can't hold anyone, why you want to let go of life. You know, in your heart of hearts, we all know, aye, where we stand, in the eye of the great judge, Life; you know you're struggling in a nightmare and you're crying out for the hand that will wake you up. But unable to respond, in a catalepsis of unreality."

"What am I to do?"

Caroline's heart was sore, she was insulted. She felt scornful but she felt there must be something very wrong with her that Nellie saw clearly; she felt herself on the edge of those abysses nervous, thin-hearted children feel, when they are growing up, she tossed and jumped like a caught fish.

"All right, Nellie, I'm weak and wrong."

Nellie said rapidly, "Our life is a mysterious thing, Caroline: we must listen to it as a seashell. There are cycles and moments. There are fatal hours. If a man's destined to die young, he dies. The world is not what it seems. Does an airman, up above the low atmospheres, see what we see? He hasn't even the same sunset and sunrise. But we think ourselves the center of the world and the world is painted on our eyes. It's a fact, pet. One can't shut one's eyes. You may talk about forgetting yourself and losing yourself in a lot of cock-and-bull stories of the golden rule, like an infant child, but it isn't worthy of you and it isn't worthy of someone I call my friend. Your life's moving in cycles to a certain end and you can't escape it; though you run howling and bawling through the universe that's closing in on you. Can you escape? For you're no airman, no, pet; you're an earth creature. No, it's a fateful thing you came to Roseland, it's a fateful thing you met me, it's a fateful thing you met those who sucked your heart dry, and the hour is now, pet: it's my voice that is telling you the right thing; listen. This is your last chance. It's now or never. But would you have the strength for it, even that? If I told you: that's the thing to do, the great thing."

"What, what?" said Caroline wearily.

"Have the courage to deal with your own life?"

"I don't know."

Nellie assured her, "You're priceless to me. I'm proud of you. I'm intensely interested in you. You give me what I've never had. You've been given to me and I feel such joy and satisfaction, Caroline, for the beautiful thing you have in you, the courage to face life and stark death; you're one of the rare ones."

She told Caroline they'd miss nothing together. They were getting somewhere now.

"You haven't my courage but you can lean on me. I'm your friend, your true friend. I know now that you never had a friend. . I am going through everything with you, all the bitterness, the black path of ashes, where the air's unbreathable and you're suffocating—"

Where would it end? The air was becoming unbreathable, filling with the smoke of Nellie's endless cigarettes; ash lay on the bed and pillows, it fell on Caroline's face and hair. Caroline brushed it away, Nellie leaning closer to brush her hair, dropped more ash. Once Nellie hung over the bed, her turnip head down to the floor, while she choked in spasms. But the night wore through and Nellie was wrestling still with her; for everything she said came back to the one thing, to face her loneliness bravely, not seeking pitiable expedients, to listen to the words from a true tongue, not the despicable lies and sensual fantasies of vain, depraved inconstant men, "the shameful expedient, a man's plaything. They made the world; and you believe in them? A woman knows what is in your heart and is your true sister and friend. With them is death, with me your friend is understanding at last, release, a bright morning, the first bright morning of your life." And gradually it began to come out, the story of Venna and the satanic world she had seen. "I'll tell you all—you must know everything."

When morning came, Nellie lay on her back on the bed smoking and listening to the first birds. Caroline lay face downwards with her arms under her, all about her her loose long hair.

"Are you asleep?" enquired Nellie at length.

After a time, Caroline muttered, "Yes, I will die. You are right. That's the thing. You've torn the world away from me. There's nothing else."

Nellie was incapable of saying anything, her face shining with the light of a planet. She asked in an intense low tone, controlling her excitement, "Will you die for me, Caroline? Because you understand death through me? It would be a great triumph. It would set me on my path. Your life would go along with me in me. Have you a great passion for me, Caroline? Will you do what I say? What I need is the confidence your beautiful sacrifice would give me. Then I would be the thing I am meant to be, the great leader—some saw in me. When I was a child, they saw it in me. My brother believed in me then; he knew he had nothing and I had the power. But he wandered away from me, inconstant and incredulous. But you believe. If you made the sacrifice I would look straight in the face of my destiny. Sacrifice, the blood of one dear and devoted—"

Caroline turned on her side away from her friend and looked outwards into the room without any thought in her face. Nellie, short of complete victory, became restless. She changed her clothes, made breakfast and brought it in. Caroline pushed it away. Nellie looked at her, left her to herself except occasionally to ask her questions in a low tone as if to a sleeper.

Caroline said suddenly, "I must go to work. I'm not going to let them down."

"But you're sick, you're feverish."

"You didn't care about that."

"Eh, love! I'll be your slave. Well, go then, but come home here. But you'll come then, Caroline," she said with a sudden pang. "You'll surely not run into the traps and ambushes again."

"Yes, all places are the same: why not here?"

Nellie kept murmuring anxiously and watching her; and in the end they both went off to work at the same time. Caroline had a pale glaring face, but there were many pale skinny anxious staring faces in the city going to work; and the same sort of faces sprinkled among those waiting on the benches in the outer room of the housing office. And all day, when she could hardly read or write, she heard their terrible stories, "two children, my husband and I in one room, and one child tubercular, I make two tents out of sheets to close in the children's cots"; she listened, with bent and burning head and it was just as if she saw these things for the first time.

"In a way Nellie is right; it's what I'm going through myself for the first time—if I'm to live to sixty, seventy and only then find out something for the first time, mistaken all my life, ignorant—"

When she got out of the office, Tom was there.

"I couldn't believe it when my sister said you had gone to work. I'm taking you straight home. I just got back. When I heard I drove here."

"I promised Nellie not to see you again. But I must get home somehow."

He said nothing.

"I must get home, I must get into bed."

"I must take care of you."

"That's what Nellie says. I think it's a put-up job between you. I've always suspected it. You work hand in hand."

He listened in silence to her ramblings, and at last said, "None of this is true and I ought not to leave you there; but I'm stumped. I can't take you to Blackstone now."

"I won't let you hurt me again. I won't suffer any more. I don't believe in you or in her or in anyone. Are there just vultures and ravens?"

Nellie had made an excuse and come home early. When she saw them she was speechless with rage and would not look at Tom, took the girl upstairs herself.

"I'll be back to have a talk with you, Nellie," said Tom.

But when Nellie got the girl upstairs, she flung herself into her arms and burst into a loud sobbing, "It's too much for me, Caroline. I do me best. I wish I could go with you, make a death pact and out. But there's something burning in me won't let me. And I haven't the strength for what the flame tells me to do."

Presently she became calmer and told Caroline her troubles at work; and she went on denouncing and fighting against other, darker, unnamed beings who hated her, friends who had turned against her.

"Oh, I thank my stars that I have found you."

[267]

Caroline sat listening and shivering.

"I need you, Caroline, above all: now that I have found you; now that I can give you what I need to give, a pure and lovely thing."

Caroline, fully dressed, rolled on to the bed and seemed to be asleep.

Nellie who had no notions of sick-nursing, went out and left her there, for she had heard Eliza come in from work. They made a pot of tea and sat long over it; and Nellie quieter now, murmured about her troubles to Eliza. There was a conspiracy at the office to get rid of her. The doctor had come round again and after a short examination, said she must try to get to the country.

"I kept me peace, for I respect the unselfish souls who give up their lives to the sick but I know the thought had been put in his head by Robert Peebles, to pay me out because I wouldn't attend his classes on theory. I would not. It's against me principles."

She spluttered, threw away her wet cigarette and started another and said quietly, "He says he thought I had an ulcer on me lung; but it's the asthma. It's just asthma. I told him me old Uncle was a martyr to it. And he said I was to watch it and not smoke or drink. But I don't know what color life would be without that? But, Eliza, if it's the asthma, why do I have this pain? There's a pain there, sometimes, like a knife. I think to myself, The old surgeon death is there cutting away at me without an anaesthetic. So I'm glad to know it's only the asthma. I can live to eighty with the asthma, eighty and more."

Eliza wrote that night to George.

Tom, later, sleepless, in his bedroom thought much about Caroline and about Nellie. He was very much touched by her appeal to his purity and chastity. He shed tears. He now for the first time saw that she had always wanted to protect his innocence, after she had ignorantly destroyed it, in the Jago time. She had appealed to him often enough, condemned him too; but he had never seen that she meant it, she honored him for his strangeness; and he thought that it showed how pure she was.

Wasn't she deeply wounded, shocked by all the wantonness she saw? She campaigned against it, but he had thought it an eccentricity; now he saw she was a simple-hearted priestess. She believed she was protecting women. He had often wanted to believe that Nellie was good-hearted and honest; now it seemed she was. The rest was the braggadocio she so dearly loved: "the old man over again." Nellie had passions for a great many things. She could not consider a thing without passion, for and against; yet none of these things was her true passion. For instance, her passion about the working class; it was true in its way but she melted into it all kinds of incompatible ideas. Then he thought she was in danger of dying for, or going to jail for, or becoming a total ruin for things which had nothing to do with what she thought was socialism. To her it was all one: those who disagreed with her on any count at all in this sacred miscellany were her enemies and enemies of the working class. People understood her passion and weakness, and were patient with her: but she never knew that. She felt herself a conqueror: or if she failed, groaned at the bitter struggle.

Tom had gone round with her on some assignments, sometimes to meetings. It was she who was the pitiful waif, the stray, the strange elf, all the things she saw in others. Nellie at a meeting of working women, for example, cut a grotesque figure. In a green peaked cap with cock's feathers, in boots lined with lamb's wool against the cold and hardness of the streets and stairs she had to tramp, a muffler round her starved and diseased throat, some old dress she felt easy in, her bodice loose either so that she could cough more easily or because she thought a tight figure bourgeois, something of the sort, her perpetual cigarette, her terrible stoop and lunging stride—there was not one woman there of the hard-pressed working sort, who looked anything like her or who understood her: and her weary old reporter's drawl, her perpetual outlandish chick, pet, sweetheart, and northern affectations, set her apart, a draggled peacock in a serious busy barnyard.

Tom went around and watched the proceedings; the meetings interested him a little. He thought she was a good reporter; he admired her courage. Still he knew there was something wrong and that she would get into a smash-up some day, any day. She didn't know what she was doing; she admired everything she did. There was something missing in her; she lacked self-criticism. She was always talking about introspection by which she meant drool; and confession, by which she meant spinning interesting lies, or sifting out people's secrets. To her that was truth: that was what she meant by truth. She had a horror and suspicion of naked fact. It seemed to her it lacked humanity: she felt that someone selfish was extracting a profit from things when he talked about facts; that he was trying to blind you and lie to you.

When Tom looked at her he felt his heart growing large and full of regret and lament. Poor Nellie, reckless, wrong-headed and long ago led astray. It was a very good thing, an unlooked for bit of luck that she had met and married George, so strong and whole. She was unprincipled, though she didn't know it; George was a rock. She was very slowly changing, though bad old habits combined with starvation, stimulants and disease and early old age, meant that she could not change much. She had met George in youth, but then the glamour of Pop Cotter had been too strong. If she had had a strong upstanding brother, thought Tom, a big chunk of brother, she would have retreated a little more and admired him, been more marriageable: as it was, she had to wait till Pop Cotter was half dead before the great light shining on her face and blinding her to other men waned. It was only then she could run after George enough to fascinate him. Poor Nellie! "If George leaves her there will be nobody but me!" thought Tom. He wasn't anxious to be left with her. He was a very poor man and would never, having Estelle to support, and sending money up home, see his way clear. He supposed he could marry a woman with money, but he was too independent for that. He was already a little cold to the idea of marrying Caroline. It did not mean much to him: and he did not want to hurt Nellie too much. He must look for a working girl.

One Saturday morning when, having traveled on a night train, he came in for breakfast, Tom found that Nellie had invited a number of friends for a party for Caroline.

[270]

"I've taken your advice, Tom: I thought some company and a drink might cheer her up. You had better go back to Blackstone tomorrow afternoon. I thought, chick, you might take poor Eliza to the station with you. She'll be here tomorrow and she's fond of you lad; she'd like to cheer you on your way and you can have the stirrup cup at Liverpool Street with her."

"What do I want to take Eliza Cook to the station for?" he said with annoyance, for the stirrup cup was a custom of Nellie and himself.

"Ah, well, you're safe with her, at any rate," said Nellie; screwing up her face and pretending to give herself away with a smirk.

"If you'd stop conspiring, Nellie, you'd find that things would work out just the same: you always walk a hundred miles to get to the next corner."

She smirked again at this tribute to her cleverness.

"It's a pity, lad, you didn't walk a hundred miles or so to get home; for if you'd your job in Bridgehead, we both could stop worrying."

"Yes, you fancy if I was there, I'd never get a chance to get a wife again," he said without bitterness; just for the pleasure of showing her he knew her. He continued, "As a matter of fact, I'm glad I'm away from you all, because I'm afraid you're going to lose your job any day now and I don't want me to be here. If George sees you ripe for the dole, he'll have to come and look after you. If I'm here, he'll pile the responsibility on Tom."

"They can't get a better journalist than me, they can't do without me, darling. They've tried a whole row of petty-bourgeois intellectuals and hacks who are so far into the groove they're writing with mud and they know I'm a damned good newspaper woman."

"O.K. Nellie: will you try to hang on at least till George finds you something over there? And whatever you think, I want you to go. They'll look after your health over there: they do. I'm not happy about you."

She cried, "I'll make no promises, this side or that. I'll not compromise my honor. I've been speaking my idea all my life; I wouldn't go back now; that would give the lie to my life. My life's my pride. I told that to Robert Peebles: Fleet Street couldn't buy my principles with money or threats and he can't with cant. And neither can they—the socialist bureaucrats, a nationload of Robert Peebles. Man is free. That's what I'm for."

Tom said, "Well, be careful for my sake."

"Ah, bless you Tom; but even for you I wouldn't eat my words."

"I wouldn't know what to think of you if you did. It wouldn't be Nellie."

She kissed him, "Bless you! You believe in me. I'd be lost without you. There's only one like you. I don't know why when Nature found this pattern, she didn't keep on making them that way."

His face turned pink. But now Nellie had no more time for talk. She was excited about the party. Women were coming. There were some women George had never allowed in the house. He was a very prejudiced man and all was black and white to him. She had a lot of messages for Tom to do before she was ready. He was to clean up the back yard. Eliza was coming to help today and tomorrow but not staying the night. She kept making sure that Tom was going early on Sunday evening: "I wouldn't have room for you, pet," she came out with. "You'll be nice and fresh for work on Monday morning."

"And I won't be able to clink glasses with Caroline," said he laughing.

She turned black at that and he did not make any more jokes. She got over it and came running back to him because she wanted him for a message.

"You aren't losing anything here, Tom," she urged. "You'll be coming down to us every weekend. There's nothing to do in a place like that. But stay away two weekends while I'm away at the conference. I'll be looking for you, chick; three weeks from today."

"Am I to stay in Blackstone two weekends?" said Tom in a burst of laughter.

"But it'll keep you straight, Tom. We can have a grand old talk when I come back."

"Well, I don't like to leave all my London women," he teased, "I don't think Blackstone women can be as good."

She pursed up her face. He laughed.

"Aye, lad, but there's too much bitter truth in it."

He picked up a few things, then sat in the back yard quietly looking at the tree tops, house-backs, the back of the Cooks' little house. At the half moon there had been three or four beautiful days and they had had perfect weather since, cloudless skies except for the geometric clouds made by airmen: the night skies, fields of daisies, with the searchlights deepening them, exploring upwards. There was an old tall yew tree not far away which stood up in the evenings, in sharp darkness. The little budding and flowering bushes in the neighboring yards were soft and light: the smells of earth, grass and flowers streamed through wall chinks and breaks. The time would be pleasant at Ilger's orchard: like other years. He began humming, reflecting and scribbling on an envelope. The country would be beautiful soon. It would not perhaps be so bad, except that a lonely country summer was painful and he always felt nervous about a new job: there were always problems and they had to be met in a haphazard way. He had conquered such things so far, but he always wondered about the next time. If he did not find company in Blackstone, he could go to King's Lynn on the weekends, or even Bury or Cambridge. He didn't know about spending all that money coming to London. He wanted to keep a little stock of money for family emergencies: he was the man of the family. He smiled. "Sir, I said, I'm Thomas Cotter—" The orotund old pub voice came to him, one single strain on the afternoon air. "Now you say, Sir, you don't need life insurance, but just let me tell you of a thing that happened this week. Now Sir, I was on the road to Berwick—" the simple flamboyant life streamed past him, on another track. There he sat, waiting for the next thing in his life, prepared not to be surprised at anything.

NELLIE HURRIED about, telephoned. Nellie had various reasons why Mrs. McMahon could not come and Eliza had to go to friends. Camilla, she explained, was in a somber mood, depressed. Mrs. McMahon, bless her honest heart, could not be trusted nor asked not to mention to George, whom she adored, about the party.

"How is Caroline?"

She was in a very bad way.

Tom went out and came back with four bottles of wine.

"Stirrup cup," said he. "I'm going to split these with Eliza, Caroline and you: it's my contribution. It'll cheer me up on the train to be a bit dizzy."

"I'm afraid you've got her wrong, pet: Caroline doesn't want to see you. She told me that."

He flushed, "I'm going to see she drinks farewell with me. She told me what was wrong with her was starvation. Every time she's had a fair wage you've argued her out of it. I owe her reparation. It's that adolescent idea of sacrifice, self immolation you have: you're a proselytizing masochist."

"I'm afraid you can't shrug this one off, Tom. No, chick. This is one case you can't flatter yourself you're curing with an anecdote and a glass of Beaujolais. You can't cure an incurable malady with that technique. This time you've met your match who doesn't care for your formulas. You're struggling with the Angel of Death himself," said Nellie through her cigarette.

"I wouldn't mention that name so lightly if I were you," said Tom; "he's the only deity we're sure exists: we know him by his works."

"You can't mend broken hearts with a callous joke," said Nellie.

Nellie ran about the garden picking up things, looking like

a freebooter on a desert isle, rakish, raffish, uneasy, masterful, dissolute. At ten in the morning she had already crooked the elbow. When Eliza came, she walked straight through to the back, a little red hat on her round flushed face, and in a bursting summer suit. Nellie with one arm on her hip, waved to her and, tossing her head, stalked into the house.

"How happy Nellie is, acting cock of the walk," said Tom.

Eliza told him everything. Nell was so down about George's absence that she felt she had to give a party before she went off to the Labour Party conference. Nellie did not want George to know. George was such a nagging puritan about liquor and fun and so hard on the purse strings that Nellie couldn't have a real party with him in the house.

"So I shall be king of the May," said Tom with a poky little smile.

Eliza got up to go inside to help. She went to a rose bush that struggled through a mass of vine and picked a flower which she threw to him. He put it over his ear.

"Now you are king of the May."

"You'll see me wear it."

His sister called Eliza. He picked a book out of his pocket and went on reading it. It was *Belchamber* by Howard O. Sturgis. He liked it. And the author did embroidery. That reminded him of Constantine Ilger. He knew life was not conventional and he liked any author who noticed it, too. Ilger was no Sturgis; but he had remarkable qualities which Marion had known how to uncover. And Marion had given him, Tom, courage and belief in himself.

The guests began to come from their work. Some would not be free till the next day. They were all working women. Of them all, only Eliza and Nellie's friend Flo, from Bridgehead, were born in real poverty. There were one or two others he knew slightly whom he didn't like at all, Nellie's rough gang, women of forty or thereabouts, all hard workers, but too tough, even depraved and licentious, who lived like disorderly men. They gave Tom scarcely a glance. Nellie was gay, accommodating, even a little obsequious to some. Good-hearted Nellie! The mother of every stray cat. In her brave bohemian democracy she allowed no questions of morality. Tom dragged a canvas stretcher out of the shed and put it under the trees.

The women sat round talking in the front room or helped themselves to things in the kitchen. They had all brought food and drink. Tom was not regretted, he saw, when he went out to the pub. There was a pub not far away; expensive, but it was worth it. The favorite drink there was gin in beer; and there were some really old fellows who came in regularly for it. Tom liked to see bent old men having some fun, getting a little unsteady. It always went to their heads; they got their money's worth. Tom sat on his bench with his beer and watched them for quite a time. When he re-entered the house, the women all looked as if he had broken in on a board meeting.

"Have a good time," he said as he passed on his way to the kitchen.

They stared at him without appreciation. Even Nellie said nothing and stared. He felt like Uncle Simon.

"But I'm no Simon. Not even for Nell," said he to himself, seeing years ahead in a moment, George lost, Nell aging, the cynical, aging women.

"So it will have to be Blackstone and I'll get a responsibility up there; and Nell will realize she can't be so scatter-brained."

He got something to eat and went to the door of the front room to say to Nell that he was tired and going to bed on the stretcher in the bicycle shed. No one took any notice of him. He undressed in the bicycle shed and put on his overcoat to read a bit in the kitchen. When one of them came out, he retired for the night. He lay for a long time looking at the slightly veiled sky. It was the first night of full moon; there was a chip off it yet. The moon had a great significance for him, which he did not understand. He would be watching the third night of full moon from some Blackstone window or hummock. A new life. He had seen Blackstone in war days. In winter it was the worst place in England, leaving out Wales; black, wild, open land, low young forests, winds rushing across, the bitter east wind making them all "bluenoses."

In spring and summer motoring through the brecklands and

forest lands it looked perhaps the finest place in England, broad rolling lands, long forested valleys and tops. The eye roved over grasslands, rushlands, heaths, preserves. They rushed through his mind now, and the great cloud fields. And not far away, the North Sea breaking into and crumbling the cliffs. Black flashing storms, the lowings and bellowings of the old sanded forest, the whistling and hooning of nameless birds, the lonesome moons, the weird fifteen-foot stone dwellers of the Old Priory, soft grassy slopes on which lovers lay, the humblest of workers by day, ecstatics by night. There were mounds everywhere on the plain: no one knew what they meant. There were remains of a Roman Road, a barrow; rivers and marshes full of fish. You had to be careful motoring on account of the pheasants, quail, rabbits, sitting out in full view quite undisturbed or running through tufts.

"I can be happy there, too, I am just an ordinary man. You can't be vain and arrogant there. It's like slipping into healing waters, pine-waters, cold and fleshy, rich-smelling, from which you come out feeling strong. The secret of joy is to be nobody."

In spite of wondering about what little room he'd get, for the present one was unsatisfactory, and how he'd manage with his various responsibilities on the salary, whether he'd be able to live in another town, buy a bike, sell his car, he soon fell asleep and was glad of the fresh air on his skin. He did not hear anything all night.

In the morning, Nellie was exhausted but devilishly gay, as the mood sometimes took her, and kept teasing him about his sleeping: a little anxiously perhaps.

"Sleeping like the dead all night. We called you for some brandy, didn't you hear?"

He hadn't heard and he didn't think he'd been called, either.

The women got up at various times and lounged round the house in careless undress, except one, called by her surname of Hardcast, who wore a business suit all the time, and Caroline in a cream blouse and dark blue slacks. He stared at her: his jaw dropped.

"Are you ill?"

"I didn't sleep. I haven't slept for three whole nights. Yet I feel quite lively."

"Oh, everyone sleeps without knowing it."

"No, I couldn't."

She looked it.

Nellie darted sharp glances at them when they were talking, twisting her beak and tufted head all the time.

"And did we keep you awake, pet?" she said to Caroline. "We stayed up a bit late carousing, I'm afraid, like a pack of adolescents, stealing a night out."

"No, I didn't hear you," said Caroline distantly. Nellie looked at her anxiously.

"That's like Nell," thought Tom; "so very tough in her own opinion: but as soon as anyone's cold to her, she can't take it."

He was a little annoyed with Caroline, even in her illness, for being unfriendly to his sister. Nellie worried about her like a foolish mother. It was true she had cost her a few jobs: that was Nell's idea of what was right and wrong.

Caroline had slept in the back attic, not much more than a box-room, with a low ceiling, a half-sized square-paned window looking out over the back yard. Nellie had drunk too much perhaps. She was in an overriding humor. She kept dashing in and out, teasing. She was hard to take in such a mood.

The girl did not want any lunch with them and went out to sit on the grass patch with Tom.

"I've never felt so calm," she said. "I can't sleep and it's as if that's what I've been craving. I manage to get up to go to work. While I'm riding in the bus I look at the others and think, How will I get to be like them: have so little and keep going? Going up the street I feel like collapsing between each step. I see young men like me, too: workmen. They put a foot forward, the body doesn't follow in the ordinary way but it comes forward afterwards. I'm finished."

"When you suffer, you think, I wish I could go back to that moment when it started, I would know how to choose. But what would you choose?"

She didn't hear him. She went on playing with a blade of grass. Her cheeks were thin and glowing, the skin on her neck

[279]

was drooping: there were gray hairs. Her eyes had fallen into hollows. She looked up and he once more looked through their transparent lenses into her mind. He felt her feebleness, nervous incoherence, himself gave up the ghost for her. At this moment, an idea he had about her slipped loose from him. They knew they were thinking of the same evil thing: he suspected her of depravity, she suspected him of being his sister's accomplice. She drew back and looked meanly, personally accusing.

"Do you think someone has taken advantage of you?" Tom asked involuntarily.

She shrank back farther and he could see that for her he was convicted. Her interpretation was that he and Nell, not to mention the others, had taken advantage of her loneliness, nervous collapse, for an abomination of their own. Shrunk like old age, she looked at him with contempt too.

"What you think is not so!" said Tom.

She turned her eyes away. Then she looked back and said, low, hurriedly, "I'm alone in the world and I've agreed to everything Nellie wants, and I've lost my sense of honor: she can't want any more than that, so I've given everything and what have I to give anyone else? She's taken everything from me. I've ruined myself."

"Would it help you if I made her talk to you? I'll talk to her."

"You must never mention it. Never. You will be the only one to understand. I'm getting old, I'm weak, I'm like the things at Stonehenge that frightened you. I am bad, lost. She wants it."

She again gave him a dark look, indignant.

"Not you, Caroline."

"The others must do the work. I can't."

The light wind played with her wasting hair. Tom went inside and said to Nellie that there was something very wrong with Caroline. Her depression and inanition were not normal.

The women were sitting in the front room eating and drinking, smoking.

"You talk her into bed, Tom, you're good at that," said Nellie.

Tom was filling a glass, stopped with the bottle poised, looked at Nellie enquiringly.

"But what does he do when he gets her there?" said their friend Flo, a short, handsome, plump woman with white arms. Tom picked up two glasses and a bottle.

"Tom's the darling of the middle-aged women;" said Nellie: "he smiles shyly and deprecatingly and buys them bull's-eyes."

"The only bull's-eyes they'll get from him," said one of the others.

Flo sat easily, smiling at him: she liked him: but she was altogether under Nellie's thumb.

Tom went out to Caroline. Nellie entered into a roistering mood. She came to the door and blackguarded him, ordering him to come in. He came in. Nellie then went to Caroline and very roughly ordered her to come in, too. She gave Nellie a strange look, but Nellie took no notice, picked up the things, came in cursing; what did she mean turning down all her guests? What was the new phase? She didn't like masochism. Was she superior to them all? She could drink with Tom? Then she could drink with them. She had been respecting Caroline's feelings and now she found out it was a ladylike pet. None of that here, it wouldn't go. Tom was shocked and acquiescent. He had never known Nellie like this: she was rough and ready as a tart. Was there a woman of that sort among the women? He eyed them. Nellie would do anything in her rough, bohemian democracy: she would never make herself out superior to other people. Once she had lived in a prostitutes' hotel. All the girls were prostitutes. She was very friendly with one.

There was some rough joking going on to which he listened half-surprised, half-amused. He did not believe women could be really rough. "You can take a horse to water but you cannot make him drink," said Flo to Tom; it was a rough joke.

"Don't take any notice of the hags," said Hardcast, the woman in the business suit, in a loud dry voice. It was the first time she had looked at him. Tom was eating, his wind-roughened lank red face bent over his plate. Hardcast always sat stiffly about with a long-distance look; never facing people, riding sidesaddle. She had black hair plastered down. She was head of a very big, city office. She was in a position to take bread from people's mouths. Some of the women there were her subordinates. Nellie had once been one of them.

"Tom doesn't mind: he's used to our style of humor," said Flo. "I suffered enough from him and Nell when we were children. They'd always be running ahead, leaving me behind and throwing back smart cracks over their shoulders. They thought they ran Bridgehead in those days."

"I never said anything unkind to you," protested Nellie shaking her topknot eagerly.

"Everyone did. You gave me a sense of inferiority."

"Didn't I work to get you out of Bridgehead?" cried Nellie indignantly; "you owe it to me!"

"I came of myself," said Flo in an easy-going style. She was very untidy, but her chalk-blue angora sweater blazed round her beautiful arms and neck; her greasy black hair framed a fine white forehead. She was an attractive slut, uneasy when she washed. She had a good nose and missed the numerous familiar scents from her own body.

"I have a lot of the dog in me," she always said; "I like to find my way about my own house by smell. I like to smell my own children. It's healthy and natural. I feel twice the woman. Besides, I'm not strong enough to keep things clean."

Her skirt, slipping from her waist and without a fastening, gaped showing a white hip. She sat next to Tom who glanced at her flesh appreciatively and smiled at what she said. Then he began talking to the woman on his other hand, Binnie, a soft plump reddish woman about thirty-eight, dressed carelessly but in a city style, with tossed well-kept hair. She was a rover, had been all over Europe, visited every danger spot, had lovers there, probably gone there to pick up lovers. She was energetic, headed committees, made speeches, had a number of children, wrote books, spoke languages, met statesmen, gave parties, introduced one circle to another and showed no sign of it at present when she was like an effusive, garrulous, top-heavy girl.

"Tell me how you do it," she said to Tom.

"Do what?"

"Make the women dance, what's the tune?"

"I do nothing."

"Is that it?"

He laughed.

"Perhaps that's it," she said lifting her voice with a slight domineering affected accent.

"We know he does nothing," said Nellie who with sharp, jealous, glances followed every word of the conversation.

"He flirts, that's enough," said Flo eating big dollops of pie. "He's the darndest flirt I ever met. The playboy of the Western World. Look at the footlights face!"

"A glitter like a Woolworth ring," said Hardcast, looking out of the window.

"Is that your mother's?" asked Binnie rudely of Hardcast, who wore a heavy gold wedding ring.

"My grandmother's, my mother had it," said Hardcast: "my grandmother wanted her to go into a convent."

"Better a mother than a mother superior," said Binnie.

This coarse joke made the women nervous. Binnie began to talk about the health of her children with Tom.

"Don't you ever miss children?" said one of the women teasing, to Tom.

"I have a child," said Tom. "I had one when I was twenty-one years old."

"A summer with but one rose," said the same woman.

Tom was angry.

"Leave him alone," said Nellie, who was watching everything.

"I bet you're happy now, surrounded by seven women," said the same tease.

Tom looked at the seventh woman longingly. She was a startling creature, flat and slender, with flaxen hair that she wore in an unbecoming but surprising style. She was elegant, in a plain Paris silk suit of yellow, stitched in white. Her eyelashes, eyebrows and the skin-hairs were pale. The light bathed her, soaked through her. She kept an unnatural stillness and coolness, sat in a sunny spot when she could, or lay on what golden, yellow, white, mustard, ocher lounges and cushions she could find. She was not saying anything, but knitting. She ate little and dry, at

[283]

least when in public. She was knitting men's socks of thin natural wool, in a variety of fine stitches. Tom could not keep his eyes off them.

"I think I know something about knitting," he said, rising and drawing nearer. "But I've never seen anyone like you. Why don't you go in for these national knitting prizes?"

"I shouldn't care for that," she said in a sharp chiming voice.

"Stop flirting in your corner," called Nellie.

"I'm not flirting," said the yellow girl, Marilyn.

"Where are you from?" she asked Tom.

"Upstairs," said Tom, laughing.

"Bridgehead? What's it like? Would I like it?"

"In autumn, about October, just before Guy Fawkes Day it's all dark at eight, quite dark. There are a few boys and girls playing quietly round the few street lamps like moths, the rest dark, no lights, all have retreated to the back fire for high tea, curtains are drawn tight across the windows. Go down the backways and you'll see a bright stream of light through the crack of the back gate and hear the yard being scrubbed. The air is sickening, you're right in an aerial coal seam, a slowly blowing, vaguely stirring mist of coal: and the next day will be rain. In the meantime you can see the stars through a ceiling of about ten feet of coal mist."

"Don't let him put you off," cried Nell impatiently, "it's a grand old town, it's our home. It's our mother, we owe everything to it: and they think hardly of us for deserting it. We're very proud of Bridgehead."

Tom did not turn his head but continued to the yellow girl, Marilyn, "And you'll meet a ragged, grotesque troop of children with stockings of flour or sawdust or earth, saying 'A Penny for the Guy.' I always go about with a pocketful of pennies, I don't know if I got it from that time. I always have about a hundred pennies on me. I used to go about myself. I got quite a bit of money. People liked me. I was bashful, my boots were always in holes, I used to sew up the holes in my pockets myself first to be sure not to lose any pennies. The others often had this stocking bludgeon but I never wanted to bludgeon anyone; it's like a big sausage they dangle in their hands," he explained, laughing.

"Are you telling your tales?" said Nellie contemptuously from the other corner of the table. "Quit your flirting there."

"I'm not flirting," complained Tom.

He remained turned to the girl. "They used to get me to sing too: I sang willingly. I had a good voice then. I used to get money."

"Sing now," said Marilyn, looking at him with curiosity.

"It's lost now."

"Come pipe up, brother," called Nellie wildly. "Let's hear the broken pipe."

"It's broken."

"Well, croak it, but let us hear you," she cried jealously.

They were surprised. He turned round, opened his mouth, and sang,

"Early in the month of May,
In the taverns slopped with ale,
Broken-footed from the way,
Loud sing I my threadbare tale,
There I stand, all red and pale,
Clowning in the month of May.
The bramble grows a wild white rose,
Late lay snows in Ilger's plot.
Look, my wreath is heavy with death,
All black beneath with loamy clot.
Sorrow, sorrow, sorrow, sorrow, sorrow till the end!
My heart is broken, none can mend; I must sorrow till the end."

He sang to simple quavering strains he had made up. Nellie laughed loudly and boldly.

"Aye, he can chirp like a bird in a cage: he sings to them, aye!"

"Do you sing to them?" enquired Flo, surprised.

He looked awkward, touching, outlandish. He looked queerer and stranger and twisted his mouth and eyes into odd shapes. He turned round and looked piteously across the room at Caroline who was sitting in a cold sulk by the hearth.

"You are a strange man," said Marilyn.

"Don't flatter him, sweetheart," called out Nellie: "or you'll be hearing nothing else for the rest of the weekend but his heartbreaking tales. He's not all there: there's a part missing."

"It's my heart," said Tom; "you're jealous of my heart."

At first he was angry and then he gave Nellie a splintered smile, very sly. She did not know where to look. Marilyn affected a snowy cold.

"Venus is the star I like most," Tom informed Marilyn in his ordinary tones, "it's like the mooring light of a ship that seems to be moving and isn't. I noticed last night through the roof."

"You write poetry I suppose," said Marilyn.

He assured her eagerly that he did. "In my Logbook. I never show it though. And I have ideas that wouldn't do for stories I suppose. I once knew a woman who wrote stories. She's dead now. This is an idea: a woman tall as the air and white, shaped like bells, and she has chains of rubies: you pull them off and she dies. Then I once knew a man who was fond of spiders, he told me all about them; what they felt."

Nellie began to make a great clatter, bang the china about, pour out wine, shout, swear, roughhouse, like a stableboy. Tom took no notice and went on confiding in Marilyn.

Nellie banged her plate with her knife, shouted, "Eh, young Cotter, throw me that rose, you daft fool, you do look silly in it!"

Tom took no notice but bent his head nearer and went on chatting.

"Thomas is not a good name for you," said Marilyn.

"It's not my name, it's my father's name. I have no name of my own," he replied.

"What do you do?"

"I can heal some people," he said. "I should have been a doctor I expect. If I knew how, combined with my feeling for people, and if I practiced, I could cure people. I'd like to do that."

"What's your brother saying?" asked Flo of Nellie.

"I don't know," said Nellie, "but he's bogus."

"He's saying that he can heal," Hardcast's voice was heard.

"He can give women children, I suppose, that's the kind of miracle he can perform," said Binnie.

"No, pet, he can't, but he can get the women thinking about children. They have only to look at those big eyes sailing right out of his head and they start sighing for a boy," said Nellie, "a boy under a flowering May tree, isn't that so, Tom?"

Tom stopped talking and stared at her.

She cackled, "Eh, eh, I made you stop the sweet drool."

He looked at her sternly.

"Eh, Cushie, you remind me too much of Bridgehead," said Eliza; "don't do it."

Nellie laughed, was so pleased she seemed to fly, eyes winking, hair sticking out like straws, arms akimbo, legs flying about, shoulders waggling, she sketched a fairy hobbledehoy, a woman cut free from the earth.

"Airmen are a great blessing, they can drop in on a woman anywhere," said Flo.

"You can make your selection as they parachute past," said someone else.

"Let them go past," said Nellie; "we're all right."

Tom got up to go out. He stepped through their crossed legs. They were drawn away from the table, close together. Their legs, the stool legs, the chair legs, the bottles and glasses formed a series of circles and the late sun coming through the back, spread its rays through them. He had to cross the empty space to get out. He stopped in the middle, looked round and taking the rose from his ear, threw it to Eliza. Nellie instantly threw her wineglass at his hand as if to stop him. She was half drunk: it was one of George's best wineglasses. A few drops of blood fell fell onto George's green carpet. He took his hand with the other hand and caressed it, held up the smear of blood.

"You fool," she said.

"Bad thing," said Tom.

"What's that for?" said Marilyn.

"It's just something they do in their family," said Florence.

Tom made his way out.

"I'm sorry, pet," said Nellie, rushing round.

"No, you're not," said Tom.

"Did I hurt you, pet?"

"You didn't kill me."

"Forgive your dumb sister, Tom."

"I don't mind horseplay."

"I'm a beast to you, Tom."

"You're a sweir beast," he said and went out.

Flo laughed and sang from the old ballad, "For Nellie is a sweir beast and canna cross the wa-ter."

Nellie gave her a dark look.

He went for the earliest of his trains, leaving the house about five; and Nellie did not try to keep him back. He was rather angry at being forced out and at the neglect. He had folded up his canvas bed and stood it in the shed, pushing his little tin trunk into a corner of the attic; and put out some canvas shoes, a flying suit and an old leather flying-jacket for Nellie to give to the bazaar. He mentioned these things to Nellie as he was leaving.

"Do you mind if I give them to poor Walter the window cleaner, Tom? I know you don't take to him, but he needs them."

"You know me better."

"You're leaving me in anger, Tom."

"Don't do anything I wouldn't do."

"You'll telephone me tomorrow night, won't you, Tom? Before I go."

"I'll do my best."

"And write to me, pet, give me all the news."

"Yes."

"And don't forget Eliza! She's going to the station with you. I forgot to mention it to you, Eliza. Would you go with the poor lad, Eliza sweetheart? Would ye darling? Oh, that would be glorious. Bless ye, darling. And then I know you're spending the evening with your Irish friends. We'll miss you."

Tom picked up his leather and canvas grips, swung them out to the front steps and waited patiently for Eliza. Nellie, standing in the doorway leaning her backbone against the doorpost, smiled at him under lowered lids. Tom smiled back. Nellie, he supposed, wanted a report on him. What girl was seeing him off at the station? No one was.

Eliza came stoutly along with her red hat and handbag.

"I hope you don't mind," said Nellie, "I know you want to get an early night, Lize, I know you've got to start early tomorrow. I know you don't think much of carousing, pet. It's a weakness, you're right, Lize: it's in me blood. Will you be round tomorrow night sweetheart? I'm expecting your remote-control troubadour of a George to put in an appearance, tomorrow night. Will ye come then, Lize? That'll be glorious darling. Ah, it's sweet of you to go with Tom: I'm eternally grateful."

She got them off and shut the door. Tom went loping along.

"Then you're not going back to the party, Eliza?"

"Well, you can see for yourself, she didn't expect me back."

Tom became somber. They said nothing while they walked up to the bus, nothing at the bus stop, till Eliza said, "Didn't you want me to come?"

"Yes."

"I am quite ashamed, Tom. It was like the old days. You know Nellie: she has to dominate."

Tom said, "But she would never do me any real harm. She's true to me."

Eliza felt upset. She said suddenly, "I don't know if she is, always."

"Nellie has got to come first," said Tom: "I don't mind."

"Do you mind going off?"

"Well, I'm glad you came too. A new job is always a bit of a worry: you feel nervous. You don't know what will happen. But I like to work. I know I'm going to be buried alive up there, but it's the same anywhere."

"Well, you could try to get to London for a job."

"I might try. But I must see how it is up there first. I don't suppose I'll stay."

"Don't you think you made a mistake to take a lower salary than before?"

He was annoyed, but said after a moment, "I don't care. What does it matter? I don't get the money, anyway. I don't need anything. I can live on bread and tea and I like it."

"Oh, well, I can too. But what I miss most, is the hahm, if I can't afford it," said Eliza, in her longing for ham, speaking in a deep voice.

At the station they had the final cup of tea. Tom was suddenly unwilling to go, said, Why was he going? They could go to the movies, go to a lunchroom—he could put up somewhere for the night, anything not to quit London too early. But he hopped on the old-fashioned country train at the last moment, with a book by C. E. Montague that he had heard was good and entertaining. She saw his boyish, peaked, blue-eyed face leaning, full of yearning for London, out of the square train-window. Even as the train moved, he said, "Shall I jump off? We'll go somewhere. I can go tomorrow." But the train moved faster. "I'm so glad you came," he called back: "I'm glad it was you."

The women in Lamb Street sat round talking, smoking, eating and were, in their relations with Caroline, stand-offish, friendly, curious, reticent, according to what they thought of her. Some of the women were journalists. They were all, but the yellow girl, central London women. They talked about political chances, news of the day, Fleet Street secrets, journalists who had lost their jobs, of special interest to them who were mostly middle-aged or on the verge of it. They were somewhat reserved in this matter towards the yellow girl, who was the youngest of them all and avid and, so it was said by them, unscrupulous: but perhaps that only meant she was younger.

They were least aware of Caroline, but she looked at them as through a block of ice, a woman lost in a glacier and some time after ten, she said she must go up to her bed in the attic: she did not know if she could sleep this night.

"The attic population always goes to bed early," said Nellie.

Caroline did not sleep but was swept along in the deep river of a lucid delirium, and, meanwhile, she vaguely heard noises in the house, music played, voices. After some length of time, she heard footsteps on the attic landing. They stopped outside her door which was presently, after some breathing pause, gently opened and shut. She lay for a while and then got up, went to the door, opened it. There was no one there. The stairs creaked, but the ceiling, stairs and walls always creaked there. The ceiling, for instance, in the attic room creaked all night. She looked over the banisters and saw nothing, though the bottom hallway was light with moon. The attic landing was dark, there being no window at the back there but moonlight fell in the empty room beside her through the skylight. The skylight was slightly raised and a soft air blew through the room. There was a bare grocery box standing under the skylight. A slender, male figure lurked just inside the open door.

"Caroline," said a voice.

She had a moment of excruciating fear. She saw in a moment that it was Nellie dressed in an airman's suit and that her open gash of a mouth was smiling and that her long hand had beckoned her. She had a thought that Nellie meant her some harm in the room, even to kill her. Nellie moved over and was standing stooping under the skylight, and nodded to her to come in: she smiled like a clown in the moonshade. Caroline went and stood on the box Nellie showed her and looked out from the skylight first at the late light of the sky and then down, down said the nod and the finger, into the back yard. Nellie also struggled for a place on the box: their hands gripped the window frame and the moon shone on Nellie's pointed face. Nellie looked quickly at her, excited, sharp, the clever smirk. The box tipped and Nellie quickly caught her round the waist. Caroline kept looking down with astonishment, and Nellie gripped her harder.

A number of naked women were rounding, breaking, wrestling, weaving together in the back yard between the brick walls, the high fence and the tree. The moonlight showed that some were rosy in the daytime, others were the colors of night-lighted fish and they were like queer fish, a seahorse, an old man snapper, a gar, a toadfish, a puffball and one rather awkward and hesitant was as yet, only a woman: and what was more ludicrous, partly dressed.

Nellie laid her beak and her chin over her shoulder with a sharp penetrating smile, her face wore its highest look of animal intelligence. Caroline looked at this human living and moon-flowering wreath in the back yard a moment till she distinguished the creatures, then she disengaged herself from the strong embrace and climbed down while Nellie after a poignant glance looked once more out of the skylight. She clung to the frame, her gaunt snowy face poked forward and with passion, surveyed the tenants of the globular moony night.

She put out her hand to touch Caroline's head, nothing was there; Caroline had gone. She looked still, expecting to see Caroline join them downstairs: she didn't. With a slight smile still she stalked after her like a shadow in the close-fitting and becoming dark suit. Was there a movement just off the stairs? She kept smiling, and followed for she thought Caroline had gone down. She went out and looked about among the women who were not excited enough to keep that slow rhythm up long.

"Where is Caroline?" her clear voice called. She went back and looked in the rooms, beginning with the ground floor. "Caroline, Caroline darling!" The house was still and living. The moon struck the faces of the little houses opposite and shone on the square panes.

"Caroline's there!" said a voice from the back yard.

She went hurrying out with her yearning intense face full of delight. "Ah, pet, where are you?"

But she was not there at all, someone had seen her at the upstairs window for a moment.

Caroline had dressed. She went down one flight and sat on the stairs, thinking she was going to fall because her heart was beating so heavily: she got up again, staggered into the empty front room, and sat down in the armchair. It was dark. Someone stood at the back entry: a voice said, "I'll get her, it'll do her good: we must help her," and footsteps thudded, a strange-shaped naked woman began to appear above the hall floor through the banisters, hank of hair, half-moon face, neck like a can, thickset shoulders, spidery arm after spidery arm, long shank after long shank. The woman complete, some sort of crab, moved past the dark door and went up the other stairs. This sight pulled Caroline together. She heard the fleshy footsteps on the next floor and the voice. In the back yard was a sweet poignant whistling, which to her mind grew louder and louder, seemed to whistle

[292]

through the walls and meanwhile upstairs she heard her name. A woman, too, came in from the yard.

She gently pushed the door to. She was lazy with terror, her heart bursting. There were steps on the stairs coming up, she heard her name in various parts of the house. The door came slowly open. Nellie stood there smiling, her gaunt jaws slightly open. There were some whispered words. Nellie came in and Caroline groaned. She got up, pushed past Nellie and went downstairs, while Nellie stood watching. The staircase came down facing the front door. The soft old lock opened easily. She began to run, fell down the steps which she had forgotten. She fell flat knocking her breath out, so that for a while she lay rolling there, and tried to roll to the road. No one came out, she heard only soft urgent voices through the door, held to.

She got up and walked clumsily away. She walked about the streets in that area and then as if the streets unrolled themselves before her in one direction only, she walked that way, rapidly as if she had an address in another part of London to go to. Her head was empty and she knew she was exhausted but found it strange how well she could keep going. She passed miles, acres. In the streets were the odors of summer and aged housing. The moon shifted. In these houses were strangers occupied in struggling for breath, not much more. She did not want to know any more about them, the wretchedness and fatigue were too general. There was something else. She had seen the riot, scandal that was the flowering of the force of nature in some, the strong wildness, that was anger, the perversity, the nonchalant feeble depravity, the indifference to degradation in others. Though she burned purer and hotter than ever, and detested vice more than before, she had also become gentle and indifferent about it: it was their way and they were human. If people had tuberculosis or cancer they were still entirely human. Her dislike of all these things, misery, perversity and disease was stronger than ever; and she knew that she had got into the wrong circle.

She was sorry she had come to London, but there was nothing to go back to. Differently from Nellie, she could see that Nellie had an idea in her constant advice about submitting. It might seem strange in a beaky, restless, gabby person like Nellie to chatter about submission, hypocrisy with an aim in it, but Nellie in her blue half-lights lit on aspects of existence. Was it because she had never submitted and could not, that she had not kept Barry and never had a friend? "Sink the turbulent selfish soul," said Nellie, who never did that—or did she sometimes in her excesses? Caroline had no temperament for excesses. "You are afraid of beauty," said Nellie, "you just want grand, impetuous life to provide you with a living; you'll never be an artist."

Caroline had taken submission as a word that Nellie used for her own purposes as she used Introspection and Friendship. By introspection she meant a shameless curiosity and crafty use of her knowledge; by friendship what only a clique meant; and it was dishonest since she trapped people that way. But Nellie was ill, and by submission she might mean death, it might be a preconception of death which only the sick could have. And this chilling submission was what Caroline for the first time was feeling now. Caroline now floated along over-shadowed by the lank, hobbling stride of the woman who had taken her up, haunted her, and ruined her. She was walking away from her, but Nellie was someone she carried with her, as you carry a bad parent always with you; Nellie had got into her being, like the knowledge of drunkenness. There had been nothing in Bridgehead, Nellie said, to satisfy their youthful intellectual and moral hungers, so they had taken to drink, vice, unbridled chaotic speculation and gnawing at each other. Hunger will prey on garbage, rather than be extinguished in death. But Nellie had not called it garbage, she called it knowledge.

George and Eliza Cook and a good many others, plain folk with strong natures and tempers, had seen things were wrong and they wanted to save humanity, their nation in particular and the greater part of the nation, the poor worker, to which they belonged, from making a terrible mistake. Many mistakes had been made by the workers. But Nellie had chosen Bedlam and the lazaret as brothers and sisters. Nellie hammered at Caroline, "What answer have you for the individual? You yourself are an individual. I think of the individual, and I've spent my life among the poor creatures. Textbook answers won't do and crusades won't do except to exculpate the smug. The individual lives, suffers, his heart is beaten out of him, he dies. Society does not die and I don't care about society. Society is a villain. It keeps on living and social arts and social sciences are only charitable dames. Marxism is cruel, because it doesn't care about the individual. Can I go to a man eating garbage out of the gutter and say, The dole is only a palliative. What you need is to starve so that you'll see your position clear and revolt? No decent person would say that, but the Marxists say that and so I say they're self-satisfied black-coated bureaucrats, a petty-bourgeois sect with canting deacons."

"But George then?"

"I'm a better revolutionist than he is."

The revolutionists she saw as fragments of men, all at fault. She went so far as to think of the fighters, the sane, healthy, as thick-skinned Philistines. She was maimed and glad of it. "The most pitiful figure, the most beautiful soul is a woman standing on the scaffold and looking down at the people around her who are going to kill her; she's inherited a heavy burden, she's suffered every disappointment, she's tried to get out of it and they've killed her for it. When she looks down at them she sees into their transparent souls: she knows them. She knows what is under every move of theirs. And so they hang her for witchcraft, for poisoning."

Nellie for a while had been absorbed by the strange life and sufferings of a woman named Mary who had been a follower of Joanna Southcott and perhaps had imagined herself a savior. Nellie had not understood the story at all and given it to Caroline eagerly with her hurried, nervous high voice, "What's the explanation, sweetheart? Do you understand her? I don't know whether she's an innocent victim that they got after, or whether she was guilty. Was she a real healer or a charlatan or self-deceived?"

Caroline read the history and rejected it, "Of course she was a poisoner."

"Ah, but she suffered. And they came to her to be healed."

Then Nellie lost all interest. But it was clear from many things that with Nellie a naïve, fresh-faced pathos was the visage of criminals. She thought that reason was a cloud hiding bad motives and society a wheel to break individuals upon.

"As you have been broken, Caroline. An individual is born into society only for society to seize it, crush it, plunder it, force it to work, marry, produce; only to rob the fruit of its labor, marriage, creation, to make it old and empty and shovel it into the grave. Society should live for the individual, but it never will. All those who agree that society is right and who try to follow its rules are mugs or ignorant. And if you understand, you can't escape, sweetheart, but you can penetrate the meaning of things, enjoy yourself in your own way and when you die it is in your own time, as you wish, not squeezed out and trodden out like an orange rind, but if you want to, when you're young. Isn't it better to die as an individual, when you want to, than to wait till you're something else, just a hulk with a cargo of disease and pain?"

Nellie herself expected to live long. "I feel it in me, Caroline: a gypsy once told me, You've a long life ahead."

And Nellie was impatient with "revolutionary pipe dreams." No City of the Future! The here and now of pain! Can a slum-mother look beyond the next rat-squeak, or an invalid beyond the next ache? "Most of their rebel talk, sweetheart, is whistling down the wind. It may be heard and may cheer a heart in an orchard two miles away or it may be lost altogether for eternity. You can't feed the hungry on maybes. For those whose torments are like ours, who understand as we do, there is sometimes only one answer." Death was the answer. "How do we know there is nothing beyond? No one ever returned. Perhaps there is something totally unlike anything ever imagined. I'm a materialist, pet, remember, but still we know nothing: there is the Unknowable. It would be an intoxication, the best, to plunge into the unknowable. When you're watching a bird, sweetheart, and see it spread its wings and fly off so easily, don't you want to do the same? To think of it; nothing more! And charity! Understanding! The accounts all settled. All the worries settled. No one to ask you for rent. Supposing there were a world like that, it would be glorious. But who can imagine a world like that? We all fight for life: that's blind animal impulse. The-Bride-of-

Death. That would be something glorious to experience, the last submission, the splendid last breath, the sacred swoon. They say it's nothing at all if it's swift, a blinding flash of light, a total darkness, something like that."

But there was a book in her library by Charles Duff which indicated that sudden death must not be like that, but a long pain.

"Aye, but that's the animal pain, the consciousness is gone."

"Who knows?"

"No one has returned from there to tell us."

It was strange that months and months they had talked around this theme and how Nellie could harmonize upon it. She had read fitfully in the last few months and brought up all the ideas she had read. Everything Nellie had read had seemed to bear upon death and to confirm her ideas.

"It would be a great and glorious thing if one of us turned out to have a soul of that quality: I always thought it might be you, Caroline. It would stretch out the measure of existence for us. And to leave a message for us all from the edge of the Unknowable! Oh, Caroline—it's a great vision."

Nellie could become exalted, and then return downwards as if to examine her listener's strength and faith.

"There were suicides and deaths when we were young, that was hunger, and despair, the bleak reality." Nellie's hunger for death had come from then. "But I will live old, it's in my bones."

The woman now began to address Nellie directly. She was taking leave of everything and Nellie was the last one lingering.

"Go away, go away, Nellie, don't talk to me, don't call me. I am gone. Let me be alone. I am alone."

As she walked she became aware of someone behind her. She stood still. The moon was still slanting and a faint wind blowing like a drapery, touching her off and on. She heard a giant stride behind her, very soft; it came from up the street towards her. An agreeable nondescript young man with cropped hair was there and wearing something loose, like coolie trousers and coat and a yard or so of uncut pale material over his shoulders. He stood faintly dark against the moonlight which slanted behind him. Caroline knew all this without seeing it. It was behind her. She heard two more strides behind her, an enormous, silent gust and his hand touched her coat lightly, with a wave of air and motion.

"Is it an unknown or death? Is it real?"

She waited but nothing more happened. She walked on, seeing behind her, without looking, the long moonlit and shadowy street. "Three great sighs, three great strides." She began to rest as she walked. Morning was coming into the moonlight, two fluids which did not mix well. There were a lot of people everywhere about at first, and she sat down to have tea in a place full of men. On the dirty table top she wrote a letter to Nellie. She had to write to Nellie who wanted it and who understood her. Then she wrote a note to the office telling them she was ill and they had better not expect her that day. They gave her envelopes and stamps and she posted the letters outside and began to walk again, though her head was turning.

She went down to the canal and had a look at it. People were about, there were trams full of people going to work and also sightseers. Everything seemed so strange. It was as if she had just come into this world.

Now the men had gone and there were women about. She walked; she could not think. Only to lie down or to climb.

At last she saw an immense apartment building, large rooms, steel girders, brickwork and the frames of windows; everything was rented in advance, a notice said in front. She climbed up a long way through the building and when the first man questioned her she said calmly she was going to see Mr. Whistler, the name of a man in an office she had worked in. "Whistler? Who's he?" were the last words she heard. She went as far up as she could and jumped onto a terrain of the sort she had always liked to play on when a child, clay, lime and sand pits, wheelbarrows, piles of bricks, and plenty of lost nails everywhere. She died that day and was not identified for two days since no one was looking for her; she had at that moment no settled address and she was a long way from Islington.

I T WAS a Sunday when Nellie returned from her conference. The door in Lamb Street was opened by Mrs. McMahon. Nellie said cheerfully, "Hello, Gwen, what are you doing here? Aren't you cooking for your family today?"

"I've given Bernard a picnic lunch and he's gone to Mrs. Bobsey's for the weekend; Mr. Cook insisted."

"Well, who's home, pet? You don't know what it is to be home. Make me a cup o' tea, pet. Where's my brother?"

"Mr. Cook's in the back yard reading the paper in his battledress," said Mrs. McMahon very merry.

George was stretched out on Tom's cot under the tree, and dressed in an army surplus jungle warfare battledress. He was reading from a pile of dainty foreign books, each a quarter of an inch thick and covered with fancy paper in small light designs. George did not get up. He was reddish brown all over from the sun. The graying strands of his hair had also burned yellow again.

He called, "Hello, darling; don't throw yourself on my stomach; Mrs. McMahon has been stuffing me for two weeks."

"You've been here for two weeks?"

"I stayed at Bob's at first; but not to wear out my welcome I came home about ten days ago. I want to use the farm as a rest home if they chuck me out of my continental office."

"What's wrong with this rest home? Get up from there, and give us a hug and a kiss. I've been working all hours for two weeks."

Her voice was hoarse. In her excitement she brought on a fit of coughing, through which she continued to sputter to her husband. He took no notice of her remarks or the coughing. He had dropped one book which was on the art of pottery and had begun on another, about G. Bernard Shaw, that Fabian he had admired as a young boy. Nellie went into a series of coughing spasms and sat down on the grass to finish them off.

George drawled, "It's witty. It's funny I used to think Shaw was a great man. I wrote to him once, telling him how to improve his style for the workingman."

Nellie said dryly, "I never fell for him, chick. To me he was just another Irishman pulling the wool over English eyes. I never saw it, pet. From the very first play I denounced him as a mountebank."

"I'd like to see you write a play half as good as Man and Superman," roared George, not because he was angry.

Mrs. McMahon's face looked round the open doorway smiling, to hear George laughing; Nellie laughed.

"It's himself in residence again. Home, home, home!" said Nellie.

The telephone rang in the front room and Nellie was up the kitchen steps, overturning a chair, throwing her hat on the ground, knocking a cup of tea to the floor and dragging the cloth half off the table, all in one moment. She cried, "It's me brother."

In a minute they heard her joyous, "Hell-o-o darling!" and the long excited chatter; her voice went down to a contralto croon, became grave and excited again. "And were ye down last weekend, pet? Ah, blast it, I missed you! Did ye sleep here?" and so on. Conversation languished; there were silences, but they still stayed at the phone, in contact. At last she came away.

"Tom was down! He never told me. Caroline's never come back? There must be a letter for me."

Very much excited, she looked for her letters, and having run briefly through them, selected some, when she noticed one from Joanna Sterker. This she slid into her dress. She went into the front room, closed the door and read this note.

Cush—Well, you see me taking up your standing invite two in a row. Not very wise your standing invite was it? Or was it? I didn't take it up when I was in town two weeks ago. Perhaps I missed something. I never thought of you. Not very

[300]

flattering was it? I was staying with a nice little pal. Expect me Saturday or Sunday. Yrs. Johnny, Broke but Game.

PS/ What about that item in the papers?

Mrs. McMahon stayed to dinner, and with them was a friend from Wales who was to stay the night, Lewis, a miners' representative.

Mrs. McMahon was doing the dishes. Inside, they were quarreling. Lewis was a flatfaced, big, serious man of about forty-two, dark and of good complexion.

George and he were saying the men had changed; "When I was a docker in Cardiff, men in pubs were interested in any kind of topic and the things they talked about intelligently would surprise you; but not now. And the same with singing. When they got a bit drunk and I was a drinking man, then they would all start up and sing and they all could; but not now. It's just silly talk, the pools, what was on telly last night. I was in a pub this evening with a couple of members of the Board; I've just got on, you know, I'm junior member; and they asked one of the men there to give a song. He went to the piano and began to strum on it and then sang a song, but not well; a man can't sing who needs an instrument. And that was to show me people could still sing!"

George agreed. It was true the men weren't serious in pubs any more. Nellie disagreed. She said the workers were just as serious, but they didn't express it in the old-fashioned sententious way.

"Wait for the event, Lew; don't get too uppity because you're on the Board. Don't take after George here, who's getting mighty critical of the workers. They're just the same and they'll soon show it."

"What will they do?" said Lewis, seriously.

"You'll see, by June, next year, there'll be a general strike."

"I don't agree with you. The old spirit's gone," said Lewis.

"The men certainly did talk more seriously twenty years ago," said George.

Nellie said perhaps it was the radio and TV.

[301]

"It's gone by in a flash: you can't discuss it."

Mrs. McMahon had finished and came in to listen, her peachy face lighted up. Said she, "The English do not sing as much as the Welsh."

Lewis noticed she was Welsh and turned a little towards her. Mrs. McMahon said, "The men think they've paid their way. They pay out their responsibilities in taxes, insurance, all kinds of contributions. They feel they've done their bit; and the little bit over is for the pub and the pools."

George had his teeth into it, though, "Well, but I remember very well when I first came to London from Tyneside. It wasn't hard to get up an argument then and I did it purposely wherever I went, to learn to speak. I learned a lot from the talking and joking in pubs. I learned to meet the serious opponent, the surly or angry man without temper: I learned to show my temper; I learned the tricks of the heckler. I'm a heckler myself. But now I couldn't learn the soapbox or the platform in the pubs and I never go near them. It's all blamed hush-hush and respect and don't say that. What's happened to men like Cobden? They must still be with us."

Nellie said there were young fellows coming up but they were not allowed up. Lewis had his teeth into it, too. He said, "It is a smug determination to take what is coming to them. The workers are determined to get what is coming to them, though they don't think for a moment the Labour Government is really their government. They're greedy for their rights. It's a lingering memory of the bad days. Now the job of social democracy is to make use of just this tendency. It's no good saying it was the war. They had much more war on the Continent and over there there are strong revolutionary parties."

Nellie became very excited at the suggestion that anything on the Continent was better than anything in England; and she theatrically and noisily scolded George when he said the food was better, revolutionary feeling was better and there was a hundred thousand times better discussion. Nellie became angry and went out with Mrs. McMahon to make tea for them and cut some cake.

"It makes me boil, Gwen, to see them stretching their legs

and denouncing their own workers and praising foreigners up. I can't understand what gets into them as soon as they leave the pit and the dockside and become representatives. They're bloody retired. They're looking for a socialist Cheltenham."

She sulked and smoked for a while. Presently Mrs. McMahon went home, Lewis went to bed and George said he'd turn in too. Nellie sat smoking and in a while her eye fell on her bundle of mail. She said she'd just run through the stuff, get another pot of tea and hop into bed. George said to give him a cup when she made it, if he wasn't snoring.

"Whether you're snoring or not, pet, I'll wake you up if I have to throw the clock at you."

She went over and kissed his face all over with endearments under which his face expanded; he relaxed. He commanded, Come to bed and stop fiddling.

Nellie was anxious to, but Johnny Sterker's note stuck in her mind. She was sorry the evening had gone by without her telephoning Vi Butters or Eliza to get the news. She had been so busy thinking of trades union affairs, that she had not had a minute to think of herself. She had written to Caroline, received no answer, been very angry, because she thought Caroline must have been taken in by one of the women guests. They would do anything. She had already been upstairs and found that nothing of Caroline's had been touched; her own letters to her were there unopened.

She was very tired. She took the letters to the kitchen, glanced at one or two and went in with the pot of tea. George was not asleep and gave her sly, soft glances.

"Come to bed, blast you, you night bat; am I going to stay awake all night while you chainsmoke?"

George would not allow her to smoke in bed. During his absence she had smoked half the night and now she was, in fact, trying to get through a few cigarettes before turning in.

"You know too much about me," said she, sitting down to her tea. He lay there, yawning and holding out his hand for his cup of tea. She gave it to him and as she returned, noticed a letter under the clock. She made a pretext and took it to the kitchen, for she knew the handwriting: but whose was it? She read,

This will be perfection and the water is rushing over the dam, it is roaring deep smooth all the threads twisting into the fabric, continuous splendid dark—I can say nothing to you, for you are inside your cell of glass this is the only message I can give—from the glorious power—think of me as grief, I will not be thinking and not grief—the end not submission rushing intensity, not what you think, everything there rankles, here is living—quiet rushing over the edge out thousands of stars so many that they are daylight, all lives stars, myriads are one. I lost my honor. I said that once to you. Honor went down the wind a rag. It turns round, flies in my face—it is returning coming at me, what it is I don't know. I lived for honor and love and—dishonor only—(there was a stroke of the pen after this and some watermarks, perhaps tear marks. Some way under she had written in big letters,) I am dying, Nellie, where is honor.

Nellie read it again and again. She felt a gust of joy, anger and fear. If Caroline had really died, what a triumph for Nellie! If she had written to others, what danger! And without understanding it, the word, honor, honor, displeased her. In a shining storm, a fierce new life in her, she came in to George, mumbled through her cigarette "I've had a cryptic announcement from Caroline that she's changed her residence. There's a woman who never caught the blue bird! Have you heard from her darling? Has she been around?"

"Come to bed and stop smoking and fidgeting."

"You heard nothing from Caroline?"

"No."

Nellie undressed, put on the faded men's pajamas she wore, an old pair of George's turned up at wrists and ankles. Round the waist she tied, like a rope, some three yards of pale blue satin ribbon Caroline had once given her, seeing her pajamas pinned up with two large safety pins. This ribbon she wound three times round her thin waist and knotted in front. She then put a boot-lace round her "bunch of scallions," ate three small raw onions, smoked a last cigarette so hastily as to bring on a spasm, spat blood, took a glass of brandy, dropped paper and ash into the fender, put Caroline's letter in her shoe, and got into bed. As soon as she got into bed, she lighted another cigarette, with a twist to her mouth and a starry eye, blew smoke in George's face.

George shouted.

"Want a real good fight, pet?"

"No, I don't: let me nap," said George.

Nellie said with a come-hither grin, "No, let's have a quarrel." She pawed him on the side of the head, pulled the pillow away, "Lazy bugger, traitor, living on foreign handouts, living on women, I've no use for you."

"Shut up. The house is swarming with people."

"Suits me, pet," she said and she went for him, teasing and insulting till he became furious and half rose to fight her. They shouted at each other, filling and exhausting their lungs. The whole house was stirred up, wakened, kept awake. When they were quite satisfied with what they had done, they fell asleep. Nellie woke up suddenly some hours later and began to think of Caroline's letter, "Your cell of glass"—"Nellie I am dying where is honor?" and suddenly of Johnny's nasty pert tone. She got up and went downstairs to the kitchen, to ferret out meanings, to plan explanations. She believed that Caroline was dead; and she felt a blow on the heart; she was very much afraid. And yet of the wonderful letter, her achievement, she was very proud. She made a copy of the suicide note for Johnny: when someone had killed herself for Johnny long ago, there had been no such beauty in it. She left out the words about honor which she did not understand.

This morning, Monday, Mrs. McMahon was washing up. George had gone off to see seniors in his organization, about difficulties abroad; and Mrs. McMahon's little girl, Georgiana, clung in teasing affection round Nellie's legs as the two women spoke. Nellie gave Mrs. McMahon a cigarette and went inside with a pot of tea. She closed the door and did a lot of telephoning. She sat down and thought for a long time. She then took up her pen and wrote fluently:

Dear old Tom,

You ought to hear this from a friend of Caroline's who feels it as much as you will. You were a playmate of Caroline's. I don't know how well you knew her. She had been under the weather morally and physically for some time and took her life some weeks ago. Friends saw that little appeared in the press and all the details are not known. There is a page missing from the diary she kept, the last day. For those who knew her it was a great tragedy and a great loss. She was so reticent and shy that she did not impinge very much until one got to know her; and that was difficult. She was a grand fellow but her tragedy was supersensitivity and fastidiousness and an ineradicable disbelief in her own worth. She was a born saint and a born victim. She believed in people as well as causes. She survived several terrible ordeals; for she had a fatal instinct for picking out paranoiacs of the selfish kind. She tried to fuse her personal incompatibles by falling "in love" with a black-coat bureaucratic climber who used everyone as a brick in the wall he was building for himself to stand on. She was born only to dedication. She couldn't take disillusionment, Tom; that was her tragedy. She tried to take it. The struggle went on for months, and she wasn't the sort of pal you can help by getting drunk together. Fate set her a problem she couldn't solve and so she cut the Gordian knot, just because there was no pal standing by at the psychological moment. And Tom it was a hard blow to take. I'll be glad of a word of comfort. I wish I had you here to pour out my thoughts. I need a good bout of introspection to relieve my feelings. Will you come down?

Bless you darling,

Your devoted Nellie.

Nellie sat smoking in the front room by the empty hearth, ruminating. She got some fresh tea and a piece of custard tart.

Georgiana came running in. She was thin, agile, wily, the kind of child that a number of serious illnesses has made avid for life. The single chest of drawers they had at home, with two small and three long drawers, was mostly given up to Georgie's toys. Nellie gave her some caramels out of a vase. The playthings which she had brought in a new red beach bag, were scattered about the rug. She entreated, "Tell me a story about the sparrows."

"Not today, pet."

The child began to tell the story about the sparrows herself. "First they all fly in a flock in winter and when spring comes they separate, mm, mm, mm." She began to play with two loose-legged wooden dolls, one a sailor, one a gypsy girl in whose wooden head Nellie had fixed an old paste buckle. Georgiana danced the dolls and chanted interminably, "Up she goes, down she goes, up he goes, down he goes. One little darling, one little husband. Nellie, what is a husband?"

"It's like a father, pet."

"One little sailor, one little princess, sitting in a corner, poor Georgie's mother doing all the work, poor Georgie's mummy doing the work. Patacake, patacake, patacake what are you doing, what are you doing? Kissing, kissing, kissing, ha-ha-ha! I kissed him on his noseypeg, sailor! I kissed him on his wooden leg, sailor, sailor, sailor!"

She sighed, "Sigh sigh. He can sigh properly."

She began to sing again, "I went down the lane, never could come back again. Georgie-porgie pudding and pie kissed the girls and made them cry. Georgie, Georgie, Georgie, here comes Georgie. Cookie, cookie, cookie, here comes cookie. Oh—"

"That's enough, pet. Go and ask your mother for an orange."

"I've got an orange here. Look! Look-cook! I bring my own oranges and biscuits and everything."

Suddenly, she rose and went to Nellie's knee, which she leaned on as she asked affectionately, "Is Mr. Cook going away again?"

"Yes, pet."

"Is he coming back again to see me?"

"I'm afraid not, pet. Not for a long time, You'll be a big girl. You won't remember him."

"But he's going to leave me all his money, isn't he?"

"Go and ask your mother, Georgie."

"But she told me yes."

"Well, now run and play in the hall."

She rambled away singing and took her dolls for a walk in the hall.

Presently Mrs. McMahon and the child went. The woman wore her usual thin black coat of some damask-surfaced rayon and underneath a shabby black jacket and skirt with a little dusty black hat on her head. She wore the same outfit summer and winter and it killed all the color in her glowing skin, brought out the first signs of fading and age. The red gold of her beautiful hair stuck out raw beneath this miserable hat. She had a worn brown leather purse which served for a shopping bag also, a string bag, brown canvas shoes and heavily bandaged though solid legs, upon which she was obliged to wear cotton stockings. She was a pretty woman and liked dress. In a thin silk dress she looked like a nicely shaped girl.

They were a pathetic pair. The child wore a pretty blue coat which her mother had cut out and made from a coat given to her, and underneath was a red and white cotton dress which cost thirty-five shillings in a local fancy goods shop. She had a white lace collar, new patent leather shoes and new white socks with red stitchings. The parents both went exceedingly shabby to dress the little girl. Georgiana was swinging a red handbag which George Cook had given her for Christmas. Nellie noticed that the child was in all its best and that Mrs. McMahon was wearing a new soft green silk blouse.

"Goodbye, Gwen," she said briefly, "come Tuesday will ye, pet?"

She sat smoking and thinking till George came in and began to take books from the bookcases and put them in stacks on the floor. He then began to look into them and sort them. He lay down on the sofa with a book.

Nellie burst out suddenly, "You're betraying me, George Cook. I can't stand it. I've no home and no husband. I've nothing."

George went on reading.

Nellie said, "I see, I've nothing to lose. I've made up my mind. It's for me to give the ultimatum. I was ashamed to play the woman's part, snivel and talk about the rights of a married woman. I've never mentioned them nor asked you to look after me. I've never tried to keep you at home or asked for a home. Our home just came together of itself and it's been my joy, my only great joy in all my life. You came, it was a miracle; it came, it was a great joy. If I've lost that I thought, I'm not going to try any tantrums or groveling tactics. You were free to pick me and you picked me. I never did believe my joy, but I felt my pride. I felt so high and sweet. Oh, my dear boy!" She straightened up, however, and began to abuse him: now she would fight. Perhaps later she'd become brave again but at present she felt sore and she was fighting. "And not for myself only, but if you quit on the British working class, which has been your life, I'll quit you. That's how I feel about it."

George had his mind made up and was unmoved by anyone's arguments. He had no apologies to make to the working class. He knew what he was doing and he had not gone back on anyone he said, unless it was on Nellie and that was her fault. She had only to follow him.

"And leave England?"

"Why not?"

"Then it's you or England?"

"What's wrong with that?"

"What about my family? My brother."

"Don't try to fool me," said George laughing, "you don't give twopence for any of them: you get exalted about them but they're nothing to you."

"I never betrayed anyone," said Nellie.

"No, you'll never betray anyone," said George, "but you'll kill people with your curious ideas of loyalty. I'd rather you weren't so loyal."

Nellie looked at him intently. "How's that pet?"

At this moment, there was so great a sound that they thought some bomb must have fallen by mistake, perhaps a mock war or a real war started. The house shook and screams and shouts were heard. They ran out and the air, as in wartime, was full of fine dust. Mrs. Yates with her baby in her arms appeared on the landing and rushed outside. Lewis, the dockers' representative, came tearing down from the top landing, covered with white and holding his hand to his face. A short crash followed.

"The ceiling fell down," called Lewis who had been sleeping in the front attic.

This was not surprising as the ceiling had fallen down in the top hallway a few months before. The cellar was blocked up from war days when a bomb fell, crushing entirely the house next door.

No one cared very much, except George who kept laughing angrily and saying he was glad he was getting out of it. He'd sell the wreck if he could. No one would want to inherit it. But Nellie wept and said it was her only home, the only home she'd ever had, it was happiness, security, peace to her. It was love. What else had she? she asked George.

If the house went, there was George and if George went, what else was there for her in life.

"You see," remarked George calmly, "all this about England is more smoke than flame. Unless it's your friends," he said in an inquisitive tone, trying to look at her face.

"My friends!" she cried passionately: "they mean nothing to me. I'm alone. I've always been alone. They don't understand me. There's only you George. You understand me."

George laughed. "It's not so hard."

"And you don't take me seriously, you bugger!"

"That's the way to understand you!"

"Ah, you belittling blighter! We're going to have a real fight."

She bit his ear. George howled and jumped off the sofa. He hotly resented physical attack. They tumbled about, smacking and tussling, shouting and insulting.

Lewis, with plaster on his face, stood in the hallway and shouted up, "Hey!"

Nellie looked over the banisters cheerfully, "Don't fret, sweetheart. We're all right."

"The roof will be coming down on you," cried Lewis anxiously.

Nellie shouted with laughter, and so did George. They made it up, but they started again. Nellie flew off to work without tea, because George had thrown the teapot on the floor saying the tea was all water.

As soon as she got to work she received a telephone call from George, but she was at that moment in the canteen having breakfast. Later she had to call him back and they spent ten minutes loveydoveying. Before she left work she received a love letter from George, left downstairs as he was on his way to some consulate.

When she got home in the evening, she found another love note in her dressing-gown, "My dearest darlingest angel, how do you put up with a rotten-tempered pug like me? Forgive me darling sweetheart? I adore you."

When George came home with a few more necessary signatures and permits for his job abroad, she flew at him and they went into a long series of embraces. She wept and got supper for him. They abused everyone in the Labour movement, all their friends. She told him scandal and gossip, he retailed his conversations with people, in which he had come off best and chortled over his very near departure.

"And I'm taking you along in the baggage so don't pull that dear old England stuff on me any more. I know it's eyewash. You read it somewhere in a schoolbook. You're a fighting woman. You don't want their England."

"It's my England too," she said proudly. "Why don't you stay at home and help take it from them."

"I've got no time: Life is too short now," said George. "Supposing I only live till ninety-two? I'm not going to spend the best years of my life fighting the police."

They growled a bit but neither was ready for a fight at that moment.

George, who said cheerfully that he'd be gone for two or three years he hoped and expected, had bought presents for several people. He was a generous man and had spent a lot of money—a clock, a purse, a blouse, some wine glasses and for Mrs. McMahon a soft-hued Shetland blanket which must have cost him eight pounds or more. It was glorious, but for the money, said Nellie, though it was beautiful of him, he could have bought two blankets, which she so sorely needed. The McMahons had only one blanket and he could have got bargains. But George said stubbornly he wanted to give Mrs. McMahon some lovely thing, not blankets for her bed. This was a blanket, too.

"What would her husband think if I start giving her blankets?"

Mrs. McMahon did not show the gifts to Nellie and went about her duties with wet eyes. After George's departure she would come no more; Nellie could not afford her. George gave her a month's pay and told her to go to Bob's farm when she could arrange her summer holiday with her husband.

"George is a pet, a sweetheart," said Nellie to Eliza, "you would not think the big block of northern granite had it in him, but underneath he's soft as honey."

Nevertheless she was surprised and moved softly as a bird, watching, and two days before George went she found Mrs. McMahon standing at the mantelpiece in front of George's photograph. It was a fine one, taken at a street corner meeting, George with his mouth open and his arm in a gesture, but it was very George. "The old docker come to life," George had written in his pretty, bold hand underneath.

"It's so very like him, isn't it, Madam?" said Mrs. McMahon. "You haven't got another? My husband and I would like to have it."

"No, pet, I haven't," said Nellie dryly.

"If Mrs. McMahon would like any piece of pottery, let her have a piece," said George the same evening, "she's got fine taste for a working girl. I want her to develop her taste."

"For a working girl me foot," cried Nellie, "you big humbug. You've been making sheep's eyes at her. The woman's crying tears all over the place. It's the noble old baron himself making free with the servant-lasses! You've got beyond yourself, George Cook. I think it's the bloody absolute limit, while I'm out at me job, you staying at home seducing the woman. She's an honest working woman or she was. Now she's thinking about sex all the time. You've been making love to her as you call it, you bloody hypocrite, for years. I wondered, it stuck in me mind that you were in no hurry to tell me you were home. It was the soldier's farewell to his lass, eh? Ah, it's a bloody shame, there's not a drop of honest blood in you, you went straight from her to me, I can't credit it, I can't understand why, if not for perversity. You take a woman that's satisfied though she's miserable, an honest girl bearing her burden bravely, with a husband and kiddie and you wreck her home. Do you think McMahon doesn't notice, that she's weeping for you?"

George threw himself down on the daybed with a pleased expression.

Nellie continued to rave and cry about her hard luck, the faithlessness of all men, and that he couldn't even wait till he shook the dust of England from his feet to betray her again.

"I can't look in the faces of my friends without thinking, Has George been sweethearting here too? It's poisoned friendship for me."

George had shut his eyes and now pretended to be asleep, but they had a great fight.

Mrs. McMahon came the next day and Nellie opened the door to her, saying, "I'm glad you came early, Gwen, there's a lot to be done."

The little girl was there too. They made the same pathetic group on the doorstep. Mrs. McMahon wore her usual black coat.

"Come into the kitchen and you can play in the front room, Georgie," Nellie said briefly, not unkindly.

Mrs. McMahon was cheerful but pale.

"You've been seeing a good bit of my husband while I've been away on jobs," said she while the worker was putting her clothes, as usual, in the front room. "What has he been doing?"

"He mostly reads the paper, Madam," said Mrs. McMahon. "Or he sits in the back yard."

She did not look at Nellie, but without haste put her things away and put on her apron.

"We'll all miss him now he's going. It's a great pity but it's got to be: a man's work comes first," said Nellie. "Men must work and women must weep for the buggers: we're fools, Gwen, to get involved with them."

Mrs. McMahon said nothing for she was on her way to the kitchen.

[313]

"Aye, pet," said Nellie entering the kitchen, "what you can do first if you're a good soul, is to make a good pot o' tea, me angel: I'm starving; and thirsty as an old boot in a storm. We'll have a cup o' tea, sweetheart, and then I've got to be off, duty calls. Aye, it's a damn hard life, Gwen. You work and the minute your back's turned the bastards play you false."

Gwen made the tea, set the tray and poured out two cups, handing one to Nellie and putting the other beside the washing-up basin.

"No, sit down a minute, pet, and let's have a talk," said Nellie. "I've got to be going. Are you very upset then, Gwen, chick, that me old man's leaving us? Ah, the bastard, leaving his harem high and dry, a traitor, eh?"

"I'm sorry, we're both sorry," said Mrs. McMahon: "and Georgie's been talking about it ever since she heard. She thinks the world of Mr. Cook. Here comes Cookie, she sings, you ought to hear her; it's cute."

"Aye, it must be," said Nellie.

"He's been so generous to her, talking to her. He told her a long story about the sparrows one day and she's been talking about it ever since and teasing him, Tell me about a squirrel. He's like a father, an uncle to her."

"Aye, I get it, pet."

"And always so kind and noticing everything you do for him."

"Yes, he's lovable," said Nellie.

"Do you think he'll stay away so long, Madam?"

"He'll stay too long for us," said Nellie amiably.

Mrs. McMahon looked at her questioningly.

"Eh, chick, don't be building up hopes on George Cook's coming back to lie to you. You've been kissing him haven't you, Gwen?"

Mrs. McMahon flushed and looked away. Then she looked at Nellie, "Yes, we kissed," she said proudly.

"Well, when you've finished your work today you can leave here for good, Gwen, I think it's a damn shame and I've got no use for traitors. Do your work, I'll not rob you of the money, and then let us say goodbye."

"I'd rather not stay."

[314]

"I want you to stay, I've got to go in half an hour, and George has got to have his lunch if the house burns down. I'm disgusted with you, I'm revolted: there's no friendship in you."

Nellie took the money out of her purse and put it down.

Mrs. McMahon left it on the table, and as Nellie turned to go up the steps out of the kitchen, she said, "Mrs. Cook! It's not what you think. It's that he loves me."

"And he's proved it to you," said Nellie; "is he going to marry you, Gwen?"

Mrs. McMahon said nothing.

"Let's not talk about it any more. It's the dirtiest trick that's been played yet and I ought to be able to take it, but I don't feel very generous at the moment. I am Mrs. Cook and I'm going to stay Mrs. Cook."

Mrs. McMahon looked after her, at the strange cut and strange dress, the wild and dirty bohemian, cursing and smoking, disorderly and perverse and she felt just as if a wild cat had come snarling into a decent household. She was an innocent woman and believed George meant her for his wife. All the stages between, two divorces, all the arrangements, were wiped away by George's splendid, easy manhood. She had great trust in him. She never doubted that she was the next wife and she looked upon Nellie as the unworthy woman.

Mrs. McMahon for some little time now had been encouraged in her daily struggle with penury. She put money aside in various forms of door-to-door insurance and saved up the clothing her married sister sent her, so that she would have provision for Georgiana and a little clothing for herself, when the break between George and Nellie occurred. She was prepared to wait a long time for George. Her own husband, Bernard, would have all his salary for himself, and would be able to get along, she considered. He was middle-aged, he had few wants. He loved the child and so did she, but she was sure some arrangement could be made. All this she had planned in her mind. George Cook had also suggested that as she was very bright, had a clear memory of all she had ever learned, she should study in evening school and learn office work. Then she would get off her feet and get better pay. She did not see at the moment how, after working in houses all day and doing her own housework, cutting, sewing, knitting and mending for her two at home, she could study at night. Nellie had lent her her own lesson books in typing and shorthand and Gwen tried to study while she was sewing.

She was twenty-eight; George was over fifty: it seemed to her that they would be happy. With grave confidence and patience she faced the prospect of all that was to be done before they could marry.

When she left the house in Lamb Street where she had worked for years and where she had been happy and in love, she was weeping.

Nellie saw the downcast, downtrodden figure in the limp black rags go past the window. She saw her afterwards passing along the other side of the street with her shopping bag half full of greens. She always tried to give her family milk, greens, fruit. Nellie noticed that she trod weakly and looked pale. The little girl's thin fingers curled into Gwen's and Georgiana skipped. They did not look at the house. Nellie felt a pang realizing several things, Gwen's pain, her patience, her weakness. She thought of George's cool tricks.

In a few minutes, with her tea, smoke and ruminations, she had forgotten and presently she was fooling herself. What was between them was a bit of flirtation.

When George came, she began on him. Their quarrels at present were not so pleasant. George wore a pleased tranquillity.

"Leave me alone, don't bother me," he said often, unlike himself, "I'm quitting, you're getting rid of me. You can't get rid of me any quicker, I'm doing my best."

He kept spending money and had a fine outfit now, the outfit of a clerk going out to India, say.

Nellie confided some of her anxieties and doubts to Eliza who was now often in the house. To George she said sharply, "You're treating me like a second-best wife."

Nellie waited for the weekend and her brother's trip down with the bodily impatience of a lover. Tom had the trick of satisfying her love and although they quarreled, she could never lose him. Her boy! He never changed, never grew older, and from him she got the illusion of being young. The women interested in him filled her with savage indignation. On the telephone, she pressed Tom to get a London job. Here she could watch over him, save him from trouble.

Tom did not answer Nellie's letter about Caroline; and when she telephoned, he told them to say he was out, a thing he had never done to anyone. He did not go to London. But because of this, he lived in misery and was only happy at work.

The bird that howled in the heath was howling in the heath. There was a wind blowing. Tom slept badly, got up early and the landlady made trouble about his getting in so late. He had only been walking and walking, looking for a site for a caravan. But the only hotel left in town that suited his purse was this, the River-Ouse; so he took her scolding and smiled at her.

The River-Ouse was a building from the previous century built for and always used by poor travelers and locals with a small pocket. There was a lantern and a table with old magazines in the lobby, which had once been the carriage entrance to a yard. This lobby was the roomiest and most cheerful part of the house.

It was a night of broad moonlight; the smell of the heath drifted in. The bedroom was small, narrow. There was a table under the window. Tom always wrote in his diary there till the light faded. He could write by the faint bulb but not see what he was writing.

A button had come off the middle of his shirt. He cut off a button lower down and sewed it in the middle. His dress was always spotless and in order. If anything went wrong, even a spot of grease or an ink scratch, the girls would laugh and try to attract his attention. He thought for days about what people said of him, though he knew it was just lonely anxiety.

He woke up in terror in the early hours. The yawning weary moon was flat over the shrunk houses. There had been voices in the room; he had heard voices calling him. It was still; the light was so gray. What needed him? He trembled because he could not answer. What thing called him? If it would swallow him up, yet he would answer it, if he knew what it was. He could not bear to be called on and not to respond. He got back into bed, fell asleep, once more heard calls and woke up. Was it Nellie?

He telephoned her Monday after work but she was at work.

He was so exhausted the next night that he slunk up to bed at nine thirty, tidied his room, moved his valises from the fireplace and was asleep by ten. He woke up suddenly about two. The moonlight was retreating quickly from his room and now shone, in its last beam, on the hearthstone, where he seemed to see words freshly engraved. He stared without moving, trying to make out the words before they faded. What he saw was a date, 1679. The moonlight moved like a spotlight; and at first he thought it might be a spotlight or a searchlight. It lighted the old gas bracket, withdrew, made merely a block of moonlight where the window really was. He got up and went over to the hearthstone. It was an engraved stone and read: *Here lies Joel Gammon of this parish, died Mar. 12, 1679. R.I.P.*

Tom could hardly sleep all night, wondering how a dead man had got into his bedroom. He did not like to mention it to the landlord, for it might have meant his moving again and there was no other cheap hotel in town.

When he got back for dinner at six thirty, he went upstairs first and, having seen at lunch that there were only two or three guests, he tried the door of another room, thinking he'd ask for it, if empty. It was bigger and ready for a guest, but to his amazement, the hearthstone read: *Sacred to the memory of Job Blondel, who departed this life, September 9, 1693. At rest.*

He went back to his room and, sitting on the bed, began to laugh mutely, "Dead guests! It is the first time I've heard of a hostelry being so reverent."

He could not help a flitting thought that the voices he had heard were those of Job and Joel; yet their dust had flown long ago; it must have reached other planets by this time; he was not afraid of the poor men. But then, he reasoned, this hotel was not standing on those dates.

He went down to his eating as if he had not observed the hearthstones; and became acquainted with the other boarders, an engineer from another factory, a forester.

After dinner he began talking to the engineer and said, "Do you have an odd hearthstone in your room?"

The engineer had heard that the man who built the hotel had bought an old graveyard and no doubt the tombstones had gone along with the site; "If he was a practical man that would explain it."

"I'll try to stand it," said Tom.

In his diary he wrote a letter to a woman, no name, telling her about the voices and the gravestones. He wrote, "I should like to have a hotel like this, a poor hotel, and run it well and call it The Weary Traveler."

TOM WAS working in Blackstone some months when the old mother died. Nellie and George Cook, over on a visit, and Tom, went up to Bridgehead for the funeral and to decide on family matters. For the moment there was enough, with contributions from Nellie and Tom, for Peggy to live on comfortably, but they had to look to the future.

The aunts, Peggy and Tom sat in the back room having tea. Two cakes had been brought and the fruits, cheeses and fancy breads on the table showed that Cushie was in the house. Peggy held court. Tom, reduced to back room routine, had shrunk into a corner by the radio. "Now I have the house to myself," said Peggy, sitting by the fire with her knitting and the dog on the floor in front of her. "There's no reason why any more meat should enter this house, except a bit for the dog, he's without reason and ye can't make him understand; but human beings who know what they're doing are another matter. I think I'll try my hand at preserving fruit and vegetables."

"Well, you might try your hand at it but it's troublesome," said Tom.

"Do you know how it's done?"

"I know how they're canned. The vegetables must be absolutely fresh, have a double cooking and some injection because they have no acids to prevent the development of bacteria. Fruits have that."

The aunts and Peggy were fervidly interested and pressed him for details.

"And how are the tops put on? By machine?"

"You'd think they'd spill if they're full to the top," said Peggy thoughtfully looking at the fire and unconsciously imitating her mother, "we didn't see many peas this year, hardly any. Mother was always asking for them. Uncle Sime bought her some canned peas. I said, What's the use of canned peas? So they have no bacteria, is that it?"

"Where's Simon, Peggy?" said Aunt Bessie.

"I told him to keep to his room for a bit. We've had enough trouble round here, with two deaths in the house. We want the place to ourselves for a bit, I told him. Don't be always sitting in other people's furniture."

"That was heartless, Peggy. You forget that he's lost his sister."

She crooned, "It's no use pampering him, Tom man, or he'll be going to bed and expecting nursing: and there's no one going to do it for him. We've had enough real sickness: we don't want shamming. You go away and stay and you lose your sense of reality, man. You ought to live in the house with people like I do. You never know a person till you've lived with them, man, then you know the ins and outs of their selfishness and their scheming."

"He likes his bed, he'll learn nothing new there," said Aunt Bessie looking round for approval of this old joke. For some reason, it fell flat.

"I saw the old man with the blind dog," said Aunt Jeanie. "He was asking me about my sister, just like every day and I told him she left us. He said he was very sorry to hear it, she was a nice woman. He never saw her in his life. Why, was she an old flame of yours? I said: you never saw her in your life. He-he. No, he said but I'm sorry when a nice woman goes; she was Tom Cotter's widow; he always had a good word for me."

"How did the dog get blind?" said Peggy, with a censorious, pale, strict face, putting herself forward again. "How was it then? Is it old? But it always was blind. Then how was it?"

"Ask no questions and I'll tell you no lies," said Aunt Bessie.

"It was blinded," said Mrs. Duncan, "it was a cruel deed. Some boys flung pepper in its eyes and it was blinded. It nearly went mad and it was ill, but it got better. It never trusted a boy near it again."

"Do you mean they blinded the dog?" said Peggy in a strange hypocritical voice. "Oh, I never understood why the dog was like that. Isn't it funny? I asked and asked and they never told me. Mother refused to tell me but she must have known. Oh, how cruel. And was it blinded by boys, Aunt Jeanie?"

"Yes, dear. That was the way of it. There's no need to talk about it."

"Oh, how cruel! Oh, I think that's terrible don't you? There are such terribly cruel people. But did you see the dog recently this week then, Aunt Bessie?"

"Yes, like I told you, with the old man, hinny."

"Oh, there are such wicked people in the world. Doesn't it show a cruel nature?"

"I went to see Mrs. Laws," said Aunt Jeanie. "She was always interested in Mary. She had an attack of asthma and, as usual, was spraying."

"Yes, isn't it an affliction! It spoils the joy of life," said Mrs. Duncan.

"That sort of thing makes you not want to go on living," said Aunt Jeanie.

"Yes, it's a cruel thing," said Tom, "I don't know how they get their work done."

"Oh, I don't think it could be as bad as that," said Peggy naïvely, "as not to want to go on living. People all want to go on living, don't they? I don't think you should let anything get you down like that, should you? Should you, Tom? After all, it can't be as bad as that? Nothing can be as bad as that, isn't that so, Aunt Jeanie? People shouldn't lose their grip like that. You need a sense of measure, don't you?"

"Well, it's serious, Peggy. It can be very bad. Look at your Uncle Simon. Mr. Pike's is a very bad case," said the neighbor, Mrs. Duncan.

"People may suffer a little, but everyone wants to go on living, why if they've got one foot in the grave, they want to go on living: why if you push them right into the grave, they're clinging on with their fingers to the edge. There's no such thing as an invalid giving up the battle for life."

"Well, but people d—" began one of the aunts. "Well, dear, of course, they fight for life."

"Aye, we all fight for life. We hang on long after we ought to be thinking about dying," said she, "aye. It's human nature, I know: and to hang on where you're not wanted you've got to be deaf and blind and old and daft, you've got to get a thick skin and hear the voices of the long ago, so you'll blind yourself to reality. Aye, fantasy's a bad thing, it blinds you to reality. And they say the sicknesses you get are what you wish for, that's the latest theory, isn't it, Tom? Aye, that's it. For if you remained normal, you'd have to have to see how things are, that you're taking up the lives of the young. It's a wonder they don't see what they're doing, wanting to be waited on when they've had their turn. It's like guests who came early and stayed late. It's a sad thing to see an old man trying to edge back when he's being put to the door."

"Where's Mr. Cook?" Aunt Jeanie said in joking tone.

"He's out somewhere with a bottle of sherry. He can't stand the house of mourning any more," said Peggy. "And I'm glad he is. As soon as he comes in, he swarms over us all to get to the fireside chair and there he sits for all the world like Pop Cotter himself. No wonder Nellie grovels before him, exactly like Ma Cotter herself. Get me this and do this and hurry my dinner and where's my tea? It was a dark day for this house the day that man crossed the threshold. Nellie gave up a good fifteen-pound-a-week job to please him and now she's down to five pounds a week, he's sick of it and he's wanting to leave her. It's only to be expected when a woman has no sense."

"Hush, pet, she's your sister and a sister's a sister," said Aunt Jeanie.

"A sister's a sister. That's funny: a sister's a sister. What are we coming to?"

"All right, pet: now I'll clear the table," said Aunt Bessie.

"Better watch her, send Tom out to watch her," giggled Aunt Jeanie, "or she'll eat the rest of the cake. Bessie's always the one to volunteer and then she stops a long time in the kitchen. Send Tom out and he'll bark when he sees her at it."

"Leave the cake alone, Aunt Bessie," said Peggy; "George'll be in soon and he eats everything in the house."

Aunt Jeanie sighed, "It's strange sitting here without Mary. The nights she was bad, she'd say, Don't leave me. She'd know who you were then and know he'd gone and she'd beg you not to leave her."

"You were good and patient with her, Peggy dear," said the neighbor. "You were a real good daughter."

"We're all very grateful: you did a wonderful job," said Aunt Bessie.

"Yes, you did; I couldn't have stood it," said Tom.

"She needs a good holiday now," said Aunt Jeanie. They all became attentive, for that was the anxiety. What was to become of the household? "You couldn't take her down to London, Tom, you and Nellie, for a couple of weeks?"

"You know I won't hear of London, man, what makes you harp on it?" said Peggy to her. "I can't stand the place. I'm sorry I ever saw it: the south is no good for me."

Well, they said, but she couldn't live here alone. "I have my plans," said Peggy. "I'm going to surprise you all. You think I'm a poor lass, a bit daft—"

At their protests she said, as if they'd insulted her, "Please don't yell at me, I'm normal, I'm saner than any of you ever were in your lives; I'm the smart one and you'll come to your senses one of these days. You'll find it out. I'll send you a letter; or you'll see it in the papers."

"We wouldn't want to do that, Peggy," said Tom.

"Some funny things get into the papers," said Aunt Bessie laughing, "you wouldn't like to be in one of those items, pet."

"All right," said Tom, "but you'll have to let us into the secret. We'll have to fix up something before Nellie and I go back. Nellie's got her own troubles and I'm a workingman."

Uncle Simon had just come downstairs. He was very pale, but he was neatly dressed and shaved. His eyes were red. He greeted them in a weak voice.

"How are you feeling, Mr. Pike?" said Mrs. Duncan.

"A took a good bowl of prunes this marnin' and ye knaw it went right through me, did a good job; and now A feel much better. A got a thorough clean out."

Tom and the women laughed. Peggy said "Ugh!"

"Well, you're looking better, Uncle Sime," said Tom, "your color has improved."

"Oh, A'm dyin' slowly. The doctor came and saw me and she said that's about the best way to die. Can ye whistle, Mr. Pike? she said. Then it's all right. That's an old one. A heard me grandfather say it, Can ye whistle? Then you're alive yet. Me grandfather was a big man, he came from a big southern duke's estate. He was steward. He was an educated man."

"Now stop your silly bragging and blowing, Uncle Sime, don't make yourself ridiculous. You belong to another day and age, man. Dukes are not popular now, man. You'd better not let your relation George Cook hear your boasting about flunkeying for dukes."

"George Cook!" said Uncle Simon, looking round the circle. He addressed himself to Tom, as one man to another. "It was a black day for this house the day that man crossed our threshold. Her father thought a lot of her, he was proud of her; he took a pride in her doin's. There she was a big earnin' woman and she gave it up to please George Cook. She dropped ten pounds a week, he said; and we could have used it in this house; she could have dropped it into me pocket, he said. Aye, it was a terrible blow to him. He was quite crestfallen. It was a sad day for this house, he said. And now," cried Uncle Simon trembling, "now he's gettin' mixed up with trades unions and foreigners and such things are not good for people. He'll end up in jail, George Cook will, that'll be the end of it; he'll go to jail."

"Maybe he won't, Uncle Sime," said Tom gently. "He won't be doing any fighting in this job he's landed: it's quite a gentlemanly job." He laughed. The aunts listened carefully.

"Then he won't be in any danger?" said one of them. "Well, I'll be better pleased when he's out of the country, then Nellie'll stay out of trouble too."

"I wouldn't bet on Nellie," said Tom tenderly. "Nellie feels she's wasting her time if there isn't trouble in the air."

"All the young people used to be so happy and contented and lead their young lives without worries and now these foreigners have come in and it's nothin' but trouble," Uncle Simon lamented.

"What foreigners, Uncle Sime?" teased Tom.

"Eh," he burst out, baited, "these Bolshe-viks, these Commune-ists."

"Why, you crazy old man, go and sit by your fire and don't trouble us any more," cried Peggy. "And see if you can whistle, for maybe you can't."

"Ye don't know," he said, looking at her with scornful pity, "what it was like in my day, lass. If A got up before six and warked hard, A liked to do it. A had no complaints: A was that strong; A felt champion. We used to go campin' on the moors and go far out towards the Cheviot, and we'd take with us a flitch of bacon and a ham and a side of mutton, a bag of potatoes and a sack of sugar and many other things and we'd do as we pleased and eat all a man can eat. And ye've never seen any such things and ye don't believe in them. A pity ye, lass, because ye think there's nothin' but what ye've seen in your lifetime; and ye've all been starved. Your father was quite right: he was used to his plate of meat. He and A came from another time. And there ye are standin' up for the foreigners who are makin' all the trouble for you. Why, when a man doesn't do his work, they cut down his wages and he can't eat proper. A woman told me A looked twenty years younger; and the doctor says A'm wonderfully young for me age. A had a happy youth; A wasna troubled like ye all are today. A'm sorry for ye."

"You're young because you do nothing but sleep. I don't call that being alive. It's fit for a baby with its life in front of it, not for a grown adult."

"Well A was disturbed in the night. A was thinkin' of me poor sister and all the days of her life. She had it hard long before ye knew her, Peggy."

"All right, man, get along now to your kitchen! Don't be making us cry with your sentimental speeches."

The aunts spoke with mild reproach to her but their attitude had changed since her mother's death; they no longer treated her as a child. She said, scolding, "And I didn't sleep so well either, I'm not blaming the old man. It's just selfishness and indifference to others, the night scenes those two make, never a thought for others." And while Tom stared unseeing ahead, their questions brought out that she meant Nellie and George.

"You'd think someone was holding a strike meeting in the house. It was the same the time father died." The aunts so enlightened did not know which way to look and hastily changed the subject; but Tom said calmly, "Yes, they quarrel too much, it's not healthy in a marriage; but Nellie has got to have her excitement at all costs."

"I'm not talking about quarreling," said Peggy, "I'm talking about keeping people awake, with domestic scenes in a house like this where you can hear a pin drop in the attic. It's a poorly built house, like all the rest: they give us the worst here in Bridgehead. If this house didn't have a house on each side of it holding it up, it would fold up like a playbook. I'm not talking about quarreling; there's been enough quarreling in this house for it to have deaf ears."

Tom sat looking frail and young, in every way diminished by the powerful scrum of women which wrangled about him. He felt like a flabby football. When the aunts had gone he talked to Peggy about discussing private matters with them, "Where's your modesty, Peggy?"

"I'll be modest, if other people are modest; why do they drag us into their private lives? Because they like it to be public. I know Nellie," she said, beginning her singsong, "I know what's going on, man. He's as indifferent as a block of wood and Nellie feels she's doing us a favor giving us a notion of what real life is like; not the life of ghosts in this house which we've all led and you lead too, Tom, for you're not a real man, like the others. I know ye all. Nellie always was an exhibitionist: there's nothing she won't do to be cock o' the walk. I see into ye all, man. Ye never pulled the wool over my eyes, though I had to sit back and pretend to know nothing when ye were all soothsaying."

"Soothsaying," said Tom puzzled.

"Eh, what is it, man, than soothsaying?" she said naïvely. "It's soft talk back and forth, isn't it? Aye, she's the spitting image of Pop Cotter, Tom, man; don't ye see it? She's unscrupulous, man," she singsonged, "wanting to be the star performer. I see people for what they are. You can't buy me off, man. It's all there in the back of me head. I'm polite and decent to ye, but you don't know, none of ye, what I'm thinking."

[328]

"That's likely, Peggy: that's what thinking is for, to be hidden."

"Aye, I know, you're a twisted crowd, you'd make a hairpin look straight: the Cotters and the Pikes are a twisted crowd, honeying and hinnying, but I see what they've got in their minds, why it's as clear as day, man, it's selfishness; there's nothing but it."

But though Tom was patient and Cushie cajoling, neither of them could find out what Peggy had in the back of her mind, and they were obliged to go back to London leaving her with Uncle Simon. She promised to write when she was ready. "You'll have a lot of surprises: I've been waiting on others and now I'm going to change things a bit."

George went down to London some days before the brother and sister. They left one morning in time for the ten o'clock morning down train and as soon as they had gone Peggy said to Uncle Simon, "Now, I'm going to paint the inside of the house, Uncle Sime, and you'll have to get ready to move your things. Just make a little bundle of what's necessary. I don't know where I'll put you yet. I'm the lady of the house now, Uncle Sime, and you must obey orders."

"It's not right what you're doin' and it's not right what they did," complained the old man. "They came here twice, those young people, when your father died and when me sister died and they consulted each other and fixed everythin' and signed papers and disposed of everythin' and never asked me advice nor consent."

"What would they ask a silly old man like you for, with no future? You'll be dead soon, man, what good is your advice? It's no concern of yours what the young do."

"Your sister Nellie asked me to be good to you, Peggy, because you're good stuff underneath; those were her words. She was always devoted to ye. Why don't ye show it, lass? A'd not bother ye if ye would be a little more like a woman."

"What do you know of women, you poor old man? Don't talk to me about women; you don't know what the thing is. Do you want me to laugh in your face?" Laughing, hearty, she pushed him out of the way, leaving the dog to jump and tear at his jacket as they went by, and turned back to say, "Now, don't forget your bundle, Uncle Sime, man, or I'll throw your old things out into the street, out of the window and you'll have to go and pick them up and then maybe I won't let you in again."

The old man, crying, went upstairs and sitting down, getting up, coughing in spasms, he rolled his bedding, his shaving things, his pension papers and pocketbook in a bundle and put his alarm clock in the pocket of his overcoat. Meantime Peggy was whistling away in the kitchen, like a blackbird in full throat. She had a beautiful whistle, a fine musical ear. She was happy. She took down the curtains, emptied out old drawers and cupboards. The sun was shining on the leaves of the sickly tree in the back yard and the dwarfed hollybush. The sparrows were chirping, flying in and out of the roofs with Uncle Simon's crumbs: all through the house was light and cheerful sound. Uncle Simon had climbed to the attic and opened one of the windows. The view was cheerful and even the sound of his alarm clock ticking away in the silence was gay. It reminded him of old days when he had been in the attic, as a younger man. He looked from the window over the rooftops up into the blue spring sky with fast-sailing clouds on a wind streaming in from the coast. The windows of small dark backrooms glittered, birds sat on chimneypots; through a chink of the red roofs, he saw a man on a bike balancing a long ladder on his shoulder, a broom, a pail and a paintpot balancing on that. He loved the attic and would have been glad to live there, but for the bitterness of winter.

Presently, he heard Peggy and the dog on the stairs. "What are you doing up in the attic, Uncle Sime? Are you counting your money?" When she saw him in the front room, she looked relieved and smiled: she looked round at the bundles. "You've not taken out your money have you, Uncle Sime, have you? Leave it in the toolbox, man. It's safe there. It's in good hands, the hands it's intended for. Why, come on, Uncle Sime, you're not going to get anywhere piling your things up in the attic. It's old days you're thinking of, man. Come on, I'll help you down."

She took up the bundle of soiled bedclothes, making a face

and remarking upon their condition. "A'm not strong enough to wash them proper," said the old man.

Peggy scolded him, but not very unkindly, as she helped him downstairs with his things, until she got them all into the front hall.

"Now," she said, "ye can go where you like, man, you're free as the wind. It's all yours."

"Where do ye want me to put them, lass?"

"I don't care: you can send someone for the bedclothes. I'm going to let you have them. You've got to have something with you or no one'll take you in."

"What do you mean, lass?" he asked turning to her, standing as straight as he could, but his hands hanging to his sides and his face open with fear.

"Why, get out, Uncle Sime, I don't know where. You've lived long enough to know. You know better than me. Go to the old men's home. You've got your pension. They get along on it and so can you. I'm not bad or cruel. I'm only taking my rights for no one'll give them to me. A young woman doesn't want to be bothered with you, man, don't flatter yourself you're a gay companion."

"But where can A go?" said Simon Pike frightened.

"It's good weather, man: I'm not putting you out in a storm, it's spring. Now, don't bother me, Uncle Sime, you've had your time, so get out and let me me have the place to myself. I've never had a moment to myself since I was born, with the whole crowd of you round my ears, quarreling and groaning and snatching. Eh, it was agony, man. Don't you realize yourself, what a burden you've been? It's kindness to you to put you out so you must shift for yourself and find your right place. You've got into a rut, Uncle Sime, man. You'll be in your place, you'll be no longer a nuisance, people won't hate ye. You're better off than Mother who's in the churchyard: you're better off than the dead, or you must think so."

"Where am A to go, a poor old man like me?" cried the aged workman. "You're out of your senses with pride, Peggy. Why, no one will let ye put me out! They'll bring me back again!"

"Aye, I've got me pride. But you've got none, aren't you

ashamed of yourself, a whole lifetime spent in other people's furniture? Now get going, or I'll set the dog on you. I'm only holding him in: he's impatient to get at you."

"No," he cried. "A'm not goin', ye mad girl. Ye don't know what you're doin'." He resolutely picked up his bundle of clothes and made towards the kitchen.

She laughed, "I'm crazy you say. Why, man, well, hadn't ye better take to your heels and leave me your toolbox? You don't want me to do something desperate to you, do you? It's all coming to me, isn't it? You'd do better to let me have it now, when I want it. If I'm tormented and worried by the thought of it, when I need it for the house, why I'll hate you, I'll have to get rid of you some way: and isn't this the better way? I'm being kind to you. Now clear out, Uncle Sime, get over to Jeanie's, or where you like, don't bother me. I've work to do."

"A'll go to Tom. He'll take care of me. He's the only decent one of ye," said Simon, turning towards the door.

"Well, that'll be a pretty picture. For when all's said and done, he's just half a man himself and together you'll make less than one. I'd like to be there, the two of you taking a walk on Sundays."

With this, she opened the door. In the door, he said, "Peggy, you're going to get into trouble. The house'll be in the papers yet. Now you mind your step. A've never said the truth about your goin's-on. A've been true to ye; now don't you let those men into the house. A've not opened me mouth to your aunts and A won't, but A'm warnin' ye. You're only a lass alone; ye don't know what you're doin'. Ye need a man here, Peggy, A'm old but A can protect ye; A'm a man."

She pushed him out onto the path with a joke and put his bundles after him. "You can leave them there to be called for, no one will run off with them," said she and closed the door.

Simon Pike stood for some time in front of the rented house where he had spent forty years and the rent of which he had paid since the beginning. He had shared the house with his sister after her marriage, filling the empty rooms, shared a bed, a blanket and an old army coat with young Tom in the hard times, in the attic, and given his wages over and over again to help them. The fine furniture that Thomas Cotter had bought in his pride and that Nellie talked about, that his poor sister Mary had struggled and pinched to keep, pinching even the children's bellies to keep it, those fine sitting room and back room and bedroom pieces would have been sold many years before if he had not paid their debts. He had once been a respected, highly-paid man. He was not a man to whine. He thought for a while where to go. Spare beds were rare. Aunt Jeanie's daughter had married but that did not make much room in the crowded little flat. Still he had to go and talk to her. While he stood there, he heard Peggy turn the key and bolt the door. He put on his overcoat and hat and looked neat, respectable, almost dapper. He straightened himself, felt for his pocketbook and papers, and as alertly as he could, he went down the street towards his sister Jeanie's; she lived about fifteen minutes' walk away.

Peggy did not answer the front door or the back yard door that day, though they heard the dog barking at one time. At another time, doubtless she was out, for there was no sound. The next day, it was obvious that there was painting going on and when Jeanie rang, Peggy appeared at the door in overalls, looking very merry; and the dog beside her barking savagely. "There are painters in, I'm sorry I can't ask you in," said she.

"You have got to take Uncle Simon back," said Aunt Jeanie, "I never heard of such a thing in my life, turning out an old man when you've got an empty house. I can't keep him."

"Why," said Peggy merrily, "I wonder what sad tale he's been pitching. It's only that I've got painters all over the house, Aunt Jeanie, man, and I'm going to let rooms. You've no objection to my becoming independent, I hope? But you've got to keep him till I'm ready. The paint will be bad for his asthma; and I can't have his terrible bedclothes in the house, what will the painters think of me? Hang them out for a few weeks on your clothesline, Aunt Jeanie, do that for me and I'll take the poor old man back when I'm ready. I wonder now what tale he's been spinning? Eh, the poor old lad, he's not quite right in his senses any more; he's got a persecution mania, ye'd better put him

[333]

away in the old men's home. The strange things he said to me. I was quite frightened to stay with him here alone. I'm only a girl alone, Jeanie, you've got to think of me too; you can't think only of yourself. You've got to get over the selfishness, Jeanie, and look at reality. Now just keep the silly old man till I'm ready and then I'll take him back. You know me, I'm soft and I'm used to him and I need the help, though he's more trouble than any money he ever brought into this house."

"Where did ye get the money to paint the house, lass?"

"I've got my ways and means. I don't throw money away like some people. I'm practical; I've got the money, so don't worry and I'll never be short."

"Simon says you've kept his savings, Peggy."

"Why, didn't I tell you he's foolish? It's paranoia, Jeanie, man. Does he look like a man of means? Eh, you'd believe anything. Now get along, woman, man. I've got work to do and I must get lunch for the painter."

Aunt Jeanie went hurrying along to see Mrs. Duncan and ask if she had a spare bed. "Eh, that Peggy, that Peggy!" she muttered to herself.

They wrote to Tom, who came on a weekend.

"I shall have to take him with me; but my heart is stone cold," he said.

"And what about Peggy?"

"I can't give up this job. You'd think there'd be somewhere to put a harmless enough girl and a decent old man. I've been all over town. They all just look blankly at me."

He went back to Hadrian's Grove to see his sister. This time she let him in. She had a strange, glad, lecherous smile.

"I'm letting rooms. I'm taking only men. Women are trouble washing their smalls and running in for pots of water; and bringing in their boys. There are no morals nowadays. But men I can look after. Do you think I'll find myself a husband? I think so. You can't blame me for looking out for myself. What would I do with Uncle Sime? He'd only be against everything. I know him. He wants his old age in comfort, and nothing happening and nobody living. You must manage otherwise, man. Don't count on me. I've done my bit."

[334]

But Tom had won a white lace scarf in a raffle, given it to a girl he met at a factory dance. Now he was engaged to her and looking for a couple of rooms. So he went to the family doctor and asked him to get Uncle Simon into a home. And this is what was done in the end.

Peggy went her way, Tom looked for rooms for himself and his wife-to-be and Uncle Simon sat with fifty others, whose stories were not much different, in the old men's home. They went to bed early, for the cold; and hoped for the present of a quarter of a pound of tea when visitors came.

George for the third time had gone to Geneva. Nellie and Eliza saw him off at the airport and he had a few words with Eliza alone. Then he asked them both to promise to go and see Mrs. McMahon. He did not think she was as fit as before.

"I know you can't afford to have her now, Nellie; and I gave her a little money; but I've written to my old friends to take her back; the ones I got her from. And you," he blustered to Nell, "try to keep calm for once; and get rid of that old crow Johnny. Stay away from her. I can't bear a dirty woman."

She said, "It's me blinking gregariousness, darling. I've got to run about raising Cain and I'm the first to suffer."

On the way home, Eliza said, "What is the matter with Gwen McMahon? Did you quarrel? George says you did."

"Yes, we had a few words."

"What about? George wouldn't say."

"He didn't know, Lize. It was a women's quarrel."

Eliza went over to see Mrs. McMahon on the way home and the following day, a Saturday, when she was free, Eliza came and said Gwen looked very queer; she didn't like the look of her. She had caught a chill perhaps and gone to bed the day before George left. The doctor said she was run down and needed a holiday. He might get her into hospital for her legs; she had bad varicose veins. Her husband earned ten pounds and she about two pounds a week. Georgiana was delicate and they had to pamper her. Besides, she liked to keep her looking nice; it made the child happy. Just now they were having folk dancing at school and the child needed a clean pair of white socks every

day, sometimes twice in the day. When Gwen had done the outside work, she worked at home, of course. She had said, so
faintly, turning her head away,

"I have a good husband, he's a good man," as if she were
speaking in an empty room. He wore cast-off clothes cheerfully,
said they were good. The landlady let him work in the back
garden for vegetables when he came home. But she had ended,
"It's only the child that keeps me alive. Georgiana needs me."

Eliza said, "What is wrong with her? I remember her as such
a lovely looking woman, quite healthy. She's not quite thirty."

"Aye, she was a fine looking girl. Your bloom washes off in
the wash pail, pet."

Eliza said, "I say malnutrition. She eats nothing and works
too hard. But it's not that: something has got at her. She looked
wan, she tried to smile and kept looking away as if she had no
expectations."

"Aye, pet, aye: it's a tragedy."

"She said to me twice, I'd like to do what I promised Mr.
Cook but I don't see how I can." But she said it in a low voice as
if she were just telling me because she didn't want to fail me.
So I dropped to it that George had told her he'd send me; I
asked her and she said, Yes, Mr. Cook was always very kind. But
again with that worn hopelessness. I think George seemed a big
man to her. She kept saying, How kind, how good!"

Eliza looked at Nellie.

"Aye, pet, he's very good. He always praised her to her face
with his courtly Bridgehead grace, the old humbug. I'm afraid,
pet, she took it seriously; she's not a woman of the world."

"Ah, I thought so. It's a damned shame!" cried Eliza.

"Eh, pet, you can't blame the lads; the girls run after them
when they're fine and big and butter with both sides of their
tongues. The temptation's too great. He thought she saw him
as a hero; she asked him how to vote, she depended on his judgment, and she would have given up the Catholic Church if he'd
asked her. And that's the story. Aye, I knew it before you. It's a
damn shame, Eliza. For she never meant a thing to him. He
brought sunshine into her back-street life. It's a case of misun-
derstanding, chick. Aye, poor woman, poor woman."

"I said you'd go to see her."

"She thought she was going to step into my boots!"

Eliza searched Nellie's face.

"I had it out with her, Lize. To see me would not cheer her up; and I wouldn't want to see her. She tried to take my man."

"You're sure?"

"She was here in tears. I should be Christian, pet, but I'm not."

Nellie then said she was going over to see Vi. "Eh, that's the girl for me when I'm blue and depressed, darling, excuse me for leaving you, pet. You're wonderful company, you're me heart's darling, but I haven't seen Vi Butters to cheer her up since before me bold sailor came home and she doesn't know the latest news on deserted wives. Will you forgive me, chick? I'll be galloping home again to see you as soon as I eat the bread and salt over in Carpentaria Grove, one of the sweetest rat-perfumed groves we sport in this glittering metropolis. A stirrup cup, my lass, and I'm off."

With an enthusiastic smack on Eliza's lips and a manly pat on the shoulder Nellie loped round the corner, but only to the next street, where she called upon Mrs. McMahon.

Miss Rose McMahon, the sister-in-law, let her in and seemed surprised, but Nellie, taking no notice, strode in swinging her postman's bag and puffing out her smoke.

"How are ye, pet? How's the world treating you? Well, well, well, here's my darling Georgie, here's me little sweetheart? And how's your mother, pet? Is she better, pet? That's too bad, chick."

She stopped in the doorless doorway, quickly eying her rival, who lay in bed against a pillow. The three-quarter bed, in which the couple slept, was pushed into a corner of the room between a wall and the small chest of drawers, which was given over to Georgiana's innumerable treasures. There was no rug. Next to the door, beside the window, was Georgiana's bed. Both beds were of the institution sort. Mrs. McMahon was in a plain white nightdress with a rose-colored sweater pulled over her shoulders. The broad and long wool Shetland scarf George had once given her was stretched over the bed, as a blanket.

"Hello, Gwen," said Nellie, fixing her sparkling eye upon her. Mrs. McMahon smiled. "Hello, Madam."

Nellie straddled her way in puffing smoke. She reached for her cigarettes and offered Mrs. McMahon one.

"I'd be glad of it," said Mrs. McMahon; "I don't often get them. Mr. Cook brought me two packets," she said trustingly to Nellie, "he's very kind, very thoughtful."

"Aye, pet, he's a good man."

At this Mrs. McMahon looked aside in one of those strange wan pauses mentioned by Eliza.

"Eliza was here to see you then, pet?"

"Eliza? Yes, Miss Cook—she was very kind. She's a very nice woman."

"Aye, pet, she's a jewel, aye, she's a precious jewel, aye, she is that. Now chick, are ye going to get up? Are ye going to get better, are ye, chick? Now that's the spirit, me love. Now what's this lying about Gwen, chick? Eh, ye'll take a little rest and then ye'll get up, won't ye? Ye'll get up and sing and chirp like ye did before, won't ye?"

"Yes, Madam," said Mrs. McMahon smiling.

"That's the spirit. Why, Gwen, I never saw ye so weak and so pale. It won't do, Gwen. Eh, life's difficult to take but ye must take it. Ye can't go dying on us, can ye pet? Eh, now there's a good girl, ye'll do that to please me, won't ye?"

Mrs. McMahon looking a little more ordinary, smiled but said nothing.

"Eh, pet?"

Mrs. McMahon laughed faintly.

"Eh, well, then," said Nellie, "so me bold sailor boy came to see you, eh? Me husband was over? It's like him, Gwen; that's like him. He'll never forget ye, pet, and the way ye polished those brasses for him: that went right to his heart: the brasses and the pottery. Him and his pots. It was a pleasure to see him worrying about whether a blue daisy had five petals or six; I used to get fat looking at him. But it's all over now, Gwen. No more polishing and dusting. The lad's run out on us, Gwen, me dear. Eh, the men, Gwen, not a good one in a bushel. Well, you've got your good man, you've nothing to worry about. He's

[338]

good to you, Gwen. He's loyal. He gives you his money; he never asks anything of you. You're lucky, my girl. Not like my man running all over the universe. Why not? For he must conquer the world of today; nothing must escape him. That's my darling. Now you're blessed, aren't you pet? A good man who's working not ten streets away and who'll be here on the tick of six fifteen. Eh, I wouldn't cry if I were you, Gwen; I'd not take it to heart. Things could be worse. That's me advice to ye, Gwen. Ye've got a good solid man who'll stick to ye until ye get old; and you're young now. And your sweet little kiddie here, she'll be growing up with ye. Partings are hard, now. I won't like to lose you, Georgiana pet: what'll I give you when I go? When I fly off to Geneva, to me husband? What would you like, Georgiana?"

"Are you going by airplane?" said the child. "Will you take me? Mr. Cook said he'd see me again one day."

Mrs. McMahon lay back on the pillow and her eyes were thoughtfully raised to the wall above the door. She did not seem to care about those present.

Nellie cast her a reptile look. "No, pet, I'm afraid not. No, you won't see him again, sweetheart, but you'll forget him. You're going to grow up and be a big lovely girl, have lots of good times. Aren't you? And you won't be worrying about any sweethearting sailor boy if you've any sense. They get round the girls, they get round the women, they get round the grandmothers, so you keep off them when you're a grown-up sensible girl. I'll buy you a jigsaw puzzle, pet, will that do? And you'll do it on Sunday night with your father."

She then turned to press questions and advice upon Mrs. McMahon and presently took her leave after giving Miss McMahon a tin of salmon for the invalid.

"And cheer her up, Rose, keep her cheerful, that's the thing."

When she got home she wrote to Tom saying she had teleponed him at the factory, but found him out and the rest of the week with the whirl of George's coming and going had no time to think about him: "and you've let me down too, a bit, Tom. Thank goodness George came in the nick of time. But now, Tom, I'm afraid it's all over. You must come down, Tom, when you can and let's have a look at you. Or has some siren with a pretty face pleased you in the flowering brecklands?"

To this she got a reply,

Dear Nell,

I hope you'll be able to make arrangements to go out with George soon. I think it would be best for you and I hope it'll be easy. Let me know if I can do anything. I don't think I can get down for a while. It's true I'd be glad to get out of the mental and emotional morass and the dullness of work at this moment, but I can't see that I'd do better in London. I'll soon lose my glamorous reputation as "the London man" but sic transit gloria mundi and as a matter of fact I'm putting on a little weight, not too much and am brighter than usual on Mondays. This confirms the local view that London is a dangerous place for a man. I'll let you know when I can come down. I'm glad you've got Eliza.

Yours, Tom.

"I'll pay the bugger out for that, I won't write until I've made him grovel," cried Nellie. "It's like his cheek. He'll let me know. What's in the man? I must be losing my charm," and this started her off once more on her visiting. She would leave Eliza home, for Eliza was often too tired after work to visit.

Long, long into the night Nellie talked out her troubles. "Everyone thinks it's all over. They're even thinking of getting up a subscription to send me out. Let me come close to you Eliza and cry my heart out. You know him, I feel nearer to him with you."

Eliza received no letter from Tom. She thought she had cut herself off from Tom; he could not write to her in Lamb Street perhaps. She grieved so deeply that Nellie noticed it and supposed she was fretting for her last lover, a young man. At last when Nellie had to go away for two weeks on an assignment, Eliza wrote a note to Tom, "It's a long time since I've seen you. If you feel like coming to London, come and stay in the house while Nellie's away, you'll be free and can go down to the farm if you like, and see your friends. But if you do come, send me a letter or send a letter to Nellie saying you can't come for she would be hurt to think you came in her absence."

She hesitated about posting it, but posted it. "He can always say he can't come."

After three days, she received a letter from Tom which was handed to her with an evil questioning look by Nellie from the morning mail, "Ah, here's a billet-doux for you from me little brother!"

Tom wrote:

Dear Eliza,

I never answered the letter you wrote me weeks and weeks ago and I am sorry you got in before I did. I had much to think of and was troubled and confused. I made up my mind I wouldn't come. I wasn't going to come, but I had to come down the other weekend to see someone, a woman you understand, and tell her it was all over. It couldn't be helped. I'm a Blackstone man now. I just couldn't take Lamb Street that weekend. I see I missed George. I had to tell someone to get the hell out of my life. I didn't seem to have anything for any woman, until just now. I'm afraid I won't be seeing London for a long time now. It's not only the distance and such minor things, but I have a responsibility, an attachment here and this sweetens for me the black-walled town and the lonely forest. It's quite a different thing with a sympathetic companion. May the world go well with you. I'll be writing to Nellie one of these days.

Yours, Tom

Eliza, with a chuckle, passed this letter over to Nellie saying, "Well, we've got your little brother off our hands! He'll be writing to you he says there," she pointed and rose smiling, brushing the crumbs off her lap. She put her things in the sink and went out.

Nellie at first suspected some sarcastic triumph in this unusual action and read Tom's letter with jealous disgust and curiosity.

Eliza, who had instantly thought how cunning Tom was to

take her invitation and transform it, and how in his purity and uprightness he was now punishing her for many things, and especially for betraying his sister, at once determined to shed any further interest in him. Her interest had always been very tender and pitying. What a terrible thrust the man had! Well, she thought, everything passes over in three days, that's my experience: I only must now live through three days. She got up from the sewing she was doing, and went upstairs to her room.

Nellie called her, but she did not answer. Nellie came upstairs and stood in the door looking at her. She took no notice for a while but began to find this presence in the doorway unbearable and suddenly looked up. Nellie's expression of curiosity was just changing to a devilish triumphant cunning. It flashed into her face and disappeared, leaving its trace in the impish smirk, the first thing that Eliza ever remembered of Nellie, when she had been a woman of twenty and Nellie only seven. Eliza thought angrily that she had given herself away to this imp of Satan, and then she recalled her first impressions of Nellie adult, a mummer, a liar. Gradually she had lost them and become very fond of her, tender towards her. Tom, too, she hadn't liked at all at first, another curious being with a floating soul, neither man nor woman, and not human; neither of them human. She tried hard, all in this moment, to recall and retain her first impressions of the fatal brother and sister.

Nellie was joyful; but she had brushed away the smirk now and came in in her graceful lope, reassuring her, "Was it a shock to you as to me, Eliza? Well, maybe it's better to have him pinned down to Blackstone and we know where he is, the reckless fool. If it's not some old harpy again, it's a wonder. Come, we'll drop tears in our gin, me dear: let's go out and celebrate. I'll not write to the ungrateful monkey though till he tells me, but you will, eh?"

"No," said Eliza.

"Eh, that's wrong, chick. You mustn't let him see you're wounded," said Nellie, looking at her sideways with a laugh.

"What's it to me?" said Eliza; "don't be foolish, Nellie."

"Ye can't conceal it from me, sweetheart, why shouldn't ye admit it? It's no disgrace. It's a maternal affection, you feel. It's no disgrace in an older woman. We all come to it. I'll be seeing myself in a few years no doubt, sighing and mewing after someone in knickerbockers."

At this brutality, Eliza burst out laughing and putting on her red hat and her jacket and very red, with her hair a little loose, looking like, as Nellie said, "a guid ould wife," she went out with Tom's sister to the nearest pub.

But in the night Nellie could not sleep now that George had gone and came to Eliza with her troubles. Tom had been a disappointment to her all his life and now he was stuck away in a cabbage patch with some hobbledehoy girl or village spinster or luring old landlady. A girl in every port and she had pinned her faith to him for he'd been a bonny lad though silly, so silly they thought him simple; they called him girlish.

For a long time she sang the old strain about Tom, his weakness, his breaking her father's pride and his mother's faith. But Eliza roused herself to say to Nellie that he had his own life and they were two old fools to be sitting there weeping over him, like village biddies themselves.

"It's all like a lost village, all of it," said she. "Would you think we were really in the heart of London?"

Nellie said no, and she talked Eliza to utter weariness telling her about the great epochs of her life. She saw it now looking back as from a hill to a glittering plain, the triumphs, the mistakes; how she had been led astray by early ones and late ones. It was a story of thickets, brigands and enchanters; and herself riding some bare-boned nag through it all, but always forward on a straight path through it all to the present moment; "the moment of my downfall, for where am I with it all, all I had? What I have to give and no one wants! I'm a genius, Eliza, and always knew it. I felt it in me and everyone felt it, they all expected great things of me; even old Pop Cotter, the old humbug, was proud of me. Me hour's come now, Eliza, perhaps: and if me George shelves me, we'll face the world together. Ye'll stand by me and I'll write me great play, Lize. I've got it in me. I see things that have never been said or not said the right way. They're all humbugs, and when they'd tell the truth, they put in the hard cruel cutting word, the unnecessary revelation, all misplaced, scorn where there should be love and hate where there should be understanding. How do I see life, Eliza? With a rosy tender veil. It's the palpitating heart of life, I must put in, with the language of love. I feel it, the rich thing like a rose. I've had terrible experiences, no one can ever know. I've had strange things happen to me, strange loves that nothing can explain, that can only be explained in their own terms, in terms of themselves. Yes, darling, I can express it all to you, it's strange, you're my only friend. We only go two by two and my brother is not as fine as you, Eliza, sweet angel," she said pausing for breath and having lost hold of the idea. She mused for a while in the dark and went on, "Loves! That is what hasn't been expressed, Eliza love, and it is hard to express: love. If I could express it, for that's the message in me, I'd be far beyond them with their rule-of-thumb explanations of the universe. What can Marxism say to a lover, or to a mother? Or what can Einstein? Aye, he can say more, for there's something wonderful and beautiful in the idea that we have an attic window only, open on the swamp of stars."

"The way you talk is so lovely," said Eliza struck by this. "I believe in you Nellie."

"Do you believe in me, pet?" said Nellie, excitedly squeezing her. "Then that's all right; then, that's all right on your side. We'll be all right together. You and me armed to the teeth with understanding, facing the bitter mocking world. Is that it? Is that how you feel? Eh, you're cured of that little stab of Tom's unfeeling letter, aren't you? I can cure you, sweetheart. I have a gift: it's given to me. I have it in me. Stay with me. We'll live together in the wilderness of London and it will be like an ideal forest, it was a lover and his lass with a hey and a ho and a hey-nonino! Ha-ha," she said, placing her long legs together and jumping up, "I can't sleep tonight, but you sleep, Eliza chick, if you must."

"I'm a heavy woman, I must sleep," said Eliza.

She slept but Nellie poured herself some brandy, and spent the night smoking and looking out of the black window to see if she could get another idea like that about the stars which had so pleased Eliza. She could not. Black curtains of fatigue dropped all over her mind. She sat in the double dark till morning, with fiery tongues of desire, brain-flame licking the roots of her skull. She had perhaps made another conquest in Eliza but it was not sufficient. The drawback of her easy conquests, she thought to herself, was that they left her dissatisfied: she wanted more. She felt greatness in herself, limitless possibilities: "Me great black and rosy wings."

Sprawling in the great armchair by the empty downstairs fireplace in which were heaped ashes and cigarette butts and some old letters, she fell into a dizzy doze, and was awakened by Eliza standing over her.

"What is it? Stop! I tried to stop you, but you hung on to whatever it was."

"It's nothing, sweetheart," said Nellie, smiling innocently at Eliza, "it was just a nightmare, nothing to be told. It was a staircase. I was going down and there was a long curtain with a flap or skirt trailing on the stair to trip me, and on that part of the stair there was no light and I was saying, There's no light, there's no light."

"It didn't sound like any words," said Eliza: "it was groaning and a scream."

"And yet in the depths of my dream it was quiet, safe and peace, peace," ruminated Nellie.

N O ONE ever got out of the country as fast as Nellie. When the news came that George had a place for her, the newspaper, all her friends hastened to do what they could, pull wires, run messages, buy the outfit, promise to keep an eye open, organize a farewell party and reserve a seat in a plane. Everyone from Robert Peebles to Bob Bobsey had been so much afraid of a crack-up, and saw so gloomy a future for Nellie, probably dependent upon a pauperized Tom, that they did all in their power to help her to get off. Delightfully rattled, in the middle of her packing party, with Tom packing a big trunk he had got for her on the way from the station, Vi Butters passing judgment on her old clothes, condemning her cherished turbans and scarves, "You can't wear things like that in Geneva!" and even Camilla, who had been told and had come round with gifts of clothes, Nellie, though never more bowed or bony, yet tinkled and gleamed with charm. She was surrounded with love and fuss, and the unbelievable had happened. George, whom she, and frankly all the others, had thought lost forever, had made a right about turn and was calling for her.

"They won't let me stay here as a bachelor, they insist upon wives!" he cried over the phone in his well-known way. "They put beautiful girls in my office and then say, Bring your wife! I was brought here under false pretences."

"God bless Europe," said Nellie.

Tom was all smiles. Everyone said some complimentary thing about his sister. He had very much the aspect of a young bridegroom. He did not know which way to look, and whether to blush or clear his throat, and said in a deep voice, "Yes, I know!"

People from the newspaper were there, dropping hasty appreciations in his ear about her good work, all the friends were there, jolly, tender, relieved from the bottom of their hearts that anything so fortunate could happen to poor Nellie. Their minds were engaged, as well with her good fortune, as upon the problem, "Will Geneva, a continental world be able to change the old Nellie? Is it too late? Was it ever possible? Is she cast, not formed?" But all were bent on one thing, to get her away before she became too ill to go, and as old friends and total strangers were united in this urgent, intense purpose, it worked.

Nellie saw in it all nothing but love; and Tom was not far from that.

"You will write Peggy a letter," said Nellie drawing Vi aside. "I don't dare tell the poor pet, I feel so guilty; she will feel she's abandoned."

"Well, she is," said Vi, "and what about me? Haven't you a thought for me too, Cushie?"

"Ah, pet, yes, but you would think that England had died for me with the old soldier, poor old Tommy Atkins. Now George is my country. I'm a traitor I'm afraid. But you'll do that for me? Write to the poor pet?"

"I will."

"She's a noble woman, a grand girl, Vi, she'll forgive me. She'll know my place is with my husband."

"Yes, I suppose they'll grudgingly say that even in Hadrian's Grove."

"There's a letter and a packet for you, Tom," cried Nellie, turning away, "it's somewhere around, look inside the piano. Some one of your sweethearts has been knitting for you." She shrugged one shoulder and eyed him sarcastically. "You're the only thing that worries me, sweetheart, but I've got to leave you to your fate, a ship without a rudder. Will you take care of him for me, pet?" she said with equal sarcasm, winking at Eliza. "I know you've got a soft spot for the changeling lad."

"Don't worry about me," said Tom in a deep voice. He had now laid his hand upon the packet and the letter.

"A girl's writing," said Nellie winking, "and a tearspot as large as a shilling on the address!"

"Ah!" cried Tom, "I didn't want to reopen that. I didn't ever want to think about it again!" He drew out a knitted waistcoat.

"Who's knitting for ye, darling?" jeered Nellie, rushing

round with seven half-pounds of tea which she packed in a tin box.

But Tom was sitting down opposite Vi reading a long letter, and after a while, he handed it to Vi. She read:

Dear Tom,

I said I'd write to you and never kept my promise. I tried to sometimes, but never felt I could. However, now I feel better about it and as I finished the waistcoat some time ago I thought I'd send it and my news. I hope you haven't got any fatter or thinner. If you got thinner, you can easily change the buttons, as I thought of that in the design. Now for my news. I was in London quite a bit, going gay you would think. But I got someone to help me on the orchard, a very good man. I saw Patrick a few times for tea but he always had an appointment afterwards and I suspected, you know, a lady in the case and so there was. Now he has written to me to say he is going to get married. He did not join the air force after all: too old I suspect; but he says he is going to settle down. This is a sort of preface to my own news, Tom. I am going to get married myself. The lady is very charming, I think, and I think anyone would think so; not in her first youth though. She has domestic ways but is more a bird of paradise than a modest hen, I think, and I wonder what you would think! I cannot understand how it was she waited for me, as it were. Of course, we didn't know each other until recently. Well, I was nervous about putting the question, for one never knows, but one day after Patrick had left me, I thought, It is now or never, I must take the plunge and I went in and won through. We are being married in a month and I want you to come. I asked Patrick but he will be in the country with his beloved! Isn't this exciting and unexpected news? I am a happy man.

Yours sincerely, Connie."

"I don't understand this," said Vi, "is it a man or a woman?"
"That's the husband! I took his wife from him!" said Tom.
"What husband?"
Tom frowned. "Marion's husband."

"Did she have a husband?"

"Good heavens, of course; where did you think she lived?"

"I thought she was trailing round the country with you in a —heavens knows in what. Oh, I don't know. You and Nellie never tell me anything. You just led me by the nose all my life. I'm a fool to you."

Tom said proudly, "Nellie did it to protect me. She has always been faithful to me." After a while he smiled, "It is quite a coincidence, because I am going to get married myself." And at this he smiled, looking for a compliment, up at Eliza who was standing by.

Eliza turned away and went into the back yard. She thought, "Well, that's a good thing, now he's off my shoulders. I feel free again."

Later, however, she felt as if she had been cracked on the head. She was dizzy and in pain. She thought that it was a good thing there was so much to do.

Nellie saw her upset and was delighted and moved, "I'll write to you, pet," she said, kissing Eliza several times, "we're great pals, we'll be pen pals, won't we?"

But that was all the time she had for Eliza in her flurry. She went off in the early morning and with her, most of the helpers. Only Tom and Eliza were left.

He and Eliza discussed what they should do about the house which neither of them could keep up. They breakfasted and presently Tom said he must get back to Blackstone.

A horrifying thing had happened there. There were three old men who called him The Engineer, and who used to wait for him on a seat on the London Road. They sat in the same places every day. The middle old man thought he owned houses and had troubles with imaginary tenants. A local lad, a dark middle-sized young fellow of football build with a thick chapped skin and narrow eyes was very contentious, had a bone to pick with everyone, "an unspeakable nuisance," and he swooped down on the middle old man. He was a smallish, rather good-looking old man, with wide cheekbones, blue eyes; he had a cap like a Chelsea Pensioner's and his white hair stuck out unwashed, underneath. Sometimes the three old men would take a walk and the landlord in dream would point down a street, "My houses are just down there, three of them in a row." The others would agree. The young busybody got to work on this harmless old man and after weeks of destroying his arguments and his proofs, had convinced him that he had no houses.

"The poor old cove tried to drown himself in the swamp and is in the hospital now. I must see him."

And so Tom went. Eliza went to the station with him, to have the stirrup cup, but he said, "I won't be coming down now, Eliza. I won't have the money. I must look for a home."

"Aye, Tom."

The two women, friends of George, who had once employed Mrs. McMahon, took her back but they were disappointed in the change in her. She was dull, inattentive, stupid, it must be admitted. She did her best but she was not as clean as before. Still, because they had made the promise to George, they kept her on, complaining about her behind her back.

After she had been there about a year, she said timidly to one of them, "Do you ever hear from Mr. Cook, Madam?"

The woman started, looked keenly at Mrs. McMahon: she thought her mind had gone.

"But Gwen, he died nearly a year ago."

"He died?" she said faintly, stood there with the pail in her hand, turned and went out to the kitchen. The woman felt upset.

She went to Gwen, who was standing by the kitchen sink, her mouth slightly open, "Didn't you know, Gwen? I didn't mean to blurt it out. He died in a skiing accident. He shouldn't have tried at his age; but he would try anything."

"And is he over there, buried, Madam?"

"Yes, Gwen. Far away."

Gwen did her work and went away, quietly. The women talked about the changes in her and one said, I think she was in love with George Cook; but they could not accept this idea; a servant in love with George Cook who had been described in the foreign press, when he died, as a "great fighter for the British working class, who turned many to socialism by his ready forceful expositions."

Nellie had invited Tom to that foreign funeral and they had brought back a photograph: Nellie gay with success as a hero's widow and Tom smiling, hand in hand. This is a problem the press always meets, people smiling for the camera in disasters; and the paper did not publish this one. Nellie bought the paper. There was a picture of Anthony Butters, husband of her friend Vi, a man whom Nellie always described as "a puir thing, a frail waif, unable to cope, an out-of-work mechanic"; but who was, as she knew, the organizer of one of the largest unions in the country. Anthony was leading a strike in a basic industry. Nellie read about Vi's husband and dropped the paper into the next litter basket on the street. Her heart turned to bitter water.

Not long after Nellie returned, Walter the window washer came to the door to ask about the Mister. Nellie told him all about it at length and he was charmed by her with all her bells swinging at him. He was a dull, respectable man who thought well of himself. He told her he belonged to a circle which was interested in consolation, in the human heart, in solving unsolved problems that the professors and scientists could not solve. She smoked, listened to him, laughed, said balderdash, but in the end thought she might go along; and that week, one evening, he took her to what she called a "Nabob villa," porch, pillars, fine windows, to a side door, over which was nailed a horseshoe. They rang and went in. Nellie, slowly at first, became interested in the problems of the unknowable.